RETURN FROM THE DEAD
A Collection of Classic Mummy Stories

RETURN FROM THE DEAD

A Collection of Classic Mummy Stories

———— ◆ ————

Selected and Introduced by
DAVID STUART DAVIES

WORDSWORTH CLASSICS

This edition published 2004 by Wordsworth Editions Limited
8B East Street, Ware, Hertfordshire SG12 9HJ

ISBN 1 84022 452 5

Text © Wordsworth Editions Limited 2004
Introduction © David Stuart Davies 2004

Wordsworth ® is a registered trademark of
Wordsworth Editions Limited

2 4 6 8 10 9 7 5 3 1

Typeset by Antony Gray
Printed and bound in Great Britain by
Mackays of Chatham, Chatham, Kent

Contents

GENERAL INTRODUCTION

Wordsworth Classics are inexpensive editions designed to appeal to the general reader and students. We commissioned teachers and specialists to write wide ranging, jargon-free introductions and to provide notes that would assist the understanding of our readers rather than interpret the stories for them. In the same spirit, because the pleasures of reading are inseparable from the surprises, secrets and revelations that all narratives contain, we strongly advise you to enjoy this book before turning to the Introduction.

General Adviser
KEITH CARABINE

INTRODUCTION

Life is precious. And it is difficult to accept that once we lose it, there is nothing more – that in fact Death is really the end. Throughout history, every religion, every civilisation has sought to prognosticate some loophole in this pessimistic scenario – some escape from the inevitable. Whether it be Judgement Day, the transmogrification of souls, reincarnation, spiritualism, the land of milk and honey, vampirism even, the human mind has clung to a belief that there is something beyond the dark curtain. But it was the Ancient Egyptians whose unshakeable belief in a life after death had such an impact on their daily lives and culture. To the Egyptians life was almost a preparation for the voyage to the afterlife. Tombs were built during their lifetime and were crammed with their earthly possessions, furnishings, treasures and artefacts, useful to them on their journey through the Underworld to their 'life' beyond in the idyllic 'Field of Reeds'.

The bodies of the wealthier Egyptians underwent a mummification process to preserve their earthly shell, believing that in the afterlife they kept their human form. The ritual of mummification was a lengthy and a physically brutal one. Although the exterior of the body was held sacred, the corpse's innards – the lungs, the stomach, the liver, the intestines – were removed. Perhaps the most horrendous part of the mummification ceremony was the extraction of the brain. To begin with a special tool with a hooked end was inserted into the skull cavity. The brain tissue was then severed from the skull, cut into small pieces and extracted through the nostrils.

Once the embalming stage had been completed, the corpse was swathed in strips of linen; over this, a preparation of pasteboard known as cartonnage was fitted. Next came the coffin which was shaped like the mummified body. These were often decorated with paintings, sometimes beaten with gold and silver and inlaid with precious stones, depending on the wealth and status of the deceased. Finally, the coffin was placed in a sarcophagus.

After this elaborate process was complete, the mummy was ready to be sealed up within its tomb. It could now begin the journey to that 'undiscover'd country, from whose bourn no traveller returns'.

But, of course, fear of death is closely allied to the dread of the dead returning, coming back to haunt the living – or worse. It is therefore not surprising that legends and stories grew up concerning those travellers who do in fact return from that 'undiscover'd country'. In the case of the Ancient Egyptians we are dealing with reanimated mummies. One legend has it that an Egyptian priest named Khamaus from third century BC who, in the process of his search for the god Thoth's great book of magic held many conversations with dead mummies. And a Coptic bishop from the sixth century AD also communicated with bandaged ghouls; they told him blood-curdling tales of their pains and miseries in the after world and, apparently, he was able to comfort them with Christian reassurances.

The mystique that surrounds this ancient world and its magical death rituals has fascinated the storyteller for centuries. Long before the first celluloid mummy rose from its dusty sarcophagus on movie sets to thrill and scare millions of cinema-goers, writers were conjuring their own brand of terror, examining and exploiting the mummy who would not lie down: the bandaged creature who had returned from the dead. This volume presents a collection of early mummy stories, seminal tales that directly or indirectly helped to establish this type of resurrection tale as a potent sub-genre of horror fiction.

The main feature on our mummy bill is a novel by Bram Stoker,

The Jewel of the Seven Stars, which is generally regarded as his best work after Dracula. However, *The Jewel of the Seven Stars* is more than just a mummy story, the writing is imbued with ideas of mysticism and spiritualism and, typical of so many *fin de siecle* novels (it was published in 1904), it raises questions as to the future of mankind.

The idea of writing a story featuring a reanimated mummy had been with Stoker a long time before he actually put pen to paper. It was Sir William Wilde, father of Oscar and amateur archaeologist, who first impressed the young Stoker with the imaginative possibilities of this supernatural tale. In the 1860s and early 1870s Stoker was a regular visitor to the Wilde house in Merrion Square where he would have heard at first hand Sir William's dramatised accounts of his expeditions to Egypt. Wilde told the tale of how he slept in the outer chamber of a tomb and was woken by whispers in the night. Wilde's house, rather like Abel Trelawney in the novel, was filled with Egyptian relics including a mummy, which Wilde had brought back from one of his digs. Over the years Stoker supplemented these vivid and inspirational memories with scholarly research in ancient Egyptian culture, myths, legends and magic. At the turn of the century Egyptian magic was in vogue with occultists. Scottish writer J. W. Brodie Innes, one of the leading members, along with Aleister Crowley, of that centre of occult practises, the Amen-Ra Temple of the Hermetic Order of the Golden Dawn, said that *Jewel of Seven Stars* ' . . . is not only a good book, it is a great book.'

The story, which concerns the resurrection of the ancient Egyptian Queen Tera, opens like an eerie detective story that might be a case for Sherlock Holmes who would find a rational explanation for the baffling events. But like so many incidents in this novel, the facts are deceptive. In the early hours of the morning, a visitor hammering on his door wakens Malcolm Ross from a strange and powerful dream involving a fascinating young woman called Margaret Trelawney whom he has just met. His nocturnal visitor turns out to be this woman's groom who bears a note seeking Malcolm's help. Apparently an attempt has been made on her father's life at their home in Notting Hill. Margaret has discovered her father Abel Trelawney unconscious in his bedroom study, which is full of Egyptian curios that he has spent his life collecting. He was lying in front of the safe, evidently after being dragged bleeding from his bed. The unopened safe suggests her father's attackers were interrupted before they could finish their work and so they escaped. Standard fare for a crime novel, one might think, but there are two baffling aspects to this situation that no detective would be able to explain. To begin with, 'there is no possible sign of [the robbers'] escape; no clue, no disturbance of anything; no open door or window; no sound.' Added to this, Trelawney's doctors are as perplexed as the police when it becomes clear that their patient's comatose state is due neither to a blow on the head nor to the loss of blood from the deep wound in his wrist. Neither has he been drugged nor hypnotised. As it transpires, the magical power of Queen Tera is already at work, even reaching out into Malcolm's dreams to entwine him invisibly to the life and fortunes of Margaret Trelawney. Her father is not simply a collector of Egyptian artefacts. He has a darker purpose. He is engaged in the dangerous pursuit of everlasting life, to discover the magical power that has control over life and death. To do this he must learn the secrets of the old Egyptian mystical arts by bringing back to life one of the adepts of the ancient lore. This is the Wizard Queen Tera, 'a woman skilled in all the science of her time . . . nearly two thousand years before Saul'.

Once Trelawney has returned to consciousness, as mysteriously as he was struck down, he continues his obsessive quest, drawing in as his assistants Malcolm Ross and his daughter Margaret, who bears a remarkable resemblance to Tera. To his growing horror, Malcolm realises that the ancient Queen is taking over Margaret's mind and body: 'In such a case Margaret would not be an individual at all, but simply a phase of Queen Tera herself: an astral body obedient to her will.'

This may be fiction, but Stoker employs learned material in constructing the various arguments and theories concerned with the resurrection and spiritual power of Tera. *The Jewel of the Seven Stars* climaxes with an elaborately ritualised reanimation, heralded as 'The Great Experiment'. The power and uncompromising pessimism of the novel's finale disturbed the publishers and no doubt many readers, and in 1912 a more up beat ending was substituted. It is not clear whether the new ending is Stoker's own work or not. Critics disagree on this point. At the time Stoker was very ill – he died that year after suffering a stroke – and in his weakened condition he may have simply agreed to what in essence is the substitution of a few pages. In this collection, we provide you with both endings so that you can judge for yourself which you consider to be the more satisfactory conclusion to this haunting and unsettling tale.

Of the remaining four stories in the collection, the earliest and perhaps the strangest is Jane Webb's *The Mummy*. In fact this is an extract from a labyrinthine three-volume novel entitled *The Mummy! A Tale of the Twenty-Second Century* which was published in 1827. Webb was but a young girl of nineteen when, heavily influenced and inspired by Mary Shelley's *Frankenstein* (1818), she put pen to paper and created this story, which is a weird mix of adventure, the supernatural and science fiction. As the title suggests, the novel is set in the future – 2126 to be precise – when man has total control of the weather, television provides the primary means of communication, and air travel in giant balloons is commonplace. Amazing concepts in the early nineteenth century. The main characters include Dr Entwerfen, 'a clownish genius' and inventor; Edric, the hero, an Indiana Jones prototype; and their manservant, Gregory. They fly to Egypt with the intention of reviving the body of the long dead pharaoh Cheops to prove the effectiveness of an electrical animation machine which Dr Entwerfen has invented. Reanimating dead tissue is obviously a steal from Shelley's *Frankenstein* but the imaginative slant which Jane Webb places on the process excuses any criticism of plagiarism. Once he has returned from the dead Cheops escapes by balloon and flies to England where he becomes involved in the power struggle for the throne. Some six hundred pages later the novel ends with Cheops returning happily to Egypt and his tomb.

Some Words with a Mummy by Edgar Allan Poe was first published in 1845 and although it is written in Poe's usual style of dark melancholy, the story is really meant as a satire rather than a horror piece. The conversation with the mummy is designed to point up the superiority of the ancient Egyptian civilisation to that of the American in the nineteenth century.

The narrator (one presumes this to be Poe himself) rather like Malcolm Ross in *The Jewel of Seven Stars*, is rudely awakened from his slumbers by a summons in the night. A messenger has brought a letter from his friend Dr Ponnonner inviting him to attend the official unswathing and opening up of a mummy at his house at eleven o'clock. The mummy is one of a pair recently brought back from Egypt. Poe hastens to his friend's house to find the mummy 'extended upon the dining table'. There follows a remarkable and detailed description of the mummy. The dead creature is eventually galvanised into life by electricity and it becomes clear that this mummy has suffered the terrible fate that Poe most feared himself: he had been buried alive.

The final two tales are real chillers from the prolific pen of Arthur Conan Doyle. The first story *The Ring of Thoth* (1890) concerns the idea of immortality and its torment. Through magic the ancient

Egyptian Sosra has achieved everlasting life. This has become a curse, preventing him from dying and in death becoming reunited with his loved one, Atma. Doyle cleverly turns the search for life after death on its head. Sosra is not the bandaged mummy of popular conception, but a 'gnarled heavy-eyed' figure haunting the Egyptian room in the Louvre where the remains of his lost love rest. This is both a horror and a love story and the essential ingredients in *The Ring of Thoth* were used by Hollywood in the 1932 movie *The Mummy* featuring a desiccated Boris Karloff. Indeed, elements of Doyle's story have found their way into most of the mummy movies that followed Karloff's success, including the big hit of 1999 bearing the same name.

On reading *Lot 249* (1894) Rudyard Kipling said that it had given him a nightmare for the first time in years. In the early part of Doyle's story we are presented with all the elements that M. R. James was to use later in his ghost stories: a measured pace and intellectual characters involved in strange, inexplicable events within a university setting. Doyle takes his time to create a growing sense of horror and unreality. The fear is manifested not so much by what he describes as by what he does not describe:

> It moved in the shadow of the hedge, silently and furtively, a dark crouching figure, dimly visible against the black background. Even as he gazed back at it, it had lessened its distance by twenty paces, and was fast closing on him. Out of the darkness he had a glimpse of a scraggy neck and of two eyes that will ever haunt him in his dreams.

The subtlety of the writing here generates fear and unease. Doyle is carrying on the tradition of the great ghost story writers – although this isn't a ghost story – of allowing the reader's own imagination to enhance the misty picture painted by the writer. And our own imagination can be far worse than words upon a page.

The fascination with the mummy as a creature of mystery and mysticism still holds sway in the twenty-first century. Perhaps it is because we know that the mummy we see in the modern museum still contains the fragile remains of a human being who existed so far back in the dark, secretive mists of time. In a sense, like the mummies of fiction, they do live on.

DAVID STUART DAVIES

DAVID STUART DAVIES is the Editor of SHERLOCK magazine. He is a playwright and crime writer and has written several novels and non-fiction books about Sherlock Holmes. His other titles for Wordsworth are: *The Best of Sherlock Holmes, Shadows of Sherlock Holmes* (a collection of stories featuring detectives, criminal agents and debonair crooks from the golden age of crime fiction), *Short Stories from the Nineteenth Century* and *Tales of Unease*.

THE JEWEL OF THE SEVEN STARS

CHAPTER I

A Summons in the Night

IT ALL SEEMED so real that I could hardly imagine that it had ever occurred before; and yet each episode came, not as a fresh step in the logic of things, but as something expected. It is in such wise that memory plays its pranks for good or ill; for pleasure or pain; for weal or woe. It is thus that life is bitter-sweet, and that which has been done becomes eternal.

Again, the light skiff, ceasing to shoot through the lazy water as when the oars flashed and dripped, glided out of the fierce July sunlight into the cool shade of the great drooping willow branches – I standing up in the swaying boat, she sitting still and with deft fingers guarding herself from stray twigs or the freedom of the resilience of moving boughs. Again, the water looked golden-brown under the canopy of translucent green; and the grassy bank was of emerald hue. Again, we sat in the cool shade, with the myriad noises of nature both without and within our bower merging into that drowsy hum in whose suffing environment the great world with its disturbing trouble, and its more disturbing joys, can be effectually forgotten. Again, in that blissful solitude the young girl lost the convention of her prim, narrow upbringing, and told me in a natural, dreamy way of the loneliness of her new life. With an undertone of sadness she made me feel how in that spacious home each one of the household was isolated by the personal magnificence of her father and herself; that there confidence had no altar, and sympathy no shrine; and that there even her father's face was as distant as the old country life seemed now. Once more, the wisdom of my manhood and the experience of my years laid themselves at the girl's feet. It was seemingly their own doing; for the individual 'I' had no say in the matter, but only just obeyed imperative orders. And once again the flying seconds multiplied themselves endlessly. For it is in the arcana of dreams that existences merge and renew themselves, change and yet keep the same – like the soul of a musician in a fugue. And so memory swooned, again and again, in sleep.

It seems that there is never to be any perfect rest. Even in Eden the snake rears its head among the laden boughs of the tree of knowledge. The silence of the dreamless night is broken by the roar of the avalanche; the hissing of sudden floods; the clanging of the engine bell marking its sweep through a sleeping American town; the clanking of distant paddles over the sea . . . Whatever it is, it is breaking the charm of my Eden. The canopy of greenery above us, starred with diamond-points of light, seems to quiver in the ceaseless beat of paddles; and the restless bell seems as though it would never cease . . .

All at once the gates of Sleep were thrown wide open, and my waking ears took in the cause of the disturbing sounds. Waking existence is prosaic enough – there was somebody knocking and ringing at someone's street door.

I was pretty well accustomed in my Jermyn Street chambers to passing sounds; usually I did not concern myself, sleeping or waking, with the doings, however noisy, of my neighbours. But this noise was too continuous, too insistent, too imperative to be ignored. There was some active intelligence behind that ceaseless sound; and some stress or need behind the intelligence. I was not altogether selfish, and at the thought of someone's need I was, without premeditation, out of bed. Instinctively I looked at my watch. It was just three o'clock; there was a faint edging of grey round the green blind which darkened my room. It was evident that the knocking and ringing were at the door of our own house; and it was evident, too, that there was no one awake to answer the call. I slipped on my dressing-gown and slippers, and went down to the hall door. When I opened it there stood a dapper groom, with one hand pressed unflinchingly on the electric bell whilst with the other he raised a ceaseless clangour with the knocker. The instant he saw me the noise ceased; one hand went up instinctively to the brim of his hat, and the other produced a letter from his pocket. A neat brougham was opposite the door, the horses were breathing heavily as though they had come fast. A policeman, with his night lantern still alight at his belt, stood by attracted to the spot by the noise.

'Beg pardon, sir, I'm sorry for disturbing you, but my orders was imperative; I was not to lose a moment, but to knock and ring till someone came. May I ask you, sir, if Mr Malcolm Ross lives here?'

'I am Mr Malcolm Ross.'

'Then this letter is for you, sir, and the bro'am is for you too, sir!'

I took, with a strange curiosity, the letter which he handed to me. As a barrister I had had, of course, odd experiences now and then, including sudden demands upon my time; but never anything like this. I stepped back into the hall, closing the door to, but leaving it ajar; then I switched on the electric light. The letter was directed in a strange hand, a woman's. It began at once without 'dear sir' or any such address:

> You said you would like to help me if I needed it; and I believe you meant what you said. The time has come sooner than I expected. I am in dreadful trouble, and do not know where to turn, or to whom to apply. An attempt has, I fear, been made to murder my Father; though, thank God, he still lives. But he is quite unconscious. The doctors and police have been sent for; but there is no one here whom I can depend on. Come at once, if you are able to; and forgive me if you can. I suppose I shall realise later what I have done in asking such a favour; but at present I cannot think. Come! Come at once!
>
> MARGARET TRELAWNY

Pain and exultation struggled in my mind as I read; but the mastering thought was that she was in trouble and had called on me – me! My dreaming of her, then, was not altogether without a cause. I called out to the groom: 'Wait! I shall be with you in a minute!' Then I flew upstairs.

A very few minutes sufficed to wash and dress; and we were soon driving through the streets as fast as the horses could go. It was market morning, and when we got out on Piccadilly there was an endless stream of carts coming from the west; but for the rest the roadway was clear, and we went quickly. I had told the groom to come into the brougham with me so that he could tell me what had happened as we went along. He sat awkwardly, with his hat on his knees as he spoke.

'Miss Trelawny, sir, sent a man to tell us to get out a carriage at once; and when we was ready she come herself and gave me the letter and told Morgan – the coachman, sir – to fly. She said as I was to lose not a second, but to keep knocking till someone come.'

'Yes, I know, I know – you told me! What I want to know is, why she sent for me. What happened in the house?'

'I don't quite know myself, sir; except that master was found in his room senseless, with the sheets all bloody, and a wound on his head. He couldn't be waked nohow. 'Twas Miss Trelawny herself as found him.'

'How did she come to find him at such an hour? It was late in the night, I suppose?'

'I don't know, sir; I didn't hear nothing at all of the details.'

As he could tell me no more, I stopped the carriage for a moment to let him get out on the box; then I turned the matter over in my mind as I sat alone. There were many things which I could have asked the servant; and for a few moments after he had gone I was angry with myself for not having used my opportunity. On second thought, however, I was glad the temptation was gone. I felt that it would be more delicate to learn what I wanted to know of Miss Trelawny's surroundings from herself, rather than from her servants.

We bowled swiftly along Knightsbridge, the small noise of our well-appointed vehicle sounding hollowly in the morning air. We turned up the Kensington Palace Road and presently stopped opposite a great house on the left-hand side, nearer, so far as I could judge, the Notting Hill than the Kensington end of the avenue. It was a truly fine house, not only with regard to size but to architecture. Even in the dim grey light of the morning, which tends to diminish the size of things, it looked big.

Miss Trelawny met me in the hall. She was not in any way shy. She seemed to rule all around her with a sort of high-bred dominance, all the more remarkable as she was greatly agitated and as pale as snow. In the great hall were several servants, the men standing together near the hall door, and the women clinging together in the further corners and doorways. A police superintendent had been talking to Miss Trelawny; two men in uniform and one plain-clothes man stood near him. As she took my hand impulsively there was a look of relief in her eyes, and she gave a gentle sigh of relief. Her salutation was simple.

'I knew you would come!'

The clasp of the hand can mean a great deal, even when it is not intended to mean anything especially. Miss Trelawny's hand somehow became lost in my own. It was not that it was a small hand; it was fine and flexible, with long delicate fingers – a rare and beautiful hand; it was the unconscious self-surrender. And though at the moment I could not dwell on the cause of the thrill which swept me, it came back to me later.

She turned and said to the police superintendent: 'This is Mr Malcolm Ross.'

The police officer saluted as he answered: 'I know Mr Malcolm Ross, miss. Perhaps he will remember I had the honour of working with him in the Brixton Coining case.' I had not at first glance noticed who it was, my whole attention having been taken with Miss Trelawny.

'Of course, Superintendent Dolan, I remember very well!' I said as we shook hands. I could not but note that the acquaintanceship seemed a relief to Miss Trelawny. There was a certain vague uneasiness in her manner which took my attention; instinctively I felt that it would be less embarrassing for her to speak with me alone. So I said to the superintendent: 'Perhaps it will be better if Miss Trelawny will see me alone for a few minutes. You, of course, have already heard all she knows; and I shall understand better how things are if I may ask some questions. I will then talk the matter over with you if I may.'

'I shall be glad to be of what service I can, sir,' he answered heartily.

Following Miss Trelawny, I moved over to a dainty room which opened from the hall and looked out on the garden at the back of the house. When we had entered and I had closed the door she said: 'I will thank you later for your goodness in coming to me in my trouble; but at present you can best help me when you know the facts.'

'Go on,' I said. 'Tell me all you know and spare no detail, however trivial it may at the present time seem to be.'

She went on at once: 'I was awakened by some sound; I do not know what. I only know that it came through my sleep; for all at once I found myself awake, with my heart beating wildly, listening anxiously for some sound from my father's room. My room is next Father's, and I can often hear him moving about before I fall asleep. He works late at night, sometimes very late indeed; so that when I wake early, as I do occasionally, or in the grey of the dawn, I hear him still moving. I tried once to remonstrate with him about staying up so late, as it cannot be good for him; but I never ventured to repeat the experiment. You know how stern and cold he can be – at least you may remember what I told you about him; and when he is polite in this mood he is dreadful. When he is angry I can bear it much better; but when he is slow and deliberate, and the side of his mouth lifts up to show the sharp teeth, I think I feel – well, I don't know how! Last night I got up softly and stole to the door, for I really feared to disturb him. There was not any noise of moving, and no kind of cry at all; but there was a queer kind of dragging sound, and a slow, heavy breathing. Oh! it was dreadful, waiting there in the dark and the silence, and fearing – fearing I did not know what!

'At last I took my courage *à deux mains*, and turning the handle of the door as softly as I could, I opened the door a tiny bit. It was quite dark within; I could just see the outline of the windows. But in the darkness the sound of breathing, becoming more distinct, was appalling. As I listened, this continued; but there was no other sound. I pushed the door open all at once. I was afraid to open it slowly; I felt as if there might be some dreadful thing behind it ready to pounce out on me! Then I switched on the electric light, and stepped into the room. I looked first at the bed. The sheets were all crumpled up, so that I knew Father had been in bed; but there was a great dark red patch in the centre of the bed, and spreading to the edge of it, that made my heart stand still. As I was gazing at it the sound of the breathing came across the room, and my eyes followed to it. There was Father on his right side with the other arm under him, just as if his dead body had been thrown there all in a heap. The track of blood went across the room up to the bed, and there was a pool all around him which looked terribly red and glittering as I bent over to examine him. The place where he lay was right in front of the big safe. He was in his pyjamas. The left sleeve was torn, showing his bare arm, and stretched out toward the safe. It looked – oh! so terrible, patched all with blood, and with the flesh torn or cut all around a gold chain bangle on his wrist. I did not know he wore such a thing, and it seemed to give me a new shock of surprise.'

She paused a moment; and as I wished to relieve her by a moment's divergence of thought, I said: 'Oh, that need not surprise you. You will see the most unlikely men wearing bangles. I have seen a judge condemn a man to death, and the wrist of the hand he held up had a gold bangle.'

She did not seem to heed much the words or the idea; the pause, however, relieved her somewhat, and she went on in a steadier voice: 'I did not lose a moment in summoning aid, for I feared he might bleed to death. I rang the bell, and then went out and called for help as loudly as I could. In what must have been a very short time – though it seemed an incredibly long one to me – some of the servants came running up; and then others, till the room seemed full of staring eyes, and dishevelled hair, and night clothes of all sorts.

'We lifted Father on a sofa; and the housekeeper, Mrs Grant, who seemed to have her wits about her more than any of us, began to look where the flow of blood came from. In a few seconds it became apparent that it came from the arm which was bare. There was a deep wound – not clean-cut as with a knife, but like a jagged rent or tear – close to the wrist, which seemed to have cut into the vein. Mrs Grant tied a handkerchief round the cut, and screwed it up tight with a silver paper-cutter; and the flow of blood seemed to be checked at once. By this time I had come to my senses – or such of them as remained; and I sent off one man for the doctor and another for the police. When they had gone, I felt that, except for the servants, I was all alone in the house, and that I knew nothing – of my Father or anything else; and a great longing came to me to have someone with me who could help me. Then I thought of you and your kind offer in the boat under the willow-tree; and, without waiting to think, I told the men to get a carriage ready at once, and I scribbled a note and sent it on to you.'

She paused. I did not like to say just then anything of how I felt. I looked at her; I think she understood, for her eyes were raised to mine for a moment and then fell, leaving her cheeks as red as peony roses. With a manifest effort she went on with her story: 'The doctor was with us in an incredibly short time. The groom had met him letting himself into his house with his latchkey, and he came here running. He made a proper tourniquet for poor Father's arm, and then went home to get some appliances. I dare say he will be back almost immediately. Then a policeman came, and sent a message to the station; and very soon the superintendent was here. Then you came.'

There was a long pause, and I ventured to take her hand for an instant. Without a word more we opened the door, and joined the superintendent in the hall. He hurried up to us, saying as he came: 'I have been examining everything myself, and have sent off a message to Scotland Yard. You see, Mr Ross, there seemed so much that was odd about the case that I thought we had better have the best man of the Criminal Investigation Department that we could get. So I sent a note asking to have Sergeant Daw sent at once. You remember him, sir, in that American poisoning case at Hoxton.'

'Oh yes,' I said, 'I remember him well; in that and other cases, for I have benefited several times by his skill and acumen. He has a mind that works as truly as any that I know. When I have been for the defence, and believed my man was innocent, I was glad to have him against us!'

'That is high praise, sir!' said the superintendent gratified: 'I am glad you approve of my choice; that I did well in sending for him.'

I answered heartily: 'Could not be better. I do not doubt that between you we shall get at the facts – and what lies behind them!'

We ascended to Mr Trelawny's room, where we found everything exactly as his daughter had described.

There came a ring at the house bell, and a minute later a man was shown into the room. A young man with aquiline features, keen grey eyes, and a forehead that stood out square and broad as that of a thinker. In his hand he had a black bag which he at once opened. Miss Trelawny introduced us: 'Dr Winchester, Mr Ross, Superintendent Dolan.' We bowed mutually, and he, without a moment's delay, began his work. We all waited, and eagerly watched him as he proceeded to dress the wound. As he went on he turned now and again to call the superintendent's attention to some point about the wound, the latter proceeding to enter the fact at once in his notebook.

'See! several parallel cuts or scratches beginning on the left side of the wrist and in some places endangering the radial artery.

'These small wounds here, deep and jagged, seem as if made with a blunt instrument. This in particular would seem as if made with some kind of sharp wedge; the flesh round it seems torn as if with lateral pressure.'

Turning to Miss Trelawny he said presently: 'Do you think we might remove this bangle? It is not absolutely necessary, as it will fall lower on the wrist where it can hang loosely; but it might add to the patient's comfort later on.'

The poor girl flushed deeply as she answered in a low voice: 'I do not know. I – I have only recently come to live with my father; and I know so little of his life or his ideas that I fear I can hardly judge in such a matter. The doctor, after a keen glance at her, said in a very kindly way: 'Forgive me! I did not know. But in any case you need not be distressed. It is not required at present to move it. Were it so I should do so at once on my own responsibility. If it be necessary later on, we can easily remove it with a file. Your father doubtless has some object in keeping it as it is. See! there is a tiny key attached to it . . . ' As he was speaking he stopped and bent lower, taking from my hand the candle which I held and lowering it till its light fell on the bangle. Then motioning me to hold the candle in the same position, he took from his pocket a magnifying-glass which he adjusted. When he had made a careful examination he stood up and handed the magnifying-glass to Dolan, saying as he did so: 'You had better examine it yourself. That is no ordinary bangle. The gold is wrought over triple steel links; see where it is worn away. It is manifestly not meant to be removed lightly; and it would need more than an ordinary file to do it.'

The superintendent bent his great body; but not getting close enough that way knelt down by the sofa as the doctor had done. He examined the bangle minutely, turning it slowly round so that no particle of it escaped observation. Then he stood up and handed the magnifying-glass to me. 'When you have examined it yourself,' he said, 'let the lady look at it if she will,' and he commenced to write at length in his notebook.

I made a simple alteration in his suggestion. I held out the glass toward Miss Trelawny, saying: 'Had you not better examine it first?'

She drew back, slightly raising her hand in disclaimer, as she said impulsively: 'Oh no! Father would doubtless have shown it to me had he wished me to see it. I would not like to without his consent.' Then she added, doubtless fearing lest her delicacy of view should give offence to the rest of us: 'Of course it is right that you should see it. You have to examine and consider everything; and indeed – indeed I am grateful to you . . . '

She turned away; I could see that she was crying quietly. It was evident to me that even in the midst of her trouble and anxiety there was a chagrin that she knew so little of her father; and that her ignorance had to be shown at such a time and amongst so many strangers. That they were all men did not make the shame more easy to bear, though there was a certain relief in it. Trying to interpret her feelings I could not but think that she must have been glad that no woman's eyes – of understanding greater than man's – were upon her in that hour.

When I stood up from my examination, which verified to me that of the doctor, the latter resumed his place beside the couch and went on with his ministrations. Superintendent Dolan said to me in a whisper: 'I think we are fortunate in our doctor!' I nodded, and was about to add something in praise of his acumen, when there came a low tapping at the door.

CHAPTER 2

Strange Instructions

SUPERINTENDENT DOLAN went quietly to the door; by a sort of natural understanding he had taken possession of affairs in the room. The rest of us waited. He opened the door a little way; and then with a gesture of manifest relief threw it wide, and a young man stepped in. A young man clean-shaven, tall and slight; with an eagle face and bright, quick eyes that seemed to take in everything around him at a glance. As he came in, the superintendent held out his hand; the two men shook hands warmly.

'I came at once, sir, the moment I got your message. I am glad I still have your confidence.'

'That you'll always have,' said the superintendent heartily. 'I have not forgotten our old Bow Street days, and I never shall!' Then, without a word of preliminary, he began to tell everything he knew up to the moment of the newcomer's entry. Sergeant Daw asked a few questions – a very few – when it was necessary for his understanding of circumstances or the relative positions of persons; but as a rule Dolan, who knew his work thoroughly, forestalled every query, and explained all necessary matters as he went on. Sergeant Daw threw occasionally swift glances round him; now at one of us; now at the room or some part of it; now at the wounded man lying senseless on the sofa.

When the superintendent had finished, the sergeant turned to me and said: 'Perhaps you remember me, sir. I was with you in that Hoxton case.'

'I remember you very well,' I said as I held out my hand. The superintendent spoke again: 'You understand, Sergeant Daw, that you are put in full charge of this case.'

'Under you I hope, sir,' he interrupted. The other shook his head and smiled as he said: 'It seems to me that this is a case that will take all a man's time and his brains. I have other work to do; but I shall be more than interested, and if I can help in any possible way I shall be glad to do so!'

'All right, sir,' said the other, accepting his responsibility with a sort of modified salute; straightway he began his investigation.

First he came over to the doctor and, having learned his name and address, asked him to write a full report which he could use, and which he could refer to headquarters if necessary. Dr Winchester bowed gravely as he promised. Then the sergeant approached me and said *sotto voce*: 'I like the look of your doctor. I think we can work together!' Turning to Miss Trelawny he asked: 'Please let me know what you can of your father; his ways of life, his history – in fact of anything of whatsoever kind which interests him, or in which he may be concerned.' I was about to interrupt to tell him what she had already said of her ignorance in all matters of her father and his ways, but her warning hand was raised to me pointedly and she spoke herself.

'Alas! I know little or nothing. Superintendent Dolan and Mr Ross know already all I can say.'

'Well, ma'am, we must be content to do what we can,' said the officer genially. 'I'll begin by making a minute examination. You say that you were outside the door when you heard the noise?'

'I was in my room when I heard the queer sound – indeed it must have been the early part of whatever it was which woke me. I came out of my room at once. Father's door was shut, and I could see the whole landing and the upper slopes of the staircase. No one could have left by the door unknown to me, if that is what you mean!'

'That is just what I do mean, miss. If everyone who knows anything will tell me as well as that, we shall soon get to the bottom of this.'

He then went over to the bed, looked at it carefully, and asked: 'Has the bed been touched?'

'Not to my knowledge,' said Miss Trelawny, 'but I shall ask Mrs Grant – the housekeeper,' she added as she rang the bell. Mrs Grant answered it in person. 'Come in,' said Miss Trelawny. 'These gentlemen want to know, Mrs Grant, if the bed has been touched.'

'Not by me, ma'am.'

'Then,' said Miss Trelawny, turning to Sergeant Daw, 'it cannot have been touched by anyone. Either Mrs Grant or I myself was here all the time, and I do not think any of the servants who came when I gave the alarm were near the bed at all. You see, Father lay here just under the great safe, and everyone crowded round him. We sent them all away in a very short time.' Daw, with a motion of his hand, asked us all to stay at the other side of the room whilst with a magnifying-glass he examined the bed, taking care as he moved each fold of the bedclothes to replace it in exact position. Then he examined with his magnifying-glass the floor beside it, taking especial pains where the blood had trickled over the side of the bed, which was of heavy red wood handsomely carved. Inch by inch, down on his knees, carefully avoiding any touch with the stains on the floor, he followed the blood-marks over to the spot, close under the great safe, where the body had lain. All around and about this spot he went for a radius of some yards; but seemingly did not meet with anything to arrest special attention. Then he examined the front of the safe; round the lock, and along the bottom and top of the double doors, more especially at the places of their touching in front.

Next he went to the windows, which were fastened down with the hasps.

'Were the shutters closed?' he asked Miss Trelawny in a casual way as though he expected the negative answer, which came.

All this time Dr Winchester was attending to his patient; now dressing the wounds in the wrist or making minute examination all over the head and throat, and over the heart. More than once he put his nose to the mouth of the senseless man and sniffed. Each time he did so he finished up by unconsciously looking round the room, as though in search of something.

Then we heard the deep strong voice of the detective: 'So far as I can see, the object was to bring that key to the lock of the safe. There seems to be some secret in the mechanism that I am unable to guess at, though I served a year in Chubb's before I joined the police. It is a combination lock of seven letters; but there seems to be a way of locking even the combination. It is one of Chatwood's; I shall call at their place and find out something about it.' Then turning to the doctor, as though his own work were for the present done, he said: 'Have you anything you can tell me at once, doctor, which will not interfere with your full report? If there is any doubt I can wait, but the sooner I know something definite the better.'

Dr Winchester answered at once: 'For my own part I see no reason in waiting. I shall make a full report of course. But in the meantime I shall tell you all I know – which is after all not very much, and all I think – which is less definite. There is no wound on the head which could account for the state of stupor in which the patient continues. I must, therefore, take it that either he has been drugged or is under some hypnotic influence. So far as I can judge, he has not been drugged – at least by means of any drug of whose qualities I am aware. Of course, there is ordinarily in this room so much of mummy smell that it is difficult to be certain about anything having a delicate aroma. I dare say that you have noticed the peculiar Egyptian scents, bitumen, nard, aromatic gums and spices, and so forth. It is quite possible that somewhere in this room, amongst the curios and hidden by stronger scents, is some substance or liquid which may have the effect we see. It is possible that the patient has taken some drug, and that he may in some sleeping phase have injured himself. I do not think this is likely; and circumstances, other than those which I have myself been investigating, may prove that this surmise is not correct. But in the meantime it is possible; and must, till it be disproved, be kept within our purview.' Here Sergeant Daw interrupted: 'That may be, but if so, we should be able to find the instrument with which the wrist was injured. There would be marks of blood somewhere.'

'Exactly so!' said the doctor, fixing his glasses as though preparing for an argument. 'But if it be that the patient has used some strange drug, it may be one that does not take effect at once. As we are as yet ignorant of its potentialities – if, indeed, the whole surmise is correct at all – we must be prepared at all points.'

Here Miss Trelawny joined in the conversation: 'That would be quite right, so far as the action of the drug was concerned; but according to the second part of your surmise the wound may have been self-inflicted, and this *after* the drug had taken effect.'

'True!' said the detective and the doctor simultaneously.

She went on. 'As however, doctor, your guess does not exhaust the possibilities, we must bear in mind that some other variant of the same root-idea may be correct. I take it, therefore, that our first search, to be made on this assumption, must be for the weapon with which the injury was done to my Father's wrist.'

'Perhaps he put the weapon in the safe before he became quite unconscious,' said I, giving voice foolishly to a half-formed thought.

'That could not be,' said the doctor quickly. 'At least I think it could hardly be,' he added cautiously, with a brief bow to me. 'You see, the left hand is covered with blood; but there is no blood mark whatever on the safe.'

'Quite right!' I said, and there was a long pause.

The first to break the silence was the doctor.

'We shall want a nurse here as soon as possible; and I know the very one to suit. I shall go at once to get her if I can. I must ask that till I return some of you will remain constantly with the patient. It may be necessary to remove him to another room later on; but in the meantime he is best left here. Miss Trelawny, may I take it that either you or Mrs Grant will remain here – not merely in the room, but close to the patient and watchful of him – till I return?'

She bowed in reply, and took a seat beside the sofa. The doctor gave her some directions as to what she should do in case her father should become conscious before his return.

The next to move was Superintendent Dolan, who came close to Sergeant Daw as he said: 'I had better return now to the station – unless, of course, you should wish me to remain for a while.'

He answered, 'Is Johnny Wright still in your division?'

'Yes! Would you like him to be with you?' The other nodded reply. 'Then I will send him on to you as soon as can be arranged. He shall then stay with you as long as you wish. I will tell him that he is to take his instructions entirely from you.'

The sergeant accompanied him to the door, saying as he went: 'Thank you, sir; you are always thoughtful for men who are working with you. It is a pleasure to me to be with you again. I shall go back to Scotland Yard and report to my chief. Then I shall call at Chatwood's; and I shall return here as soon as possible. I suppose I may take it, miss, that I may put up here for a day or two, if required. It may be some help, or possibly some comfort to you, if I am about, until we unravel this mystery.'

'I shall be very grateful to you.' He looked keenly at her for a few seconds before he spoke again.

'Before I go have I permission to look about your father's table and desk? There might be something which would give us a clue – or a lead at all events.' Her answer was so unequivocal as almost to surprise him.

'You have the fullest possible permission to do anything which may help us in this dreadful trouble – to discover what it is that is wrong with my father, or which may shield him in the future!'

He began at once a systematic search of the dressing-table, and after that of the writing-table in the room. In one of the drawers he found a letter sealed; this he brought at once across the room and handed to Miss Trelawny.

'A letter – directed to me – and in my Father's hand!' she said as she eagerly opened it. I watched her face as she began to read; but seeing at once that Sergeant Daw kept his keen eyes on her face, unflinchingly watching every flitting expression, I kept my eyes henceforth fixed on his. When Miss Trelawny had read her letter through, I had in my mind a conviction, which, however, I kept locked in my own heart. Amongst the suspicions in the mind of the detective was one, rather perhaps potential than definite, of Miss Trelawny herself.

For several minutes Miss Trelawny held the letter in her hand with her eyes downcast, thinking. Then she read it carefully again; this time the varying expressions were intensified, and I thought I could easily follow them. When she had finished the second reading, she paused again. Then, though with some reluctance, she handed the letter to the detective. He read it eagerly but with unchanging face; read it a second time, and then handed it back with a bow. She paused a little again, and then handed it to me. As she did so she raised her eyes to mine for a single moment appealingly; a swift blush spread over her pale cheeks and forehead.

With mingled feelings I took it, but, all said, I was glad. She did not show any perturbation in giving the letter to the detective – she might not have shown any to anyone else. But to me . . . I feared to follow the thought further; but read on, conscious that the eyes of both Miss Trelawny and the detective were fixed on me.

My Dear Daughter – I want you to take this letter as an instruction – absolute and imperative, and admitting of no deviation whatever – in case anything untoward or unexpected by you or by others should happen to me. If I should be suddenly and mysteriously stricken down – either by sickness, accident or attack – you must follow these directions implicitly. If I am not already in my bedroom when you are made cognisant of my state, I am to be brought there as quickly as possible. Even should I be dead, my body is to be brought there. Thenceforth, until I am either conscious and able to give instructions on my own account, or buried, I am never to be left alone – not for a single instant. From nightfall to sunrise at least two persons must remain in the room. It will be well that a trained nurse be in the room from time to time, and will note any symptoms, either permanent or changing, which may strike her. My solicitors, Marvin & Jewkes, of 27b Lincoln's Inn, have full instructions in case of my death; and Mr Marvin has himself undertaken to see personally my wishes carried out. I should advise you, my dear daughter, seeing that you have no relative to apply to, to get some friend whom you can trust to either remain within the house where instant communication can be made, or to come nightly to aid in the watching, or to be within call. Such friend may be either male or female; but, whichever it may be, there should be added one other watcher or attendant at hand of the opposite sex. Understand, that it is of the very essence of my wish that there should be, awake and exercising themselves to my purposes, both masculine and feminine intelligences. Once more, my dear Margaret, let me impress on you the need for observation and just reasoning to conclusions, howsoever strange. If I am taken ill or injured, this will be no ordinary occasion; and I wish to warn you, so that your guarding may be complete.

Nothing in my room – I speak of the curios – must be removed or displaced in any way, or for any cause whatever. I have a special reason and a special purpose in the placing of each; so that any moving of them would thwart my plans.

Should you want money or counsel in anything, Mr Marvin will carry out your wishes; to the which he has my full instructions.

ABEL TRELAWNY

I read the letter a second time before speaking, for I feared to betray myself. The choice of a friend might be a momentous occasion for me. I had already ground for hope, in that she had asked me to help her in the first throe of her trouble; but love makes its own doubtings, and I feared. My thoughts seemed to whirl with lightning rapidity, and in a few seconds a whole process of reasoning became formulated. I must not volunteer to be the friend that the father advised his daughter to have to aid in her vigil; and yet that one glance had a lesson which I must not ignore. Also, did not she, when she wanted help, send to me – to me a stranger, except for one meeting at a dance and one brief afternoon of companionship on the river? Would it not humiliate her to make her ask me twice? Humiliate her! No! that pain I could at all events save her; it is not humiliation to refuse. So, as I handed her back the letter, I said: 'I know you will forgive me, Miss Trelawny, if I presume too much; but if you will permit me to aid in the watching I shall be proud. Though the occasion is a sad one, I shall be so far happy to be allowed the privilege.'

Despite her manifest and painful effort at self-control, the red tide swept her face and neck. Even her eyes seemed suffused, and in stern contrast with her pale cheeks when the tide had rolled back. She answered in a low voice: 'I shall be very grateful for your help!' Then in an afterthought she added: 'But you must not let me be selfish in my need! I know you have many duties to engage you; and though I shall value your help highly – most highly – it would not be fair to monopolise your time.'

'As to that,' I answered at once, 'my time is yours. I can for today easily arrange my work so that I can come here in the afternoon and stay till morning. After that, if the occasion still demands it, I can so arrange my work that I shall have more time still at my disposal.'

She was much moved. I could see the tears gather in her eyes, and she turned away her head. The detective spoke: 'I am glad you will be here, Mr Ross. I shall be in the house myself, as Miss Trelawny will allow me, if my people in Scotland Yard will permit. That letter seems to put a different complexion on everything; though the mystery remains greater than ever. If you can wait here an hour or two I shall go to headquarters, and then to the safe makers. After that I shall return; and you can go away easier in your mind, for I shall be here.'

When he had gone, we two, Miss Trelawny and I, remained in silence. At last she raised her eyes and looked at me for a moment; after that I would not have exchanged places with a king. For a while she busied herself round the extemporised bedside of her father. Then, asking me to be sure not to take my eyes off him till she returned, she hurried out.

In a few minutes she came back with Mrs Grant and two maids and a couple of men, who bore the entire frame and furniture of a light iron bed. This they proceeded to put together and to make. When the work was completed, and the servants had withdrawn, she said to me: 'It will be well to be all ready when the doctor returns. He will surely want to have Father put to bed; and a proper bed will be better for him than the sofa.' She then got a chair close beside her father, and sat down watching him.

I went about the room, taking accurate note of all I saw. And truly there were enough things in the room to evoke the curiosity of any man – even though the attendant circumstances were less strange.

The whole place, excepting those articles of furniture necessary to a well-furnished bedroom, was filled with magnificent curios, chiefly Egyptian. As the room was of immense size there was opportunity for the placing of a large number of them, even if, as with these, they were of huge proportions.

Whilst I was still investigating the room there came the sound of wheels on the gravel outside the house. There was a ring at the hall door, and a few minutes later, after a preliminary tap at the door and an answering 'Come in!' Dr Winchester entered, followed by a young woman in the dark dress of a nurse.

'I have been fortunate!' he said as he came in. 'I found her at once and free. Miss Trelawny, this is Nurse Kennedy!'

CHAPTER 3

The Watchers

I WAS STRUCK by the way the two young women looked at each other. I suppose I have been so much in the habit of weighing up in my own mind the personality of witnesses and of forming judgment by their unconscious action and mode of bearing themselves, that the habit extends to my life outside as well as within the court-house. At this moment of my life anything that interested Miss Trelawny interested me; and as she had been struck by the newcomer I instinctively weighed her up also. By comparison of the two I seemed somehow to gain a new knowledge of Miss Trelawny. Certainly, the two women made a good contrast. Miss Trelawny was of fine figure; dark, straight-featured. She had marvellous eyes; great, wide-open, and as black and soft as velvet, with a mysterious depth. To look in them was like gazing at a black mirror such as Dr Dee used in his wizard rites. I heard an old gentleman at the picnic, a great oriental traveller, describe the effect of her eyes 'as looking at night at the great distant lamps of a mosque through the open door'. The eyebrows were typical. Finely arched and rich in long curling hair, they seemed like the proper architectural environment of the deep, splendid eyes. Her hair was black also, but was as fine as silk. Generally black hair is a type of animal strength and seems as if some strong expression of the forces of a strong nature; but in this case there could be no such thought. There were refinement and high breeding; and though there was no suggestion of weakness, any sense of power there was, was rather spiritual than animal. The whole harmony of her being seemed complete. Carriage, figure, hair, eyes; the mobile, full mouth, whose scarlet lips and white teeth seemed to light up the lower part of the face – as the eyes did the upper; the wide sweep of the jaw from chin to ear; the long, fine fingers; the hand which seemed to move from the wrist as though it had a sentience of its own. All these perfections went to make up a personality that dominated either by its grace, its sweetness, its beauty, or its charm.

Nurse Kennedy, on the other hand, was rather under than over a woman's average height. She was firm and thickset, with full limbs and broad, strong, capable hands. Her colour was in the general effect that of an autumn leaf. The yellow-brown hair was thick and long, and the golden-brown eyes sparkled from the freckled, sun-burnt skin. Her rosy cheeks gave a general idea of rich brown. The red lips and white teeth did not alter the colour scheme, but only emphasised it. She had a snub nose – there was no possible doubt about it; but like such noses in general it showed a nature generous, untiring, and full of good-nature. Her broad white forehead, which even the freckles had spared, was full of forceful thought and reason.

Dr Winchester had on their journey from the hospital, coached her in the necessary particulars, and without a word she took charge of the patient and set to work. Having examined the new-made bed and shaken the pillows, she spoke to the doctor, who gave instructions; presently we all four, stepping together, lifted the unconscious man from the sofa.

Early in the afternoon, when Sergeant Daw had returned, I called at my rooms in Jermyn Street, and sent out such clothes, books and papers as I should be likely to want within a few days. Then I went on to keep my legal engagements.

The Court sat late that day as an important case was ending; it was striking six as I drove in at the gate of the Kensington Palace Road. I found myself installed in a large room close to the sick chamber.

That night we were not yet regularly organised for watching, so that the early part of the evening showed an unevenly balanced guard. Nurse Kennedy, who had been on duty all day, was lying down, as she had arranged to come on again by twelve o'clock. Dr Winchester, who was dining in the house, remained in the room until dinner was announced; and went back at once when it was over. During dinner Mrs Grant remained in the room, and with her Sergeant Daw, who wished to complete a minute examination which he had undertaken of everything in the room and near it. At nine o'clock Miss Trelawny and I went in to relieve the doctor. She had lain down for a few hours in the afternoon so as to be refreshed for her work at night. She told me that she had determined that for this night at least she would sit up and watch. I did not try to dissuade her, for I knew that her mind was made up. Then and there I made up my mind that I would watch with her – unless, of course, I should see that she really did not wish it. I said nothing of my intentions for the present. We came in on tiptoe, so silently that the doctor, who was bending over the bed, did not hear us, and seemed a little startled when suddenly looking up he saw our eyes upon him. I felt that the mystery of the whole thing was getting on his nerves, as it had already got on the nerves of some others of us. He was, I fancied, a little annoyed with himself for having been so startled, and at once began to talk in a hurried manner as though to get over our idea of his embarrassment: 'I am really and absolutely at my wits'-end to find any fit cause for this stupor. I have made again as accurate an examination as I know how, and I am satisfied that there is no injury to the brain, that is, no external injury. Indeed, all his vital organs seem unimpaired. I have given him, as you know, food several times and it has manifestly done him good. His breathing is strong and regular, and his pulse is slower and stronger than it was this morning. I cannot find evidence of any known drug, and his unconsciousness does not resemble any of the many cases of hypnotic sleep which I saw in the Charcot Hospital in Paris. And as to these wounds' – he laid his finger gently on the bandaged wrist which lay outside the coverlet as he spoke, 'I do not know what to make of them. They might have been made by a carding-machine; but that supposition is untenable. It is within the bounds of possibility that they might have been made by a wild animal if it had taken care to sharpen its claws. That too is, I take it, impossible. By the way, have you any strange pets here in the house; anything of an exceptional kind, such as a tiger-cat or anything out of the common?' Miss Trelawny smiled a sad smile which made my heart ache, as she made answer: 'Oh no! Father does not like animals about the house, unless they are dead and mummied.' This was said with a touch of bitterness – or jealousy, I could hardly tell which. 'Even my poor kitten was only allowed in the house on sufferance; and though he is the dearest and best-conducted cat in the world, he is now on a sort of parole, and is not allowed into this room.'

As she was speaking a faint rattling of the door handle was heard. Instantly Miss Trelawny's face brightened. She sprang up and went over to the door, saying as she went: 'There he is! That is my Silvio.

He stands on his hind legs and rattles the door handle when he wants to come into a room.' She opened the door, speaking to the cat as though he were a baby: 'Did him want his movver? Come then; but he must stay with her!' She lifted the cat, and came back with him in her arms. He was certainly a magnificent animal. A chinchilla grey Persian with long silky hair; a really lordly animal with a haughty bearing, despite his gentleness; and with great paws which spread out as he placed them on the ground. Whilst she was fondling him, he suddenly gave a wriggle like an eel and slipped out of her arms. He ran across the room and stood opposite a low table on which stood the mummy of an animal, and began to mew and snarl. Miss Trelawny was after him in an instant and lifted him in her arms, kicking and struggling and wriggling to get away; but not biting or scratching, for evidently he loved his beautiful mistress. He ceased to make a noise the moment he was in her arms; in a whisper she admonished him: 'O you naughty Silvio! You have broken your parole that mother gave for you. Now, say goodnight to the gentlemen, and come away to mother's room!' As she was speaking she held out the cat's paw to me to shake. As I did so I could not but admire its size and beauty. 'Why,' said I, 'his paw seems like a little boxing-glove full of claws.'

She smiled: 'So it ought to. Don't you notice that my Silvio has seven toes, see!' she opened the paw; and surely enough there were seven separate claws, each of them sheathed in a delicate, fine, shell-like case. As I gently stroked the foot the claws emerged and one of them accidentally – there was no anger now and the cat was purring – stuck into my hand. Instinctively I said as I drew back: 'Why, his claws are like razors!'

Dr Winchester had come close to us and was bending over looking at the cat's claws; as I spoke he said in a quick, sharp way: 'Eh!' I could hear the quick intake of his breath. Whilst I was stroking the now quiescent cat, the doctor went to the table and tore off a piece of blotting-paper from the writing-pad and came back. He laid the paper on his palm and, with a simple 'pardon me!' to Miss Trelawny, placed the cat's paw on it and pressed it down with his other hand. The haughty cat seemed to resent somewhat the familiarity, and tried to draw its foot away. This was plainly what the doctor wanted, for in the act the cat opened the sheaths of its claws and made several reefs in the soft paper. Then Miss Trelawny took her pet away.

She returned in a couple of minutes; as she came in she said: 'It is most odd about that mummy! When Silvio came into the room first – indeed I took him in as a kitten to show to Father – he went on just the same way. He jumped up on the table, and tried to scratch and bite the mummy. That was what made Father so angry, and brought the decree of banishment on poor Silvio. Only his parole, given through me, kept him in the house.'

Whilst she had been gone, Dr Winchester had taken the bandage from her father's wrist. The wound was now quite clear, as the separate cuts showed out in fierce red lines. The doctor folded the blotting-paper across the line of punctures made by the cat's claws, and held it down close to the wound. As he did so, he looked up triumphantly and beckoned us over to him.

The cuts in the paper corresponded with the wounds in the wrist! No explanation was needed, as he said: 'It would have been better if master Silvio had not broken his parole!'

We were all silent for a little while. Suddenly Miss Trelawny said: 'But Silvio was not in here last night!'

'Are you sure? Could you prove that if necessary?' She hesitated before replying: 'I am certain of it; but I fear it would be difficult to prove. Silvio sleeps in a basket in my room. I certainly put him to bed last night; I remember distinctly laying his little blanket over him, and tucking him in. This morning I took him out of the basket myself. I certainly never noticed him in here; though, of course, that would not mean much, for I was too concerned about poor father, and too much occupied with him, to notice even Silvio.'

The doctor shook his head as he said with a certain sadness: 'Well, at any rate it is no use trying to prove anything now. Any cat in the world would have cleaned blood-marks – did any exist – from his paws in a hundredth part of the time that has elapsed.'

Again we were all silent; and again the silence was broken by Miss Trelawny: 'But now that I think of it, it could not have been poor Silvio that injured Father. My door was shut when I first heard the sound; and Father's was shut when I listened at it. When I went in, the injury had been done; so that it must have been before Silvio could possibly have got in.' This reasoning commended itself, especially to me as a barrister, for it was proof to satisfy a jury. It gave me a distinct pleasure to have Silvio acquitted of the crime – possibly because he was Miss Trelawny's cat and was loved by her. Happy cat! Silvio's mistress was manifestly pleased as I said: 'Verdict, "not guilty"! Dr Winchester after a pause observed: 'My apologies to master Silvio on this occasion; but I am still puzzled to know why he is so keen against that mummy. Is he the same toward the other mummies in the house? There are, I suppose, a lot of them. I saw three in the hall as I came in.'

'There are lots of them,' she answered. 'I sometimes don't know whether I am in a private house or the British Museum. But Silvio never concerns himself about any of them except that particular one. I suppose it must be because it is of an animal, not a man or a woman.'

'Perhaps it is of a cat!' said the doctor as he started up and went across the room to look at the mummy more closely. 'Yes,' he went on, 'it is the mummy of a cat; and a very fine one, too. If it hadn't been a special favourite of some very special person it would never have received so much honour. See! A painted case and obsidian eyes – just like a human mummy. It is an extraordinary thing, that knowledge of kind to kind. Here is a dead cat – that is all; it is perhaps four or five thousand years old – and another cat of another breed, in what is practically another world, is ready to fly at it, just as it would if it were not dead. I should like to experiment a bit about that cat if you don't mind, Miss Trelawny.' She hesitated before replying: 'Of course, do anything you may think necessary or wise; but I hope it will not be anything to hurt or worry my poor Silvio.' The doctor smiled as he answered: 'Oh, Silvio would be all right: it is the other one that my sympathies would be reserved for.'

'How do you mean?'

'Master Silvio will do the attacking; the other one will do the suffering.'

'Suffering?' There was a note of pain in her voice. The doctor smiled more broadly: 'Oh, please make your mind easy as to that. The other won't suffer as we understand it; except perhaps in his structure and outfit.'

'What on earth do you mean?'

'Simply this, my dear young lady, that the antagonist will be a mummy cat like this one. There are, I take it, plenty of them to be had in Museum Street. I shall get one and place it here instead of that one – you won't think that a temporary exchange will violate your Father's instructions, I hope. We shall then find out, to begin with, whether Silvio objects to all mummy cats, or only to this one in particular.'

'I don't know,' she said doubtfully. 'Father's instructions seem very uncompromising.' Then after a pause she went on: 'But of course under the circumstances anything that is to be ultimately for his good must be done. I suppose there can't be anything very particular about the mummy of a cat.'

Dr Winchester said nothing. He sat rigid, with so grave a look on his face that his extra gravity passed on to me; and in its enlightening perturbation I began to realise more than I had yet done the strangeness of the case in which I was now so deeply concerned. When once this thought had begun there was no end to it. Indeed it grew, and blossomed, and reproduced itself in a thousand different ways. The room and all in it gave grounds for strange thoughts. There were so many ancient relics that unconsciously one was taken back to strange lands and strange times. There were so many mummies or mummy objects, round which there seem to cling for ever the penetrating odours of bitumen, and spices and gums – 'Nard and Circassia's balmy smells' – that one was unable to forget the past. Of course, there was but little light in the room, and that carefully shaded; so that there was no glare anywhere. None of that direct light which can manifest itself as a power or an entity, and so make for companionship. The room was a large one, and lofty in proportion to its size. In its vastness was place for a multitude of things not often found in a bedchamber. In far corners of the room were shadows of uncanny shape. More than once as I thought, the multitudinous presence of the dead and the past took such hold on me that I caught myself looking round fearfully as though some strange personality or influence was present. Even the manifest presence of Dr Winchester and Miss Trelawny could not altogether comfort or satisfy me at such moments. It was with a distinct sense of relief that I saw a new personality in the room in the shape of Nurse Kennedy. There was no doubt that that business-like, self-reliant, capable young woman added an element of security to such wild imaginings as my own. She had a quality of common sense that seemed to pervade everything around her, as though it were some kind of emanation. Up to that moment I had been building fancies around the sick man; so that finally all about him, including myself, had become involved in them, or enmeshed, or saturated, or . . . But now that she had come, he relapsed into his proper perspective as a patient; the room was a sick-room, and the shadows lost their fearsome quality. The only thing which it could not altogether abrogate was the strange Egyptian smell. You may put a mummy in a glass case and hermetically seal it so that no corroding air can get within; but all the same it will exhale its odour. One might think that four or five thousand years would exhaust the olfactory qualities of anything; but experience teaches us that these smells remain, and that their secrets are unknown to us. Today they are as much mysteries as they were when the embalmers put the body in the bath of natron . . . All at once I sat up. I had become lost in an absorbing reverie. The Egyptian smell had seemed to get on my nerves – on my memory – on my very will.

At that moment I had a thought which was like an inspiration. If I was influenced in such a manner by the smell, might it not be that the sick man, who lived half his life or more in the atmosphere, had gradually and by slow but sure process taken into his system something which had permeated him to such degree that it had a new power derived from quantity – or strength – or . . .

I was becoming lost again in a reverie. This would not do. I must take such precaution that I could remain awake, or free from such entrancing thought. I had had but half a night's sleep last night; and this night I must remain awake. Without stating my intention, for I feared that I might add to the trouble and uneasiness of Miss Trelawny, I went downstairs and out of the house. I soon found a chemist's shop, and came away with a respirator. When I got back, it was ten o'clock; the doctor was going for the night. The nurse came with him to the door of the sick-room, taking her last instructions. Miss Trelawny sat still beside the bed. Sergeant Daw, who had entered as the doctor went out, was some little distance off.

When Nurse Kennedy joined us, we arranged that she should sit up till two o'clock, when Miss Trelawny would relieve her. Thus, in accordance with Mr Trelawny's instructions, there would always be a man and a woman in the room; and each one of us would overlap, so that at no time would a new set of watchers come on duty without someone to tell of what – if anything – had occurred. I lay down on a sofa in my own room, having arranged that one of the servants should call me a little before twelve. In a few moments I was asleep.

When I was waked, it took me several seconds to get back my thoughts so as to recognise my own identity and surroundings. The short sleep had, however, done me good, and I could look on things around me in a more practical light than I had been able to do earlier in the evening. I bathed my face, and thus refreshed went into the sick-room. I moved very softly. The nurse was sitting by the bed, quiet and alert; the detective sat in an armchair across the room in deep shadow. He did not move when I crossed, until I got close to him, when he said in a dull whisper: 'It is all right; I have not been asleep!' An unnecessary thing to say, I thought – it always is, unless it be untrue in spirit. When I told him that his watch was over; that he might go to bed till I should call him at six o'clock, he seemed relieved and went with alacrity. At the door he turned and, coming back to me, said in a whisper: 'I sleep lightly and I shall have my pistols with me. I won't feel so heavy-headed when I get out of this mummy smell.'

He too, then, had shared my experience of drowsiness!

I asked the nurse if she wanted anything. I noticed that she had a vinaigrette in her lap. Doubtless she, too, had felt some of the influence which had so affected me. She said that she had all she required, but that if she should want anything she would at once let me know. I wished to keep her from noticing my respirator, so I went to the chair in the shadow where her back was toward me. Here I quietly put it on, and made myself comfortable.

For what seemed a long time, I sat and thought and thought. It was a wild medley of thoughts, as might have been expected from the experiences of the previous day and night. Again I found myself thinking of the Egyptian smell; and I remember that I felt a delicious satisfaction that I did not experience it as I had done. The respirator was doing its work.

It must have been that the passing of this disturbing thought made for repose of mind, which is the corollary of bodily rest, for, though I really cannot remember being asleep or waking from it, I saw a vision – I dreamed a dream, I scarcely know which.

I was still in the room, seated in the chair. I had on my respirator and knew that I breathed freely. The nurse sat in her chair with her back toward me. She sat quite still. The sick man lay as still as the dead. It was rather like the picture of a scene than the reality; all were still and silent; and the stillness and silence were continuous. Outside, in the distance I could hear the sounds of a city, the occasional roll of wheels, the shout of a reveller, the far-away echo of whistles and the rumbling of trains. The light was very, very low; the reflection of it under the green-shaded lamp was a dim relief to the darkness, rather than light. The green silk fringe of the lamp had merely the colour of an emerald seen in the moonlight. The room, for all its darkness, was full of shadows. It seemed in my whirling thoughts as though all the real things had become shadows – shadows which moved, for they passed the dim outline of the high windows. Shadows which had sentience. I even thought there was sound, a faint sound as of the mew of a cat – the rustle of drapery and a metallic clink as of metal faintly touching metal. I sat as one entranced. At last I felt, as in nightmare, that this was sleep, and that in the passing of its portals all my will had gone.

All at once my senses were full awake. A shriek rang in my ears. The room was filled suddenly with a blaze of light. There was the sound of pistol shots – one, two; and a haze of white smoke in the room. When my waking eyes regained their power, I could have shrieked with horror myself at what I saw before me.

CHAPTER 4

The Second Attempt

THE SIGHT which met my eyes had the horror of a dream within a dream, with the certainty of reality added. The room was as I had seen it last; except that the shadowy look had gone in the glare of the many lights, and every article in it stood stark and solidly real.

By the empty bed sat Nurse Kennedy, as my eyes had last seen her, sitting bolt upright in the armchair beside the bed. She had placed a pillow behind her, so that her back might be erect; but her neck was fixed as that of one in a cataleptic trance. She was, to all intents and purposes, turned into stone. There was no special expression on her face – no fear, no horror; nothing such as might be expected of one in such a condition. Her open eyes showed neither wonder nor interest. She was simply a negative existence, warm, breathing, placid; but absolutely unconscious of the world around her. The bedclothes were disarranged, as though the patient had been drawn from under them without throwing them back. The corner of the upper sheet hung upon the floor; close by it lay one of the bandages with which the doctor had dressed the wounded wrist. Another and another lay further along the floor, as though forming a clue to where the sick man now lay. This was almost exactly where he had been found on the previous night, under the great safe. Again, the left arm lay toward the safe. But there had been a new outrage, an attempt had been made to sever the arm close to the bangle which held the tiny key. A heavy 'kukri' knife – one of the leaf - shaped knives which the Gurkhas and others of the hill tribes of India use with such effect – had been taken from its place on the wall, and with it the attempt had been made. It was manifest that just at the moment of striking, the blow had been arrested, for only the point of the knife and not the edge of the blade had struck the flesh. As it was, the outer side of the arm had been cut to the bone and the blood was pouring out. In addition, the former wound in front of the arm had been cut or torn about terribly, one of the cuts seemed to jet out blood as if with each pulsation of the heart. By the side of her father knelt Miss Trelawny, her white nightdress stained with the blood in which she knelt. In the middle of the room Sergeant Daw, in his shirt and trousers and stocking feet, was putting fresh cartridges into his revolver in a dazed mechanical kind of way. His eyes were red and heavy, and he seemed only half awake, and less than half conscious of what was going on around him. Several servants, bearing lights of various kinds, were clustered round the doorway.

As I rose from my chair and came forward, Miss Trelawny raised her eyes toward me. When she saw me she shrieked and started to her feet, pointing towards me. Never shall I forget the strange picture she made, with her white drapery all smeared with blood which, as she rose from the pool, ran in streaks toward her bare feet. I believe that I had only been asleep; that whatever influence had worked on Mr Trelawny and Nurse Kennedy – and in less degree on Sergeant Daw – had not touched me. The respirator had been of some service, though it had not kept off the tragedy whose dire evidences were before me. I can understand now – I could understand even then – the fright, added to that which had gone before, which my appearance must have evoked. I had still on the respirator, which covered mouth and nose; my hair had been tossed in my sleep. Coming suddenly forward, thus enwrapped and dishevelled, in that horrified crowd, I must have had, in the strange mixture of lights, an extraordinary and terrifying appearance. It was well that I recognised all this in time to avert another catastrophe; for the half-dazed, mechanically-acting detective put in the cartridges and had raised his revolver to shoot at me when I succeeded in wrenching off the respirator and shouting to him to hold his hand. In this also he acted mechanically; the red, half-awake eyes had not in them even then the intention of conscious action. The danger, however, was averted. The relief of the situation, strangely enough, came in a simple fashion. Mrs Grant, seeing that her young mistress had on only her nightdress, had gone to fetch a dressing-gown, which she now threw over her. This simple act brought us all back to the region of fact. With a long breath, one and all seemed to devote themselves to the most pressing matter before us, that of staunching the flow of blood from the arm of the wounded man. Even as the thought of action came, I rejoiced; for the bleeding was very proof that Mr Trelawny still lived.

Last night's lesson was not thrown away. More than one of those present knew now what to do in such an emergency, and within a few seconds willing hands were at work on a tourniquet. A man was at once despatched for the doctor, and several of the servants disappeared to make themselves respectable. We lifted Mr Trelawny on to the sofa where he had lain yesterday; and, having done what we could for him, turned our attention to the nurse. In all the turmoil she had not stirred; she sat there as before, erect and rigid, breathing softly and naturally and with a placid smile. As it was manifestly of no use to attempt anything with her till the doctor had come, we began to think of the general situation.

Mrs Grant had by this time taken her mistress away and changed her clothes; for she was back presently in a dressing-gown and slippers, and with the traces of blood removed from her hands. She was now much calmer, though she trembled sadly; and her face was ghastly white. When she had looked at her father's wrist, I holding the tourniquet, she turned her eyes round the room, resting them now and again on each one of us present in turn, but seeming to find no comfort. It was so apparent to me that she did not know where to begin or whom to trust that, to reassure her, I said: 'I am all right now; I was only asleep.' Her voice had a gulp in it as she said in a low voice: 'Asleep! You! and my father in danger! I thought you were on the watch!' I felt the sting of justice in the reproach; but I really wanted to help her, so I answered: 'Only asleep. It is bad enough, I know; but there is something more than an 'only' round us here. Had it not been that I took a definite precaution I might have been like the nurse there.' She turned her eyes swiftly on the weird figure, sitting grimly upright like a painted statue; and then her face softened. With the action of habitual courtesy she said: 'Forgive me! I did not mean to be rude. But I am in such distress and fear that I hardly know what I am saying. Oh, it is dreadful! I fear for fresh trouble and horror and mystery every moment.' This cut me to the very heart, and out of the heart's fullness I spoke: 'Don't give me a thought! I don't deserve it. I was on guard, and yet I slept. All that I can say is that I didn't mean to, and I tried to avoid it; but it was over me before I knew it. Anyhow, it is done now; and can't be undone. Probably someday we may understand it all; but now let us try to get at some idea of what has happened. Tell me what you remember!' The effort to recollect seemed to stimulate her; she became calmer as she spoke: 'I was asleep, and woke suddenly with the same horrible feeling on me that Father was in great and immediate danger. I jumped up and ran, just as I was, into his room. It was nearly pitch dark, but as I opened the door there was light enough to see Father's nightdress as he lay on the floor under the safe, just as on that first awful night. Then I think I must have gone mad for a moment.' She stopped and shuddered. My eyes lit on Sergeant Daw, still fiddling in an aimless way with the revolver. Mindful of my work with the tourniquet, I said calmly: 'Now tell us, Sergeant Daw, what did you fire at?' The policeman seemed to pull himself together with the habit of obedience. Looking around at the servants remaining in the room, he said with that air of importance which, I take it, is the regulation attitude of an official of the law before strangers: 'Don't you think, sir, that we can allow the servants to go away? We can then better go into the matter.' I nodded approval; the servants took the hint and withdrew, though unwillingly, the last one closing the door behind him. Then the detective went on: 'I think I had better tell you my impressions, sir, rather than recount my actions. That is, so far as I remember them.' There was a mortified deference now in his manner, which probably arose from his consciousness of the awkward position in which he found himself. 'I went to sleep half-dressed – as I am now, with a revolver under my pillow. It was the last thing I remember thinking of. I do not know how long I slept. I had turned off the electric light, and it was quite dark. I thought I heard a scream; but I can't be sure, for I felt thick-headed as a man does when he is called too soon after an extra long stretch of work. Not that such was the case this time. Anyhow my thoughts flew to the pistol. I took it out, and ran on to the landing. Then I heard a sort of scream, or rather a call for help, and ran into this room. The room was dark, for the lamp beside the nurse was out, and the only light was that from the landing, coming through the open door. Miss Trelawny was kneeling on the floor beside her father, and was screaming. I thought I saw something move between me and the window; so, without thinking, and being half dazed and only half awake, I shot at it. It moved a little more to the right between the windows, and I shot again. Then you came up out of the big chair with all that muffling on your face. It seemed to me, being as I say half dazed and only half awake – I know, sir, you will take this into account – as if it had been you, being in the same direction as the thing I had fired at. And so I was about to fire again when you pulled off the wrap.' Here I asked him – I was cross-examining now and felt at home: 'You say you thought I was the thing you fired at. What thing?' The man scratched his head, but made no reply.

'Come, sir,' I said, 'what thing; what was it like?' The answer came in a low voice: 'I don't know, sir. I thought there was something; but what it was, or what it was like, I haven't the faintest notion. I suppose it was because I had been thinking of the pistol before I went to sleep, and because when I came in here I was half dazed and only half awake – which I hope you will in future, sir, always remember.' He clung to that formula of excuse as though it were his sheet-anchor. I did not want to antagonise the man; on the contrary I wanted to have him with us. Besides, I had on me at that time myself the shadow of my own default; so I said as kindly as I knew how: 'Quite right! sergeant. Your impulse was correct; though of course in the half-somnolent condition in which you were, and perhaps partly affected by the same influence – whatever it may be – which made me sleep and which has put the nurse in that cataleptic trance, it could not be expected that you would pause to weigh matters. But now, whilst the matter is fresh, let me see exactly where you stood and where I sat. We shall be able to trace the course of your bullets.' The prospect of action and the exercise of his habitual skill seemed to brace him at once; he seemed a different man as he set about his work. I asked Mrs Grant to hold the tourniquet, and went and stood where he had stood and looked where, in the darkness, he had pointed. I could not but notice the mechanical exactness of his mind, as when he showed me where he had stood, or drew, as a matter of course, the revolver from his pistol pocket, and pointed with it. The chair from which I had risen still stood in its place. Then I asked him to point with his hand only, as I wished to move in the track of his shot.

Just behind my chair, and a little back of it, stood a high buhl cabinet. The glass door was shattered. I asked: 'Was this the direction of your first shot or your second?' The answer came promptly: 'The second; the first was over there!'

He turned a little to the left, more toward the wall where the great safe stood, and pointed. I followed the direction of his hand and came to the low table whereon rested, amongst other curios, the mummy of the cat which had raised Silvio's ire. I got a candle and easily found the mark of the bullet. It had broken a little glass vase and a tazza of black, basalt, exquisitely engraved with hieroglyphics, the graven lines being filled with some faint green cement and the whole thing being polished to an equal surface. The bullet, flattened against the wall, lay on the table.

I then went to the broken cabinet. It was evidently a receptacle for valuable curios; for in it were some great scarabs of gold, agate, green jasper, amethyst, lapis lazuli, opal, granite, and blue-green china. None of these things happily were touched. The bullet had gone through the back of the cabinet; but no other damage, save the shattering of the glass, had been done. I could not but notice the strange arrangement of the curios on the shelf of the cabinet. All the scarabs, rings, amulets, etc. were arranged in an uneven oval round an exquisitely-carved golden miniature figure of a hawk-headed god crowned with a disk and plumes. I did not wait to look further at present, for my attention was demanded by more pressing things; but

I determined to make a more minute examination when I should have time. It was evident that some of the strange Egyptian smell clung to these old curios; through the broken glass came an added whiff of spice and gum and bitumen, almost stronger than those I had already noticed as coming from others in the room.

All this had really taken but a few minutes. I was surprised when my eye met, through the chinks between the dark window blinds and the window cases, the brighter light of the coming dawn. When I went back to the sofa and took the tourniquet from Mrs Grant, she went over and pulled up the blinds.

It would be hard to imagine anything more ghastly than the appearance of the room with the faint grey light of early morning coming in upon it. As the windows faced north, any light that came was a fixed grey light without any of the rosy possibility of dawn which comes in the eastern quarter of the heavens. The electric lights seemed dull and yet glaring; and every shadow was of a hard intensity. There was nothing of morning freshness; nothing of the softness of night. All was hard and cold, and inexpressibly dreary. The face of the senseless man on the sofa seemed of a ghastly yellow; and the nurse's face had taken a suggestion of green from the shade of the lamp near her. Only Miss Trelawny's face looked white; and it was of a pallor which made my heart ache. It looked as if nothing on God's earth could ever again bring back to it the colour of life and happiness.

It was a relief to us all when Dr Winchester came in, breathless with running. He only asked one question: 'Can anyone tell me anything of how this wound was gotten?' On seeing the headshake which went round us under his glance, he said no more, but applied himself to his surgical work. For an instant he looked up at the nurse sitting so still; but then bent himself to his task, a grave frown contracting his brows. It was not till the arteries were tied and the wounds completely dressed that he spoke again, except, of course, when he had asked for anything to be handed to him or to be done for him. When Mr Trelawny's wounds had been thoroughly cared for, he said to Miss Trelawny: 'What about Nurse Kennedy?' She answered at once: 'I really do not know. I found her when I came into the room at half-past two o'clock, sitting exactly as she does now. We have not moved her, or changed her position. She has not wakened since. Even Sergeant Daw's pistol-shots did not disturb her.' 'Pistol-shots? Have you then discovered any cause for this new outrage?' The rest were silent, so I answered: 'We have discovered nothing. I was in the room watching with the nurse. Earlier in the evening I fancied that the mummy smells were making me drowsy, so I went out and got a respirator. I had it on when I came on duty; but it did not keep me from going to sleep. I awoke to see the room full of people; that is, Miss Trelawny and Sergeant Daw and the servants. The nurse was sitting in her chair just as I had seen her. Sergeant Daw, being only half awake and still stupefied by the same scent or influence which had affected us, fancied that he saw something moving through the shadowy darkness of the room, and fired twice. When I rose out of my chair, with my face swathed in the respirator, he took me for the cause of the trouble. Naturally enough, he was about to fire again, when I was fortunately in time to manifest my identity. Mr Trelawny was lying beside the safe, just as he was found last night; and was bleeding profusely from the new wound in his wrist. We lifted him on the sofa, and made a tourniquet. That is, literally and absolutely, all that any of us know as yet. We have not touched the knife, which you see lies close by the pool of blood. Look!' I said, going over and lifting it, 'The point is red with the blood which has dried.'

Dr Winchester stood quite still a few minutes before speaking: 'Then the doings of this night are quite as mysterious as those of last night?'

'Quite!' I answered. He said nothing in reply, but turning to Miss Trelawny said: 'We had better take Nurse Kennedy into another room. I suppose there is nothing to prevent it?'

'Nothing! Please, Mrs Grant, see that Nurse Kennedy's room is ready; and ask two of the men to come and carry her in.' Mrs Grant went out immediately; and in a few minutes came back saying: 'The room is quite ready; and the men are here.' By her direction two footmen came into the room and, lifting up the rigid body of Nurse Kennedy under the supervision of the doctor, carried her out of the room. Miss Trelawny remained with me in the sick chamber, and Mrs Grant went with the doctor into the nurse's room.

When we were alone Miss Trelawny came over to me, and taking both my hands in hers, said: 'I hope you won't remember what I said. I did not mean it, and I was distraught.' I did not make reply; but I held her hands and kissed them. There are different ways of kissing a lady's hands. This way was intended as homage and respect; and it was accepted as such in the high-bred, dignified way which marked Miss Trelawny's bearing and every movement. I went over to the sofa and looked down at the senseless man. The dawn had come much nearer in the last few minutes, and there was something of the clearness of day in the light. As I looked at the stern, cold, set face, now as white as a marble monument in the pale grey light, I could not but feel that there was some deep mystery beyond all that had happened within the last twenty-six hours. Those beetling brows screened some massive purpose; that high, broad forehead held some finished train of reasoning, which the broad chin and massive jaw would help to carry into effect. As I looked and wondered, there began to steal over me again that phase of wandering thought which had last night heralded the approach of sleep. I resisted it, and held myself sternly to the present. This was easier to do when Miss Trelawny came close to me, and, leaning her forehead against my shoulder, began to cry silently. Then all the manhood in me woke, and to present purpose. It was of little use trying to speak; words were inadequate to thought. But we understood each other; she did not draw away when I put my arm protectingly over her shoulder as I used to do with my little sister long ago when in her childish trouble she would come to her big brother to be comforted. That very act or attitude of protection made me more resolute in my purpose, and seemed to clear my brain of idle, dreamy wandering in thought. With an instinct of greater protection, however, I took away my arm as I heard the doctor's footstep outside the door.

When Dr Winchester came in he looked intently at the patient before speaking. His brows were set, and his mouth was a thin, hard line. Presently he said: 'There is much in common between the sleep of your father and Nurse Kennedy. Whatever influence has brought it about has probably worked the same way in both cases. In Kennedy's case the coma is less marked. I cannot but feel, however, that with her we may be able to do more and more quickly than with this patient, as our hands are not tied. I have placed her in a draught; and already she shows some signs, though very faint ones, of ordinary unconsciousness. The rigidity of her limbs is less, and her skin seems more sensitive – or perhaps I should say less insensitive – to pain.'

'How is it, then,' I asked, 'that Mr Trelawny is still in this state of insensibility; and yet, so far as we know, his body has not had such rigidity at all?'

'That I cannot answer. The problem is one which we may solve in a few hours; or it may need a few days. But it will be a useful lesson in diagnosis to us all; and perhaps to many and many others after us, who knows!' he added, with the genuine fire of an enthusiast.

As the morning wore on, he flitted perpetually between the two rooms, watching anxiously over both patients. He made Mrs Grant remain with the nurse, but either Miss Trelawny or I, generally both of us, remained with the wounded man. We each managed, however, to get bathed and dressed; the doctor and Mrs Grant remained with Mr Trelawny whilst we had breakfast.

Sergeant Daw went off to report at Scotland Yard the progress of the night; and then to the local station to arrange for the coming of his comrade, Wright, as fixed with Superintendent Dolan. When he returned I could not but think that he had been hauled over the coals for shooting in a sick-room; or perhaps for shooting at all without certain and proper cause. His remark to me enlightened me in the matter: 'A good character is worth something, sir, in spite of what some of them say. See! I've still got leave to carry my revolver.'

That day was a long and anxious one. Toward nightfall Nurse Kennedy so far improved that the rigidity of her limbs entirely disappeared. She still breathed quietly and regularly; but the fixed expression of her face, though it was a calm enough expression, gave place to fallen eyelids and the negative look of sleep. Dr Winchester had, towards evening, brought two more nurses, one of whom was to remain with Nurse Kennedy and the other to share in the watching with Miss Trelawny, who had insisted on remaining up herself. She had, in order to prepare for the duty, slept for several hours in the afternoon. We had all taken counsel together, and had arranged thus for the watching in Mr Trelawny's room. Mrs Grant was to remain beside the patient till twelve, when Miss Trelawny would relieve her. The new nurse was to sit in Miss Trelawny's room, and to visit the sick chamber each quarter of an hour. The doctor would remain till twelve; when I was to relieve him. One or other of the detectives was to remain within hail of the room all night; and to pay periodical visits to see that all was well. Thus, the watchers would be watched; and the possibility of such events as last night, when the watchers were both overcome, would be avoided.

When the sun set, a strange and grave anxiety fell on all of us; and in our separate ways we prepared for the vigil. Dr Winchester had evidently been thinking of my respirator, for he told me he would go out and get one. Indeed, he took to the idea so kindly that I persuaded Miss Trelawny also to have one which she could put on when her time for watching came.

And so the night drew on.

CHAPTER 5

More Strange Instructions

WHEN I CAME from my room at half-past eleven o'clock I found all well in the sick-room. The new nurse, prim, neat, and watchful, sat in the chair by the bedside where Nurse Kennedy had sat last night. A little way off, between the bed and the safe, sat Dr Winchester alert and wakeful, but looking strange and almost comic with the respirator over mouth and nose. As I stood in the doorway looking at them I heard a slight sound; turning round I saw the new detective, who nodded, held up the finger of silence and withdrew quietly. Hitherto no one of the watchers was overcome by sleep.

I took a chair outside the door. As yet there was no need for me to risk coming again under the subtle influence of last night. Naturally my thoughts went revolving round the main incidents of the last day and night, and I found myself arriving at strange conclusions, doubts, conjectures; but I did not lose myself, as on last night, in trains of thought. The sense of the present was ever with me, and I really felt as should a sentry on guard. Thinking is not a slow process; and when it is earnest the time can pass quickly. It seemed a very short time indeed till the door, usually left ajar, was pulled open and Dr Winchester emerged, taking off his respirator as he came. His act, when he had it off, was demonstrative of his keenness. He turned up the outside of the wrap and smelled it carefully.

'I am going now,' he said. 'I shall come early in the morning; unless, of course, I am sent for before. But all seems well tonight.'

The next to appear was Sergeant Daw, who went quietly into the room and took the seat vacated by the doctor. I still remained outside; but every few minutes looked into the room. This was rather a form than a matter of utility, for the room was so dark that coming even from the dimly-lighted corridor it was hard to distinguish anything.

A little before twelve o'clock Miss Trelawny came from her room. Before coming to her father's she went into that occupied by Nurse Kennedy. After a couple of minutes she came out, looking, I thought, a trifle more cheerful. She had her respirator in her hand, but before putting it on, asked me if anything special had occurred since she had gone to lie down. I answered in a whisper – there was no loud talking in the house tonight – that all was safe, was well. She then put on her respirator, and I mine; and we entered the room. The detective and the nurse rose up, and we took their places. Sergeant Daw was the last to go out; he closed the door behind him as we had arranged.

For a while I sat quiet, my heart beating. The place was grimly dark. The only light was a faint one from the top of the lamp which threw a white circle on the high ceiling, except the emerald sheen of the shade as the light took its under edges. Even the light only seemed to emphasise the blackness of the shadows. These presently began to seem, as on last night, to have a sentience of their own. I did not myself feel in the least sleepy; and each time I went softly over to look at the patient, which I did about every ten minutes, I could see that Miss Trelawny was keenly alert. Every quarter of an hour one or other of the policemen looked in through the partly opened door. Each time both Miss Trelawny and I said through our mufflers, 'all right,' and the door was closed again.

As the time wore on, the silence and the darkness seemed to increase. The circle of light on the ceiling was still there, but it seemed less brilliant than at first. The green edging of the lampshade became like Maori greenstone rather than emerald. The sounds of the night without the house, and the starlight spreading pale lines along the edges of the window-cases, made the pall of black within more solemn and more mysterious.

We heard the clock in the corridor chiming the quarters with its silver bell till two o'clock; and then a strange feeling came over me. I could see from Miss Trelawny's movement as she looked round, that she also had some new sensation. The new detective had just looked in; we two were alone with the unconscious patient for another quarter of an hour.

My heart began to beat wildly. There was a sense of fear over me. Not for myself; my fear was impersonal. It seemed as though some new person had entered the room, and that a strong intelligence was awake close to me. Something brushed against my leg. I put my hand down hastily and touched the furry coat of Silvio. With a very faint far-away sound of a snarl he turned and scratched at me. I felt blood on my hand. I rose gently and came over to the bedside. Miss Trelawny, too, had stood up and was looking behind her, as though there was something close to her. Her eyes were wild, and her breast rose and fell as though she were fighting for air. When I touched her she did not seem to feel me; she worked her hands in front of her, as though she was fending off something.

There was not an instant to lose. I seized her in my arms and rushed over to the door, threw it open, and strode into the passage, calling loudly: 'Help! Help!'

In an instant the two detectives, Mrs Grant, and the nurse appeared on the scene. Close on their heels came several of the servants, both men and women. Immediately Mrs Grant came near enough, I placed Miss Trelawny in her arms, and rushed back into the room, turning up the electric light as soon as I could lay my hand on it. Sergeant Daw and the nurse followed me.

We were just in time. Close under the great safe, where on the two successive nights he had been found, ray Mr Trelawny with his left arm, bare save for the bandages, stretched out. Close by his side was a leaf-shaped Egyptian knife which had lain amongst the curios on the shelf of the broken cabinet. Its point was stuck in the parquet floor, whence had been removed the blood-stained rug.

But there was no sign of disturbance anywhere; nor any sign of anyone or anything unusual. The policemen and I searched the room accurately, whilst the nurse and two of the servants lifted the wounded man back to bed; but no sign or clue could we get. Very soon Miss Trelawny returned to the room. She was pale but collected. When she came close to me she said in a low voice: 'I felt myself fainting. I did not know why; but I was afraid!'

The only other shock I had was when Miss Trelawny cried out to me, as I placed my hand on the bed to lean over and look carefully at her father: 'You are wounded. Look! look! your hand is bloody. There is blood on the sheets!' I had, in the excitement, quite forgotten Silvio's scratch. As I looked at it, the recollection came back to me; but before I could say a word Miss Trelawny had caught hold of my hand and lifted it up. When she saw the parallel lines of the cuts she cried out again: 'It is the same wound as Father's!' Then she laid my hand down gently but quickly, and said to me and to Sergeant Daw: 'Come to my room! Silvio is there in his basket.' We followed her, and found Silvio sitting in his basket awake. He was licking his paws. The detective said: 'He is there sure enough; but why licking his paws?'

Margaret – Miss Trelawny – gave a moan as she bent over and took one of the forepaws in her hand; but the cat seemed to resent it and snarled. At that Mrs Grant came into the room. When she saw that we were looking at the cat she said: 'The nurse tells me that Silvio was asleep on Nurse Kennedy's bed ever since you went to your father's room until a while ago. He came there just after you had gone to master's room. Nurse says that Nurse Kennedy is moaning and muttering in her sleep as though she had a nightmare. I think we should send for Dr Winchester.'

'Do so at once, please!' said Miss Trelawny; and we went back to the room.

For a while Miss Trelawny stood looking at her father, with her brows wrinkled. Then, turning to me, as though her mind were made up, she said: 'Don't you think we should have a consultation on Father? Of course I have every confidence in Dr Winchester; he seems an immensely clever young man. But he *is* a young man; and there must be men who have devoted themselves to this branch of science. Such a man would have more knowledge and more experience; and his knowledge and experience might help to throw light on poor father's case. As it is, Dr Winchester seems to be quite in the dark. Oh! I don't know what to do. It is all so terrible!' Here she broke down a little and cried; and I tried to comfort her.

Dr Winchester arrived quickly. His first thought was for his patient; but when he found him without further harm, he visited Nurse Kennedy. When he saw her, a hopeful look came into his eyes. Taking a towel, he dipped a corner of it in cold water and flicked her on the face. The skin coloured, and she stirred slightly. He said quietly to the new nurse – Sister Doris he called her: 'She is all right. She will wake in a few hours at latest. She may be dizzy and distraught at first, or perhaps hysterical. If so, you know how to treat her.'

'Yes, sir!' answered Sister Doris demurely; and we went back to Mr Trelawny's room. As soon as we had entered, Mrs Grant and the nurse went out so that only Dr Winchester, Miss Trelawny, and myself remained in the room. When the door had been closed Dr Winchester asked me as to what had occurred. I told him fully, giving exactly every detail so far as I could remember. Throughout my narrative, which did not take long, however, he kept asking me questions as to who had been present and the order in which each one had come into the room. He asked other things, but nothing of any importance; these were all that took my attention, or remained in my memory. When our conversation was finished, he said, in a very decided way indeed, to Miss Trelawny: 'I think, Miss Trelawny, that we had better have a consultation on this case.' She answered at once, seemingly a little to his surprise: 'I am glad you have mentioned it. I quite agree. Who would you suggest?'

'Have you any choice yourself?' he asked. 'Anyone to whom your Father is known? Has he ever consulted anyone?'

'Not to my knowledge. But I hope you will choose whoever you think would be best. My dear father should have all the help that can be had; and I shall be deeply obliged by your choosing. Who is the best man in London – anywhere else – in such a case?'

'There are several good men; but they are scattered all over the world. Somehow, the brain specialist is born, not made; though a lot of hard work goes to the completing of him and fitting him for his work. He comes from no country. The most daring investigator up to the present is Chiuni, the Japanese; but he is rather a surgical experimentalist than a practitioner. Then there is Zammerfest of Upsala, and Fenelon of the University of Paris, and Morfessi of Naples. These, of course, are in addition to our own men, Morrison of Aberdeen and Richardson of Birmingham. But before them all I would put Frere of King's College. Of all that I have named he best unites theory and practice. He has no hobbies – that have been discovered at all events; and his experience is immense. It is the regret of all of us who admire him that the nerve so firm and the hand so dexterous must yield to time. For my own part I would rather have Frere than anyone living.'

'Then,' said Miss Trelawny decisively, 'let us have Dr Frere – by the way, is he Dr or Mr? – as early as we can get him in the morning!'

A weight seemed removed from him, and he spoke with greater ease and geniality than he had yet shown: 'He is Sir James Frere. I shall go to him myself as early as it is possible to see him, and shall ask him to come here at once.' Then turning to me he said: 'You had better let me dress your hand.'

'It is nothing,' I said.

'Nevertheless it should be seen to. A scratch from any animal might turn out dangerous; there is nothing like being safe.' I submitted; forthwith he began to dress my hand. He examined with a magnifying-glass the several parallel wounds, and compared them with the slip of blotting-paper, marked with Silvio's claws, which he took from his pocket-book. He put back the paper, simply remarking: 'It's a pity that Silvio slips in – and out – just when he shouldn't.'

The morning wore slowly on. By ten o'clock Nurse Kennedy had so far recovered that she was able to sit up and talk intelligibly. But she was still hazy in her thoughts; and could not remember anything that had happened on the previous night, after her taking her place by the sick-bed. As yet she seemed neither to know nor care what had happened.

It was nearly eleven o'clock when Dr Winchester returned with Sir James Frere. Somehow I felt my heart sink when from the landing I saw them in the hall below; I knew that Miss Trelawny was to have the pain of telling yet another stranger of her ignorance of her father's life.

Sir James Frere was a man who commanded attention followed by respect. He knew so thoroughly what he wanted himself, that he placed at once on one side all wishes and ideas of less definite persons. The mere flash of his piercing eyes, or the set of his resolute mouth, or the lowering of his great eyebrows, seemed to compel immediate and willing obedience to his wishes. Somehow, when we had all been introduced and he was well amongst us, all sense of mystery seemed to melt away. It was with a hopeful spirit that I saw him pass into the sick-room with Dr Winchester.

They remained in the room a long time; once they sent for the nurse, the new one, sister Doris, but she did not remain long. Again they both went into Nurse Kennedy's room. He sent out the nurse attendant on her. Dr Winchester told me afterward that Nurse Kennedy, though she was ignorant of later matters, gave full and satisfactory answers to all Dr Frere's questions relating to her patient up to the time she became unconscious. Then they went to the study, where they remained so long, and their voices raised in heated discussion seemed in such determined opposition, that I began to feel uneasy. As for Miss Trelawny, she was almost in a state of collapse from nervousness before they joined us. Poor girl! she had had a sadly anxious time of it, and her nervous strength had almost broken down.

They came out at last, Sir James first, his grave face looking as unenlightening as that of the sphinx. Dr Winchester followed him closely; his face was pale, but with that kind of pallor which looked like a reaction. It gave me the idea that it had been red not long before. Sir James asked that Miss Trelawny would come into the study. He suggested that I should come also. When we had entered, Sir James turned to me and said: 'I understand from Dr Winchester that you are a friend of Miss Trelawny, and that you have already considerable knowledge of this case. Perhaps it will be well that you should be with us. I know you already as a keen lawyer, Mr Ross, though I never had the pleasure of meeting you. As Dr Winchester tells me that there are some strange matters outside this case which seem to puzzle him – and others – and in which he thinks you may yet be specially interested, it might be as well that you should know every phase of the case. For myself I do not take much account of mysteries – except those of science; and as there seems to be some idea of an attempt at assassination or robbery, all I can say is that if assassins were at work they ought to take some elementary lessons in anatomy before their next job, for they seem thoroughly ignorant. If robbery were their purpose, they seem to have worked with marvellous inefficiency. That, however, is not my business.' Here he took a big pinch of snuff, and turning to Miss Trelawny, went on: 'Now as to the patient. Leaving out the cause of his illness, all we can say at present is that he appears to be suffering from a marked attack of catalepsy. At present nothing can be done, except to sustain his strength. The treatment of my friend Dr Winchester is mainly such as I approve of; and I am confident that should any slight change arise he will be able to deal with it satisfactorily. It is an interesting case – most interesting; and should any new or abnormal development arise I shall be happy to come at any time. There is just one thing to which I wish to call your attention; and I put it to you, Miss Trelawny, directly, since it is your responsibility. Dr Winchester informs me that you are not yourself free in the matter, but are bound by an instruction given by your Father in case just such a condition of things should arise. I would strongly advise that the patient be removed to another room; or, as an alternative, that those mummies and all such things should be removed from his chamber. Why, it's enough to put any man into an abnormal condition, to have such an assemblage of horrors round him, and to breathe the atmosphere which they exhale. You have evidence already of how such mephitic odour may act. That nurse – Kennedy, I think you said, doctor – isn't yet out of her state of catalepsy; and you, Mr Ross, have, I am told, experienced something of the same effects. I know this' – here his eyebrows came down more than ever, and his mouth hardened – 'if I were in charge here I should insist on the patient having a different atmosphere; or I would throw up the case. Dr Winchester already knows that I can only be again consulted on this condition being fulfilled. But I trust that you will see your way, as a good daughter to my mind should, to looking to your Father's health and sanity rather than to any whim of his – whether supported or not by a foregoing fear, or by any number of 'penny dreadful' mysteries. The day has hardly come yet, I am glad to say, when the British Museum and St Thomas's Hospital have exchanged their normal functions. Good-day, Miss Trelawny. I earnestly hope that I may soon see your Father restored. Remember, that should you fulfil the elementary condition which I have laid down, I am at your service day or night. Good-morning, Mr Ross. I hope you will be able to report to me soon, Dr Winchester.'

When he had gone we stood silent, till the rumble of his carriage wheels died away. The first to speak was Dr Winchester: 'I think it well to say that to my mind, speaking purely as a physician, he is quite right. I feel as if I could have assaulted him when he made it a condition of not giving up the case; but all the same he is right as to treatment. He does not understand that there is something odd about this special case; and he will not realise the knot that we are all tied up in by Mr Trelawny's instructions. Of course – ' He was interrupted by Miss Trelawny: 'Dr Winchester, do you, too, wish to give up the case; or are you willing to continue it under the conditions you know?'

'Give it up! Less now than ever. Miss Trelawny, I shall never give it up, so long as life is left to him or any of us!' She said nothing, but held out her hand, which he took warmly.

'Now,' said she, 'if Sir James Frere is a type of the cult of specialists, I want no more of them. To start with, he does not seem to know any more than you do about my Father's condition; and if he were a hundredth part as much interested in it as you are, he would not stand on such punctilio. Of course, I am only too anxious about my poor Father; and if I can see a way to meet either of Sir James Frere's conditions, I shall do so. I shall ask Mr Marvin to come here today, and advise me as to the limit of Father's wishes. If he thinks I am free to act in any way on my own responsibility, I shall not hesitate to do so.' Then Dr Winchester took his leave.

Miss Trelawny sat down and wrote a letter to Mr Marvin, telling him of the state of affairs, and asking him to come and see her and to bring with him any papers which might throw any light on the subject. She sent the letter off with a carriage to bring back the solicitor; we waited with what patience we could for his coming.

It is not a very long journey for oneself from Kensington Palace Gardens to Lincoln's Inn Fields; but it seemed endlessly long when waiting for someone else to take it. All things, however, are amenable to time; it was less than an hour all told when Mr Marvin was with us.

He recognised Miss Trelawny's impatience, and when he had learned sufficient of her father's illness, he said to her: 'Whenever you are ready I can go with you into particulars regarding your father's wishes.'

'Whenever you like,' she said, with an evident ignorance of his meaning. 'Why not now?' He looked at me, as to a fellow man of business, and stammered out: 'We are not alone.'

'I have brought Mr Ross here on purpose,' she answered. 'He knows so much at present, that I want him to know more.' The solicitor was a little disconcerted, a thing which those knowing him only in courts would hardly have believed. He answered, however, with some hesitation: 'But, my dear young lady – Your father's wishes! – Confidence between father and child – '

Here she interrupted him; there was a tinge of red in her pale cheeks as she did so: 'Do you really think that applies to the present circumstances, Mr Marvin? My father never told me anything of his affairs; and I can now, in this sad extremity, only learn his wishes through a gentleman who is a stranger to me and of whom I never even heard till I got my father's letter, written to be shown to me only in extremity. Mr Ross is a new friend; but he has all my confidence, and I should like him to be present. Unless, of course,' she added, 'such a thing is forbidden by my father. Oh! forgive me, Mr Marvin, if I seem rude; but I have been in such dreadful trouble and anxiety lately, that I have hardly command of myself.' She covered her eyes with her hand for a few seconds; we two men looked at each other and waited, trying to appear unmoved. She went on more firmly; she had recovered herself: 'Please! please do not think I am ungrateful to you for your kindness in coming here and so quickly. I really am grateful; and I have every confidence in your judgment. If you wish, or think it best, we can be alone.' I stood up; but Mr Marvin made a dissentient gesture. He was evidently pleased with her attitude; there was geniality in his voice and manner as he spoke: 'Not at all! Not at all! There is no restriction on your Father's part; and on my own I am quite willing. Indeed, all told, it may be better. From what you have said of Mr Trelawny's illness, and the other – incidental – matters, it will be well in case of any – grave – eventuality, that it was understood from the first, that circumstances were ruled by your father's own imperative instructions. For, please, understand me, his instructions are imperative – most imperative. They are so unyielding that he has given me a power of attorney, under which I have undertaken to act, authorising me to see his written wishes carried out. Please believe once for all, that he intended fully everything mentioned in that letter to you! Whilst he is alive he is to remain in his own room; and none of his property is to be removed from it under any circumstances whatever. He has even given an inventory of the articles which are not to be displaced.'

Miss Trelawny was silent. She looked somewhat distressed; so, thinking that I understood the immediate cause, I asked: 'May we see the list? Miss Trelawny's face at once brightened; but it fell again as the lawyer answered promptly – he was evidently prepared for the question: 'Not unless I am compelled to take action on the Power of Attorney. I have brought that instrument with me. You will recognise, Mr Ross' – he said this with a sort of business conviction which I had noticed in his professional work, as he handed me the deed – 'how strongly it is worded, and how the grantor made his wishes apparent in such a way as to leave no loophole. It is his own wording, except for certain legal formalities; and I assure you I have seldom seen a more iron-clad document. Even I myself have no power to make the slightest relaxation of the instructions, without committing a distinct breach of faith. And that, I need not tell you, is impossible.' He evidently added the last words in order to prevent an appeal to his personal consideration. He did not like the seeming harshness of his words, however, for he added: 'I do hope, Miss Trelawny, that you understand that I am willing – frankly and unequivocally willing – to do anything I can, within the limits of my power, to relieve your distress. But your father had, in all his doings, some purpose of his own which he did not disclose to me. So far as I can see, there is not a word of his instructions that he had not thought over fully. Whatever idea he had in his mind was the idea of a lifetime; he had studied it in every possible phase, and was prepared to guard it at every point.

'Now I fear I have distressed you, and I am truly sorry for it; for I see you have much – too much – to bear already. But I have no alternative. If you want to consult me at any time about anything, I promise you I will come without a moment's delay, at any hour of the day or night. There is my private address,' he scribbled in his pocket-book as he spoke, 'and under it the address of my club, where I am generally to be found in the evening.' He tore out the paper and handed it to her. She thanked him. He shook hands with her and with me and withdrew.

As soon as the hall door was shut on him, Mrs Grant tapped at the door and came in. There was such a look of distress in her face that Miss Trelawny stood up, deadly white, and asked her: 'What is it, Mrs Grant? What is it? Any new trouble?'

'I grieve to say, miss, that the servants, all but two, have given notice and want to leave the house today. They have talked the matter over among themselves; the butler has spoken for the rest. He says as how they are willing to forego their wages, and even to pay their legal obligations instead of notice; but that go today they must.'

'What reason do they give?'

'None, miss. They say as how they're sorry, but that they've nothing to say. I asked Jane, the upper housemaid, miss, who is not with the rest but stops on; and she tells me confidential that they've got some notion in their silly heads that the house is haunted!'

We ought to have laughed, but we didn't. I could not look in Miss Trelawny's face and laugh. The pain and horror there showed no sudden paroxysm of fear; there was a fixed idea of which this was a confirmation. For myself, it seemed as if my brain had found a voice. But the voice was not complete; there was some other thought, darker and deeper, which lay behind it, whose voice had not sounded as yet.

CHAPTER 6

Suspicions

THE FIRST TO GET full self-command was Miss Trelawny. There was a haughty dignity in her bearing as she said: 'Very well, Mrs Grant; let them go! Pay them up to today, and a month's wages. They have hitherto been very good servants; and the occasion of their leaving is not an ordinary one. We must not expect much faithfulness from anyone who is beset with fears. Those who remain are to have in future double wages; and please send these to me presently when I send word.' Mrs Grant bristled with smothered indignation; all the housekeeper in her was outraged by such generous treatment of servants who had combined to give notice: 'They don't deserve it, miss; them to go on so, after the way they have been treated here. Never in my life have I seen servants so well treated or anyone so good to them and gracious to them as you have been. They might be in the household of a king for treatment. And now, just as there is trouble, to go and act like this. It's abominable, that's what it is!'

Miss Trelawny was very gentle with her, and smothered her ruffled dignity; so that presently she went away with, in her manner, a lesser measure of hostility to the undeserving. In quite a different frame of mind she returned presently to ask if her mistress would like her to engage a full staff of other servants, or at any rate try to do so. 'For you know, ma'am,' she went on, 'when once a scare has been established in the servants' hall, it's wellnigh impossible to get rid of it. Servants may come; but they go away just as quick. There's no holding them. They simply won't stay; or even if they work out their month's notice, they lead you that life that you wish every hour of the day that you hadn't kept them. The women are bad enough, the huzzies; but the men are worse!' There was neither anxiety nor indignation in Miss Trelawny's voice or manner as she said: 'I think, Mrs Grant, we had better try to do with those we have. Whilst my dear father is ill we shall not be having any company, so that there will be only three now in the house to attend to. If those servants who are willing to stay are not enough, I should only get sufficient to help them to do the work. It will not, I should think, be difficult to get a few maids; perhaps some that you know already. And please bear in mind, that those whom you get, and who are suitable and will stay, are henceforth to have the same wages as those who are remaining. Of course, Mrs Grant, you well understand that though I do not group you in any way with the servants, the rule of double salary applies to you too.' As she spoke she extended her long, fine-shaped hand, which the other took and then, raising it to her lips, kissed it impressively with the freedom of an elder woman to a younger. I could not but admire the generosity of her treatment of her servants. In my mind I endorsed Mrs Grant's *sotto voce* remark as she left the room: 'No wonder the house is like a king's house, when the mistress is a princess!'

'A princess!' That was it. The idea seemed to satisfy my mind, and to bring back in a wave of light the first moment when she swept across my vision at the ball in Belgrave Square. A queenly figure! tall and slim, bending, swaying, undulating as the lily or the lotus. Clad in a flowing gown of some filmy black material shot with gold. For ornament in her hair she wore an old Egyptian jewel, a tiny crystal disk, set between rising plumes carved in lapis lazuli. On her wrist was a broad bangle or bracelet of antique work, in the shape of a pair of spreading wings wrought in gold, with the feathers made of coloured gems. For all her gracious bearing toward me, when our hostess introduced me, I was then afraid of her. It was only when later, at the picnic on the river, I had come to realise her sweet and gentle nature, that my awe changed to something else.

For a while she sat, making some notes or memoranda. Then putting them away, she sent for the faithful servants. I thought that she had better have this interview alone, and so left her. When I came back there were traces of tears in her eyes.

The next phase in which I had a part was even more disturbing, and infinitely more painful. Late in the afternoon Sergeant Daw came into the study where I was sitting. After closing the door carefully and looking all round the room to make certain that we were alone, he came close to me.

'What is it?' I asked him. 'I see you wish to speak to me privately.'

'Quite so, sir! May I speak in absolute confidence?'

'Of course you may. In anything that is for the good of Miss Trelawny – and of course of Mr Trelawny – you may be perfectly frank. I take it that we both want to serve them to the best of our powers.' He hesitated before replying: 'Of course you know that I have my duty to do; and I think you know me well enough to know that I will do it. I am a policeman – a detective; and it is my duty to find out the facts of any case I am put on, without fear or favour to anyone. I would rather speak to you alone, in confidence if I may, without reference to any duty of anyone to anyone, except mine to Scotland Yard.'

'Of course! of course!' I answered mechanically, my heart sinking, I did not know why. 'Be quite frank with me. I assure you of my confidence.'

'Thank you, sir. I take it that what I say is not to pass beyond you – not to anyone. Not to Miss Trelawny herself, or even to Mr Trelawny when he becomes well again.'

'Certainly, if you make it a condition!' I said a little more stiffly. The man recognised the change in my voice or manner, and said apologetically: 'Excuse me, sir, but I am going outside my duty in speaking to you at all on the subject. I know you, however, of old; and I feel that I can trust you. Not your word, sir, that is all right; but your discretion!'

I bowed. 'Go on!' I said. He began at once: 'I have gone over this case, sir, till my brain begins to reel; but I can't find any ordinary solution of it. At the time of each attempt no one has seemingly come into the house; and certainly no one has got out. What does it strike you is the inference?'

'That the somebody – or the something – was in the house already,' I answered, smiling in spite of myself.

'That's just what I think,' he said, with a manifest sigh of relief. 'Very well! Who can be that someone?'

' "Someone, or something," was what I said,' I answered.

'Let us make it "someone", Mr Ross! That cat, though he might have scratched or bit, never pulled the old gentleman out of bed, and tried to get the bangle with the key off his arm. Such things are all very well in books where your amateur detectives, who know everything before it's done, can fit them into theories; but in Scotland Yard, where the men aren't all idiots either, we generally find that when crime is done, or attempted, it's people, not things, that are at the bottom of it.'

'Then make it "people" by all means, sergeant.'

'We were speaking of "someone", sir.'

'Quite right. *Someone*, be it!'

'Did it ever strike you, sir, that on each of the three separate occasions where outrage was effected, or attempted, there was one person who was the first to be present and to give the alarm?'

'Let me see! Miss Trelawny, I believe, gave the alarm on the first occasion. I was present myself, if fast asleep, on the second; and so was Nurse Kennedy. When I woke there were several people in the room; you were one of them. I understand that on that occasion also Miss Trelawny was before you. At the last attempt I was in the room when Miss Trelawny fainted. I carried her out and went back. In returning, I was first; and I think you were close behind me.'

Sergeant Daw thought for a moment before replying: 'She was present, or first, in the room on all the occasions; there was only damage done in the first and second!'

The inference was one which I, as a lawyer, could not mistake. I thought the best thing to do was to meet it half-way. I have always found that the best way to encounter an inference is to cause it to be turned into a statement.

'You mean,' I said, 'that as on the only occasions when actual harm was done, Miss Trelawny's being the first to discover it is a proof that she did it; or was in some way connected with the attempt, as well as the discovery?'

'I didn't venture to put it as clear as that; but that is where the doubt which I had leads.' Sergeant Daw was a man of courage; he evidently did not shrink from any conclusion of his reasoning on facts.

We were both silent for a while. Fears began crowding in on my own mind. Not doubts of Miss Trelawny, or of any act of hers; but fears lest such acts should be misunderstood. There was evidently a mystery somewhere; and if no solution to it could be found, the doubt would be cast on someone. In such cases the guesses of the majority are bound to follow the line of least resistance; and if it could be proved that any personal gain to anyone would follow Mr Trelawny's death, should such ensue, it might prove a difficult task for anyone to prove innocence in the face of suspicious facts. I found myself instinctively taking that deferential course which, until the plan of battle of the prosecution is unfolded, is so safe an attitude for the defence. It would never do for me, at this stage, to combat any theories which a detective might form. I could best help Miss Trelawny by listening and understanding. When the time should come for the dissipation and obliteration of the theories, I should be quite willing to use all my militant ardour, and all the weapons at my command.

'You will of course do your duty, I know,' I said, 'and without fear. What course do you intend to take?'

'I don't know as yet, sir. You see, up to now it isn't with me even a suspicion. If anyone else told me that that sweet young lady had a hand in such a matter, I would think him a fool; but I am bound to follow my own conclusions. I know well that just as unlikely persons have been proved guilty, when a whole court – all except the prosecution who knew the facts, and the judge who had taught his mind to wait – would have sworn to innocence. I wouldn't, for all the world, wrong such a young lady; more especial when she has such a cruel weight to bear. And you will be sure that I won't say a word that'll prompt anyone else to make such a charge. That's why I speak to you in confidence, man to man. You are skilled in proofs; that is your profession. Mine only gets so far as suspicions, and what we call our own proofs – which are nothing but *ex parte* evidence after all. You know Miss Trelawny better than I do; and though I watch round the sick-room, and go where I like about the house and in and out of it, I haven't the same opportunities as you have of knowing the lady and what her life is, or her means are; or of anything else which might give me a clue to her actions. If I were to try to find out from her, it would at once arouse her suspicions. Then, if she were guilty, all possibility of ultimate proof would go; for she would easily find a way to baffle discovery. But if she be innocent, as I hope she is, it would be doing a cruel wrong to accuse her. I have thought the matter over according to my lights before I spoke to you; and if I have taken a liberty, sir, I am truly sorry.'

'No liberty in the world, Daw,' I said warmly, for the man's courage and honesty and consideration compelled respect. 'I am glad you have spoken to me so frankly. We both want to find out the truth; and there is so much about this case that is strange – so strange as to go beyond all experiences – that to aim at truth is our only chance of making anything clear in the long-run – no matter what our views are, or what object we wish to achieve ultimately!' The sergeant looked pleased as he went on: 'I thought, therefore, that if you had it once in your mind that somebody else held to such a possibility, you would by degrees get proof; or at any rate such ideas as would convince yourself, either for or against it. Then we would come to some conclusion; or at any rate we should so exhaust all other possibilities that the most likely one would remain as the nearest thing to proof, or strong suspicion, that we could get. After that we should have to – '

Just at this moment the door opened and Miss Trelawny entered the room. The moment she saw us she drew back quickly, saying: 'Oh, I beg pardon! I did not know you were here, and engaged.' By the time I had stood up, she was about to go back.

'Do come in,' I said; 'Sergeant Daw and I were only talking matters over.'

Whilst she was hesitating, Mrs Grant appeared, saying as she entered the room: 'Dr Winchester is come, miss, and is asking for you.'

I obeyed Miss Trelawny's look; together we left the room.

When the doctor had made his examination, he told us that there was seemingly no change. He added that nevertheless he would like to stay in the house that night if he might. Miss Trelawny looked glad, and sent word to Mrs Grant to get a room ready for him. Later in the day, when he and I happened to be alone together, he said suddenly: 'I have arranged to stay here tonight because I want to have a talk with you. And as I wish it to be quite private, I thought the least suspicious way would be to have a cigar together late in the evening when Miss Trelawny is watching her father.' We still kept to our arrangement that either the sick man's daughter or I should be on watch all night. We were to share the duty at the early hours of the morning. I was anxious about this, for I knew from our conversation that the detective would watch in secret himself, and would be particularly alert about that time.

The day passed uneventfully. Miss Trelawny slept in the afternoon; and after dinner went to relieve the nurse. Mrs Grant remained with her, Sergeant Daw being on duty in the corridor. Dr Winchester and I took our coffee in the library. When we had lit our cigars he said quietly: 'Now that we are alone I want to have a confidential talk. We are "tiled", of course; for the present at all events?'

'Quite so!' I said, my heart sinking as I thought of my conversation with Sergeant Daw in the morning, and of the disturbing and harrowing fears which it had left in my mind. He went on: 'This case is enough to try the sanity of all of us concerned in it. The more I think of it, the madder I seem to get; and the two lines, each continually strengthened, seem to pull harder in opposite directions.'

'What two lines?' He looked at me keenly for a moment before replying. Dr Winchester's look at such moments was apt to be disconcerting. It would have been so to me had I had a personal part, other than my interest in Miss Trelawny, in the matter. As it was, however, I stood it unruffled. I was now an attorney in the case; an *amicus curiœ* in one sense, in another retained for the defence. The mere thought that in this clever man's mind were two lines, equally strong and opposite, was in itself so consoling as to neutralise my anxiety as to a new attack. As he began to speak, the doctor's face wore an inscrutable smile; this, however, gave place to a stern gravity as he proceeded: 'Two lines: Fact and – Fancy! In the first there is this whole thing: attacks; attempts at robbery and murder; stupefyings; organised catalepsy which points to either criminal hypnotism and thought suggestion, or some simple form of poisoning unclassified yet in our toxicology. In the other there is some influence at work which is not classified in any book that I know – outside the pages of romance. I never felt in my life so strongly the truth of Hamlet's words: "There are more things in heaven and earth . . . Than are dreamt of in your philosophy".

'Let us take the "fact" side first. Here we have a man in his home; amidst his own household; plenty of servants of different classes in the house, which forbids the possibility of an organised attempt made from the servants' hall. He is wealthy, learned, clever. From his physiognomy there is no doubting that he is a man of iron will and determined purpose. His daughter – his only child, I take it, a young girl bright and clever – is sleeping in the very next room to his. There is seemingly no possible reason for expecting any attack or disturbance of any kind; and no reasonable opportunity for any outsider to effect it. And yet we have an attack made; a brutal and remorseless attack, made in the middle of the night. Discovery is made quickly; made with that rapidity which in criminal cases generally is found to be not accidental, but of premeditated intent. The attacker, or attackers, are manifestly disturbed before the completion of their work, whatever their ultimate intent may have been. And yet there is no possible sign of their escape; no clue, no disturbance of anything; no open door or window; no sound. Nothing whatever to show who had done the deed, or even that a deed has been done; except the victim, and his surroundings incidental to the deed!

'The next night a similar attempt is made, though the house is full of wakeful people; and though there are on watch in the room and around it a detective officer, a trained nurse, an earnest friend, and the man's own daughter. The nurse is thrown into a catalepsy, and the watching friend – though protected by a respirator – into a deep sleep. Even the detective is so far overcome with some phase of stupor that he fires off his pistol in the sick-room, and can't even tell what he thought he was firing at. That respirator of yours is the only thing that seems to have a bearing on the "fact" side of the affair. That you did not lose your head as the others did – the effect in such case being in proportion to the amount of time each remained in the room – points to the probability that the stupefying medium was not hypnotic, whatever else it may have been. But again, there is a fact which is contradictory. Miss Trelawny, who was in the room more than any of you – for she was in and out all the time and did her share of permanent watching also – did not seem to be affected at all. This would show that the influence, whatever it is, does not affect generally – unless, of course, it was that she was in some way inured to it. If it should turn out that it be some strange exhalation from some of those Egyptian curios, that might account for it; only, we are then face to face with the fact that Mr Trelawny, who was most of all in the room – who, in fact, lived more than half his life in it – was affected worst of all. What kind of influence could it be which would account for all these different and contradictory effects? No! the more I think of this form of the dilemma, the more I am bewildered! Why, even if it were that the attack, the physical attack, on Mr Trelawny had been made by someone residing in the house and not within the sphere of suspicion, the oddness of the stupefyings would still remain a mystery. It is not easy to put anyone into a catalepsy. Indeed, so far as is known yet in science, there is no way to achieve such an object at will. The crux of the whole matter is Miss Trelawny, who seems to be subject to none of the influences, or possibly of the variants of the same influence at work. Through all she goes unscathed, except for that one slight semi-faint. It is most strange!'

I listened with a sinking heart; for, though his manner was not illuminative of distrust, his argument was disturbing. Although it was not so direct as the suspicion of the detective, it seemed to single out Miss Trelawny as different from all others concerned; and in a mystery to be alone is to be suspected, ultimately if not immediately. I thought it better not to say anything. In such a case silence is indeed golden; and if I said nothing now I might have less to defend, or explain, or take back later. I was, therefore, secretly glad that his form of putting his argument did not require any answer from me – for the present, at all events. Dr Winchester did not seem to expect any answer – a fact which, when I recognised it, gave me pleasure, I hardly knew why. He paused for a while, sitting with his chin in his hand, his eyes staring at vacancy, whilst his brows were fixed. His cigar was held limp between his fingers; he had apparently forgotten it. In an even voice, as though commencing exactly where he had left off, he resumed his argument: 'The other horn of the dilemma is a different affair altogether; and if we once enter on it we must leave everything in the shape of science and experience behind us. I confess that it has its fascinations for me; though at every new thought I find myself romancing in a way that makes me pull up suddenly and look facts resolutely in the face. I sometimes wonder whether the influence or emanation from the sick-room at times affects me as it did the others – the detective, for instance. Of course it may be that if it is anything chemical, any drug, for example, in vaporeal form, its effects may be cumulative. But then, what could there be that could produce such an effect? The room is, I know, full of mummy smell; and no wonder, with so many relics from the tomb, let alone the actual mummy of that animal which Silvio attacked. By the way, I am going to test him tomorrow; I have been on the trace of a mummy cat, and am to get possession of it in the morning. When I bring it here we shall find out if it be a fact that racial instinct can survive a few thousand years in the grave. However, to get back to the subject in hand. These very mummy smells arise from the presence of substances, and combinations of substances, which the Egyptian priests, who were the learned men and scientists of their time, found by the experience of centuries to be strong enough to arrest the natural forces of decay. There must be powerful agencies at work to effect such a purpose; and it is possible that we may have here some rare substance or combination whose qualities and powers are not understood in this later and more prosaic age. I wonder if Mr Trelawny has any knowledge, or even suspicion, of such a kind? I only know this for certain, that a worse atmosphere for a sick chamber could not possibly be imagined; and I admire the courage of Sir James Frere in refusing to have anything to do with a case under such conditions. These instructions of Mr Trelawny to his daughter, and from what you have told me, the care with which he has protected his wishes through his solicitor, show that he suspected something, at any rate. Indeed, it would almost seem as if he expected something to happen . . . I wonder if it would be possible to learn anything about that! Surely his papers would show or suggest something . . . It is a difficult matter to tackle; but it might have to be done. His present condition cannot go on for ever; and if anything should happen there would have to be an inquest. In such case full examination would have to be made into everything . . . As it stands, the police evidence would show a murderous attack more than once repeated. As no clue is apparent, it would be necessary to seek one in a motive.'

He was silent. The last words seemed to come in a lower and lower tone as he went on. It had the effect of hopelessness. It came to me as a conviction that now was my time to find out if he had any definite suspicion; and as if in obedience to some command, I asked: 'Do you suspect anyone?' He seemed in a way startled rather than surprised as he turned his eyes on me: 'Suspect anyone? Any thing, you mean. I certainly suspect that there is some influence; but at present my suspicion is held within such limit. Later on, if there be any sufficiently definite conclusion to my reasoning, or my thinking – for there are not proper data for reasoning – I may suspect; at present, however – '

He stopped suddenly and looked at the door. There was a faint sound as the handle turned. My own heart seemed to stand still. There was over me some grim, vague apprehension. The interruption in the morning, when I was talking with the detective, came back upon me with a rush.

The door opened, and Miss Trelawny entered the room.

When she saw us, she started back; and a deep flush swept her face. For a few seconds she paused; at such a time a few succeeding seconds seem to lengthen in geometrical progression. The strain upon me, and, as I could easily see, on the doctor also, relaxed as she spoke: 'Oh, forgive me, I did not know that you were engaged. I was looking for you, Dr Winchester, to ask you if I might go to bed tonight with safety, as you will be here. I feel so tired and worn-out that I fear I may break down; and tonight I would certainly not be of any use.' Dr Winchester answered heartily: 'Do! Do go to bed by all means, and get a good night's sleep. God knows! you want it. I am more than glad you have made the suggestion, for I feared when I saw you tonight that I might have you on my hands a patient next.'

She gave a sigh of relief, and the tired look seemed to melt from her face. Never shall I forget the deep, earnest look in her great, beautiful black eyes as she said to me: 'You will guard Father tonight, won't you, with Dr Winchester? I am so anxious about him that every second brings new fears. But I am really worn-out; and if I don't get a good sleep, I think I shall go mad. I will change my room for tonight. I'm afraid that if I stay so close to Father's room I shall multiply every sound into a new terror. But, of course, you will have me waked if there be any cause. I shall be in the bedroom of the little suite next the boudoir off the hall. I had those rooms when first I came to live with Father, and I had no care then . . . It will be easier to rest there; and perhaps for a few hours I may forget. I shall be all right in the morning. Good-night!'

When I had closed the door behind her and come back to the little table at which we had been sitting, Dr Winchester said: 'That poor girl is overwrought to a terrible degree. I am delighted that she is to get a rest. It will be life to her; and in the morning she will be all right. Her nervous system is on the verge of a breakdown. Did you notice how fearfully disturbed she was, and how red she got when she came in and found us talking? An ordinary thing like that, in her own house with her own guests, wouldn't under normal circumstances disturb her!'

I was about to tell him, as an explanation in her defence, how her entrance was a repetition of her finding the detective and myself alone together earlier in the day, when I remembered that that conversation was so private that even an allusion to it might be awkward in evoking curiosity. So I remained silent.

We stood up to go to the sick-room; but as we took our way through the dimly-lighted corridor I could not help thinking, again and again, and again – ay, and for many a day after – how strange it was that she had interrupted me on two such occasions when touching on such a theme.

There was certainly some strange web of accidents, in whose meshes we were all involved.

CHAPTER 7

The Traveller's Loss

THAT NIGHT everything went well. Knowing that Miss Trelawny herself was not on guard, Dr Winchester and I doubled our vigilance. The nurses and Mrs Grant kept watch, and the detectives made their visit each quarter of an hour. All night the patient remained in his trance. He looked healthy, and his chest rose and fell with the easy breathing of a child. But he never stirred; only for his breathing he might have been of marble. Dr Winchester and I wore our respirators, and irksome they were on that intolerably hot night. Between midnight and three o'clock I felt anxious, and had once more that creepy feeling to which these last few nights had accustomed me; but the grey of the dawn, stealing round the edges of the blinds, came with inexpressible relief. In the cool, hopeful darkness, with the east quickening into pallor, I could breathe freely; the same relief, followed by restfulness, went through the household. During the hot night my ears, strained to every sound, had been almost painfully troubled; as though my brain or sensoria were in anxious touch with them. Every breath of the nurse or the rustle of her dress; every soft pat of slippered feet, as the policeman went his rounds; every moment of watching life, seemed to be a new impetus to guardianship. Something of the same feeling must have been abroad in the house; now and again I could hear upstairs the sound of restless feet, and more than once downstairs the opening of a window. With the coming of the dawn, however, all this ceased, and the whole household seemed to rest. Dr Winchester went home when Sister Doris came to relieve Mrs Grant. He was, I think, a little disappointed or chagrined that nothing of an exceptional nature had happened during his long night vigil.

At eight o'clock Miss Trelawny joined us, and I was amazed as well as delighted to see how much good her night's sleep had done her. She was fairly radiant; just as I had seen her at our first meeting and at the picnic. There was even a suggestion of colour in her cheeks, which, however, looked startlingly white in contrast with her black brows and scarlet lips. With her restored strength, there seemed to have come a tenderness even exceeding that which she had at first shown to her sick father. I could not but be moved by the loving touches as she fixed his pillows and brushed the hair from his forehead.

I was wearied out myself with my long spell of watching; and now that she was on guard I started off to bed, blinking my tired eyes in the full light and feeling the weariness of a sleepless night on me all at once.

I had a good sleep, and after lunch I was about to start out to walk to Jermyn Street, when I noticed an importunate man at the hall door. The servant in charge was the one called Morris, formerly the 'odd man', but since the exodus of the servants promoted to be butler *pro tem*. The stranger was speaking rather loudly, so that there was no difficulty in understanding his grievance. The servant man was respectful in both words and demeanour; but he stood squarely in front of the great double door, so that the other could not enter. The first words which I heard from the visitor sufficiently explained the situation: 'That's all very well, but I tell you I must see Mr Trelawny! What is the use of your saying I can't, when I tell you I must. You put me off, and off, and off! I came here at nine; you said then that he was not up, and that as he was not well he could not be disturbed. I came at twelve; and you told me again he was not up. I asked then to see any of his household; you told me that Miss Trelawny was not up. Now I come again at three, and you tell me he is still in bed, and is not awake yet. Where is Miss Trelawny? "She is occupied and must not be disturbed!" Well, she must be disturbed! Or someone must. I am here about Mr Trelawny's special business; and I have come from a place where servants always begin by saying "No". "No" isn't good enough for me this time! I've had three years of it, waiting outside doors and tents when it took longer to get in than it did into the tombs; and then you would think, too, the men inside were as dead as the mummies. I've had about enough of it, I tell you. And when I come home, and find the door of the man I've been working for barred, in just the same way and with the same old answers, it stirs me up the wrong way. Did Mr Trelawny leave orders that he would not see me when I should come?'

He paused and excitedly mopped his forehead. The servant answered very respectfully: 'I am very sorry, sir, if in doing my duty I have given any offence. But I have my orders, and must obey them. If you would like to leave any message, I will give it to Miss Trelawny; and if you will leave your address, she can communicate with you if she wishes.' The answer came in such a way that it was easy to see that the speaker was a kind-hearted man, and a just one.

'My good fellow, I have no fault to find with you personally; and I am sorry if I have hurt your feelings. I must be just, even if I am angry. But it is enough to anger any man to find himself in the position I am. Time is pressing. There is not an hour – not a minute – to lose! And yet here I am, kicking my heels for six hours; knowing all the time that your master will be a hundred times angrier than I am, when he hears how the time has been fooled away. He would rather be waked out of a thousand sleeps than not see me just at present – and before it is too late. My God! it's simply dreadful, after all I've gone through, to have my work spoiled at the last and be foiled in the very doorway by a stupid flunkey! Is there no one with sense in the house; or with authority, even if he hasn't got sense? I could mighty soon convince him that your master must be awakened; even if he sleeps like the Seven Sleepers – '

There was no mistaking the man's sincerity, or the urgency and importance of his business; from his point of view at any rate. I stepped forward.

'Morris,' I said, 'you had better tell Miss Trelawny that this gentleman wants to see her particularly. If she is busy, ask Mrs Grant to tell her.'

'Very good, sir!' he answered in a tone of relief, and hurried away.

I took the stranger into the little boudoir across the hall. As we went he asked me: 'Are you the secretary?'

'No! I am a friend of Miss Trelawny's. My name is Ross.'

'Thank you very much, Mr Ross, for your kindness!' he said. 'My name is Corbeck. I would give you my card, but they don't use cards where I've come from. And if I had had any, I suppose they, too, would have gone last night – '

He stopped suddenly, as though conscious that he had said too much. We both remained silent; as we waited I took stock of him. A short, sturdy man, brown as a coffee-berry; possibly inclined to be fat, but now lean exceedingly. The deep wrinkles in his face and neck were not merely from time and exposure; there were those unmistakable signs where flesh or fat has fallen away, and the skin has become loose. The neck was simply an intricate surface of seams and wrinkles, and was sun-scarred with the burning of the desert. The Far East, the tropic seasons, and the desert – each can have its colour mark. But all three are quite different; and an eye which has once known, can thenceforth easily distinguish them. The dusky pallor of one; the fierce red-brown of the other; and of the third, the dark, ingrained burning, as though it had become a permanent colour. Mr Corbeck had a big head, massive and full; with shaggy, dark red-brown hair, but bald on the temples. His forehead was a fine one, high and broad; with, to use the terms of physiognomy, the frontal sinus boldly marked. The squareness of it showed 'ratiocination'; and the fullness under the eyes 'language'. He had the short, broad nose that marks energy; the square chin – marked despite a thick, unkempt beard – and massive jaw that showed great resolution.

'No bad man for the desert!' I thought as I looked.

Miss Trelawny came very quickly. When Mr Corbeck saw her, he seemed somewhat surprised. But his annoyance and excitement had not disappeared; quite enough remained to cover up any such secondary and purely exoteric feeling as surprise. But as she spoke he never took his eyes off her; and I made a mental note that I would find some early opportunity of investigating the cause of his surprise. She began with an apology which quite smoothed down his ruffled feelings: 'Of course, had my Father been well you would not have been kept waiting. Indeed, had not I been on duty in the sick-room when you called the first time, I should have seen you at once. Now will you kindly tell me what is the matter which so presses?' He looked at me and hesitated. She spoke at once: 'You may say before Mr Ross anything which you can tell me. He has my fullest confidence, and is helping me in my trouble. I do not think you quite understand how serious my Father's condition is. For three days he has not waked, or given any sign of consciousness; and I am in terrible trouble about him. Unhappily I am in great ignorance of my Father and his life. I only came to live with him a year ago; and I know nothing whatever of his affairs. I do not even know who you are, or in what way your business is associated with him.' She said this with a little deprecating smile, all conventional and altogether graceful; as though to express in the most genuine way her absurd ignorance.

He looked steadily at her for perhaps a quarter of a minute; then he spoke, beginning at once as though his mind were made up and his confidence established: 'My name is Eugene Corbeck. I am a Master of Arts and Doctor of Laws and Master of Surgery of Cambridge; Doctor of Letters of Oxford; Doctor of Science and Doctor of Languages of London University; Doctor of Philosophy of Berlin; Doctor of Oriental Languages of Paris. I have some other degrees, honorary and otherwise, but I need not trouble you with them. Those I have named will show you that I am sufficiently feathered with diplomas to fly into even a sick-room. Early in life – fortunately for my interests and pleasures, but unfortunately for my pocket – I fell in with Egyptology. I must have been bitten by some powerful scarab, for I took it bad. I went out tomb-hunting; and managed to get a living of a sort, and to learn some things that you can't get out of books. I was in pretty low water when I met your Father, who was doing some explorations on his own account; and since then I haven't found that I have many unsatisfied wants. He is a real patron of the arts; no mad Egyptologist can ever hope for a better chief!'

He spoke with feeling; and I was glad to see that Miss Trelawny coloured up with pleasure at the praise of her father. I could not help noticing, however, that Mr Corbeck was, in a measure, speaking as if against time. I took it that he wished, while speaking, to study his ground; to see how far he would be justified in taking into confidence the two strangers before him. As he went on, I could see that his confidence kept increasing. When I thought of it afterward, and remembered what he had said, I realised that the measure of the information which he gave us marked his growing trust.

'I have been several times out on expeditions in Egypt for your Father; and I have always found it a delight to work for him. Many of his treasures – and he has some rare ones, I tell you – he has procured through me, either by my exploration or by purchase – or – or – otherwise. Your father, Miss Trelawny, has a rare knowledge. He sometimes makes up his mind that he wants to find a particular thing, of whose existence – if it still exists – he has become aware; and he will follow it all over the world till he gets it. I've been on just such a chase now.'

He stopped suddenly, as suddenly as though his mouth had been shut by the jerk of a string. We waited; when he went on he spoke with a caution that was new to him, as though he wished to forestall our asking any questions: 'I am not at liberty to mention anything of my mission; where it was to, what it was for, or anything at all about it. Such matters are in confidence between Mr Trelawny and myself; I am pledged to absolute secrecy.'

He paused, and an embarrassed look crept over his face. Suddenly he said: 'You are sure, Miss Trelawny, your Father is not well enough to see me today?'

A look of wonderment was on her face in turn. But it cleared at once; she stood up, saying in a tone in which dignity and graciousness were blended: 'Come and see for yourself!' She moved toward her father's room; he followed, and I brought up the rear.

Mr Corbeck entered the sick-room as though he knew it. There is an unconscious attitude or bearing to persons in new surroundings which there is no mistaking. Even in his anxiety to see his powerful friend, he glanced for a moment round the room, as at a familiar place. Then all his attention became fixed on the bed. I watched him narrowly, for somehow I felt that on this man depended much of our enlightenment regarding the strange matter in which we were involved.

It was not that I doubted him. The man was of transparent honesty; it was this very quality which we had to dread. He was of that courageous, fixed trueness to his undertaking, that if he should deem it his duty to guard a secret he would do it to the last. The case before us was, at least, an unusual one; and it would, consequently, require more liberal recognition of bounds of the duty of secrecy than would hold under ordinary conditions. To us, ignorance was helplessness. If we could learn anything of the past we might at least form some idea of the conditions antecedent to the attack; and might, so, achieve some means of helping the patient to recovery. There were curios which might be removed . . . My thoughts were beginning to whirl once again; I pulled myself up sharply and watched. There was a look of infinite pity on the sun-stained, rugged face as he gazed at his friend, lying so helpless. The sternness of Mr Trelawny's face had not relaxed in sleep; but somehow it made the helplessness more marked. It would not have troubled one to see a weak or an ordinary face under such conditions; but this purposeful, masterful man, lying before us wrapped in impenetrable sleep, had all the pathos of a great ruin. The sight was not a new one to us; but I could see that Miss Trelawny, like myself, was moved afresh by it in the presence of the stranger. Mr Corbeck's face grew stern. All the pity died away; and in its stead came a grim, hard look which boded ill for whoever had been the cause of this mighty downfall. This look in turn gave place to one of decision; the volcanic energy of the man was working to some definite purpose. He glanced around at us; and as his eyes lighted on Nurse Kennedy his eyebrows went up a trifle. She noted the look, and glanced interrogatively at Miss Trelawny, who flashed back a reply with a glance. She went quietly from the room, closing the door behind her. Mr Corbeck looked first at me, with a strong man's natural impulse to learn from a man rather than a woman; then at Miss Trelawny, with a remembrance of the duty of courtesy, and said: 'Tell me all about it. How it began and when!' Miss Trelawny looked at me appealingly; and forthwith I told him all that I knew. He seemed to make no motion during the whole time; but insensibly the bronze face became steel. When, at the end, I told him of Mr Marvin's visit and of the power of attorney, his look began to brighten. And when, seeing his interest in the matter, I went more into detail as to its terms, he spoke: 'Good! Now I know where my duty lies!'

With a sinking heart I heard him. Such a phrase, coming at such a time, seemed to close the door to my hopes of enlightenment.

'What do you mean?' I asked, feeling that my question was a feeble one.

His answer emphasised my fears: 'Trelawny knows what he is doing. He had some definite purpose in all that he did; and we must not thwart him. He evidently expected something to happen, and guarded himself at all points.'

'Not at all points!' I said impulsively. 'There must have been a weak spot somewhere, or he wouldn't be lying here like that!' Somehow his impassiveness surprised me. I had expected that he would find a valid argument in my phrase; but it did not move him, at least not in the way I thought. Something like a smile flickered over his swarthy face as he answered me: 'This is not the end! Trelawny did not guard himself to no purpose. Doubtless, he expected this too; or at any rate the possibility of it.'

'Do you know what he expected, or from what source?' The questioner was Miss Trelawny.

The answer came at once: 'No! I know nothing of either. I can guess . . . ' He stopped suddenly.

'Guess what?' The suppressed excitement in the girl's voice was akin to anguish. The steely look came over the swarthy face again; but there was tenderness and courtesy in both voice and manner as he replied: 'Believe me, I would do anything I honestly could to relieve your anxiety. But in this I have a higher duty.'

'What duty?'

'Silence!' As he spoke the word, the strong mouth closed like a steel trap.

We all remained silent for a few minutes. In the intensity of our thinking, the silence became a positive thing; the small sounds of life within and without the house seemed intrusive. The first to break it was Miss Trelawny. I had seen an idea – a hope – flash in her eyes; but she steadied herself before speaking: 'What was the urgent subject on which you wanted to see me, knowing that my father was – not available?' The pause showed her mastery of her thoughts.

The instantaneous change in Mr Corbeck was almost ludicrous. His start of surprise, coming close upon his iron-clad impassiveness, was like a pantomimic change. But all idea of comedy was swept away by the tragic earnestness with which he remembered his original purpose.

'My God!' he said, as he raised his hand from the chair back on which it rested, and beat it down with a violence which would in itself have arrested attention. His brows corrugated as he went on: 'I quite forgot! What a loss! Now of all times! Just at the moment of success! He lying there helpless, and my tongue tied! Not able to raise hand or foot in my ignorance of his wishes!'

'What is it? Oh, do tell us! I am so anxious about my dear father! Is it any new trouble? I hope not! oh, I hope not! I have had such anxiety and trouble already! It alarms me afresh to hear you speak so! Won't you tell me something to allay this terrible anxiety and uncertainty?'

He drew his sturdy form up to his full height as he said: 'Alas! I cannot, may not, tell you anything. It is his secret.' He pointed to the bed. 'And yet – and yet I came here for his advice, his counsel, his assistance. And he lies there helpless . . . And time is flying by us! It may soon be too late!'

'What is it? what is it?' broke in Miss Trelawny in a sort of passion of anxiety, her face drawn with pain. 'Oh, speak! Say something! This anxiety, and horror, and mystery are killing me!' Mr Corbeck calmed himself by a great effort.

'I may not tell you details; but I have had a great loss. My mission, in which I have spent three years, was successful. I discovered all that I sought – and more; and brought them home with me safely. Treasures, priceless in themselves, but doubly precious to him by whose wishes and instructions I sought them. I arrived in London only last night; and when I woke this morning my precious charge was stolen. Stolen in some mysterious way. Not a soul in London knew that I was arriving. No one but myself knew what was in the shabby portmanteau that I carried. My room had but one door, and that I locked and bolted. The room was high in the house, five stories up, so that no entrance could have been obtained by the window. Indeed, I had closed the window myself and shut the hasp, for I wished to be secure in every way. This morning the hasp was untouched . . . And yet my portmanteau was empty. The lamps were gone! . . . There! it is out. I went to Egypt to search for a set of antique lamps which Mr Trelawny wished to trace. With incredible labour, and through many dangers, I followed them. I brought them safe home . . . And now!' He turned away much moved. Even his iron nature was breaking down under the sense of loss.

Miss Trelawny stepped over and laid her hand on his arm. I looked at her in amazement. All the passion and pain which had so moved her seemed to have taken the form of resolution. Her form was erect, her eyes blazed; energy was manifest in every nerve and fibre of her being. Even her voice was full of nervous power as she spoke. It was apparent that she was a marvellously strong woman, and that her strength could answer when called upon.

'We must act at once! My father's wishes must be carried out, if it is possible to us. Mr Ross, you are a lawyer. We have actually in the house a man whom you consider one of the best detectives in London. Surely we can do something. We can begin at once!' Mr Corbeck took new life from her enthusiasm.

'Good! You are your Father's daughter!' was all he said. But his admiration for her energy was manifested by the impulsive way in which he took her hand. I moved over to the door. I was going to bring Sergeant Daw; and from her look of approval, I knew that Margaret – Miss Trelawny – understood. I was at the door when Mr Corbeck called me back.

'One moment,' he said, 'before we bring a stranger on the scene. It must be borne in mind that he is not to know what you know now, that the lamps were the objects of a prolonged and difficult and dangerous search. All I can tell him, all that he must know from any source, is that some of my property has been stolen. I must describe some of the lamps, especially one, for it is of gold; and my fear is lest the thief, ignorant of its historic worth, may, in order to cover up his crime, have it melted. I would willingly pay ten, twenty, a hundred, a thousand times its intrinsic value rather than have it destroyed. I shall tell him only what is necessary. So, please, let me answer any questions he may ask; unless, of course, I ask you or refer to either of you for the answer.' We both nodded acquiescence. Then a thought struck me and I said: 'By the way, if it be necessary to keep this matter quiet it will be better to have it if possible a private job for the detective. If once a thing gets to Scotland Yard it is out of our power to keep it quiet, and further secrecy may be impossible. I shall sound Sergeant Daw before he comes up. If I say nothing, it will mean that he accepts the task and will deal with it privately.' Mr Corbeck answered at once: 'Secrecy is everything. The one thing I dread is that the lamps, or some of them, may be destroyed at once.' To my intense astonishment Miss Trelawny spoke out at once, but quietly, in a decided voice: 'They will not be destroyed; nor any of them!' Mr Corbeck actually smiled in amazement.

'How on earth do you know?' he asked. Her answer was still more incomprehensible: 'I don't know how I know it; but know it I do. I feel it all through me; as though it were a conviction which has been with me all my life!'

CHAPTER 8

The Finding of the Lamps

SERGEANT DAW at first made some demur; but finally agreed to advise privately on a matter which might be suggested to him. He added that I was to remember that he only undertook to advise; for if action were required he might have to refer the matter to headquarters. With this understanding I left him in the study, and brought Miss Trelawny and Mr Corbeck to him. Nurse Kennedy resumed her place at the bedside before we left the room.

I could not but admire the cautious, cool-headed precision with which the traveller stated his case. He did not seem to conceal anything, and yet he gave the least possible description of the objects missing. He did not enlarge on the mystery of the case; he seemed to look on it as an ordinary hotel theft. Knowing, as I did, that his one object was to recover the articles before their identity could be obliterated, I could see the rare intellectual skill with which he gave the necessary matter and held back all else, though without seeming to do so. 'Truly,' thought I, 'this man has learned the lesson of the Eastern bazaars; and with Western intellect has improved upon his masters!' He quite conveyed his idea to the detective, who, after thinking the matter over for a few moments, said: 'Pot or scale? that is the question!'

'What does that mean?' asked the other, keenly alert.

'An old thieves' phrase from Birmingham. I thought that in these days of slang everyone knew that. In old times at Brum, which had a lot of small metal industries, the gold- and silversmiths used to buy metal from almost anyone who came along. And as metal in small quantities could generally be had cheap when they didn't ask where it came from, it got to be a custom to ask only one thing – whether the customer wanted the goods melted, in which case the buyer made the price, and the melting-pot was always on the fire. If it was to be preserved in its present state at the buyer's option, it went into the scale and fetched standard price for old metal.

'There is a good deal of such work done still, and in other places than Brum. When we're looking for stolen watches we often come across the works, and it's not possible to identify wheels and springs out of a heap; but it's not often that we come across cases that are wanted. Now, in the present instance much will depend on whether the thief is a good man – that's what they call a man who knows his work. A first-class crook will know whether a thing is of more value than merely the metal in it; and in such case he would put it with someone who could place it later on – in America or France, perhaps. By the way, do you think anyone but yourself could identify your lamps?'

'No one but myself!'

'Are there others like them?'

'Not that I know of,' answered Mr Corbeck; 'though there may be others that resemble them in many particulars.' The detective paused before asking again: 'Would any other skilled person – at the British Museum, for instance, or a dealer, or a collector like Mr Trelawny, know the value – the artistic value – of the lamps?'

'Certainly! Anyone with a head on his shoulders would see at a glance that the things were valuable.'

The detective's face brightened. 'Then there is a chance. If your door was locked and the window shut, the goods were not stolen by the chance of a chambermaid or a boots coming along. Whoever did the job went after it special; and he ain't going to part with his swag without his price. This must be a case of notice to the pawnbrokers. There's one good thing about it, anyhow, that the hue and cry needn't be given. We needn't tell Scotland Yard unless you like; we can work the thing privately. If you wish to keep the thing dark, as you told me at the first, that is our chance.' Mr Corbeck, after a pause, said quietly: 'I suppose you couldn't hazard a suggestion as to how the robbery was effected?' The policeman smiled the smile of knowledge and experience.

'In a very simple way, I have no doubt, sir. That is how all these mysterious crimes turn out in the long-run. The criminal knows his work and all the tricks of it; and he is always on the watch for chances. Moreover, he knows by experience what these chances are likely to be, and how they usually come. The other person is only careful; he doesn't know all the tricks and pits that may be made for him, and by some little oversight or other he falls into the trap. When we know all about this case, you will wonder that you did not see the method of it all along!' This seemed to annoy Mr Corbeck a little; there was decided heat in his manner as he answered: 'Look here, my good friend, there is not anything simple about this case – except that the things were taken. The window was closed; the fireplace was bricked up. There is only one door to the room, and that I locked and bolted. There is no transom; I have heard all about hotel robberies through the transom. I never left my room in the night. I looked at the things before going to bed; and I went to look at them again when I woke up. If you can rig up any kind of simple robbery out of these facts you are a clever man. That's all I say; clever enough to go right away and get my things back.' Miss Trelawny laid her hand upon his arm in a soothing way, and said quietly: 'Do not distress yourself unnecessarily. I am sure they will turn up.' Sergeant Daw turned to her so quickly that I could not help remembering vividly his suspicions of her, already formed, as he said: 'May I ask, miss, on what you base that opinion?'

I dreaded to hear her answer, given to ears already awake to suspicion; but it came to me as a new pain or shock all the same: 'I cannot tell you how I know. But I am sure of it!' The detective looked at her for some seconds in silence, and then threw a quick glance at me.

Presently he had a little more conversation with Mr Corbeck as to his own movements, the details of the hotel and the room, and the means of identifying the goods. Then he went away to commence his enquiries, Mr Corbeck impressing on him the necessity for secrecy lest the thief should get wind of his danger and destroy the lamps. Mr Corbeck promised, when going away to attend to various matters of his own business, to return early in the evening, and to stay in the house.

All that day Miss Trelawny was in better spirits and looked in better strength than she had yet been, despite the new shock and annoyance of the theft which must ultimately bring so much disappointment to her father.

We spent most of the day looking over the curio treasures of Mr

Trelawny. From what I had heard from Mr Corbeck I began to have some idea of the vastness of his enterprise in the world of Egyptian research; and with this light everything around me began to have a new interest. As I went on, the interest grew; any lingering doubts which I might have had changed to wonder and admiration. The house seemed to be a veritable storehouse of marvels of antique art. In addition to the curios, big and little, in Mr Trelawny's own room – from the great sarcophagi down to the scarabs of all kinds in the cabinets – the great hall, the staircase landings, the study, and even the boudoir were full of antique pieces which would have made a collector's mouth water.

Miss Trelawny from the first came with me, and looked with growing interest at everything. After having examined some cabinets of exquisite amulets she said to me in quite a naïve way: 'You will hardly believe that I have of late seldom even looked at any of these things. It is only since Father has been ill that I seem to have even any curiosity about them. But now, they grow and grow on me to quite an absorbing degree. I wonder if it is that the collector's blood which I have in my veins is beginning to manifest itself. If so, the strange thing is that I have not felt the call of it before. Of course I know most of the big things, and have examined them more or less; but really, in a sort of way I have always taken them for granted, as though they had always been there. I have noticed the same thing now and again with family pictures, and the way they are taken for granted by the family. If you will let me examine them with you it will be delightful!'

It was a joy to me to hear her talk in such a way; and her last suggestion quite thrilled me. Together we went round the various rooms and passages, examining and admiring the magnificent curios. There was such a bewildering amount and variety of objects that we could only glance at most of them; but as we went along we arranged that we should take them *seriatim*, day by day, and examine them more closely. In the hall was a sort of big frame of floriated steel work which Margaret said her father used for lifting the heavy stone lid of the sarcophagi. It was not heavy and could be moved about easily enough. By aid of this we raised the covers in turn and looked at the endless series of hieroglyphic pictures cut in most of them. In spite of her profession of ignorance Margaret knew a good deal about them; her year of life with her father had had unconsciously its daily and hourly lesson. She was a remarkably clever and acute-minded girl, and with a prodigious memory; so that her store of knowledge, gathered unthinkingly bit by bit, had grown to proportions that many a scholar might have envied.

And yet it was all so naïve and unconscious; so girlish and simple. She was so fresh in her views and ideas, and had so little thought of self, that in her companionship I forgot for the time all the troubles and mysteries which enmeshed the house; and I felt like a boy again . . .

The most interesting of the sarcophagi were undoubtedly the three in Mr Trelawny's room. Of these, two were of dark stone, one of porphyry and the other of a sort of ironstone. These were wrought with some hieroglyphs. But the third was strikingly different. It was of some yellow-brown substance of the dominating colour effect of Mexican onyx, which it resembled in many ways, excepting that the natural pattern of its convolutions was less marked. Here and there were patches almost transparent – certainly translucent. The whole chest, cover and all, was wrought with hundreds, perhaps thousands, of minute hieroglyphics, seemingly in an endless series. Back, front, sides, edges, bottom, all had their quota of the dainty pictures, the deep blue of their colouring showing up fresh and sharply edged in the yellow stone. It was very long, nearly nine feet; and perhaps a yard wide. The sides undulated, so that there was no hard line. Even the corners took such excellent curves that they pleased the eye. 'Truly,' I said, 'this must have been made for a giant!'

'Or for a giantess!' said Margaret.

This sarcophagus stood near to one of the windows. It was in one respect different from all the other sarcophagi in the place. All the others in the house, of whatever material – granite, porphyry, ironstone, basalt, slate, or wood – were quite simple in form within. Some of them were plain of interior surface; others were engraved, in whole or part, with hieroglyphics. But each and all of them had no protuberances or uneven surface anywhere. They might have been used for baths; indeed, they resembled in many ways Roman baths of stone or marble which I had seen. Inside this, however, was a raised space, outlined like a human figure. I asked Margaret if she could explain it in any way. For answer she said: 'Father never wished to speak about this. It attracted my attention from the first; but when I asked him about it he said: 'I shall tell you all about it someday, little girl – if I live! But not yet! The story is not yet told, as I hope to tell it to you! Someday, perhaps soon, I shall know all; and then we shall go over it together. And a mighty interesting story you will find it – from first to last!' Once afterward I said, rather lightly I am afraid: 'Is that story of the sarcophagus told yet, Father?' He shook his head, and looked at me gravely as he said:

'Not yet, little girl; but it will be – if I live – if I live!' His repeating that phrase about his living rather frightened me; I never ventured to ask him again.'

Somehow this thrilled me. I could not exactly say how or why; but it seems like a gleam of light at last. There are, I think, moments when the mind accepts something as true; though it can account for neither the course of the thought, nor, if there be more than one thought, the connection between them. Hitherto we had been in such outer darkness regarding Mr Trelawny, and the strange visitation which had fallen on him, that anything which afforded a clue, even of the faintest and most shadowy kind, had at the outset the enlightening satisfaction of a certainty. Here were two lights of our puzzle. The first that Mr Trelawny associated with this particular curio a doubt of his own living. The second that he had some purpose or expectation with regard to it, which he would not disclose, even to his daughter, till complete. Again it was to be borne in mind that this sarcophagus differed internally from all the others. What meant that odd raised place? I said nothing to Miss Trelawny, for I feared lest I should either frighten her or buoy her up with future hopes; but I made up my mind that I would take an early opportunity for further investigation.

Close beside the sarcophagus was a low table of green stone with red veins in it, like bloodstone. The feet were fashioned like the paws of a jackal, and round each leg was twined a full-throated snake wrought exquisitely in pure gold. On it rested a strange and very beautiful coffer or casket of stone of a peculiar shape. It was something like a small coffin, except that the longer sides, instead of being cut off square like the upper or level part were continued to a point. Thus it was an irregular septahedron, there being two planes on each of the two sides, one end and a top and bottom. The stone, of one piece of which it was wrought, was such as I had never seen before. At the base it was of a full green, the colour of emerald without, of course, its gleam. It was not by any means dull, however, either in colour or substance, and was of infinite hardness and fineness of texture. The surface was almost that of a jewel. The colour grew lighter as it rose, with gradation so fine as to be imperceptible, changing to a fine yellow almost of the colour of 'mandarin' china. It was quite unlike anything I had ever seen, and did not resemble any stone or gem that I knew. I took it to be some unique mother-stone, or matrix of some gem. It was wrought all over, except in a few spots, with fine hieroglyphics, exquisitely done and coloured with the same blue-green cement or pigment that appeared on the sarcophagus. In length it was about two feet and a half; in breadth about half this, and was nearly a foot high. The vacant spaces were irregularly distributed about the top running to the pointed end. These places seemed less opaque than the rest of the stone. I tried to lift up the lid so that I might see if they were translucent; but it was securely fixed. It fitted so exactly that the whole coffer seemed like a single piece of stone mysteriously hollowed from within. On the sides and edges were some odd-looking protuberances wrought just as finely as any other portion of the coffer which had been sculptured by manifest design in the cutting of the stone. They had queer-shaped holes or hollows, different in each; and, like the rest, were covered with the hiero-glyphic figures, cut finely and filled in with the same blue-green cement.

On the other side of the great sarcophagus stood another small table of alabaster, exquisitely chased with symbolic figures of gods and the signs of the zodiac. On this table stood a case of about a foot square composed of slabs of rock crystal set in a skeleton of bands of red gold, beautifully engraved with hieroglyphics, and coloured with a blue green, very much the tint of the figures on the sarcophagus and the coffer. The whole work was quite modern.

But if the case was modern what it held was not. Within, on a cushion of cloth of gold as fine as silk, and with the peculiar softness of old gold, rested a mummy hand, so perfect that it startled one to see it. A woman's hand, fine and long, with slim tapering fingers and nearly as perfect as when it was given to the embalmer thousands of years before. In the embalming it had lost nothing of its beautiful shape; even the wrist seemed to maintain its pliability as the gentle curve lay on the cushion. The skin was of a rich creamy or old ivory colour; a dusky fair skin which suggested heat, but heat in shadow. The great peculiarity of it, as a hand, was that it had in all seven fingers, there being two middle and two index fingers. The upper end of the wrist was jagged, as though it had been broken off, and was stained with a red-brown stain. On the cushion near the hand was a small scarab, exquisitely wrought of emerald.

'That is another of my father's mysteries. When I asked him about it he said that it was perhaps the most valuable thing he had, except one. When I asked him what that one was, he refused to tell me, and forbade me to ask him anything concerning it. "I will tell you," he said, "all about it, too, in good time – if I live!" '

'If I live!' the phrase again. These three things grouped together, the sarcophagus, the coffer, and the hand, seemed to make a trilogy of mystery indeed!

At this time Miss Trelawny was sent for on some domestic matter. I looked at the other curios in the room; but they did not seem to have anything like the same charm for me, now that she was away. Later on in the day I was sent for to the boudoir where she was consulting with Mrs Grant as to the lodgment of Mr Corbeck. They were in doubt as to whether he should have a room close to Mr Trelawny's or quite away from it, and had thought it well to ask my advice on the subject. I came to the conclusion that he had better not be too near; for the first at all events, he could easily be moved closer if necessary. When Mrs Grant had gone, I asked Miss Trelawny how it came that the furniture of this room, the boudoir in which we were, was so different from the other rooms of the house.

'Father's forethought!' she answered. 'When I first came, he thought, and rightly enough, that I might get frightened with so many records of death and the tomb everywhere. So he had this room and the little suite off it – that door opens into the sitting-room – where I slept last night, furnished with pretty things. You see, they are all beautiful. That cabinet belonged to the great Napoleon.'

'There is nothing Egyptian in these rooms at all then?' I asked, rather to show interest in what she had said than anything else, for the furnishing of the room was apparent. 'What a lovely cabinet! May I look at it?'

'Of course! with the greatest pleasure!' she answered, with a smile. 'Its finishing within and without, Father says, is absolutely complete.' I stepped over and looked at it closely. It was made of tulip wood, inlaid in pattern; and was mounted in ormolu. I pulled open one of the drawers, a deep one where I could see the work to great advantage. As I pulled it, something rattled inside as though rolling; there was a tinkle as of metal on metal.

'Hullo!' I said. 'There is something in here. Perhaps I had better not open it.'

'There is nothing that I know of,' she answered. 'Some of the housemaids may have used it to put something by for the time and forgotten it. Open it by all means!'

I pulled open the drawer; as I did so, both Miss Trelawny and I started back in amazement.

There before our eyes lay a number of ancient Egyptian lamps, of various sizes and of strangely varied shapes.

We leaned over them and looked closely. My own heart was beating like a trip-hammer; and I could see by the heaving of Margaret's bosom that she was strangely excited.

Whilst we looked, afraid to touch and almost afraid to think, there was a ring at the front door; immediately afterwards Mr Corbeck, followed by Sergeant Daw, came into the hall. The door of the boudoir was open, and when they saw us Mr Corbeck came running in, followed more slowly by the detective. There was a sort of chastened joy in his face and manner as he said impulsively: 'Rejoice with me, my dear Miss Trelawny, my luggage has come and all my things are intact!' Then his face fell as he added, 'Except the lamps. The lamps that were worth all the rest a thousand times . . . ' He stopped, struck by the strange pallor of her face. Then his eyes, following her look and mine, lit on the cluster of lamps in the drawer. He gave a sort of cry of surprise and joy as he bent over and touched them: 'My lamps! My lamps! Then they are safe – safe – safe! . . . But how, in the name of God – of all the gods – did they come here?'

We all stood silent. The detective made a deep sound of in-taking breath. I looked at him, and as he caught my glance he turned his eyes on Miss Trelawny whose back was toward him.

There was in them the same look of suspicion which had been there when he had spoken to me of her being the first to find her father on the occasions of the attack.

CHAPTER 9

The Need of Knowledge

MR CORBECK seemed to go almost off his head at the recovery of the lamps. He took them up one by one and looked them all over tenderly, as though they were things that he loved. In his delight and excitement he breathed so hard that it seemed almost like a cat purring. Sergeant Daw said quietly, his voice breaking the silence like a discord in a melody: 'Are you quite sure those lamps are the ones you had, and that were stolen?'

His answer was in an indignant tone: 'Sure! Of course I'm sure. There isn't another set of lamps like these in the world!'

'So far as you know!' The detective's words were smooth enough, but his manner was so exasperating that I was sure he had some motive in it; so I waited in silence. He went on: 'Of course there may be some in the British Museum; or Mr Trelawny may have had these already. There's nothing new under the sun, you know, Mr Corbeck; not even in Egypt. These may be the originals, and yours may have been the copies. Are there any points by which you can identify these as yours?'

Mr Corbeck was really angry by this time. He forgot his reserve; and in his indignation poured forth a torrent of almost incoherent, but enlightening, broken sentences: 'Identify! Copies of them! British Museum! Rot! Perhaps they keep a set in Scotland Yard for teaching idiot policemen Egyptology! Do I know them? When I have carried them about my body, in the desert, for three months; and lay awake night after night to watch them! When I have looked them over with a magnifying-glass, hour after hour, till my eyes ached; till every tiny blotch, and chip, and dinge became as familiar to me as his chart to a captain; as familiar as they doubtless have been all the time to every thick-headed area-prowler within the bounds of mortality. See here, young man, look at these!' He ranged the lamps in a row on the top of the cabinet. 'Did you ever see a set of lamps of these shapes – of any one of these shapes? Look at these dominant figures on them! Did you ever see so complete a set – even in Scotland Yard; even in Bow Street? Look! one on each, the seven forms of Hathor. Look at that figure of the Ka, of a princess of the two Egypts, standing between Ra and Osiris in the Boat of the Dead, with the Eye of Sleep, supported on legs, bending before her; and Harmochis rising in the north. Will you find that in the British Museum – or Bow Street? Or perhaps your studies in the Gizeh Museum, or the Fitzwilliam, or Paris, or Leyden, or Berlin, have shown you that the episode is common in hieroglyphics; and that this is only a copy. Perhaps you can tell me what that figure of Ptah-Seker-Ausar holding the Tet wrapped in the Sceptre of Papyrus means? Did you ever see it before; even in the British Museum, or Gizeh, or Scotland Yard?'

He broke off suddenly; and then went on in quite a different way: 'Look here! it seems to me that the thick-headed idiot is myself! I beg your pardon, old fellow, for my rudeness. I quite lost my temper at the suggestion that I do not know these lamps. You don't mind, do you?' The detective answered heartily: 'Lord, sir, not I. I like to see folks angry when I am dealing with them, whether they are on my side or the other. It is when people are angry that you learn the truth from them. I keep cool; that is my trade! Do you know, you have told me more about those lamps in the past two minutes than when you filled me up with details of how to identify them.'

Mr Corbeck grunted; he was not pleased at having given himself away. All at once he turned to me and said in his natural way: 'Now tell me how you got them back?' I was so surprised that I said without thinking: 'We didn't get them back!' The traveller laughed openly.

'What on earth do you mean?' he asked. 'You didn't get them back! Why, there they are before your eyes! We found you looking at them when we came in.' By this time I had recovered my surprise and had my wits about me.

'Why, that's just it,' I said. 'We had only come across them, by accident, that very moment!'

Mr Corbeck drew back and looked hard at Miss Trelawny and myself; turning his eyes from one to the other as he asked: 'Do you mean to tell me that no one brought them here; that you found them in that drawer? That, so to speak, no one at all brought them back?'

'I suppose someone must have brought them here; they couldn't have come of their own accord. But who it was, or when, or how, neither of us knows. We shall have to make enquiry, and see if any of the servants know anything of it.'

We all stood silent for several seconds. It seemed a long time. The first to speak was the detective, who said in an unconscious way: 'Well, I'm damned! I beg your pardon, miss!' Then his mouth shut like a steel trap.

We called up the servants, one by one, and asked them if they knew anything of some articles placed in a drawer in the boudoir; but none of them could throw any light on the circumstance. We did not tell them what the articles were; or let them see them.

Mr Corbeck packed the lamps in cotton wool, and placed them in a tin box. This, I may mention incidentally, was then brought up to the detectives' room, where one of the men stood guard over them with a revolver the whole night. Next day we got a small safe into the house, and placed them in it. There were two different keys. One of them I kept myself; the other I placed in my drawer in the safe deposit vault. We were all determined that the lamps should not be lost again.

About an hour after we had found the lamps, Dr Winchester arrived. He had a large parcel with him, which, when unwrapped, proved to be the mummy of a cat. With Miss Trelawny's permission he placed this in the boudoir; and Silvio was brought close to it. To the surprise of us all, however, except perhaps Dr Winchester, he did not manifest the least annoyance; he took no notice of it whatever. He stood on the table close beside it, purring loudly. Then, following out his plan, the doctor brought him into Mr Trelawny's room, we all following. Dr Winchester was excited; Miss Trelawny anxious. I was more than interested myself, for I began to have a glimmering of the doctor's idea. The detective was calmly and coldly superior: but Mr Corbeck, who was an enthusiast, was full of eager curiosity.

The moment Dr Winchester got into the room, Silvio began to mew and wriggle; and, jumping out of his arms, ran over to the cat mummy and began to scratch angrily at it. Miss Trelawny had some difficulty in taking him away; but so soon as he was out of the room he became quiet. When she came back there was a clamour of comments: 'I thought so!' from the doctor.

'What can it mean?' from Miss Trelawny.

'That's a very strange thing!' from Mr Corbeck.

'Odd! but it doesn't prove anything!' from the detective.

'I suspend my judgment!' from myself, thinking it advisable to say something.

Then by common consent we dropped the theme – for the present.

In my room that evening I was making some notes of what had happened, when there came a low tap on the door. In obedience to my summons Sergeant Daw came in, carefully closing the door behind him.

'Well, sergeant,' said I, 'sit down. What is it?'

'I wanted to speak to you, sir, about those lamps.' I nodded and waited: he went on: 'You know that that room where they were found opens directly into the room where Miss Trelawny slept last night?'

'Yes.'

'During the night a window somewhere in that part of the house was opened, and shut again. I heard it, and took a look round; but I could see no sign of anything.'

'Yes, I know that!' I said; 'I heard a window moved myself.'

'Does nothing strike you as strange about it, sir?'

'Strange!' I said; 'strange! why it's all the most bewildering, maddening thing I have ever encountered. It is all so strange that one seems to wonder, and simply waits for what will happen next. But what do you mean by strange?'

The detective paused, as if choosing his words to begin; and then said deliberately: 'You see, I am not one who believes in magic and such things. I am for facts all the time; and I always find in the long-run that there is a reason and a cause for everything. This new gentleman says these things were stolen out of his room in the hotel. The lamps, I take it from some things he has said, really belong to Mr Trelawny. His daughter, the lady of the house, having left the room she usually occupies, sleeps that night on the ground floor. A window is heard to open and shut during the night. When we, who have been during the day trying to find a clue to the robbery, come to the house, we find the stolen goods in a room close to where she slept, and opening out of it!'

He stopped. I felt that same sense of pain and apprehension, which I had experienced when he had spoken to me before, creeping, or rather rushing, over me again. I had to face the matter out, however. My relations with her, and the feeling toward her which I now knew full well meant a very deep love and devotion, demanded so much. I said as calmly as I could, for I knew the keen eyes of the skilful investigator were on me: 'And the inference?'

He answered with the cool audacity of conviction: 'The inference to me is that there was no robbery at all. The goods were taken by someone to this house, where they were received through a window on the ground floor. They were placed in the cabinet, ready to be discovered when the proper time should come!'

Somehow I felt relieved; the assumption was too monstrous. I did not want, however, my relief to be apparent, so I answered as gravely as I could: 'And who do you suppose brought them to the house?'

'I keep my mind open as to that. Possibly Mr Corbeck himself; the matter might be too risky to trust to a third party.'

'Then the natural extension of your inference is that Mr Corbeck is a liar and a fraud; and that he is in conspiracy with Miss Trelawny to deceive someone or other about those lamps.'

'Those are harsh words, Mr Ross. They're so plain-spoken that they bring a man up standing, and make new doubts for him. But I have to go where my reason points. It may be that there is another party than Miss Trelawny in it. Indeed, if it hadn't been for the other matter that set me thinking and bred doubts of its own about her, I wouldn't dream of mixing her up in this. But I'm safe on Corbeck. Whoever else is in it, he is! The things couldn't have been taken without his connivance – if what he says is true. If it isn't – well! he is a liar anyhow. I would think it a bad job to have him stay in the house with so many valuables, only that it will give me and my mate a chance of watching him. We'll keep a pretty good look-out, too, I tell you. He's up in my room now, guarding those lamps; but Johnny Wright is there too. I go on before he comes off; so there won't be much chance of another house-breaking. Of course, Mr Ross, all this, too, is between you and me.'

'Quite so! You may depend on my silence!' I said; and he went away to keep a close eye on the Egyptologist.

It seemed as though all my painful experiences were to go in pairs, and that the sequence of the previous day was to be repeated; for before long I had another private visit from Dr Winchester who had now paid his nightly visit to his patient and was on his way home. He took the seat which I preferred and began at once: 'This is a strange affair altogether. Miss Trelawny has just been telling me about the stolen lamps, and of the finding of them in the Napoleon cabinet. It would seem to be another complication of the mystery; and yet, do you know, it is a relief to me. I have exhausted all human and natural possibilities of the case, and am beginning to fall back on super-human and supernatural possibilities. Here are such strange things that, if I am not going mad, I think we must have a solution before long. I wonder if I might ask some questions and some help from Mr Corbeck, without making further complications and embarrassing us. He seems to know an amazing amount regarding Egypt and all relating to it. Perhaps he wouldn't mind translating a little bit of hieroglyphic. It is child's play to him. What do you think?'

When I had thought the matter over a few seconds I spoke. We wanted all the help we could get. For myself, I had perfect confidence in both men; and any comparing notes, or mutual assistance, might bring good results. Such could hardly bring evil.

'By all means I should ask him. He seems an extraordinarily learned man in Egyptology; and he seems to me a good fellow as well as an enthusiast. By the way, it will be necessary to be a little guarded as to whom you speak regarding any information which he may give you.'

'Of course!' he answered. 'Indeed I should not dream of saying anything to anybody, excepting yourself. We have to remember that when Mr Trelawny recovers he may not like to think that we have been chattering unduly over his affairs.'

'Look here!' I said, 'why not stay for a while: and I shall ask him to come and have a pipe with us. We can then talk over things.'

He acquiesced: so I went to the room where Mr Corbeck was, and brought him back with me. I thought the detectives were pleased at his going. On the way to my room he said: 'I don't half like leaving those things there, with only those men to guard them. They're a deal sight too precious to be left to the police!'

From which it would appear that suspicion was not confined to Sergeant Daw.

Mr Corbeck and Dr Winchester, after a quick glance at each other, became at once on most friendly terms. The traveller professed his willingness to be of any assistance which he could, provided, he added, that it was anything about which he was free to speak. This was not very promising; but Dr Winchester began at once: 'I want you, if you will, to translate some hieroglyphic for me.'

'Certainly, with the greatest pleasure, so far as I can. For I may tell you that hieroglyphic writing is not quite mastered yet; though we are getting at it! We are getting at it! What is the inscription?'

'There are two,' he answered. 'One of them I shall bring here.'

He went out, and returned in a minute with the mummy cat which he had that evening introduced to Silvio. The scholar took it; and, after a short examination, said: 'There is nothing especial in this. It is an appeal to Bast, the Lady of Bubastis, to give her good bread and milk in the Elysian Fields. There may be more inside; and if you will care to unroll it, I will do my best. I do not think, however, that there is anything special. From the method of wrapping I should say it is from the Delta; and of a late period, when such mummy work was common and cheap. What is the other inscription you wish me to see?'

'The inscription on the mummy cat in Mr Trelawny's room.'

Mr Corbeck's face fell. 'No!' he said, 'I cannot do that! I am, for the present at all events, practically bound to secrecy regarding any of the things in Mr Trelawny's room.'

Dr Winchester's comment and my own were made at the same moment. I said only the one word, 'Checkmate!' from which I think he may have gathered that I guessed more of his idea and purpose than perhaps I had intentionally conveyed to him. He murmured: 'Practically bound to secrecy?'

Mr Corbeck at once took up the challenge conveyed: 'Do not misunderstand me! I am not bound by any definite pledge of secrecy; but I am bound in honour to respect Mr Trelawny's confidence, given to me, I may tell you, in a very large measure. Regarding many of the objects in his room he has a definite purpose in view; and it would not be either right or becoming for me, his trusted friend and confidant, to forestall that purpose. Mr Trelawny, you may know – or rather you do not know or you would not have so construed my remark – is a scholar, a very great scholar. He has worked for years toward a certain end. For this he has spared no labour, no expense, no personal danger or self-denial. He is on the line of a result which will place him amongst the foremost discoverers or investigators of his age. And now, just at the time when any hour might bring him success, he is stricken down!'

He stopped, seemingly overcome with emotion. After a time he recovered himself and went on: 'Again, do not misunderstand me as to another point. I have said that Mr Trelawny has made much confidence with me; but I do not mean to lead you to believe that I know all his plans, or his aims or objects. I know the period which he has been studying; and the definite historical individual whose life he has been investigating, and whose records he has been following up one by one with infinite patience. But beyond this I know nothing. That he has some aim or object in the completion of this knowledge I am convinced. What it is I may guess; but I must say nothing. Please to remember, gentlemen, that I have voluntarily accepted the position of recipient of a partial confidence. I have respected that; and I must ask any of my friends to do the same.'

He spoke with great dignity; and he grew, moment by moment, in the respect and esteem of both Dr Winchester and myself. We understood that he had not done speaking; so we waited in silence till he continued: 'I have spoken this much, although I know well that even such a hint as either of you might gather from my words might jeopardise the success of his work. But I am convinced that you both wish to help him – and his daughter,' he said this looking me fairly between the eyes, 'to the best of your power, honestly and unself-ishly. He is so stricken down, and the manner of it is so mysterious that I cannot but think that it is in some way a result of his own work. That he calculated on some set-back is manifest to us all. God knows! I am willing to do what I can, and to use any knowledge I have in his behalf. I arrived in England full of exultation at the thought that I had fulfilled the mission with which he had trusted me. I had got what he said were the last objects of his search; and I felt assured that he would now be able to begin the experiment of which he had often hinted to me. It is too dreadful that at just such a time such a calamity should have fallen on him. Dr Winchester, you are a physician; and, if your face does not belie you, you are a clever and a bold one. Is there no way which you can devise to wake this man from his unnatural stupor?'

There was a pause; then the answer came slowly and deliberately: 'There is no ordinary remedy that I know of. There might possibly be some extraordinary one. But there would be no use in trying to find it, except on one condition.'

'And that?'

'Knowledge! I am completely ignorant of Egyptian matters, language, writing, history, secrets, medicines, poisons, occult powers – all that go to make up the mystery of that mysterious land. This disease, or condition, or whatever it may be called, from which Mr Trelawny is suffering, is in some way connected with Egypt. I have had a suspicion of this from the first; and later it grew into a certainty, though without proof. What you have said tonight confirms my conjecture, and makes me believe that a proof is to be had. I do not think that you quite know all that has gone on in this house since the night of the attack – of the finding of Mr Trelawny's body. Now I propose that we confide in you. If Mr Ross agrees, I shall ask him to tell you. He is more skilled than I am in putting facts before other people. He can speak by his brief; and in this case he has the best of all briefs, the experience of his own eyes and ears, and the evidence that he has himself taken on the spot from participators in, or spectators of, what has happened. When you know all, you will, I hope, be in a position to judge as to whether you can best help Mr Trelawny, and further his secret wishes, by your silence or your speech.'

I nodded approval. Mr Corbeck jumped up, and in his impulsive way held out a hand to each.

'Done!' he said. 'I acknowledge the honour of your confidence; and on my part I pledge myself that if I find my duty to Mr Trelawny's wishes will, in his own interest, allow my lips to open on his affairs, I shall speak so freely as I may.'

Accordingly I began, and told him, as exactly as I could, everything that had happened from the moment of my waking at the knocking on the door in Jermyn Street. The only reservations I made were as to my own feeling toward Miss Trelawny and the matters of small import to the main subject which followed it; and my conversations with Sergeant Daw, which were in themselves private, and which would have demanded discretionary silence in any case. As I spoke, Mr Corbeck followed with breathless interest. Sometimes he would stand up and pace about the room in uncontrollable excitement; and then recover himself suddenly, and sit down again. Sometimes he would be about to speak, but would, with an effort, restrain himself. I think the narration helped me to make up my own mind; for even as I talked, things seemed to appear in a clearer light. Things big and little, in relation of their importance to the case, fell into proper perspective. The story up to date became coherent, except as to its cause, which seemed a greater mystery than ever. This is the merit of entire, or collected, narrative. Isolated facts, doubts, suspicions, conjectures, give way to a homogeneity which is convincing.

That Mr Corbeck was convinced was evident. He did not go through any process of explanation or limitation, but spoke right out at once to the point, and fearlessly, like a man: 'That settles me! There is in activity some force that needs special care. If we all go on working in the dark we shall get in one another's way, and by hampering each other, undo the good that any or each of us, working in different directions, might do. It seems to me that the first thing we have to accomplish is to get Mr Trelawny waked out of that unnatural sleep. That he can be waked is apparent from the way the nurse has recovered; though what additional harm may have been done to him in the time he has been lying in that room I suppose no one can tell. We must chance that, however. He *has* lain there, and whatever the effect might be, it is there now; and we have, and shall have, to deal with it as a fact. A day more or less won't hurt in the long-run. It is late now; and we shall probably have tomorrow a task before us that will require our energies fresh. You, doctor, will want to get to your sleep; for I suppose you have other work as well as this to do tomorrow. As for you, Mr Ross, I understand that you are to have a spell of watching in the sick-room tonight. I shall get you a book which will help to pass the time for you. I shall go and look for it in the library. I know where it was when I was here last; and I don't suppose Mr Trelawny has used it since. He knew long ago all that was in it which was or might be of interest to him. But it will be necessary, or at least helpful, to understand other things which I shall tell you later. You will be able to tell Dr Winchester all that would aid him. For I take it that our work will branch out pretty soon. We shall each have our own end to hold up; and it will take each of us all our time and understanding to get through his own tasks. It will not be necessary for you to read the whole book. All that will interest you – with regard to our matter I mean of course, for the whole book is interesting as a record of travel in a country then quite unknown – is the preface, and two or three chapters which I shall mark for you.'

He shook hands warmly with Dr Winchester who had stood up to go.

Whilst he was away I sat lonely, thinking. As I thought, the world around me seemed to be illimitably great. The only little spot in which I was interested seemed like a tiny speck in the midst of a wilderness. Without and around it were darkness and unknown danger, pressing in from every side. And the central figure in our little oasis was one of sweetness and beauty. A figure one could love; could work for; could die for . . . !

Mr Corbeck came back in a very short time with the book; he had found it at once in the spot where he had seen it three years before. Having placed in it several slips of paper, marking the places where I was to read, he put it into my hands, saying: 'That is what started Mr Trelawny; what started me when I read it; and which will, I have no doubt, be to you an interesting beginning to a special study – whatever the end may be. If, indeed, any of us here may ever see the end.'

At the door he paused and said: 'I want to take back one thing. That detective is a good fellow. What you have told me of him puts him in a new light. The best proof of it is that I can go quietly to sleep tonight, and leave the lamps in his care!'

When he had gone I took the book with me, put on my respirator, and went to my spell of duty in the sick-room!

CHAPTER 10

The Valley of the Sorcerer

I PLACED THE BOOK on the little table on which the shaded lamp rested, and moved the screen to one side. Thus I could have the light on my book; and by looking up, see the bed, and the nurse, and the door. I cannot say that the conditions were enjoyable, or calculated to allow of that absorption in the subject which is advisable for effective study. However, I composed myself to the work as well as I could. The book was one which, on the very face of it, required special attention. It was a folio in Dutch, printed in Amsterdam in 1650. Someone had made a literal translation, writing generally the English word under the Dutch, so that the grammatical differences between the two tongues made even the reading of the translation a difficult matter. One had to dodge backward and forward among the words. This was in addition to the difficulty of deciphering a strange handwriting of two hundred years ago. I found, however, that after a short time I got into the habit of following in conventional English the Dutch construction; and, as I became more familiar with the writing, my task became easier.

At first the circumstances of the room, and the fear lest Miss Trelawny should return unexpectedly and find me reading the book, disturbed me somewhat. For we had arranged amongst us, before Dr Winchester had gone home, that she was not to be brought into the range of the coming investigation. We considered that there might be some shock to a woman's mind in matters of apparent mystery; and further, that she, being Mr Trelawny's daughter, might be placed in a difficult position with him afterward if she took part in, or even had a personal knowledge of, the disregarding of his expressed wishes. But when I remembered that she did not come on nursing duty till two o'clock, the fear of interruption passed away. I had still nearly three hours before me. Nurse Kennedy sat in her chair by the bedside, patient and alert. A clock ticked on the landing; other clocks in the house ticked; the life of the city without manifested itself in the distant hum, now and again swelling into a roar as a breeze floating westward took the concourse of sounds with it. But still the dominant idea was of silence. The light on my book, and the soothing fringe of green silk round the shade intensified, whenever I looked up, the gloom of the sick-room. With every line I read, this seemed to grow deeper and deeper; so that when my eyes came back to the page the light seemed to dazzle me. I stuck to my work, however, and presently began to get sufficiently into the subject to become interested in it.

The book was by one Nicholas van Huyn of Hoorn. In the preface he told how, attracted by the work of John Greaves of Merton College, *Pyramidographia*, he himself visited Egypt, where he became so interested in its wonders that he devoted some years of his life to visiting strange places, and exploring the ruins of many temples and tombs. He had come across many variants of the story of the building of the Pyramids as told by the Arabian historian, Ibn Abd Alhokin, some of which he set down. These I did not stop to read, but went on to the marked pages.

As soon as I began to read these, however, there grew on me some sense of a disturbing influence. Once or twice I looked to see if the nurse had moved, for there was a feeling as though someone were near me. Nurse Kennedy sat in her place, as steady and alert as ever; and I came back to my book again.

The narrative went on to tell how, after passing for several days through the mountains to the east of Aswan, the explorer came to a certain place. Here I give his own words, simply putting the translation into modern English: 'Toward evening we came to the entrance of a narrow, deep valley, running east and west. I wished to proceed through this; for the sun, now nearly down on the horizon, showed a wide opening beyond the narrowing of the cliffs. But the fellaheen absolutely refused to enter the valley at such a time, alleging that they might be caught by the night before they could emerge from the other end. At first they would give no reason for their fear. They had hitherto gone anywhere I wished, and at any time, without demur. On being pressed, however, they said that the place was the Valley of the Sorcerer, where none might come in the night. On being asked to tell of the sorcerer, they refused, saying that there was no name, and that they knew nothing. On the next morning, however, when the sun was up and shining down the valley, their fears had somewhat passed away. Then they told me that a great

Sorcerer in ancient days – "millions of millions of years" was the term they used – a king or a queen, they could not say which, was buried there. They could not give the name, persisting to the last that there was no name; and that anyone who should name it would waste away in life so that at death nothing of him would remain to be raised again in the other world. In passing through the valley they kept together in a cluster, hurrying on in front of me. None dared to remain behind. They gave, as their reason for so proceeding, that the arms of the Sorcerer were long, and that it was dangerous to be the last. The which was of little comfort to me who of this necessity took that honourable post. In the narrowest part of the valley, on the south side, was a great cliff of rock, rising sheer, of smooth and even surface. Hereon were graven certain cabalistic signs, and many figures of men and animals, fishes, reptiles and birds; suns and stars; and many quaint symbols. Some of these latter were disjointed limbs and features, such as arms and legs, fingers, eyes, noses, ears, and lips. Mysterious symbols which will puzzle the recording angel to interpret at the Judgment Day. The cliff faced exactly north. There was something about it so strange, and so different from the other carved rocks which I had visited, that I called a halt and spent the day in examining the rock front as well as I could with my telescope. The Egyptians of my company were terribly afraid, and used every kind of persuasion to induce me to pass on. I stayed till late in the afternoon, by which time I had failed to make out aright the entry of any tomb, for I suspected that such was the purpose of the sculpture of the rock. By this time the men were rebellious; and I had to leave the valley if I did not wish my whole retinue to desert. But I secretly made up my mind to discover the tomb, and explore it. To this end I went further into the mountains, where I met with an Arab Sheik who was willing to take service with me. The Arabs were not bound by the same superstitious fears as the Egyptians; Sheik Abu Soma and his following were willing to take a part in the explorations.

'When I returned to the valley with these Bedouins, I made effort to climb the face of the rock, but failed, it being of one impenetrable smoothness. The stone, generally flat and smooth by nature, had been chiselled to completeness. That there had been projecting steps was manifest, for there remained, untouched by the wondrous climate of that strange land, the marks of saw and chisel and mallet where the steps had been cut or broken away.

'Being thus baffled of winning the tomb from below, and being unprovided with ladders to scale, I found a way by much circuitous journeying to the top of the cliff. Thence I caused myself to be lowered by ropes, till I had investigated that portion of the rock face wherein I expected to find the opening. I found that there was an entrance, closed however by a great stone slab. This was cut in the rock more than a hundred feet up, being two-thirds the height of the cliff. The hieroglyphic and cabalistic symbols cut in the rock were so managed as to disguise it. The cutting was deep, and was continued through the rock and the portals of the doorway, and through the great slab which formed the door itself. This was fixed in place with such incredible exactness that no stone chisel or cutting implement which I had with me could find a lodgment in the interstices. I used much force, however; and by many heavy strokes won a way into the tomb, for such I found it to be. The stone door having fallen into the entrance I passed over it into the tomb, noting as I went a long iron chain which hung coiled on a bracket close to the doorway.

'The tomb I found to be complete, after the manner of the finest Egyptian tombs, with chamber and shaft leading down to the corridor, ending in the mummy pit. It had the table of pictures, which seems some kind of record – whose meaning is now for ever lost – graven in a wondrous colour on a wondrous stone.

'All the walls of the chamber and the passage were carved with strange writings in the uncanny form mentioned. The huge stone coffin or sarcophagus in the deep pit was marvellously graven throughout with signs. The Arab chief and two others who ventured into the tomb with me, and who were evidently used to such grim explorations, managed to take the cover from the sarcophagus without breaking it. At which they wondered; for such good fortune, they said, did not usually attend such efforts. Indeed they seemed not over careful; and did handle the various furniture of the tomb with such little concern that, only for its great strength and thickness, even the coffin itself might have been injured. Which gave me much concern, for it was very beautifully wrought of rare stone, such as I had no knowledge of. Much I grieved that it were not possible to carry it away. But time and desert journeyings forbade such; I could only take with me such small matters as could be carried on the person.

'Within the sarcophagus was a body, manifestly of a woman, swathed with many wrappings of linen, as is usual with all mummies. From certain embroiderings thereon, I gathered that she was of high rank. Across the breast was one hand, unwrapped. In the mummies which I had seen, the arms and hands are within the wrappings, and certain adornments of wood, shaped and painted to resemble arms and hands, lie outside the enwrapped body.

'But this hand was strange to see, for it was the real hand of her who lay enwrapped there; the arm projecting from the cerements being of flesh, seemingly made as like marble in the process of embalming. Arm and hand were of dusky white, being of the hue of ivory that hath lain long in air. The skin and the nails were complete and whole, as though the body had been placed for burial over night. I touched the hand and moved it, the arm being something flexible as a live arm; though stiff with long disuse, as are the arms of those faqueers which I have seen in the Indees. There was, too, an added wonder that on this ancient hand were no less than seven fingers, the same all being fine and long, and of great beauty. Sooth to say, it made me shudder and my flesh creep to touch that hand that had lain there undisturbed for so many thousands of years, and yet was like unto living flesh. Underneath the hand, as though guarded by it, lay a huge jewel of ruby; a great stone of wondrous bigness, for the ruby is in the main a small jewel. This one was of wondrous colour, being as of fine blood whereon the light shineth. But its wonder lay not in its size or colour, though these were, as I have said, of priceless rarity; but in that the light of it shone from seven stars, each of seven points, as clearly as though the stars were in reality there imprisoned. When that the hand was lifted, the sight of that wondrous stone lying there struck me with a shock almost to momentary paralysis. I stood gazing on it, as did those with me, as though it were that fabled head of the Gorgon Medusa with the snakes in her hair, whose sight struck into stone those who beheld. So strong was the feeling that I wanted to hurry away from the place. So, too, those with me; therefore, taking this rare jewel, together with certain amulets of strangeness and richness being wrought of jewel-stones, I made haste to depart. I would have remained longer, and made further research in the wrappings of the mummy, but that I feared so to do. For it came to me all at once that I was in a desert place, with strange men who were with me because they were not over-scrupulous. That we were in a lone cavern of the dead, an hundred feet above the ground, where none could find me were ill done to me, nor would any ever seek. But in secret I determined that I would come again, though with more secure following. Moreover, was I tempted to seek further, as in examining the wrappings I saw many things of strange import in that wondrous tomb; including a casket of eccentric shape made of some strange stone, which methought might have contained other jewels, inasmuch as it had secure lodgment in the great sarcophagus itself. There was in the tomb also another coffer which, though of rare proportion and adornment, was more simply shaped. It was of ironstone of great thickness; but the cover was lightly cemented down with what seemed gum and Paris plaster, as though to insure that no air could penetrate. The Arabs with me so insisted in its opening, thinking that from its thickness much treasure was stored therein, that I consented thereto. But their hope was a false one, as it proved. Within, closely packed, stood four jars finely wrought and carved with various adornments. Of these one was the head of a man, another of a dog, another of a jackal, and another of a hawk. I had before known that such burial urns as these were used to contain the entrails and other organs of the mummied dead; but on opening these, for the fastening of wax, though complete, was thin, and yielded easily, we found that they held but oil. The Bedouins, spilling most of the oil in the process, groped with their hands in the jars lest treasure should have been there concealed. But their searching was of no avail; no treasure was there. I was warned of my danger by seeing in the eyes of the Arabs certain covetous glances. Whereon, in order to hasten their departure, I wrought upon those fears of superstition which even in these callous men were apparent. The chief of the Bedouins ascended from the Pit to give the signal to those above to raise us; and I, not caring to remain with the men whom I mistrusted, followed him immediately. The others did not come at once; from which I feared that they were rifling the tomb afresh on their own account. I refrained to speak of it, however, lest worse should befall. At last they came. One of them, who ascended first, in landing at the top of the cliff lost his foothold and fell below. He was instantly killed. The other followed, but in safety. The chief came next, and I came last. Before coming away I pulled into its place again, as well as I could, the slab of stone that covered the entrance to the tomb. I wished, if possible, to preserve it for my own examination should I come again.

'When we all stood on the hill above the cliff, the burning sun that was bright and full of glory was good to see after the darkness and strange mystery of the tomb. Even was I glad that the poor Arab who fell down the cliff and lay dead below, lay in the sunlight and not in that gloomy cavern. I would fain have gone with my companions to seek him and give him sepulture of some kind; but the Sheik made light of it, and sent two of his men to see to it whilst we went on our way.

'That night as we camped, one of the men only returned, saying that a lion of the desert had killed his companion after that they had buried the dead man in a deep sand without the valley, and had covered the spot where he lay with many great rocks, so that jackals or other preying beasts might not dig him up again as is their wont.

'Later, in the light of the fire round which the men sat or lay, I saw him exhibit to his fellows something white which they seemed to regard with special awe and reverence. So I drew near silently, and saw that it was none other than the white hand of the mummy which had lain protecting the jewel in the great sarcophagus. I heard the Bedouin tell how he had found it on the body of him who had fallen from the cliff. There was no mistaking it, for there were the seven fingers which I had noted before. This man must have wrenched it off the dead body whilst his chief and I were otherwise engaged; and from the awe of the others I doubted not that he had hoped to use it as an amulet, or charm. Whereas if powers it had, they were not for him who had taken it from the dead; since his death followed hard upon his theft. Already his amulet had had an awesome baptism; for the wrist of the dead hand was stained with red as though it had been dipped in recent blood.

'That night I was in certain fear lest there should be some violence done to me; for if the poor dead hand was so valued as a charm, what must be the worth in such wise of the rare jewel which it had guarded. Though only the chief knew of it, my doubt was perhaps even greater; for he could so order matters as to have me at his mercy when he would. I guarded myself, therefore, with wakefulness so well as I could, determined that at my earliest opportunity I should leave this party, and complete my journeying home, first to the Nile bank, and then down its course by boat to Alexandria; with other guides who knew not what strange matters I had with me.

'At last there came over me a disposition of sleep, so potent that I felt it would be resistless. Fearing attack, or that being searched in my sleep the Bedouin might find the Star Jewel which he had seen me place with others in my dress, I took it out unobserved and held it in my hand. It seemed to give back the light of the flickering fire and the light of the stars – for there was no moon – with equal fidelity; and I could note that on its reverse it was graven deeply with certain signs such as I had seen in the tomb. As I sank into the unconsciousness of sleep, the graven Star Jewel was hidden in the hollow of my clenched hand.

'I waked out of sleep with the light of the morning sun on my face. I sat up and looked around me. The fire was out, and the camp was desolate; save for one figure which lay prone close to me. It was that of the Arab chief, who lay on his back, dead. His face was almost black; and his eyes were open, and staring horribly up at the sky, as though he saw there some dreadful vision. He had evidently been strangled; for on looking, I found on his throat the red marks where fingers had pressed. There seemed so many of these marks that I counted them. There were seven; and all parallel, except the thumb mark, as though made with one hand. This thrilled me as I thought of the mummy hand with the seven fingers.

'Even there, in the open desert, it seemed as if there could be enchantments!

'In my surprise, as I bent over him, I opened my right hand, which up to now I had held shut with the feeling, instinctive even in sleep, of keeping safe that which it held. As I did so, the Star Jewel held there fell out and struck the dead man on the mouth. *Mirabile dictu* there came forth at once from the dead mouth a great gush of blood, in which the red jewel was for the moment lost. I turned the dead man over to look for it, and found that he lay with his right hand bent under him as though he had fallen on it; and in it he held a great knife, keen of point and edge, such as Arabs carry at the belt. It may have been that he was about to murder me when vengeance came on him, whether from man or God, or the gods of old, I know not. Suffice it, that when I found my ruby jewel, which shone up as a living star from the mess of blood wherein it lay, I paused not, but fled from the place. I journeyed on alone through the hot desert, till, by God's grace, I came upon an Arab tribe camping by a well, who gave me salt. With them I rested till they had set me on my way.

'I know not what became of the mummy hand, or of those who had it. What strife, or suspicion, or disaster, or greed went with it I know not; but some such cause there must have been, since those who had it fled with it. It doubtless is used as a charm of potence by some desert tribe.

'At the earliest opportunity I made examination of the Star Ruby, as I wished to try to understand what was graven on it. The symbols – whose meaning, however, I could not understand – were as follows . . . '

Twice, whilst I had been reading this engrossing narrative, I had thought that I had seen across the page streaks of shade, which the weirdness of the subject had made to seem like the shadow of a hand. On the first of these occasions I found that the illusion came from the fringe of green silk around the lamp; but on the second I had looked up, and my eyes had lit on the mummy hand across the room on which the starlight was falling under the edge of the blind. It was of little wonder that I had connected it with such a narrative; for if my eyes told me truly, here, in this room with me, was the very hand of which the traveller Van Huyn had written. I looked over at the bed; and it comforted me to think that the nurse still sat there, calm and wakeful. At such a time, with such surroundings, during such a narrative, it was well to have assurance of the presence of some living person.

I sat looking at the book on the table before me; and so many strange thoughts crowded on me that my mind began to whirl. It was almost as if the light on the white fingers in front of me was beginning to have some hypnotic effect. All at once, all thoughts seemed to stop; and for an instant the world and time stood still.

There lay a real hand across the book! What was there to so overcome me, as was the case? I knew the hand that I saw on the book – and loved it. Margaret Trelawny's hand was a joy to me to see – to touch; and yet at that moment, coming after other marvellous things, it had a strangely moving effect on me. It was but momentary, however, and had passed even before her voice had reached me.

'What disturbs you? What are you staring at the book for? I thought for an instant that you must have been overcome again!' I jumped up.

'I was reading,' I said, 'an old book from the library.' As I spoke I closed it and put it under my arm. 'I shall now put it back, as I understand that your Father wishes all things, especially books, kept in their proper places.' My words were intentionally misleading; for I did not wish her to know what I was reading, and thought it best not to wake her curiosity by leaving the book about. I went away, but not to the library; I left the book in my room where I could get it when I had had my sleep in the day. When I returned Nurse Kennedy was ready to go to bed; so Miss Trelawny watched with me in the room. I did not want any book whilst she was present. We sat close together and talked in a whisper whilst the moments flew by. It was with surprise that I noted the edge of the curtains changing from grey to yellow light. What we talked of had nothing to do with the sick man, except in so far that all which concerned his daughter must ultimately concern him. But it had nothing to say to Egypt, or mummies, or the dead, or caves, or Bedouin chiefs. I could well take note in the growing light that Margaret's hand had not seven fingers, but five; for it lay in mine.

When Dr Winchester arrived in the morning and had made his visit to his patient, he came to see me as I sat in the dining-room having a little meal – breakfast or supper, I hardly knew which it was – before I went to lie down. Mr Corbeck came in at the same time; and we resumed our conversation where we had left it the night before. I told Mr Corbeck that I had read the chapter about the finding of the tomb, and that I thought Dr Winchester should read it, too. The latter said that, if he might, he would take it with him; he had that morning to make a railway journey to Ipswich, and would read it on the train. He said he would bring it back with him when he came again in the evening. I went up to my room to bring it down; but I could not find it anywhere. I had a distinct recollection of having left it on the little table beside my bed, when I had come up after Miss Trelawny's going on duty into the sick-room. It was very strange; for the book was not of a kind that any of the servants would be likely to take. I had to come back and explain to the others that I could not find it.

When Dr Winchester had gone, Mr Corbeck, who seemed to know the Dutchman's work by heart, talked the whole matter over with me. I told him that I was interrupted by a change of nurses, just as I had come to the description of the ring. He smiled as he said: 'So far as that is concerned, you need not be disappointed. Not in Van Huyn's time, nor for nearly two centuries later, could the meaning of that engraving have been understood. It was only when the work was taken up and followed by Young and Champollion, by Birch and Lepsius and Rosellini and Salvolini, by Mariette Bey and by Wallis Budge and Flinders Petrie and the other scholars of their times that great results ensued, and that the true meaning of hieroglyphic was known.

'Later, I shall explain to you, if Mr Trelawny does not explain it himself, or if he does not forbid me to, what it means in that particular place. I think it will be better for you to know what followed Van Huyn's narrative; for with the description of the stone, and the account of his bringing it to Holland at the termination of his travels, the episode ends. Ends so far as his book is concerned. The chief thing about the book is that it sets others thinking – and acting. Amongst them were Mr Trelawny and myself. Mr Trelawny is a good linguist of the Orient, but he does not know Northern tongues. As for me I have a faculty for learning languages; and when I was pursuing my studies in Leyden I learned Dutch so that I might more easily make references in the library there. Thus it was, that at the very time when Mr Trelawny, who, in making his great collection of works on Egypt, had, through a booksellers' catalogue, acquired this volume with the manuscript translation, was studying it, I was reading another copy, in original Dutch, in Leyden. We were both struck by the description of the lonely tomb in the rock; cut so high up as to be inaccessible to ordinary seekers: with all means of reaching it carefully obliterated; and yet with such an elaborate ornamentation of the smoothed surface of the cliff as Van Huyn has described. It also struck us both as an odd thing – for in the years between Van Huyn's time and our own the general knowledge of Egyptian curios and records has increased marvellously – that in the case of such a tomb, made in such a place, and which must have cost an immense sum of money, there was no seeming record or effigy to point out who lay within. Moreover, the very name of the place, 'the Valley of the Sorcerer,' had, in a prosaic age, attractions of its own. When we met, which we did through his seeking the assistance of other Egyptologists in his work, we talked over this as we did over many other things; and we determined to make search for the mysterious valley. Whilst we were waiting to start on the travel, for many things were required which Mr Trelawny undertook to see to himself, I went to Holland to try if I could by any traces verify Van Huyn's narrative. I went straight to Hoorn, and set patiently to work to find the house of the traveller and his descendants, if any. I need not trouble you with details of my seeking – and finding. Hoorn is a place that has not changed much since Van Huyn's time, except that it has lost the place which it held amongst commercial cities. Its externals are such as they had been then; in such a sleepy old place a century or two does not count for much. I found the house, and discovered that none of the descendants were alive. I searched records; but only to one end – death and extinction. Then I set me to work to find what had become of his treasures; for that such a traveller must have had great treasures was apparent. I traced a good many to museums in Leyden, Utrecht, and Amsterdam; and some few to the private houses of rich collectors. At last, in the shop of an old watchmaker and jeweller at Hoorn, I found what he considered his chiefest treasure: a great ruby, carven like a scarab, with seven stars, and engraven with hieroglyphics. The old man did not know hiero-glyphic character, and in his old-world, sleepy life, the philological discoveries of recent years had not reached him. He did not know anything of Van Huyn, except that such a person had been, and that his name was, during two centuries, venerated in the town as a great traveller. He valued the jewel as only a rare stone, spoiled in part by the cutting; and though he was at first loth to part with such an unique gem, he became amenable ultimately to commercial reason. I had a full purse, since I bought for Mr Trelawny, who is, as I suppose you know, immensely wealthy. I was shortly on my way back to London, with the Star Ruby safe in my pocket-book; and in my heart a joy and exultation which knew no bounds.

'For here we were with proof of Van Huyn's wonderful story. The jewel was put in security in Mr Trelawny's great safe; and we started out on our journey of exploration in full hope.

'Mr Trelawny was, at the last, loth to leave his young wife whom he dearly loved; but she, who loved him equally, knew his longing to prosecute the search. So keeping to herself, as all good women do, all her anxieties – which in her case were special – she bade him follow out his bent.

CHAPTER II

A Queen's Tomb

'MR TRELAWNY's hope was at least as great as my own. He is not so volatile a man as I am, prone to ups and downs of hope and despair; but he has a fixed purpose which crystallises hope into belief. At times I had feared that there might have been two such stones, or that the adventures of Van Huyn were traveller's fictions, based on some ordinary acquisition of the curio in Alexandria or Cairo, or London or Amsterdam. But Mr Trelawny never faltered in his belief. We had many things to distract our minds from belief or disbelief. This was soon after Arabi Pasha, and Egypt was no safe place for travellers, especially if they were English. But Mr Trelawny is a fearless man; and I almost come to think at times that I am not a coward myself. We got together a band of Arabs whom one or other of us had known in former trips to the desert, and whom we could trust; that is, we did not distrust them as much as others. We were numerous enough to protect ourselves from chance marauding bands, and we took with us large impedimenta. We had secured the consent and passive co-operation of the officials still friendly to Britain; in the acquiring of which consent I need hardly say that Mr Trelawny's riches were of chief importance. We found our way in dhahabiyehs to Aswân; whence, having got some Arabs from the Sheik and having given our usual backsheesh, we set out on our journey through the desert.

'Well, after much wandering and trying every winding in the interminable jumble of hills, we came at last at nightfall on just such a valley as Van Huyn had described. A valley with high, steep cliffs; narrowing in the centre, and widening out to the eastern and western ends. At daylight we were opposite the cliff and could easily note the opening high up in the rock, and the hieroglyphic figures which were evidently intended originally to conceal it.

'But the signs which had baffled Van Huyn and those of his time – and later, were no secrets to us. The host of scholars who have given their brains and their lives to this work, had wrested open the mysterious prison-house of Egyptian language. On the hewn face of the rocky cliff we, who had learned the secrets, could read what the Theban priesthood had had there inscribed nearly fifty centuries before.

'For that the external inscription was the work of the priesthood – and a hostile priesthood at that – there could be no living doubt. The inscription on the rock, written in hieroglyphic, ran thus: "Hither the gods come not at any summons. The 'nameless one' has insulted them and is for ever alone. Go not nigh, lest their vengeance wither you away!"

'The warning must have been a terribly potent one at the time it was written and for thousands of years afterwards; even when the language in which it was given had become a dead mystery to the people of the land. The tradition of such a terror lasts longer than its cause. Even in the symbols used there was an added significance of alliteration. "For ever" is given in the hieroglyphics as "millions of years". This symbol was repeated nine times, in three groups of three; and after each group a symbol of the upper world, the under world, and the sky. So that for this lonely one there could be, through the vengeance of all the gods, resurrection in neither the world of sunlight, in the world of the dead, or for the soul in the region of the gods.

'Neither Mr Trelawny nor I dared to tell any of our people what the writing meant. For though they did not believe in the religion whence the curse came, or in the gods whose vengeance was threatened, yet they were so superstitious that they would probably, had they known of it, have thrown up the whole task and run away.

'Their ignorance, however, and our discretion preserved us. We made an encampment close at hand; but behind a jutting rock a little further along the valley, so that they might not have the inscription always before them. For even that traditional name of the place: "The Valley of the Sorcerer", had a fear for them; and for us through them. With the timber which we had brought, we made a ladder up the face of the rock. We hung a pulley on a beam fixed to project from the top of the cliff. We found the great slab of rock, which formed the door, placed clumsily in its place and secured by a few stones. Its own weight kept it in safe position. In order to enter, we had to push it in; and we passed over it. We found the great coil of chain which Van Huyn had described fastened into the rock. There were, however, abundant evidences amid the wreckage of the great stone door, which had revolved on iron hinges at top and bottom, that ample provision had been originally made for closing and fastening it from within.

'Mr Trelawny and I went alone into the tomb. We had brought plenty of lights with us; and we fixed them as we went along. We wished to get a complete survey at first, and then make examination of all in detail. As we went on, we were filled with ever-increasing wonder and delight. The tomb was one of the most magnificent and beautiful which either of us had ever seen. From the elaborate nature of the sculpture and painting, and the perfection of the workman-ship, it was evident that the tomb was prepared during the lifetime of her for whose resting-place it was intended. The drawing of the hieroglyphic pictures was fine, and the colouring superb; and in that high cavern, far away from even the damp of the Nile-flood, all was as fresh as when the artists had laid down their palettes. There was one thing which we could not avoid seeing. That although the cutting on the outside rock was the work of the priesthood, the smoothing of the cliff face was probably a part of the tomb-builder's original design. The symbolism of the painting and cutting within all gave the same idea. The outer cavern, partly natural and partly hewn, was regarded architecturally as only an antechamber. At the end of it, so that it would face the east, was a pillared portico, hewn out of the solid rock. The pillars were massive and were seven-sided, a thing which we had not come across in any other tomb. Sculptured on the architrave was the Boat of the Moon, containing Hathor, cow-headed and bearing the disk and plumes, and the dog-headed Hapi, the god of the North. It was steered by Harpocrotes towards the north, represented by the Pole Star surrounded by Draco and Ursa Major. In the latter the stars that form what we call the "Plough" were cut larger than any of the other stars; and were filled with gold so that, in the light of torches, they seemed to flame with a special significance. Passing within the portico, we found two of the architectural features of a rock tomb, the chamber, or chapel, and the pit, all complete as Van Huyn had noticed, though in his day the names given to these parts by the Egyptians of old were unknown.

'The stele, or record, which had its place low down on the western wall, was so remarkable that we examined it minutely, even before going on our way to find the mummy which was the object of our search. This stele was a great slab of lapis lazuli, cut all over with hieroglyphic figures of small size and of much beauty. The cutting was filled in with some cement of exceeding fineness, and of the colour of pure vermilion. The inscription began: "Tera, queen of the Egypts, daughter of Antef, Monarch of the North and the South". "Daughter of the Sun", "Queen of the Diadems".

'It then set out, in full record, the history of her life and reign.

'The signs of sovereignty were given with a truly feminine profusion of adornment. The united crowns of Upper and Lower Egypt were, in especial, cut with exquisite precision. It was new to us both to find the Hejet and the Desher – the white and the red crowns of Upper and Lower Egypt – on the stele of a queen; for it was a rule, without exception in the records, that in ancient Egypt either crown was worn only by a king; though they are to be found on goddesses. Later on we found an explanation, of which I shall say more presently.

'Such an inscription was in itself a matter so startling as to arrest attention from anyone anywhere at any time; but you can have no conception of the effect which it had upon us. Though our eyes were not the first which had seen it, they were the first which could see it with understanding since first the slab of rock was fixed in the cliff opening nearly five thousand years before. To us was given to read this message from the dead. This message of one who had warred against the gods of old, and claimed to have controlled them at a time when the hierarchy professed to be the only means of exciting their fears or gaining their good will.

'The walls of the upper chamber of the pit and the sarcophagus chamber were profusely inscribed; all the inscriptions, except that on the stele, being coloured with bluish-green pigment. The effect when seen sideways as the eye caught the green facets, was that of an old, discoloured Indian turquoise.

'We descended the Pit by the aid of the tackle we had brought with us. Trelawny went first. It was a deep pit, more than seventy feet; but it had never been filled up. The passage at the bottom sloped up to the sarcophagus chamber, and was longer than is usually found. It had not been walled up.

'Within, we found a great sarcophagus of yellow stone. But that I need not describe; you have seen it in Mr Trelawny's chamber. The cover of it lay on the ground; it had not been cemented, and was just as Van Huyn had described it. Needless to say, we were excited as we looked within. There must, however, be one sense of disappointment. I could not help feeling how different must have been the sight which met the Dutch traveller's eyes when he looked within and found that white hand lying lifelike above the shrouding mummy cloths. It is true that a part of the arm was there, white and ivory like.

'But there was a thrill to us which came not to Van Huyn!

'The end of the wrist was covered with dried blood! It was as though the body had bled after death! The jagged ends of the broken wrist were rough with the clotted blood; through this the white bone, sticking out, looked like the matrix of opal. The blood had streamed down and stained the brown wrappings as with rust. Here, then, was full confirmation of the narrative. With such evidence of the narrator's truth before us, we could not doubt the other matters which he had told, such as the blood on the mummy hand, or marks of the seven fingers on the throat of the strangled Sheik.

'I shall not trouble you with details of all we saw, or how we learned all we knew. Part of it was from knowledge common to scholars; part we read on the stele in the tomb, and in the sculptures and hieroglyphic paintings on the walls.

'Queen Tera was of the eleventh, or Theban dynasty of Egyptian kings which held sway between twenty-ninth and twenty-fifth centuries before Christ. She succeeded as the only child of her father, Antef. She must have been a girl of extraordinary character as well as ability, for she was but a young girl when her father died. Her youth and sex encouraged the ambitious priesthood, which had then achieved immense power. By their wealth and numbers and learning they dominated all Egypt, more especially the upper portion. They were then secretly ready to make an effort for the achievement of their bold and long-considered design, that of transferring the governing power from a kingship to a hierarchy. But King Antef had suspected some such movement, and had taken the precaution of securing to his daughter the allegiance of the army. He had also had her taught statecraft, and had even made her learned in the lore of the very priests themselves. He had used those of one cult against the other; each being hopeful of some present gain on its own part by the influence of the king, or of some ultimate gain from its own influence over his daughter. Thus, the princess had been brought up amongst scribes, and was herself no mean artist. Many of these things were told on the walls in picture or in hieroglyphic writing of great beauty; and we came to the conclusion that not a few of them had been done by the princess herself. It was not without cause that she was inscribed on the stele as "Protector of the Arts."

'But the king had gone to further lengths, and had had his daughter taught magic, by which she had power over sleep and will. This was real magic – "black" magic; not the magic of the temples, which, I may explain, was of the harmless or "white" order, and was intended to impress rather than to effect. She had been an apt pupil; and had gone further than her teachers. Her power and her resources had given her great opportunities, of which she had availed herself to the full. She had won secrets from nature in strange ways; and had even gone to the length of going down into the tomb herself, having been swathed and coffined and left as dead for a whole month. The priests had tried to make out that the real Princess Tera had died in the experiment, and that another girl had been substituted; but she had conclusively proved their error. All this was told in pictures of great merit. It was probably in her time that the impulse was given in the restoring the artistic greatness of the fourth dynasty which had found its perfection in the days of Chufu.

'In the chamber of the sarcophagus were pictures and writings to show that she had achieved victory over sleep. Indeed, there was everywhere a symbolism, wonderful even in a land and an age of symbolism. Prominence was given to the fact that she, though a queen, claimed all the privileges of kingship and masculinity. In one place she was pictured in man's dress, and wearing the white and red crowns. In the following picture she was in female dress, but still wearing the crowns of Upper and Lower Egypt, while the discarded male raiment lay at her feet. In every picture where hope, or aim, or resurrection was expressed there was the added symbol of the North; and in many places – always in representations of important events, past, present, or future – was a grouping of the stars of the Plough. She evidently regarded this constellation as in some way peculiarly associated with herself.

'Perhaps the most remarkable statement in the records, both on the stele and in the mural writings, was that Queen Tera had power to compel the gods. This, by the way, was not an isolated belief in Egyptian history; but was different in its cause. She had engraved on a ruby, carved like a scarab, and having seven stars of seven points, master words to compel all the gods, both of the upper and the under worlds.

'In the statement it was plainly set forth that the hatred of the priests was, she knew, stored up for her, and that they would after her death try to suppress her name. This was a terrible revenge, I may tell you, in Egyptian mythology; for without a name no one can after death be introduced to the gods, or have prayers said for him. Therefore, she had intended her resurrection to be after long time and in a more northern land, under the constellation whose seven

stars had ruled her birth. To this end, her hand was to be in the air –
"unwrapped"– and in it the Jewel of Seven Stars, so that wherever
was air she might move even as her Ka could move! This, after
thinking it over, Mr Trelawny and I agreed meant that her body
could become astral at command, and so move, particle by particle,
and become whole again when and where required. Then there was a
piece of writing in which allusion was made to a chest or casket in
which were contained all the gods, and will, and sleep, the two latter
being personified by symbols. The box was mentioned as with seven
sides. It was not much of a surprise to us when, underneath the feet of
the mummy, we found the seven-sided casket, which you have also
seen in Mr Trelawny's room. On the underneath part of the wrapping-
linen of the left foot was painted, in the same vermilion colour as that
used in the stele, the hieroglyphic symbol for much water: $\equiv\equiv\!\!\!\!\perp$, and
underneath the right foot the symbol of the earth: $\amalg$. We made out
the symbolism to be that her body, immortal and transferable at will,
ruled both the land and water, air and fire – the latter being
exemplified by the light of the jewel stone, and further by the flint
and iron which lay outside the mummy wrappings.

'As we lifted the casket from the sarcophagus, we noticed on its
sides the strange protuberances which you have already seen; but we
were unable at the time to account for them. There were a few
amulets in the sarcophagus, but none of any special worth or
significance. We took it that if there were such, they were within the
wrappings; or more probably in the strange casket underneath the
mummy's feet. This, however, we could not open. There were signs
of there being a cover; certainly the upper portion and the lower were
each in one piece. The fine line, a little way from the top, appeared to
be where the cover was fixed; but it was made with such exquisite
fineness and finish that the joining could hardly be seen. Certainly
the top could not be moved. We took it, that it was in some way
fastened from within. I tell you all this in order that you may
understand things with which you may be in contact later. You must
suspend your judgment entirely. Such strange things have happened
regarding this mummy and all around it, that there is a necessity for
new belief somewhere. It is absolutely impossible to reconcile certain
things which have happened with the ordinary currents of life or
knowledge.

'We stayed around the Valley of the Sorcerer, till we had copied
roughly all the drawings and writings on the walls, ceiling, and floor.
We took with us the stele of lapis lazuli, whose graven record was
coloured with vermilion pigment. We took the sarcophagus and the

mummy; the stone chest with the alabaster jars; the tables of bloodstone and alabaster and onyx and carnelian; and the ivory pillow whose arch rested on "buckles", round each of which was twisted an uraeus wrought in gold. We took all the articles which lay in the chapel, and the mummy pit; the wooden boats with crews and the ushaptiu figures, and the symbolic amulets.

'When coming away we took down the ladders, and at a distance buried them in the sand under a cliff, which we noted so that if necessary we might find them again. Then with our heavy baggage, we set out on our laborious journey back to the Nile. It was no easy task, I tell you, to bring the case with that great sarcophagus over the desert. We had a rough cart and sufficient men to draw it; but the progress seemed terribly slow, for we were anxious to get our treasures into a place of safety. The night was an anxious time with us, for we feared attack from some marauding band. But more still we feared some of those with us. They were, after all, but predatory, unscrupulous men; and we had with us a considerable bulk of precious things. They, or at least the dangerous ones amongst them, did not know why it was so precious; they took it for granted that it was material treasure of some kind that we carried. We had taken the mummy from the sarcophagus, and packed it for safety of travel in a separate case. During the first night two attempts were made to steal things from the cart; and two men were found dead in the morning.

'On the second night there came on a violent storm, one of those terrible simoons of the desert which makes one feel his helplessness. We were overwhelmed with the drifting sand. Some of our Bedouins had fled before the storm, hoping to find shelter; the rest of us, wrapped in our bournous, endured with what patience we could. In the morning, when the storm had passed, we recovered from under the piles of sand what we could of our impedimenta. We found the case in which the mummy had been packed all broken, but the mummy itself could nowhere be found. We searched everywhere around, and dug up the sand which had piled around us; but in vain. We did not know what to do, for Trelawny had his heart set on taking home that mummy. We waited a whole day in hopes that the Bedouins, who had fled, would return; we had a blind hope that they might have in some way removed the mummy from the cart, and would restore it. That night, just before dawn, Mr Trelawny woke me up and whispered in my ear: "We must go back to the tomb in the Valley of the Sorcerer. Show no hesitation in the morning when I give the orders! If you ask any questions as to where we are going it will create suspicion, and will defeat our purpose."

' "All right!" I answered. "But why shall we go there?" His answer seemed to thrill through me as though it had struck some chord ready tuned within: "We shall find the mummy there! I am sure of it!" Then anticipating doubt or argument he added: "Wait, and you shall see!" and he sank back into his blanket again.

'The Arabs were surprised when we retraced our steps; and some of them were not satisfied. There was a good deal of friction, and there were several desertions; so that it was with a diminished following that we took our way eastward again. At first the Sheik did not manifest any curiosity as to our definite destination; but when it became apparent that we were again making for the Valley of the Sorcerer, he too showed concern. This grew as we drew near; till finally at the entrance of the valley he halted and refused to go further. He said he would await our return if we chose to go on alone. That he would wait three days; but if by that time we had not returned he would leave. No offer of money would tempt him to depart from this resolution. The only concession he would make was that he would find the ladders and bring them near the cliff. This he did; and then, with the rest of the troop, he went back to wait at the entrance of the valley.

'Mr Trelawny and I took ropes and torches, and again ascended to the tomb. It was evident that someone had been there in our absence, for the stone slab which protected the entrance to the tomb was lying flat inside, and a rope was dangling from the cliff summit. Within, there was another rope hanging into the shaft of the mummy pit. We looked at each other; but neither said a word. We fixed our own rope, and as arranged Trelawny descended first, I following at once. It was not till we stood together at the foot of the shaft that the thought flashed across me that we might be in some sort of a trap; that someone might descend the rope from the cliff, and by cutting the rope by which we had lowered ourselves into the Pit, bury us there alive. The thought was horrifying; but it was too late to do anything. I remained silent. We both had torches, so that there was ample light as we passed through the passage and entered the chamber where the sarcophagus had stood. The first thing noticeable was the emptiness of the place. Despite all its magnificent adornment, the tomb was made a desolation by the absence of the great sarcophagus, to hold which it was hewn in the rock; of the chest with the alabaster jars; of the tables which had held the implements and food for the use of the dead, and the ushaptiu figures.

'It was made more infinitely desolate still by the shrouded figure of the mummy of Queen Tera which lay on the floor where the great sarcophagus had stood! Beside it lay, in the strange contorted attitudes of violent death, three of the Arabs who had deserted from our party. Their faces were black, and their hands and necks were smeared with blood which had burst from mouth and nose and eyes.

'On the throat of each were the marks, now blackening, of a hand of seven fingers.

'Trelawny and I drew close, and clutched each other in awe and fear as we looked.

'For, most wonderful of all, across the breast of the mummied queen lay a hand of seven fingers, ivory white, the wrist only showing a scar like a jagged red line, from which seemed to depend drops of blood.

CHAPTER 12

The Magic Coffer

'WHEN WE RECOVERED our amazement, which seemed to last unduly long, we did not lose any time carrying the mummy through the passage, and hoisting it up the pit shaft. I went first, to receive it at the top. As I looked down, I saw Mr Trelawny lift the severed hand and put it in his breast, manifestly to save it from being injured or lost. We left the dead Arabs where they lay. With our ropes we lowered our precious burden to the ground; and then took it to the entrance of the valley where our escort was to wait. To our astonishment we found them on the move. When we remonstrated with the Sheik, he answered that he had fulfilled his contract to the letter; he had waited the three days as arranged. I thought that he was lying to cover up his base intention of deserting us; and I found when we compared notes that Trelawny had the same suspicion. It was not till we arrived at Cairo that we found he was correct. It was the 3rd of November 1884 when we entered the mummy pit for the second time; we had reason to remember the date.

'We had lost three whole days of our reckoning – out of our lives – whilst we had stood wondering in that chamber of the dead. Was it strange, then, that we had a superstitious feeling with regard to the dead Queen Tera and all belonging to her? Is it any wonder that it rests with us now, with a bewildering sense of some power outside ourselves or our comprehension? Will it be any wonder if it go down to the grave with us at the appointed time? If, indeed, there be any graves for us who have robbed the grave!' He was silent for quite a minute before he went on: 'We got to Cairo all right, and from there to Alexandria, where we were to take ship by the *Messagerie* service to Marseilles, and go thence by express to London. But 'the best-laid schemes o' mice and men, gang aft agley.'

At Alexandria, Trelawny found waiting a cable stating that Mrs Trelawny had died in giving birth to a daughter.

'Her stricken husband hurried off at once by the Orient Express; and I had to bring the treasures alone to the desolate house. I got to London all safe; there seemed to be some special good fortune to our journey. When I got to this house, the funeral had long been over. The child had been put out to nurse, and Mr Trelawny had so far recovered from the shock of his loss that he had set himself to take up again the broken threads of his life and his work. That he had had a shock, and a bad one, was apparent. The sudden grey in his black hair was proof enough in itself; but in addition, the strong cast of his features had become set and stern. Since he received that cable in the shipping office at Alexandria I have never seen a happy smile on his face.

'Work is the best thing in such a case; and to his work he devoted himself heart and soul. The strange tragedy of his loss and gain – for the child was born after the mother's death – took place during the time that we stood in that trance in the mummy pit of Queen Tera. It seemed to have become in some way associated with his Egyptian studies, and more especially with the mysteries connected with the queen. He told me very little about his daughter; but that two forces struggled in his mind regarding her was apparent. I could see that he loved, almost idolised her. Yet he could never forget that her birth had cost her mother's life. Also, there was something whose existence seemed to wring his father's heart, though he would never tell me what it was. Again, he once said in a moment of relaxation of his purpose of silence: "She is unlike her mother; but in both feature and colour she has a marvellous resemblance to the pictures of Queen Tera."

'He said that he had sent her away to people who would care for her as he could not; and that till she became a woman she should have all the simple pleasures that a young girl might have, and that were best for her. I would often have talked with him about her; but he would never say much. Once he said to me: "There are reasons why I should not speak more than is necessary. Someday you will know – and understand!" I respected his reticence; and beyond asking after her on my return after a journey, I have never spoken of her again. I had never seen her till I did so in your presence.

'Well, when the treasures which we had – ah! – taken from the tomb had been brought here, Mr Trelawny arranged their disposition himself. The mummy, all except the severed hand, he placed in the great ironstone sarcophagus in the hall. This was wrought for the Theban high priest Uni, and is, as you may have remarked, all inscribed with wonderful invocations to the old gods of Egypt. The rest of the things from the tomb he disposed about his own room, as you have seen. Amongst them he placed, for special reasons of his own, the mummy hand. I think he regards this as the most sacred of his possessions, with perhaps one exception. That is the carven ruby which he calls the "Jewel of Seven Stars", which he keeps in that great safe which is locked and guarded by various devices, as you know.

'I dare say you find this tedious; but I have had to explain it, so that you should understand all up to the present. It was a long time after my return with the mummy of Queen Tera when Mr Trelawny reopened the subject with me. He had been several times to Egypt, sometimes with me and sometimes alone; and I had been several trips, on my own account or for him. But in all that time, nearly sixteen years, he never mentioned the subject, unless when some pressing occasion suggested, if it did not necessitate, a reference.

'One morning early he sent for me in a hurry; I was then studying in the British Museum, and had rooms in Hart Street. When I came, he was all on fire with excitement. I had not seen him in such a glow since before the news of his wife's death. He took me at once into his room. The window blinds were down and the shutters closed; not a ray of daylight came in. The ordinary lights in the room were not lit, but there were a lot of powerful electric lamps, fifty candle-power at least, arranged on one side of the room. The little bloodstone table on which the heptagonal coffer stands was drawn to the centre of the room. The coffer looked exquisite in the glare of light which shone on it. It actually seemed to glow as if lit in some way from within.

' "What do you think of it?" he asked.

' "It is like a jewel," I answered. "You may well call it the 'sorcerer's magic coffer', if it often looks like that. It almost seems to be alive."

' "Do you know why it seems so?"

' "From the glare of the light, I suppose?"

' "Light of course," he answered, "but it is rather the disposition of light." As he spoke he turned up the ordinary lights of the room and switched off the special ones. The effect on the stone box was surprising; in a second it lost all its glowing effect. It was still a very beautiful stone, as always; but it was stone and no more.

' "Do you notice anything in the arrangement of the lamps?" he asked.

' "No!"

' "They were in the shape of the stars in the Plough, as the stars are in the ruby!" The statement came to me with a certain sense of conviction. I do not know why, except that there had been so many mysterious associations with the mummy and all belonging to it that any new one seemed enlightening. I listened as Trelawny went on to explain: "For sixteen years I have never ceased to think of that adventure, or to try to find a clue to the mysteries which came before us; but never until last night did I seem to find a solution. I think I must have dreamed of it, for I woke all on fire about it. I jumped out of bed with a determination of doing something, before I quite knew what it was that I wished to do. Then, all at once, the purpose was clear before me. There were allusions in the writing on the walls of the tomb to the seven stars of the Great Bear that go to make up the Plough; and the North was again and again emphasised. The same symbols were repeated with regard to the 'magic box' as we called it. We had already noticed those peculiar translucent spaces in the stone of the box. You remember the hieroglyphic writing had told that the jewel came from the heart of an aerolite, and that the coffer was cut from it also. It might be, I thought, that the light of the seven stars, shining in the right direction, might have some effect on the box, or something within it. I raised the blind and looked out. The Plough was high in the heavens, and both its stars and the Pole Star were straight opposite the window. I pulled the table with the coffer out into the light, and shifted it until the translucent patches were in the direction of the stars. Instantly the box began to glow, as you saw it under the lamps, though but slightly. I waited and waited; but the sky clouded over, and the light died away. So I got wires and lamps – you know how often I use them in experiments – and tried the effect of electric light. It took me some time to get the lamps properly placed, so that they would correspond to the parts of the stone, but the moment I got them right the whole thing began to glow as you have seen it.

' "I could get no further, however. There was evidently something wanting. All at once it came to me that if light could have some effect there should be in the tomb some means of producing light; for there could not be starlight in the mummy pit in the cavern. Then the whole thing seemed to become clear. On the bloodstone table, which has a hollow carved in its top, into which the bottom of the coffer fits, I laid the magic coffer; and I at once saw that the odd protuberances so carefully wrought in the substance of the stone corresponded in a way to the stars in the constellation. These, then, were to hold lights.

' "*Eureka!*" I cried. "All we want now is the lamps." I tried placing the electric lights on, or close to, the protuberances. But the glow never came to the stone. So the conviction grew on me that there were special lamps made for the purpose. If we could find them, a step on the road to solving the mystery should be gained.

' "But what about the lamps?" I asked. "Where are they? When are we to discover them? How are we to know them if we do find them? What – "

'He stopped me at once: "One thing at a time!" he said quietly. "Your first question contains all the rest. Where are these lamps? I shall tell you: In the tomb!"

' "In the tomb!" I repeated in surprise. "Why you and I searched the place ourselves from end to end; and there was not a sign of a lamp. Not a sign of anything remaining when we came away the first time; or on the second, except the bodies of the Arabs."

'Whilst I was speaking, he had uncoiled some large sheets of paper which he had brought in his hand from his own room. These he spread out on the great table, keeping their edges down with books and weights. I knew them at a glance; they were the careful copies which he had made of our first transcripts from the writing in the tomb. When he had all ready, he turned to me and said slowly: "Do you remember wondering, when we examined the tomb, at the lack of one thing which is usually found in such a tomb?"

' "Yes! There was no serdâb."

'The Serdâb, I may perhaps explain,' said Mr Corbeck to me, 'is a sort of niche built or hewn in the wall of a tomb. Those which have as yet been examined bear no inscriptions, and contain only effigies of the dead for whom the tomb was made.' Then he went on with his narrative.

'Trelawny, when he saw that I had caught his meaning, went on speaking with something of his old enthusiasm: "I have come to the conclusion that there must be a serdâb – a secret one. We were dull not to have thought of it before. We might have known that the maker of such a tomb – a woman, who had shown in other ways such a sense of beauty and completeness, and who had finished every detail with a feminine richness of elaboration – would not have neglected such an architectural feature. Even if it had not its own special significance in ritual, she would have had it as an adornment. Others had had it, and she liked her own work to be complete. Depend upon it, there was – there is – a serdâb; and that in it, when it is discovered, we shall find the lamps. Of course, had we known then what we now know or at all events surmise, that there were lamps, we might have suspected some hidden spot, some cahet. I am going to ask you to go out to Egypt again; to seek the tomb; to find the serdâb; and to bring back the lamps!"

' "And if I find there is no serdâb; or if discovering it I find no lamps in it, what then?" He smiled grimly with that saturnine smile of his, so rarely seen for years past, as he spoke slowly: "Then you will have to hustle till you find them!"

' "Good!" I said. He pointed to one of the sheets.

' "Here are the transcripts from the chapel at the south and the east. I have been looking over the writings again; and I find that in seven places round this corner are the symbols of the constellation which we call the Plough, which Queen Tera held to rule her birth and her destiny. I have examined them carefully, and I notice that they are all representations of the grouping of the stars, as the constellation appears in different parts of the heavens. They are all astronomically correct; and as in the real sky the pointers indicate the Pole Star, so these all point to one spot in the wall where usually the serdâb is to be found!"

' "Bravo!" I shouted, for such a piece of reasoning demanded applause. He seemed pleased as he went on: "When you are in the tomb, examine this spot. There is probably some spring or mechanical contrivance for opening the receptacle. What it may be, there is no use guessing. You will know what best to do, when you are on the spot."

'I started the next week for Egypt; and never rested till I stood again in the tomb. I had found some of our old following; and was fairly well provided with help. The country was now in a condition very different to that in which it had been sixteen years before; there was no need for troops or armed men.

'I climbed the rock face alone. There was no difficulty, for in that fine climate the woodwork of the ladder was still dependable. It was easy to see that in the years that had elapsed there had been other visitors to the tomb; and my heart sank within me when I thought that some of them might by chance have come across the secret place. It would be a bitter discovery indeed to find that they had forestalled me; and that my journey had been in vain.

'The bitterness was realised when I lit my torches, and passed between the seven-sided columns to the chapel of the tomb.

'There, in the very spot where I had expected to find it, was the opening of a serdâb. And the serdâb was empty.

'But the chapel was not empty; for the dried-up body of a man in Arab dress lay close under the opening, as though he had been stricken down. I examined all round the walls to see if Trelawny's surmise was correct; and I found that in all the positions of the stars as given, the pointers of the Plough indicated a spot to the left hand, or south side, of the opening of the serdâb, where was a single star in gold.

'I pressed this, and it gave way. The stone which had marked the front of the serdâb, and which lay back against the wall within, moved slightly. On further examining the other side of the opening, I found a similar spot, indicated by other representations of the constellation; but this was itself a figure of the seven stars, and each was wrought in burnished gold. I pressed each star in turn; but without result. Then it struck me that if the opening spring was on the left, this on the right might have been intended for the simultaneous pressure of all the stars by one hand of seven fingers. By using both my hands, I managed to effect this.

'With a loud click, a metal figure seemed to dart from close to the opening of the serdâb; the stone slowly swung back to its place, and shut with a click. The glimpse which I had of the descending figure appalled me for the moment. It was like that grim guardian which, according to the Arabian historian Ibn Abd Alhokin, the builder of the Pyramids, King Saurid Ibn Salhouk placed in the Western Pyramid to defend its treasure: "A marble figure, upright, with lance in hand; with on his head a serpent wreathed. When any approached, the serpent would bite him on one side, and twining about his throat and killing him, would return again to his place."

'I knew well that such a figure was not wrought to pleasantry; and that to brave it was no child's play. The dead Arab at my feet was proof of what could be done! So I examined again along the wall; and found here and there chippings as if someone had been tapping with a heavy hammer. This then had been what happened: The grave-robber more expert at his work than we had been, and suspecting the presence of a hidden serdâb, had made essay to find it. He had struck the spring by chance; had released the avenging "Treasurer", as the Arabian writer designated him. The issue spoke for itself. I got a piece of wood, and, standing at a safe distance, pressed with the end of it upon the star.

'Instantly the stone flew back. The hidden figure within darted forward and thrust out its lance. Then it rose up and disappeared. I thought I might now safely press on the seven stars; and did so. Again the stone rolled back; and the "treasurer" flashed by to his hidden lair.

'I repeated both experiments several times; with always the same result. I should have liked to examine the mechanism of that figure of such malignant mobility; but it was not possible without such tools as could not easily be had. It might be necessary to cut into a whole section of the rock. Someday I hope to go back, properly equipped, and attempt it.

'Perhaps you do not know that the entrance to a serdâb is almost always very narrow; sometimes a hand can hardly be inserted. Two things I learned from this serdâb. The first was that the lamps, if lamps at all there had been, could not have been of large size; and secondly, that they would be in some way associated with Hathor, whose symbol, the hawk in a square with the right top corner forming a smaller square, was cut in relief on the wall within, and coloured the bright vermilion which we had found on the stele. Hathor is the goddess who in Egyptian mythology answers to Venus of the Greeks, in as far as she is the presiding deity of beauty and pleasure. In the Egyptian mythology, however, each god has many forms; and in some aspects Hathor has to do with the idea of resurrection. There are seven forms or variants of the goddess; why should not these correspond in some way to the seven lamps! That there had been such lamps, I was convinced. The first grave-robber had met his death; the second had found the contents of the serdâb. The first attempt had been made years since; the state of the body proved this. I had no clue to the second attempt. It might have been long ago; or it might have been recently. If, however, others had been to the tomb, it was probable that the lamps had been taken long ago. Well! all the more difficult would be my search; for undertaken it must be!

'That was nearly three years ago; and for all that time I have been like the man in the *Arabian Nights*, seeking old lamps, not for new, but for cash. I dared not say what I was looking for, or attempt to give any description; for such would have defeated my purpose. But I had in my own mind at the start a vague idea of what I must find. In process of time this grew more and more clear; till at last I almost overshot my mark by searching for something which might have been wrong.

'The disappointments I suffered, and the wild-goose chases I made, would fill a volume; but I persevered. At last, not two months ago, I was shown by an old dealer in Mossul one lamp such as I had looked for. I had been tracing it for nearly a year, always suffering disappointment, but always buoyed up to further endeavour by a growing hope that I was on the track.

'I do not know how I restrained myself when I realised that, at last, I was at least close to success. I was skilled, however, in the finesse of Eastern trade; and the Jew-Arab-Portugee trader met his match. I wanted to see all his stock before buying; and one by one he produced, amongst masses of rubbish, seven different lamps. Each of them had a distinguishing mark; and each and all was some form of the symbol of Hathor. I think I shook the imperturbability of my swarthy friend by the magnitude of my purchases; for in order to prevent him guessing what form of goods I sought, I nearly cleared out his shop. At the end he nearly wept, and said I had ruined him; for now he had nothing to sell. He would have torn his hair had he known what price I should ultimately have given for some of his stock, that perhaps he valued least.

'I parted with most of my merchandise at normal price as I hurried home. I did not dare to give it away, or even lose it, lest I should incur suspicion. My burden was far too precious to be risked by any foolishness now. I got on as fast as it is possible to travel in such countries; and arrived in London with only the lamps and certain portable curios and papyri which I had picked up on my travels.

'Now, Mr Ross, you know all I know; and I leave it to your discretion how much, if any of it, you will tell Miss Trelawny.'

As he finished a clear young voice said behind us: 'What about Miss Trelawny? She is here!'

We turned, startled; and looked at each other inquiringly. Miss Trelawny stood in the doorway. We did not know how long she had been present, or how much she had heard.

CHAPTER 13

Awaking from the Trance

THE FIRST UNEXPECTED WORDS may always startle a hearer; but when the shock is over, the listener's reason has asserted itself, and he can judge of the manner, as well as of the matter, of speech. Thus it was on this occasion. With intelligence now alert, I could not doubt of the simple sincerity of Margaret's next question.

'What have you two men been talking about all this time, Mr Ross? I suppose, Mr Corbeck has been telling you all his adventures in finding the lamps. I hope you will tell me too, someday, Mr Corbeck; but that must not be till my poor father is better. He would like, I am sure, to tell me all about these things himself; or to be present when I heard them.' She glanced sharply from one to the other. 'Oh, that was what you were saying as I came in? All right! I shall wait; but I hope it won't be long. The continuance of Father's condition is, I feel, breaking me down. A little while ago I felt that my nerves were giving out; so I determined to go out for a walk in the Park. I am sure it will do me good. I want you, if you will, Mr Ross, to be with Father whilst I am away. I shall feel secure then.'

I rose with alacrity, rejoicing that the poor girl was going out, even for half an hour. She was looking terribly wearied and haggard; and the sight of her pale cheeks made my heart ache. I went to the sick-room; and sat down in my usual place. Mrs Grant was then on duty; we had not found it necessary to have more than one person in the room during the day. When I came in, she took occasion to go about some household duty. The blinds were up, but the north aspect of the room softened the hot glare of the sunlight without.

I sat for a long time thinking over all that Mr Corbeck had told me; and weaving its wonders into the tissue of strange things which had come to pass since I had entered the house. At times I was inclined to doubt; to doubt everything and everyone; to doubt even the evidences of my own senses. The warnings of the skilled detective kept coming back to my mind. He had put down Mr Corbeck as a clever liar, and a confederate of Miss Trelawny. Of Margaret! That settled it! Face to face with such a proposition as that, doubt vanished. Each time when her image, her name, the merest thought of her, came before my mind, each event stood out stark as a living fact. My life upon her faith!

I was recalled from my reverie, which was fast becoming a dream of love, in a startling manner. A voice came from the bed; a deep, strong, masterful voice. The first note of it called up like a clarion my eyes and my ears. The sick man was awake and speaking!

'Who are you? What are you doing here?'

Whatever ideas any of us had ever formed of his waking, I am quite sure that none of us expected to see him start up all awake and full master of himself. I was so surprised that I answered almost mechanically: 'Ross is my name. I have been watching by you!' He looked surprised for an instant, and then I could see that his habit of judging for himself came into play.

'Watching by me! How do you mean? Why watching by me?' His eye had now lit on his heavily bandaged wrist. He went on in a different tone; less aggressive, more genial, as of one accepting facts: 'Are you a doctor?' I felt myself almost smiling as I answered; the relief from the long pressure of anxiety regarding his life was beginning to tell: 'No, sir!'

'Then why are you here? If you are not a doctor, what are you?' His tone was again more dictatorial. Thought is quick; the whole train of reasoning on which my answer must be based flooded through my brain before the words could leave my lips. Margaret! I must think of Margaret! This was her father, who as yet knew nothing of me; even of my very existence. He would be naturally curious, if not anxious, to know why I amongst men had been chosen as his daughter's friend on the occasion of his illness. Fathers are naturally a little jealous in such matters as a daughter's choice, and in the undeclared state of my love for Margaret I must do nothing which could ultimately embarrass her.

'I am a Barrister. It is not, however, in that capacity I am here; but simply as a friend of your daughter. It was probably her knowledge of my being a lawyer which first determined her to ask me to come when she thought you had been murdered. Afterwards she was good enough to consider me to be a friend, and to allow me to remain in accordance with your expressed wish that someone should remain to watch.'

Mr Trelawny was manifestly a man of quick thought, and of few words. He gazed at me keenly as I spoke, and his piercing eyes seemed to read my thought. To my relief he said no more on the subject just then, seeming to accept my words in simple faith. There was evidently in his own mind some cause for the acceptance deeper than my own knowledge. His eyes flashed, and there was an unconscious movement of the mouth – it could hardly be called a twitch – which betokened satisfaction. He was following out some train of reasoning in his own mind. Suddenly he said: 'She thought I had been murdered! Was that last night?'

'No! four days ago.' He seemed surprised. Whilst he had been speaking the first time he had sat up in bed; now he made a movement as though he would jump out. With an effort, however, he restrained himself; leaning back on his pillows he said quietly: 'Tell me all about it! All you know! Every detail! Omit nothing! But stay; first lock the door! I want to know, before I see anyone, exactly how things stand.'

Somehow his last words made my heart leap. 'Anyone!' He evidently accepted me, then, as an exception. In my present state of feeling for his daughter, this was a comforting thought. I felt exultant as I went over to the door and softly turned the key. When I came back I found him sitting up again. He said: 'Go on!'

Accordingly, I told him every detail, even of the slightest which I could remember, of what had happened from the moment of my arrival at the house. Of course I said nothing of my feeling towards Margaret, and spoke only concerning those things already within his own knowledge. With regard to Corbeck, I simply said that he had brought back some lamps of which he had been in quest. Then I proceeded to tell him fully of their loss, and of their rediscovery in the house.

He listened with a self-control which, under the circumstances, was to me little less than marvellous. It was not impassiveness, for at times his eyes would flash or blaze, and the strong fingers of his uninjured hand would grip the sheet, pulling it into far-extending wrinkles. This was most noticeable when I told him of the return of Corbeck, and the finding of the lamps in the boudoir. At times he spoke, but only a few words, and as if unconsciously in emotional comment. The mysterious parts, those which had most puzzled us, seemed to have no special interest for him; he seemed to know them already. The utmost concern he showed was when I told him of Daw's shooting. His muttered comment: 'Stupid ass!' together with a quick glance across the room at the injured cabinet, marked the measure of his disgust. As I told him of his daughter's harrowing anxiety for him, of her unending care and devotion, of the tender love which she had shown, he seemed much moved. There was a sort of veiled surprise in his unconscious whisper: 'Margaret! Margaret!'

When I had finished my narration, bringing matters up to the moment when Miss Trelawny had gone out for her walk – I thought of her as 'Miss Trelawny,' not as 'Margaret' now, in the presence of her father – he remained silent for quite a long time. It was probably two or three minutes; but it seemed interminable. All at once he turned and said to me briskly: 'Now tell me all about yourself!' This was something of a floorer; I felt myself grow red-hot. Mr Trelawny's eyes were upon me; they were now calm and inquiring, but never ceasing in their soul-searching scrutiny. There was just a suspicion of a smile on the mouth which, though it added to my embarrassment, gave me a certain measure of relief. I was, however, face to face with difficulty; and the habit of my life stood me in good stead. I looked him straight in the eyes as I spoke: 'My name, as I told you, is Ross, Malcolm Ross. I am by profession a barrister. I was made a Q.C. in the last year of the queen's reign. I have been fairly successful in my work.' To my relief he said: 'Yes, I know. I have always heard well of you! Where and when did you meet Margaret?'

'First at the Hay's in Belgrave Square, ten days ago. Then at a picnic up the river with Lady Strathconnell. We went from Windsor to Cookham. Mar – Miss Trelawny was in my boat. I scull a little, and I had my own boat at Windsor. We had a good deal of conversation – naturally.'

'Naturally!' there was just a suspicion of something sardonic in the tone of acquiescence; but there was no other intimation of his feeling. I began to think that as I was in the presence of a strong man, I should show something of my own strength. My friends, and sometimes my opponents, say that I am a strong man. In my present circumstances, not to be absolutely truthful would be to be weak. So I stood up to the difficulty before me; always bearing in mind, however, that my words might effect Margaret's happiness through her love for her father. I went on: 'In conversation at a place and time and amid surroundings so pleasing, and in a solitude inviting to confidence, I got a glimpse of her inner life. Such a glimpse as a man of my years and experience may get from a young girl!' The father's face grew graver as I went on; but he said nothing. I was committed now to a definite line of speech, and went on with such mastery of my mind as I could exercise. The occasion might be fraught with serious consequences to me too.

'I could not but see that there was over her spirit a sense of loneliness which was habitual to her. I thought I understood it; I am myself an only child. I ventured to encourage her to speak to me freely; and was happy enough to succeed. A sort of confidence became established between us.' There was something in the father's face which made me add hurriedly: 'Nothing was said by her, sir, as you can well imagine, which was not right and proper. She only told me in the impulsive way of one longing to give voice to thoughts long carefully concealed, of her yearning to be closer to the father whom she loved; more *en rapport* with him; more in his confidence; closer within the circle of his sympathies. Oh, believe me, sir, that it was all good! All that a father's heart could hope or wish for! It was all loyal! That she spoke it to me was perhaps because I was almost a stranger with whom there was no previous barrier to confidence.'

Here I paused. It was hard to go on; and I feared lest I might, in my zeal, do Margaret a disservice. The relief of the strain came from her father.

'And you?'

'Sir, Miss Trelawny is very sweet and beautiful! She is young; and her mind is like crystal! Her sympathy is a joy! I am not an old man, and my affections were not engaged. They never had been till then. I hope I may say as much, even to a father!' My eyes involuntary dropped. When I raised them again Mr Trelawny was still gazing at me keenly. All the kindliness of his nature seemed to wreathe itself in a smile as he held out his hand and said: 'Malcolm Ross, I have always heard of you as a fearless and honourable gentleman. I am glad my girl has such a friend! Go on!'

My heart leaped. The first step to the winning of Margaret's father was gained. I dare say I was somewhat more effusive in my words and my manner as I went on. I certainly felt that way.

'One thing we gain as we grow older: to use our age judiciously! I have had much experience. I have fought for it and worked for it all my life; and I felt that I was justified in using it. I ventured to ask Miss Trelawny to count on me as a friend; to let me serve her should occasion arise. She promised me that she would. I had little idea that my chance of serving her should come so soon or in such a way; but that very night you were stricken down. In her desolation and anxiety she sent for me!' I paused. He continued to look at me as I went on: 'When your letter of instructions was found, I offered my services. They were accepted, as you know.'

'And these days, how did they pass for you?' The question startled me. There was in it something of Margaret's own voice and manner; something so greatly resembling her lighter moments that it brought out all the masculinity in me. I felt more sure of my ground now as I said: 'These days, sir, despite all their harrowing anxiety, despite all the pain they held for the girl whom I grew to love more and more with each passing hour, have been the happiest of my life!' He kept silence for a long time; so long that, as I waited for him to speak, with my heart beating, I began to wonder if my frankness had been too effusive. At last he said: 'I suppose it is hard to say so much vicariously. Her poor mother should have heard you; it would have made her heart glad!' Then a shadow swept across his face; and he went on more hurriedly.

'But are you quite sure of all this?'

'I know my own heart, sir; or, at least, I think I do!'

'No! no!' he answered, 'I don't mean you. That is all right! But you spoke of my girl's affection for me . . . and yet . . . ! And yet she has been living here, in my house, a whole year . . . Still, she spoke to you of her loneliness – her desolation. I never – it grieves me to say it, but it is true – I never saw sign of such affection towards myself in all the year! . . . ' His voice trembled away into sad, reminiscent introspection.

'Then, sir,' I said, 'I have been privileged to see more in a few days than you in her whole lifetime!' My words seemed to call him up from himself; and I thought that it was with pleasure as well as surprise that he said: 'I had no idea of it. I thought that she was indifferent to me. That what seemed the neglect of her youth was revenging itself on me. That she was cold of heart . . . It is a joy unspeakable to me that her mother's daughter loves me too!' Unconsciously he sank back upon his pillow, lost in memories of the past.

How he must have loved her mother! It was the love of her mother's child, rather than the love of his own daughter, that appealed to him. My heart went out to him in a great wave of sympathy and kindliness. I began to understand. To understand the passion of these two great, silent, reserved natures, that successfully concealed the burning hunger for the other's love! It did not surprise me when presently he murmured to himself: 'Margaret, my child! Tender, and thoughtful, and strong, and true, and brave! Like her dear mother! like her dear mother!'

And then to the very depths of my heart I rejoiced that I had spoken frankly.

Presently Mr Trelawny said: 'Four days! The sixteenth! Then this is the twentieth of July?' I nodded affirmation; he went on: 'So I have been lying in a trance for four days. It is not the first time. I was in a trance once under strange conditions for three days; and never even suspected it till I was told of the lapse of time. I shall tell you all about it someday, if you care to hear.'

That made me thrill with pleasure. That he, Margaret's father, would so take me into his confidence made it possible . . . The business-like, everyday alertness of his voice as he spoke next quite recalled me: 'I had better get up now. When Margaret comes in, tell her yourself that I am all right. It will avoid any shock! And will you tell Corbeck that I would like to see him as soon as I can. I want to see those lamps, and hear all about them!'

His attitude towards me filled me with delight. There was a possible father-in-law aspect that would have raised me from a deathbed. I was hurrying away to carry out his wishes; when, however, my hand was on the key of the door, his voice recalled me: 'Mr Ross!'

I did not like to hear him say 'Mr'. After he knew of my friendship with his daughter he had called me Malcolm Ross; and this obvious return to formality not only pained, but filled me with apprehension. It must be something about Margaret. I thought of her as 'Margaret' and not as 'Miss Trelawny,' now that there was danger of losing her. I know now what I felt then: that I was determined to fight for her rather than lose her. I came back, unconsciously holding myself erect. Mr Trelawny, the keen observer of men, seemed to read my thought; his face, which was set in a new anxiety, relaxed as he said: 'Sit down a minute; it is better that we speak now than later. We are both men, and men of the world. All this about my daughter is very new to me, and very sudden; and I want to know exactly how and where I stand. Mind, I am making no objection; but as a father I have duties which are grave, and may prove to be painful. I – I' – he seemed slightly at a loss how to begin, and this gave me hope – 'I suppose I am to take it, from what you have said to me of your feelings towards my girl, that it is in your mind to be a suitor for her hand, later on?' I answered at once: 'Absolutely! Firm and fixed; it was my intention the evening after I had been with her on the river, to seek you, of course after a proper and respectful interval, and to ask you if I might approach her on the subject. Events forced me into closer relationship more quickly than I had dared to hope would be possible; but that first purpose has remained fresh in my heart, and has grown in intensity, and multiplied itself with every hour which has passed since then.' His face seemed to soften as he looked at me; the memory of his own youth was coming back to him instinctively. After a pause he said: 'I suppose I may take it, too, Malcolm Ross' – the return to the familiarity of address swept through me with a glorious thrill – 'that as yet you have not made any protestation to my daughter?'

'Not in words, sir.' The *arrière pensée* of my phrase struck me, not by its own inherent humour, but through the grave, kindly smile on the father's face. There was a pleasant sarcasm in his comment: 'Not in words! That is dangerous! She might have doubted words, or even disbelieved them.'

'I felt myself blushing to the roots of my hair as I went on: 'The duty of delicacy in her defenceless position; my respect for her father – I did not know you then, sir, as yourself, but only as her father – restrained me. But even had not these barriers existed, I should not have dared in the presence of such grief and anxiety to have declared myself. Mr Trelawny, I assure you on my word of honour that your daughter and I are as yet, on her part, but friends and nothing more!' Once again he held out his hands, and we clasped each other warmly. Then he said heartily: 'I am satisfied, Malcolm Ross. Of course, I take it that until I have seen her and have given you permission, you will not make any declaration to my daughter – in words,' he added, with an indulgent smile. But his face became stern again as he went on: 'Time presses; and I have to think of some matters so urgent and so strange that I dare not lose an hour.

Otherwise I should not have been prepared to enter, at so short a notice and to so new a friend, on the subject of my daughter's settlement in life, and of her future happiness.' There was a dignity and a certain proudness in his manner which impressed me much.

'I shall respect your wishes, sir!' I said as I went back and opened the door. I heard him lock it behind me.

When I told Mr Corbeck that Mr Trelawny had quite recovered, he began to dance about like a wild man. But he suddenly stopped, and asked me to be careful not to draw any inferences, at all events at first, when in the future speaking of the finding of the lamps, or of the first visits to the tomb. This was in case Mr Trelawny should speak to me on the subject; 'as, of course, he will,' he added, with a sidelong look at me which meant knowledge of the affairs of my heart. I agreed to this, feeling that it was quite right. I did not quite understand why; but I knew that Mr Trelawny was a peculiar man. In no case could one make a mistake by being reticent. Reticence is a quality which a strong man always respects.

The manner in which the others of the house took the news of the recovery varied much. Mrs Grant wept with emotion; then she hurried off to see if she could do anything personally, and to set the house in order for 'Master', as she always called him. The nurse's face fell: she was deprived of an interesting case. But the disappointment was only momentary; and she rejoiced that the trouble was over. She was ready to come to the patient the moment she should be wanted; but in the meantime she occupied herself in packing her portmanteau.

I took Sergeant Daw into the study, so that we should be alone when I told him the news. It surprised even his iron self-control when I told him the method of the waking. I was myself surprised in turn by his first words: 'And how did he explain the first attack? He was unconscious when the second was made.'

Up to that moment the nature of the attack, which was the cause of my coming to the house, had never even crossed my mind, except when I had simply narrated the various occurrences in sequence to Mr Trelawny. The detective did not seem to think much of my answer: 'Do you know, it never occurred to me to ask him!' The professional instinct was strong in the man, and seemed to supersede everything else.

'That is why so few cases are ever followed out,' he said, 'unless our people are in them. Your amateur detective never hunts down to the death. As for ordinary people, the moment things begin to mend, and the strain of suspense is off them, they drop the matter in hand. It is like seasickness,' he added philosophically after a pause; 'the moment you touch the shore you never give it a thought, but run off to the buffet to feed! Well, Mr Ross, I'm glad the case is over; for over it is, so far as I am concerned. I suppose that Mr Trelawny knows his own business; and that now he is well again, he will take it up himself. Perhaps, however, he will not do anything. As he seemed to expect something to happen, but did not ask for protection from the police in any way, I take it that he don't want them to interfere with an eye to punishment. We'll be told officially, I suppose, that it was an accident, or sleep-walking, or something of the kind, to satisfy the conscience of our Record Department; and that will be the end. As for me, I tell you frankly, sir, that it will be the saving of me. I verily believe I was beginning to get dotty over it all. There were too many mysteries, that aren't in my line, for me to be really satisfied as to either facts or the causes of them. Now, I'll be able to wash my hands of it, and get back to clean, wholesome, criminal work. Of course, sir, I'll be glad to know if you ever do light on a cause of any kind. And I'll be grateful if you can ever tell me how the man was dragged out of bed when the cat bit him, and who used the knife the second time. For master Silvio could never have done it by himself. But there! I keep thinking of it still. I must look out and keep a check on myself, or I shall think of it when I have to keep my mind on other things!'

When Margaret returned from her walk, I met her in the hall. She was still pale and sad; somehow, I had expected to see her radiant after her walk. The moment she saw me her eyes brightened, and she looked at me keenly.

'You have some good news for me?' she said. 'Is Father better?'

'He is! Why did you think so?'

'I saw it in your face. I must go to him at once.' She was hurrying away when I stopped her.

'He said he would send for you the moment he was dressed.'

'He said he would send for me!' she repeated in amazement. 'Then he is awake again, and conscious? I had no idea he was so well as that! O Malcolm!'

She sat down on the nearest chair and began to cry. I felt overcome myself. The sight of her joy and emotion, the mention of my own name in such a way and at such a time, the rush of glorious possibilities all coming together, quite unmanned me. She saw my emotion, and seemed to understand. She put out her hand. I held it hard, and kissed it. Such moments as these, the opportunities of lovers, are gifts of the gods! Up to this instant, though I knew I loved her, and though I believe she returned my affection, I had had only hope. Now, however, the self-surrender manifest in her willingness to let me squeeze her hand, the ardour of her pressure in return, and the glorious flush of love in her beautiful, deep, dark eyes as she lifted them to mine, were all the eloquences which the most impatient or exacting lover could expect or demand.

No word was spoken; none was needed. Even had I not been pledged to verbal silence, words would have been poor and dull to express what we felt. Hand in hand, like two little children, we went up the staircase and waited on the landing, till the summons from Mr Trelawny should come.

I whispered in her ear – it was nicer than speaking aloud and at a greater distance – how her father had awakened, and what he had said; and all that had passed between us, except when she herself had been the subject of conversation.

Presently a bell rang from the room. Margaret slipped from me, and looked back with warning finger on lip. She went over to her father's door and knocked softly.

'Come in!' said the strong voice.

'It is I, Father!' The voice was tremulous with love and hope.

There was a quick step inside the room; the door was hurriedly thrown open, and in an instant Margaret, who had sprung forward, was clasped in her father's arms. There was little speech; only a few broken phrases.

'Father! Dear, dear Father!'

'My child! Margaret! My dear, dear child!'

'O Father, Father! At last! At last!'

Here the father and daughter went into the room together, and the door closed.

CHAPTER 14

The Birthmark

DURING MY WAITING for the summons to Mr Trelawny's room, which I knew would come, the time was long and lonely. After the first few moments of emotional happiness at Margaret's joy, I somehow felt apart and alone; and for a little time the selfishness of a lover possessed me. But it was not for long. Margaret's happiness was all in all to me; and in the conscious sense of it I lost my baser self.

Margaret's last words as the door closed on them gave the key to the whole situation, as it had been and as it was These two proud, strong people, though father and daughter, had only come to know each other when the girl was grown up. Margaret's nature was of that kind which matures early.

The pride and strength of each, and the reticence which was their corollary, made a barrier at the beginning. Each had respected the other's reticence too much thereafter; and the misunderstanding grew to habit. And so these two loving hearts, each of which yearned for sympathy from the other, were kept apart. But now all was well, and in my heart of hearts I rejoiced that at last Margaret was happy. Whilst I was still musing on the subject, and dreaming dreams of a personal nature, the door was opened, and Mr Trelawny beckoned to me.

'Come in, Mr Ross!' he said cordially, but with a certain formality which I dreaded. I entered the room, and he closed the door again. He held out his hand, and I put mine in it. He did not let it go, but still held it as he drew me over toward his daughter. Margaret looked from me to him, and back again; and her eyes fell. When I was close to her, Mr Trelawny let go my hand, and, looking his daughter straight in the face, said: 'If things are as I fancy, we shall not have any secrets between us. Malcolm Ross knows so much of my affairs already, that I take it he must either let matters stop where they are and go away in silence, or else he must – know more. Margaret! are you willing to let Mr Ross see your wrist?'

She threw one swift look of appeal in his eyes; but even as she did so she seemed to make up her mind. Without a word she raised her right hand, so that the bracelet of spreading wings which covered the wrist fell back, leaving the flesh bare. Then an icy chill shot through me.

On her wrist was a thin red jagged line, from which seemed to hang red stains like drops of blood!

She stood there, a veritable figure of patient pride.

Oh! but she looked proud! Through all her sweetness, all her dignity, all the high-souled negation of self which I had known, and which never seemed more marked than now – through all the fire that seemed to shine from the dark depths of her eyes into my very soul, pride shone conspicuously. The pride that has faith; the pride that is born of conscious purity; the pride of a veritable queen of Old Time, when to be royal was to be the first and greatest and bravest in all high things. As we stood thus for some seconds, the deep, grave voice of her father seemed to sound a challenge in my ears: 'What do you say now?'

My answer was not in words. I caught Margaret's right hand in mine as it fell, and, holding it tight, whilst with the other I pushed back the golden cincture, stooped and kissed the wrist. As I looked up at her, but never letting go her hand, there was a look of joy on her face such as I dream of when I think of heaven. Then I faced her father.

'You have my answer, sir!' His strong face looked gravely sweet. He only said one word as he laid his hand on our clasped ones, whilst he bent over and kissed his daughter: 'Good!'

We were interrupted by a knock at the door. In answer to an impatient 'Come in!' from Mr Trelawny, Mr Corbeck entered. When he saw us grouped he would have drawn back; but in an instant Mr Trelawny had sprung forth and dragged him forward. As he shook him by both hands, he seemed a transformed man. All the enthusiasm of his youth, of which Mr Corbeck had told us, seemed to have come back to him in an instant.

'So you have got the lamps!' he almost shouted. 'My reasoning was right after all. Come to the library, where we will be alone, and tell me all about it! And while he does it, Ross,' said he, turning to me, 'do you, like a good fellow, get the key from the safe deposit, so that I may have a look at the lamps!'

Then the three of them, the daughter lovingly holding her father's arm, went into the library, whilst I hurried off to Chancery Lane.

When I returned with the key, I found them still engaged in the narrative; but Dr Winchester, who had arrived soon after I left, was with them. Mr Trelawny, on hearing from Margaret of his great attention and kindness, and how he had, under much pressure to the contrary, steadfastly obeyed his written wishes, had asked him to remain and listen. 'It will interest you, perhaps,' he said, 'to learn the end of the story!'

We all had an early dinner together. We sat after it a good while, and then Mr Trelawny said: 'Now, I think we had all better separate and go quietly to bed early. We may have much to talk about tomorrow; and tonight I want to think.'

Dr Winchester went away, taking, with a courteous forethought, Mr Corbeck with him, and leaving me behind. When the others had gone Mr Trelawny said: 'I think it will be well if you, too, will go home for tonight. I want to be quite alone with my daughter; there are many things I wish to speak of to her, and to her alone. Perhaps, even tomorrow, I will be able to tell you also of them; but in the meantime there will be less distraction to us both if we are alone in the house.' I quite understood and sympathised with his feelings; but the experiences of the last few days were strong on me, and with some hesitation I said: 'But may it not be dangerous? If you knew as we do –'

To my surprise Margaret interrupted me: 'There will be no danger, Malcolm. I shall be with my father!' As she spoke she clung to him in a protective way. I said no more, but stood up to go at once. Mr Trelawny said heartily: 'Come as early as you please, Ross. Come to breakfast. After it, you and I will want to have a word together.' He went out of the room quietly, leaving us together. I clasped and kissed Margaret's hands, which she held out to me, and then drew her close to me, and our lips met for the first time.

I did not sleep much that night. Happiness on the one side of my bed and anxiety on the other kept sleep away. But if I had anxious care, I had also happiness which had not equal in my life – or ever can have. The night went by so quickly that the dawn seemed to rush on me, not stealing as is its wont.

Before nine o'clock I was at Kensington. All anxiety seemed to float away like a cloud as I met Margaret, and saw that already the pallor of her face had given way to the rich bloom which I knew. She told me that her father had slept well, and that he would be with us soon.

'I do believe,' she whispered, 'that my dear and thoughtful Father has kept back on purpose, so that I might meet you first, and alone!'

After breakfast Mr Trelawny took us into the study, saying as he passed in: 'I have asked Margaret to come too.' When we were seated, he said gravely: 'I told you last night that we might have something to say to each other. I dare say that you may have thought that it was about Margaret and yourself. Isn't that so?'

'I thought so.'

'Well, my boy, that is all right. Margaret and I have been talking, and I know her wishes.' He held out his hand. When I had wrung it, and had kissed Margaret, who drew her chair close to mine, so that we could hold hands as we listened, he went on, but with a certain hesitation – it could hardly be called nervousness – which was new to me: 'You know a good deal of my hunt after this mummy and her belongings; and I dare say you have guessed a good deal of my theories. But these at any rate I shall explain later, concisely and categorically, if it be necessary. What I want to consult you about now is this: Margaret and I disagree on one point. I am about to make an experiment; the experiment which is to crown all that I have devoted twenty years of research, and danger, and labour to prepare for. Through it we may learn things that have been hidden from the eyes and the knowledge of men for centuries; for scores of centuries.

I do not want my daughter to be present; for I cannot blind myself to the fact that there may be danger in it – great danger, and of an unknown kind. I have, however, already faced very great dangers, and of an unknown kind; and so has that brave scholar who has helped me in the work. As to myself, I am willing to run any risk. For science, and history, and philosophy may benefit; and we may turn one old page of a wisdom unknown in this prosaic age. But for my daughter to run such a risk I am loth. Her young bright life is too precious to throw lightly away; now especially when she is on the very threshold of new happiness. I do not wish to see her life given, as her dear mother's was – '

He broke down for a moment, and covered his eyes with his hands. In an instant Margaret was beside him, clasping him close, and kissing him, and comforting him with loving words. Then, standing erect, with one hand on his head, she said: 'Father! mother did not bid you stay beside her, even when you wanted to go on that journey of unknown danger to Egypt; though that country was then upset from end to end with war and the dangers that follow war. You have told me how she left you free to go as you wished; though that she thought of danger for you and feared it for you, is proved by this!' She held up her wrist with the scar that seemed to run blood. 'Now, mother's daughter does as mother would have done herself!' Then she turned to me: 'Malcolm, you know I love you! But love is trust; and you must trust me in danger as well as in joy. You and I must stand beside Father in this unknown peril. Together we shall come through it; or together we shall fail; together we shall die. That is my wish; my first wish to my husband that is to be! Do you not think that, as a daughter, I am right? Tell my Father what you think!'

She looked like a queen stooping to plead. My love for her grew and grew. I stood up beside her; and took her hand and said: 'Mr Trelawny! in this Margaret and I are one!'

He took both our hands and held them hard. Presently he said with deep emotion: 'It is as her mother would have done!'

Mr Corbeck and Dr Winchester came exactly at the time appointed, and joined us in the library. Despite my great happiness I felt our meeting to be a very solemn function. For I could never forget the strange things that had been; and the idea of the strange things which might be, was with me like a cloud, pressing down on us all. From the gravity of my companions I gathered that each of them also was ruled by some such dominating thought.

Instinctively we gathered our chairs into a circle round Mr Trelawny, who had taken the great armchair near the window.

Margaret sat by him on his right, and I was next to her. Mr Corbeck was on his left, with Dr Winchester on the other side. After a few seconds of silence Mr Trelawny said to Mr Corbeck: 'You have told Dr Winchester all up to the present, as we arranged?

'Yes,' he answered; so Mr Trelawny said: 'And I have told Margaret, so we all know!' Then, turning to the doctor, he asked: 'And am I to take it that you, knowing all as we know it who have followed the matter for years, wish to share in the experiment which we hope to make?' His answer was direct and uncompromising: 'Certainly! Why, when this matter was fresh to me, I offered to go on with it to the end. Now that it is of such strange interest, I would not miss it for anything which you could name. Be quite easy in your mind, Mr Trelawny. I am a scientist and an investigator of phenomena. I have no one belonging to me or dependent on me. I am quite alone, and free to do what I like with my own – including my life!' Mr Trelawny bowed gravely, and turning to Mr Corbeck said: 'I have known your ideas for many years past, old friend; so I need ask you nothing. As to Margaret and Malcolm Ross, they have already told me their wishes in no uncertain way.' He paused a few seconds, as though to put his thoughts or his words in order; then he began to explain his views and intentions. He spoke very carefully, seeming always to bear in mind that some of us who listened were ignorant of the very root and nature of some things touched upon, and explaining them to us as he went on: 'The experiment which is before us is to try whether or no there is any force, any reality, in the old magic. There could not possibly be more favourable conditions for the test; and it is my own desire to do all that is possible to make the original design effective. That there is some such existing power I firmly believe. It might not be possible to create, or arrange, or organise such a power in our own time; but I take it that if in Old Time such a power existed, it may have some exceptional survival. After all, the Bible is not a myth; and we read there that the sun stood still at a man's command, and that an ass – not a human one – spoke. And if the Witch at Endor could call up to Saul the spirit of Samuel, why may not there have been others with equal powers; and why may not one among them survive? Indeed, we are told in the Book of Samuel that the Witch of Endor was only one of many, and her being consulted by Saul was a matter of chance. He only sought one among the many whom he had driven out of Israel; "all those that had familiar spirits, and the wizards". This Egyptian queen, Tera, who reigned nearly two thousand years before Saul, had a familiar, and was a wizard too. See how the priests of her time, and those after it tried to wipe out her name from the face of the earth, and put a curse over the very door of her tomb so that none might ever discover the lost name. Ay, and they succeeded so well that even Manetho, the historian of the Egyptian kings, writing in the tenth century before Christ, with all the lore of the priesthood for forty centuries behind him, and with possibility of access to every existing record, could not even find her name. Did it strike any of you, in thinking of the late events, who or what her familiar was?' There was an interruption, for Dr Winchester struck one hand loudly on the other as he ejaculated: 'The cat! The mummy cat! I knew it!' Mr Trelawny smiled over at him.

'You are right! There is every indication that the familiar of the wizard queen was that cat which was mummied when she was, and was not only placed in her tomb, but was laid in the sarcophagus with her. That was what bit into my wrist, what cut me with sharp claws.' He paused. Margaret's comment was a purely girlish one: 'Then my poor Silvio is acquitted. I am glad!' Her father stroked her hair and went on: 'This woman seems to have had an extraordinary foresight. Foresight far, far beyond her age and the philosophy of her time. She seems to have seen through the weakness of her own religion, and even prepared for emergence into a different world. All her aspirations were for the North, the point of the compass whence blew the cool invigorating breezes that make life a joy. From the first, her eyes seem to have been attracted to the seven stars of the Plough from the fact, as recorded in the hieroglyphics in her tomb, that at her birth a great aerolite fell, from whose heart was finally extracted that Jewel of Seven Stars which she regarded as the talisman of her life. It seems to have so far ruled her destiny that all her thought and care circled round it. The magic coffer, so wondrously wrought with seven sides, we learn from the same source, came from the aerolite. Seven was to her a magic number; and no wonder. With seven fingers on one hand, and seven toes on one foot. With a talisman of a rare ruby with seven stars in the same position as in that constellation which ruled her birth, each star of the seven having seven points – in itself a geological wonder – it would have been odd if she had not been attracted by it. Again, she was born, we learn in the stele of her tomb, in the seventh month of the year – the month beginning with the Inundation of the Nile. Of which month the presiding goddess was Hathor, the goddess of her own house, of the Antefs of the Theban line – the goddess who in various forms symbolises beauty, and pleasure, and resurrection. Again, in this seventh month – which, by later Egyptian astronomy began on October 28th, and ran to the 27th of our November – on the seventh day the pointer of the Plough just rises above the horizon of the sky at Thebes.

'In a marvellously strange way, therefore, are grouped into this woman's life these various things. The number seven; the Pole Star, with the constellation of seven stars; the god of the month, Hathor, who was her own particular god, the god of her family, the Antefs of the Theban dynasty, whose kings' symbol it was, and whose seven forms ruled love and the delights of life and resurrection. If ever there was ground for magic; for the power of symbolism carried into mystic use; for a belief in finite spirits in an age which knew not the living god, it is here.

'Remember, too, that this woman was skilled in all the science of her time. Her wise and cautious father took care of that, knowing that by her own wisdom she must ultimately combat the intrigues of the Hierarchy. Bear in mind that in old Egypt the science of Astronomy began and was developed to an extraordinary height; and that astrology followed astronomy in its progress. And it is possible that in the later developments of science with regard to light rays, we may yet find that Astrology is on a scientific basis. Our next wave of scientific thought may deal with this. I shall have something special to call your minds to on this point presently. Bear in mind also that the Egyptians knew sciences, of which today, despite all our advantages, we are profoundly ignorant. Acoustics, for instance, an exact science with the builders of the temples of Karnak, of Luxor, of the Pyramids, is today a mystery to Bell, and Kelvin, and Edison, and Marconi. Again, these old miracle-workers probably understood some practical way of using other forces, and amongst them the forces of light that at present we do not dream of. But of this matter I shall speak later. That magic coffer of Queen Tera is probably a magic box in more ways than one. It may – possibly it does – contain forces that we wot not of. We cannot open it; it must be closed from within. How then was it closed? It is a coffer of solid stone, of amazing hardness, more like a jewel than an ordinary marble, with a lid equally solid; and yet all is so finely wrought that the finest tool made today cannot be inserted under the flange. How was it wrought to such perfection? How was the stone so chosen that those translucent patches match the relations of the seven stars of the constellation? How is it, or from what cause, that when the starlight shines on it, it glows from within – that when I fix the lamps in similar form the glow grows greater still; and yet the box is irresponsive to ordinary light however great? I tell you that that box hides some great mystery of science. We shall find that the light will open it in some way: either by striking on some substance, sensitive in a peculiar way to its effect, or in releasing some greater power. I only trust that in our ignorance we may not so bungle things as to do harm to its mechanism; and so deprive the knowledge of our time of a lesson handed down, as by a miracle, through nearly five thousand years.

'In another way, too, there may be hidden in that box secrets which, for good or ill, may enlighten the world. We know from their records, and inferentially also, that the Egyptians studied the properties of herbs and minerals for magic purposes – white magic as well as black. We know that some of the wizards of old could induce from sleep dreams of any given kind. That this purpose was mainly effected by hypnotism, which was another art or science of Old Nile, I have little doubt. But still, they must have had a mastery of drugs that is far beyond anything we know. With our own pharmacopoeia we can, to a certain extent, induce dreams. We may even differentiate between good and bad – dreams of pleasure, or disturbing and harrowing dreams. But these old practitioners seemed to have been able to command at will any form or colour of dreaming; could work round any given subject or thought in almost any way required. In that coffer, which you have seen, may rest a very armoury of dreams. Indeed, some of the forces that lie within it may have been already used in my household.' Again there was an interruption from Dr Winchester.

'But if in your case some of these imprisoned forces were used, what set them free at the opportune time, or how? Besides, you and Mr Corbeck were once before put into a trance for three whole days, when you were in the queen's tomb for the second time. And then, as I gathered from Mr Corbeck's story, the coffer was not back in the tomb, though the mummy was. Surely in both these cases there must have been some active intelligence awake, and with some other power to wield.' Mr Trelawny's answer was equally to the point: 'There was some active intelligence awake. I am convinced of it. And it wielded a power which it never lacks. I believe that on both those occasions hypnotism was the power wielded.'

'And wherein is that power contained? What view do you hold on the subject?' Dr Winchester's voice vibrated with the intensity of his excitement as he leaned forward, breathing hard, and with eyes staring. Mr Trelawny said solemnly: 'In the mummy of the Queen Tera! I was coming to that presently. Perhaps we had better wait till I clear the ground a little. What I hold is, that the preparation of that box was made for a special occasion; as indeed were all the preparations of the tomb and all belonging to it. Queen Tera did not trouble herself to guard against snakes and scorpions, in that rocky tomb cut in the sheer cliff face a hundred feet above the level of the valley, and fifty down from the summit. Her precautions were against the disturbances of human hands; against the jealousy and hatred of the priests, who, had they known of her real aims, would have tried to baffle them. From her point of view, she made all ready for the time of resurrection, whenever that might be. I gather from the symbolic pictures in the tomb that she so far differed from the belief of her time that she looked for a resurrection in the flesh. It was doubtless this that intensified the hatred of the priesthood, and gave them an acceptable cause for obliterating the very existence, present and future, of one who had outraged their theories and blasphemed their gods. All that she might require, either in the accomplishment of the resurrection or after it, were contained in that almost hermetically sealed suite of chambers in the rock. In the great sarcophagus, which as you know is of a size quite unusual even for kings, was the mummy of her Familiar, the cat, which from its great size I take to be a sort of tiger-cat. In the tomb, also in a strong receptacle, were the canopic jars usually containing those internal organs which are separately embalmed, but which in this case had no such contents. So that, I take it, there was in her case a departure in embalming; and that the organs were restored to the body, each in its proper place – if, indeed, they had ever been removed. If this surmise be true, we shall find that the brain of the queen either was never extracted in the usual way, or, if so taken out, that it was duly replaced, instead of being enclosed within the mummy wrappings. Finally, in the sarcophagus there was the magic coffer on which her feet rested. Mark you also, the care taken in the preservance of her power to control the elements. According to her belief, the open hand outside the wrappings controlled the air, and the strange jewel stone with the shining stars controlled fire. The symbolism inscribed on the soles of her feet gave sway over land and water. About the Star Stone I shall tell you later; but whilst we are speaking of the sarcophagus, mark how she guarded her secret in case of grave-wrecking or intrusion. None could open her magic coffer without the lamps, for we know now that ordinary light will not be effective. The great lid of the sarcophagus was not sealed down as usual, because she wished to control the air. But she hid the lamps, which in structure belong to the magic coffer, in a place where none could find them, except by following the secret guidance which she had prepared for only the eyes of wisdom. And

even here she had guarded against chance discovery, by preparing a
bolt of death for the unwary discoverer. To do this she had applied
the lesson of the tradition of the avenging guard of the treasures of
the Pyramid, built by her great predecessor of the fourth dynasty of
the throne of Egypt.

'You have noted, I suppose, how there were, in the case of her
tomb, certain deviations from the usual rules. For instance, the shaft
of the mummy pit, which is usually filled up solid with stones and
rubbish, was left open. Why was this? I take it that she had made
arrangements for leaving the tomb when, after her resurrection, she
should be a new woman, with a different personality, and less inured
to the hardships that in her first existence she had suffered. So far as
we can judge of her intent, all things needful for her exit into the
world had been thought of, even to the iron chain, described by Van
Huyn, close to the door in the rock, by which she might be able to
lower herself to the ground. That she expected a long period to
elapse was shown in the choice of material. An ordinary rope would
be rendered weaker or unsafe in process of time, but she imagined,
and rightly, that the iron would endure.

'What her intentions were when once she trod the open earth
afresh we do not know, and we never shall, unless her own dead lips
can soften and speak.

CHAPTER 15

The Purpose of Queen Tera

'Now, as to the Star Jewel! This she manifestly regarded as the
greatest of her treasures. On it she had engraven words which none
of her time dared to speak.

'In the old Egyptian belief it was held that there were words,
which, if used properly – for the method of speaking them was as
important as the words themselves – could command the lords of the
upper and the lower worlds. The "hekau", or word of power, was all-
important in certain ritual. On the Jewel of Seven Stars, which, as
you know, is carved into the image of a scarab, are graven in
hieroglyphic two such hekau, one above, the other underneath. But
you will understand better when you see it! Wait here! Do not stir!'

As he spoke, he rose and left the room. A great fear for him came over me; but I was in some strange way relieved when I looked at Margaret. Whenever there had been any possibility of danger to her father, she had shown great fear for him; now she was calm and placid. I said nothing, but waited.

In two or three minutes Mr Trelawny returned. He held in his hand a little golden box. This, as he resumed his seat, he placed before him on the table. We all leaned forward as he opened it.

On a lining of white satin lay a wondrous ruby of immense size, almost as big as the top joint of Margaret's little finger. It was carven – it could not possibly have been its natural shape, but jewels do not show the working of the tool – into the shape of a scarab, with its wings folded, and its legs and feelers pressed back to its sides. Shining through its wondrous 'pigeon's blood' colour were seven different stars, each of seven

points, in such position that they reproduced exactly the figure of the Plough. There could be no possible mistake as to this in the mind of anyone who had ever noted the constellation. On it were some hieroglyphic figures, cut with the most exquisite

precision, as I could see when it came to my turn to use the magnifying-glass, which Mr Trelawny took from his pocket and handed to us.

When we all had seen it fully, Mr Trelawny turned it over so that it rested on its back in a cavity made to hold it in the upper half of the box. The reverse was no less wonderful than the upper, being carved to resemble the under side of the beetle. It, too, had some hieroglyphic figures cut on it. Mr Trelawny resumed his lecture as we all sat with our heads close to this wonderful jewel: 'As you see, there are two words, one on the top, the other underneath. The symbols on the top represent a single word, composed of one syllable prolonged, with its determinatives. You know, all of you, I suppose, that the Egyptian language was phonetic, and that the hieroglyphic symbol represented the sound. The first symbol here, the hoe, means "mer", and the two pointed ellipses the prolongation of the final r: mer-r-r. The sitting figure with the hand to its face is what we call the "determinative" of "thought"; and the roll of papyrus that of "abstraction". Thus we get the word "mer", love, in its abstract, general, and fullest sense. This is the hekau which can command the upper world.'

Margaret's face was a glory as she said in a deep, low, ringing tone: 'Oh, but it is true. How the old wonder-workers guessed at almighty Truth!' Then a hot blush swept her face, and her eyes fell. Her father smiled at her lovingly as he resumed: 'The symbolisation of the word on the reverse is simpler, though the meaning is more abstruse. The first symbol means "men", "abiding", and the second, "ab", "the heart". So that we get "abiding of heart", or in our own language "patience". And this is the hekau to control the lower world!'

He closed the box, and motioning us to remain as we were, he went back to his room to replace the jewel in the safe. When he had returned and resumed his seat, he went on: 'That jewel, with its mystic words, and which Queen Tera held under her hand in the sarcophagus, was to be an important factor – probably the most important – in the working out of the act of her resurrection. From the first I seemed by a sort of instinct to realise this. I kept the jewel within my great safe, whence none could extract it; not even Queen Tera herself with her astral body.'

'Her "astral body"? What is that, Father? What does that mean?' There was a keenness in Margaret's voice as she asked the question which surprised me a little; but Trelawny smiled a sort of indulgent parental smile, which came through his grim solemnity like sunshine through a rifted cloud, as he spoke: 'The astral body, which is a part of Buddhist belief, long subsequent to the time I speak of, and which is an accepted fact of modern mysticism, had its rise in Ancient Egypt; at least, so far as we know. It is that the gifted individual can at will, quick as thought itself, transfer his body whithersoever he chooses, by the dissolution and reincarnation of particles. In the ancient belief there were several parts of a human being. You may as well know them; so that you will understand matters relative to them or dependent on them as they occur.

'First there is the "Ka", or "Double", which, as Dr Budge explains, may be defined as "an abstract individuality of personality" which was imbued with all the characteristic attributes of the individual it represented, and possessed an absolutely independent existence. It was free to move from place to place on earth at will; and it could enter into heaven and hold converse with the gods. Then there was the "Ba", or "soul", which dwelt in the "Ka", and had the power of becoming corporeal or incorporeal at will; "it had both substance and form . . . It had power to leave the tomb . . . It could revisit the body in the tomb . . . and could reincarnate it and hold converse with it".

Again there was the "Khu", the "spiritual intelligence", or spirit. It took the form of "a shining, luminous, intangible shape of the body" . . . Then, again, there was the "Sekhem", or "power" of a man, his strength or vital force personified. These were the "Khaibit", or "shadow", the "Ren", or "name", the "Khat", or "physical body", and "Ab", the "heart", in which life was seated, went to the full making up of a man.

'Thus you will see, that if this division of functions, spiritual and bodily, ethereal and corporeal, ideal and actual, be accepted as exact, there are all the possibilities and capabilities of corporeal transference, guided always by an unimprisonable will or intelligence.' As he paused I murmured the lines from Shelley's *Prometheus Unbound*: "The Magnus Zoroaster . . . Met his own image walking in the garden." '

Mr Trelawny was not displeased. 'Quite so!' he said, in his quiet way. 'Shelley had a better conception of ancient beliefs than any of our poets.' With a voice changed again he resumed his lecture, for so it was to some of us: 'There is another belief of the ancient Egyptian which you must bear in mind; that regarding the ushaptiu figures of Osiris, which were placed with the dead to do its work in the under world. The enlargement of this idea came to a belief that it was possible to transmit, by magical formulae, the soul and qualities of any living creature to a figure made in its image. This would give a terrible extension of power to one who held the gift of magic.

'It is from a union of these various beliefs, and their natural corollaries, that I have come to the conclusion that Queen Tera expected to be able to effect her own resurrection, when, and where, and how, she would. That she may have held before her a definite time for making her effort is not only possible but likely. I shall not stop now to explain it, but shall enter upon the subject later on. With a soul with the gods, a spirit which could wander the earth at will, and a power of corporeal transference, or an astral body, there need be no bounds or limits to her ambition. The belief is forced upon us that for these forty or fifty centuries she lay dormant in her tomb – waiting. Waiting with that 'patience' which could rule the gods of the under world, for that 'love' which could command those of the upper world. What she may have dreamt we know not; but her dream must have been broken when the Dutch explorer entered her sculptured cavern, and his follower violated the sacred privacy of her tomb by his rude outrage in the theft of her hand.

'That theft, with all that followed, proved to us one thing, however: that each part of her body, though separated from the rest, can be a central point or rallying place for the items or particles of her astral body. That hand in my room could ensure her instantaneous presence in the flesh, and its equally rapid dissolution.

'Now comes the crown of my argument. The purpose of the attack on me was to get the safe open, so that the sacred Jewel of Seven Stars could be extracted. That immense door of the safe could not keep out her astral body, which, or any part of it, could gather itself as well within as without the safe. And I doubt not that in the darkness of the night that mummied hand sought often the Talisman Jewel, and drew new inspiration from its touch. But despite all its power, the astral body could not remove the jewel through the chinks of the safe. The ruby is not astral; and it could only be moved in the ordinary way by the opening of the doors. To this end, the queen used her astral body and the fierce force of her Familiar, to bring to the keyhole of the safe the master key which debarred her wish. For years I have suspected, nay, have believed as much; and I, too, guarded myself against powers of the nether world. I, too, waited in patience till I should have gathered together all the factors required for the opening of the magic coffer and the resurrection of the mummied queen!' He paused, and his daughter's voice came out sweet and clear, and full of intense feeling: 'Father, in the Egyptian belief, was the power of resurrection of a mummied body a general one, or was it limited? That is: could it achieve resurrection many times in the course of ages; or only once, and that one final?'

'There was but one resurrection,' he answered. 'There were some who believed that this was to be a definite resurrection of the body into the real world. But in the common belief, the spirit found joy in the Elysian Fields, where there was plenty of food and no fear of famine. Where there was moisture and deep-rooted reeds, and all the joys that are to be expected by the people of an arid land and burning clime.'

Then Margaret spoke with an earnestness which showed the conviction of her inmost soul: 'To me, then, it is given to understand what was the dream of this great and far-thinking and high-souled lady of old; the dream that held her soul in patient waiting for its realisation through the passing of all those tens of centuries. The dream of a love that might be; a love that she felt she might, even under new conditions, herself evoke. The love that is the dream of every woman's life; of the old and of the new; Pagan or Christian; under whatever sun; in whatever rank or calling; however may have been the joy or pain of her life in other ways. Oh! I know it! I know it! I am a woman, and I know a woman's heart. What were the lack of food or the plenitude of it; what were feast or famine to this woman, born in a palace, with the shadow of the crown of the two Egypts on her brows! What were reedy morasses or the tinkle of running water to her whose barges could sweep the great Nile from the mountains to the sea. What were petty joys and absence of petty fears to her, the raising of whose hand could hurl armies, or draw to the water-stairs of her palaces the commerce of the world! At whose word rose temples filled with all the artistic beauty of the times of old which it was her aim and pleasure to restore! Under whose guidance the solid rock yawned into the sepulchre that she designed!

'Surely, surely, such a one had nobler dreams! I can feel them in my heart; I can see them with my sleeping eyes!'

As she spoke she seemed to be inspired; and her eyes had a far-away look as though they saw something beyond mortal sight. And then the deep eyes filled up with unshed tears of great emotion. The very soul of the woman seemed to speak in her voice; whilst we who listened sat entranced.

'I can see her in her loneliness and in the silence of her mighty pride, dreaming her own dream of things far different from those around her. Of some other land, far, far away under the canopy of the silent night, lit by the cool, beautiful light of the stars. A land under that Northern star, whence blew the sweet winds that cooled the feverish desert air. A land of wholesome greenery, far, far away. Where were no scheming and malignant priesthood; whose ideas were to lead to power through gloomy temples and more gloomy caverns of the dead, through an endless ritual of death! A land where love was not base, but a divine possession of the soul! Where there might be some one kindred spirit which could speak to hers through mortal lips like her own; whose being could merge with hers in a sweet communion of soul to soul, even as their breaths could mingle in the ambient air! I know the feeling, for I have shared it myself. I may speak of it now, since the blessing has come into my own life. I may speak of it since it enables me to interpret the feelings, the very longing soul, of that sweet and lovely queen, so different from her surroundings, so high above her time! Whose nature, put into a word, could control the forces of the under world; and the name of whose aspiration, though but graven on a starlit jewel, could command all the powers in the pantheon of the high gods.

'And in the realisation of that dream she will surely be content to rest!'

We men sat silent, as the young girl gave her powerful interpretation of the design or purpose of the woman of old. Her every word and tone carried with it the conviction of her own belief. The loftiness of her thoughts seemed to uplift us all as we listened. Her noble words, flowing in musical cadence and vibrant with internal force, seemed to issue from some great instrument of elemental power. Even her tone was new to us all; so that we listened as to some new and strange being from a new and strange world. Her father's face was full of delight. I knew now its cause. I understood the happiness that had come into his life, on his return to the world that he knew, from that prolonged sojourn in the world of dreams. To find in his daughter, whose nature he had never till now known, such a wealth of affection, such a splendour of spiritual insight, such a scholarly imagination, such . . . The rest of his feeling was of hope!

The two other men were silent unconsciously. One man had had his dreaming; for the other, his dreams were to come.

For myself, I was like one in a trance. Who was this new, radiant being who had won to existence out of the mist and darkness of our fears. Love has divine possibilities for the lover's heart! The wings of the soul may expand at any time from the shoulders of the loved one, who then may sweep into angel form. I knew that in my Margaret's nature were divine possibilities of many kinds. When under the shade of the overhanging willow-tree on the river, I had gazed into the depths of her beautiful eyes, I had thenceforth a strict belief in the manifold beauties and excellences of her nature; but this soaring and understanding spirit was, indeed, a revelation. My pride, like her father's, was outside myself; my joy and rapture were complete and supreme.

When we had all got back to earth again in our various ways, Mr Trelawny, holding his daughter's hand in his, went on with his discourse: 'Now, as to the time at which Queen Tera intended her resurrection to take place! We are in contact with some of the higher astronomical calculations in connection with true orientation. As you know, the stars shift their relative positions in the heavens; but though the real distances traversed are beyond all ordinary comprehension, the effects as we see them are small. Nevertheless, they are susceptible of measurement, not by years, indeed, but by centuries. It was by this means that Sir John Herschel arrived at the date of the building of the Great Pyramid – a date fixed by the time necessary to change the star of the true north from Draconis to the Pole Star, and since then verified by later discoveries. From the above there can be no doubt whatever that astronomy was an exact science with the Egyptians at least a thousand years before the time of Queen Tera. Now, the stars that go to make up a constellation change in process of time their relative positions, and the Plough is a notable example. The changes in the position of stars in even forty centuries is so small as to be hardly noticeable by an eye not trained to minute observances, but they can be measured and verified. Did you, or any of you, notice how exactly the stars in the ruby correspond to the position of the stars in the Plough; or how the same holds with regard to the translucent places in the magic coffer?'

We all assented. He went on: 'You are quite correct. They correspond exactly. And yet when Queen Tera was laid in her tomb, neither the stars in the jewel nor the translucent places in the coffer corresponded to the position of the stars in the constellation as they then were!'

We looked at each other as he paused: a new light was breaking upon us. With a ring of mastery in his voice he went on: 'Do you not see the meaning of this? Does it not throw a light on the intention of the queen? She, who was guided by augury, and magic, and superstition, naturally chose a time for her resurrection which seemed to have been pointed out by the high gods themselves, who had sent their message on a thunderbolt from other worlds. When such a time was fixed by supernal wisdom, would it not be the height of human wisdom to avail itself of it? Thus it is' – here his voice deepened and trembled with the intensity of his feeling – 'that to us and our time is given the opportunity of this wondrous peep into the old world, such as has been the privilege of none other of our time; which may never be again.

'From first to last the cryptic writing and symbolism of that wondrous tomb of that wondrous woman is full of guiding light; and the key of the many mysteries lies in that most wondrous jewel which she held in her dead hand over the dead heart, which she hoped and believed would beat again in a newer and nobler world!

'There are only loose ends now to consider. Margaret has given us the true inwardness of the feeling of the other queen!' He looked at her fondly, and stroked her hand as he said it. 'For my own part I sincerely hope she is right; for in such case it will be a joy, I am sure, to all of us to assist at such a realisation of hope. But we must not go too fast, or believe too much in our present state of knowledge. The voice that we hearken for comes out of times strangely other than our own; when human life counted for little, and when the morality of the time made little account of the removing of obstacles in the way to achievement of desire. We must keep our eyes fixed on the scientific side, and wait for the developments on the psychical side.

'Now, as to this stone box, which we call the magic coffer. As I have said, I am convinced that it opens only in obedience to some principle of light, or the exercise of some of its forces at present unknown to us. There is here much ground for conjecture and for experiment; for as yet the scientists have not thoroughly differentiated the kinds, and powers, and degrees of light. Without analysing various rays we may, I think, take it for granted that there are different qualities and powers of light; and this great field of scientific investigation is almost virgin soil. We know as yet so little of natural forces, that imagination need set no bounds to its flights in considering the possibilities of the future. Within but a few years we have made such discoveries as two centuries ago would have sent the discoverers to the flames. The liquefaction of oxygen; the existence of radium, of helium, of polonium, of argon; the different powers of Röntgen and Cathode and Becquerel rays. And as we may finally prove that there are different kinds and qualities of light, so we may find that combustion may have its own powers of differentiation; that there are qualities in some flames non-existent in others. It may be that some of the essential conditions of substance are continuous, even in the destruction of their bases. Last night I was thinking of this, and reasoning that as there are certain qualities in some oils which are not in others, so there may be certain similar or corresponding qualities or powers in the combinations of each. I suppose we have all noticed sometime or other that the light of colza oil is not quite the same as that of paraffin, or that the flames of coal gas and whale oil are different. They find it so in the lighthouses! All at once it occurred to me that there might be some special virtue in the oil which had been found in the jars when Queen Tera's tomb was opened. These had not been used to preserve the intestines as usual, so they must have been placed there for some other purpose. I remembered that in Van Huyn's narrative he had commented on the way the jars were sealed. This was lightly, though effectually; they could be opened without force. The jars were themselves preserved in a sarcophagus which, though of immense strength and hermetically sealed, could be opened easily. Accordingly, I went at once to examine the jars. A little – very little of the oil still remained, but it had grown thick in the two and a half centuries in which the jars had been open. Still, it was not rancid; and on examining it I found it was cedar oil, and that it still exhaled something of its original aroma. This gave me the idea that it was to be used to fill the lamps. Whoever had placed the oil in the jars, and the jars in the sarcophagus, knew that there might be shrinkage in process of time, even in vases of alabaster, and fully allowed for it; for each of the jars would have filled the lamps half a dozen times. With part of the oil remaining I made some experiments, therefore, which may give useful results. You know, doctor, that cedar oil, which was much used in the preparation and ceremonials of the Egyptian dead, has a certain refractive power which we do not find in other oils. For instance, we use it on the lenses of our microscopes to give additional clearness of vision. Last night I put some in one of the lamps, and placed it near a translucent part of the magic coffer. The effect was very great; the glow of light within was fuller and more intense than I could have imagined, where an electric light similarly placed had little, if any, effect. I should have tried others of the seven lamps, but that my supply of oil ran out. This, however, is on the road to rectification. I have sent for more cedar oil, and expect to have before long an ample supply. Whatever may happen from other causes, our experiment shall not, at all events, fail from this. We shall see! We shall see!'

Dr Winchester had evidently been following the logical process of the other's mind, for his comment was: 'I do hope that when the light is effective in opening the box, the mechanism will not be impaired or destroyed.'

His doubt as to this gave anxious thought to some of us.

CHAPTER 16

The Cavern

IN THE EVENING Mr Trelawny took again the whole party into the study. When we were all attention he began to unfold his plans: 'I have come to the conclusion that for the proper carrying out of what we will call our great experiment we must have absolute and complete isolation. Isolation not merely for a day or two, but for as long as we may require. Here such a thing would be impossible; the needs and habits of a great city with its ingrained possibilities of interruption, would, or might, quite upset us. Telegrams, registered letters, or express messengers would alone be sufficient; but the great army of those who want to get something would make disaster certain. In addition, the occurrences of the last week have drawn police attention to this house. Even if special instructions to keep an eye on it have not been issued from Scotland Yard or the district station, you may be sure that the individual policeman on his rounds will keep it well under observation. Besides, the servants who have discharged themselves will before long begin to talk. They must; for they have, for the sake of their own characters, to give some reason for the termination of a service which has I should say a position in the neighbourhood. The servants of the neighbours will begin to talk, and, perhaps the neighbours themselves. Then the active and intelligent Press will, with its usual zeal for the enlightenment of the public and its eye to increase of circulation, get hold of the matter. When the reporter is after us we shall not have much chance of privacy. Even if we were to bar ourselves in, we should not be free from interruption, possibly from intrusion. Either would ruin our plans, and so we must take measures to effect a retreat, carrying all our impedimenta with us. For this I am prepared. For a long time past I have foreseen such a possibility, and have made preparation for it. Of course, I had no foreknowledge of what has happened; but I knew something would, or might, happen. For more than two years past my house in Cornwall has been made ready to receive all the curios which are preserved here. When Corbeck went off on his search for the lamps I had the old house at Kyllion made ready; it is fitted with electric light all over, and all the appliances for manufacture of the light are complete. I had perhaps better tell you, for none of you, not even Margaret, knows anything of it, that the house is absolutely shut out from public access or even from view. It stands on a little rocky promontory behind a steep hill, and except from the sea cannot be seen. Of old it was fenced in by a high stone wall, for the house which it succeeded was built by an ancestor of mine in the days when a great house far away from a centre had to be prepared to defend itself. Here, then, is a place so well adapted to our needs that it might have been prepared on purpose. I shall explain it to you when we are all there. This will not be long, for already our movement is in train. I have sent word to Marvin to have all preparation for our transport ready. He is to have a special train, which is to run at night so as to avoid notice. Also a number of carts and stone-wagons, with sufficient men and appliances to take all our packing-cases to Paddington. We shall be away before the Argus-eyed pressman is on the watch. We shall today begin our packing up; and I dare say that by tomorrow night we shall be ready. In the outhouses I have all the packing-cases which were used for bringing the things from Egypt, and I am satisfied that as they were sufficient for the journey across the desert and down the Nile to Alexandria and thence on to London, they will serve without fail between here and Kyllion. We four men, with Margaret to hand us such things as we may require, will be able to get the things packed safely; and the carrier's men will take them to the trucks.

'Today the servants go to Kyllion, and Mrs Grant will make such arrangements as may be required. She will take a stock of necessaries with her, so that we will not attract local attention by our daily needs; and will keep us supplied with perishable food from London. Thanks to Margaret's wise and generous treatment of the servants who decided to remain, we have got a staff on which we can depend. They have been already cautioned to secrecy, so that we need not fear gossip from within. Indeed, as the servants will be in London after their preparations at Kyllion are complete, there will not be much subject for gossip, in detail at any rate.

'As, however, we should commence the immediate work of packing at once, we will leave over the after proceedings till later when we have leisure.'

Accordingly we set about our work. Under Mr Trelawny's guidance, and aided by the servants, we took from the outhouses great packing-cases. Some of these were of enormous strength, fortified by many thicknesses of wood, and by iron bands and rods with screw-ends and nuts. We placed them throughout the house, each close to the object which it was to contain. When this preliminary work had been effected, and there had been placed in each room and in the hall great masses of new hay, cotton-waste and paper, the servants were sent away. Then we set about packing.

No one, not accustomed to packing, could have the slightest idea of the amount of work involved in such a task as that in which we were engaged. For my own part I had had a vague idea that there were a large number of Egyptian objects in Mr Trelawny's house; but until I came to deal with them *seriatim* I had little idea of either their importance, the size of some of them, or of their endless number. Far into the night we worked. At times we used all the strength which we could muster on a single object; again we worked separately, but always under Mr Trelawny's immediate direction. He himself, assisted by Margaret, kept an exact tally of each piece.

It was only when we sat down, utterly wearied, to a long-delayed supper that we began to realise that a large part of the work was done. Only a few of the packing-cases, however, were closed; for a vast amount of work still remained. We had finished some of the cases, each of which held only one of the great sarcophagi. The cases which held many objects could not be closed till all had been differentiated and packed.

I slept that night without movement or without dreams; and on our comparing notes in the morning, I found that each of the others had had the same experience.

By dinner-time next evening the whole work was complete, and all was ready for the carriers who were to come at midnight. A little before the appointed time we heard the rumble of carts; then we were shortly invaded by an army of workmen, who seemed by sheer force of numbers to move without effort, in an endless procession, all our prepared packages. A little over an hour sufficed them, and when the carts had rumbled away, we all got ready to follow them to Paddington. Silvio was of course to be taken as one of our party.

Before leaving we went in a body over the house, which looked desolate indeed. As the servants had all gone to Cornwall there had been no attempt at tidying-up; every room and passage in which we had worked, and all the stairways, were strewn with paper and waste, and marked with dirty feet.

The last thing which Mr Trelawny did before coming away was to take from the great safe the Ruby with the Seven Stars. As he put it safely into his pocket-book, Margaret, who had all at once seemed to grow deadly tired and stood beside her father pale and rigid, suddenly became all aglow, as though the sight of the jewel had inspired her. She smiled at her father approvingly as she said: 'You are right, Father. There will not be any more trouble tonight. She will not wreck your arrangements for any cause. I would stake my life upon it.'

'She – or something – wrecked us in the desert when we had come from the tomb in the Valley of the Sorcerer!' was the grim comment of Corbeck, who was standing by. Margaret answered him like a flash: 'Ah! she was then near her tomb from which for thousands of years her body had not been moved. She must know that things are different now.'

'How must she know?' asked Corbeck keenly.

'If she has that astral body that Father spoke of, surely she must know! How can she fail to, with an invisible presence and an intellect that can roam abroad even to the stars and the worlds beyond us!' She paused, and her father said solemnly: 'It is on that supposition that we are proceeding. We must have the courage of our convictions, and act on them – to the last!'

Margaret took his hand and held it in a dreamy kind of way as we filed out of the house. She was holding it still when he locked the hall door, and when we moved up the road to the gateway, whence we took a cab to Paddington.

When all the goods were loaded at the station, the whole of the workmen went on to the train; this took also some of the stone-wagons used for carrying the cases with the great sarcophagi. Ordinary carts and plenty of horses were to be found at Westerton, which was our station for Kyllion. Mr Trelawny had ordered a sleeping-carriage for our party; as soon as the train had started we all turned into our cubicles.

That night I slept sound. There was over me a conviction of security which was absolute and supreme. Margaret's definite announcement: 'There will not be any trouble tonight!' seemed to carry assurance with it. I did not question it; nor did anyone else. It was only afterwards that I began to think as to how she was so sure. The train was a slow one, stopping many times and for considerable intervals. As Mr Trelawny did not wish to arrive at Westerton before dark, there was no need to hurry; and arrangements had been made to feed the workmen at certain places on the journey. We had our own hamper with us in the private car.

All that afternoon we talked over the great experiment, which seemed to have become a definite entity in our thoughts. Mr Trelawny became more and more enthusiastic as the time wore on; hope was with him becoming certainty. Dr Winchester seemed to become imbued with some of his spirit, though at times he would throw out some scientific fact which would either make an *impasse* to the other's line of argument, or would come as an arresting shock. Mr Corbeck, on the other hand, seemed slightly antagonistic to the theory. It may have been that whilst the opinions of the others advanced, his own stood still; but the effect was an attitude which appeared negative, if not wholly one of negation.

As for Margaret, she seemed to be in some way overcome. Either it was some new phase of feeling with her, or else she was taking the issue more seriously than she had yet done. She was generally more or less *distraite*, as though sunk in a brown study; from this she would recover herself with a start. This was usually when there occurred some marked episode in the journey, such as stopping at a station, or when the thunderous rumble of crossing a viaduct woke the echoes of the hills or cliffs around us. On each such occasion she would plunge into the conversation, taking such a part in it as to show that, whatever had been her abstracted thought, her senses had taken in fully all that had gone on around her. Towards myself her manner was strange. Sometimes it was marked by a distance, half shy, half haughty, which was new to me. At other times there were moments of passion in look and gesture and voice which almost made me dizzy with delight. Little, however, of a marked nature transpired during the journey. There was but one episode which had in it any element of alarm, but as we were all asleep at the time it did not disturb us. We only learned it from a communicative guard in the morning. Whilst running between Dawlish and Teignmouth the train was stopped by a warning given by someone who moved a torch to and fro right on the very track. The driver had found on pulling up that just ahead of the train a small landslip had taken place, some of the red earth from the high bank having fallen away. It did not however reach to the metals; and the driver had resumed his way, none too well pleased at the delay. To use his own words, the guard thought 'there was too much bally caution on this 'ere line!'

We arrived at Westerton about nine o'clock in the evening. Carts and horses were in waiting, and the work of unloading the train began at once. Our own party did not wait to see the work done, as it was in the hands of competent people. We took the carriage which was in waiting, and through the darkness of the night sped on to Kyllion.

We were all impressed by the house as it appeared in the bright moonlight. A great grey stone mansion of the Jacobean period; vast and spacious, standing high over the sea on the very verge of a high cliff. When we had swept round the curve of the avenue cut through the rock, and come out on the high plateau on which the house stood, the crash and murmur of waves breaking against rock far below us came with an invigorating breath of moist sea air. We understood then in an instant how well we were shut out from the world on that rocky shelf above the sea.

Within the house we found all ready. Mrs Grant and her staff had worked well, and all was bright and fresh and clean. We took a brief survey of the chief rooms, and then separated to have a wash and to change our clothes after our long journey of more than four-and-twenty hours.

We had supper in the great dining-room on the south side, the walls of which actually hung over the sea. The murmur came up muffled, but it never ceased. As the little promontory stood well out into the sea, the northern side of the house was open; and the due north was in no way shut out by the great mass of rock, which, reared high above us, shut out the rest of the world. Far off across the bay we could see the trembling lights of the castle, and here and there along the shore the faint light of a fisher's window. For the rest the sea was a dark blue plain with an occasional flicker of light as the gleam of starlight fell on the slope of a swelling wave.

When supper was over we all adjourned to the room which Mr Trelawny had set aside as his study, his bedroom being close to it. As we entered, the first thing I noticed was a great safe, somewhat similar to that which stood in his room in London. When we were in the room Mr Trelawny went over to the table, and, taking out his pocket-book, laid it on the table. As he did so he pressed down on it with the palm of his hand. A strange pallor came over his face. With fingers that trembled he opened the book, saying as he did so: 'Its bulk does not seem the same; I hope nothing has happened!'

All three of us men crowded round close. Margaret alone remained calm; she stood erect and silent, and still as a statue. She had a far-away look in her eyes, as though she did not either know or care what was going on around her.

With a despairing gesture Trelawny threw open the pouch of the pocket-book wherein he had placed the Jewel of Seven Stars. As he sank down on the chair which stood close to him, he said in a hoarse voice: 'My God! it is gone. Without it the great experiment can come to nothing!'

His words seemed to wake Margaret from her introspective mood. An agonised spasm swept her face; but almost on the instant she was calm. She almost smiled as she said: 'You may have left it in your room, Father. Perhaps it has fallen out of the pocket-book whilst you were changing.' Without a word we all hurried into the next room through the open door between the study and the bedroom. And then a sudden calm fell on us like a cloud of fear.

There! on the table, lay the Jewel of Seven Stars, shining and sparkling with lurid light, as though each of the seven points of each of the seven stars gleamed through blood!

Timidly we each looked behind us, and then at each other. Margaret was now like the rest of us. She had lost her statuesque calm. All the introspective rigidity had gone from her; and she clasped her hands together till the knuckles were white.

Without a word Mr Trelawny raised the jewel, and hurried with it into the next room. As quietly as he could he opened the door of the safe with the key fastened to his wrist and placed the jewel within. When the heavy doors were closed and locked he seemed to breathe more freely.

Somehow this episode, though a disturbing one in many ways, seemed to bring us back to our old selves. Since we had left London we had all been overstrained; and this was a sort of relief. Another step in our strange enterprise had been effected.

The change back was more marked in Margaret than in any of us.

Perhaps it was that she was a woman, whilst we were men; perhaps it was that she was younger than the rest; perhaps both reasons were effective, each in its own way. At any rate the change was there, and I was happier than I had been through the long journey. All her buoyancy, her tenderness, her deep feeling seemed to shine forth once more; now and again as her father's eyes rested on her, his face seemed to light up.

Whilst we waited for the carts to arrive, Mr Trelawny took us through the house, pointing out and explaining where the objects which we had brought with us were to be placed. In one respect only did he withhold confidence. The positions of all those things which had connection with the great experiment were not indicated. The cases containing them were to be left in the outer hall, for the present.

By the time we had made the survey, the carts began to arrive; and the stir and bustle of the previous night were renewed. Mr Trelawny stood in the hall beside the massive ironbound door, and gave directions as to the placing of each of the great packing-cases. Those containing many items were placed in the inner hall where they were to be unpacked.

In an incredibly short time the whole consignment was delivered; and the men departed with a *douceur* for each, given through their foreman, which made them effusive in their thanks. Then we all went to our own rooms. There was a strange confidence over us all. I do not think that anyone of us had a doubt as to the quiet passing of the remainder of the night.

The faith was justified, for on our reassembling in the morning we found that all had slept well and peaceably.

During that day all the curios, except those required for the great experiment, were put into the places designed for them. Then it was arranged that all the servants should go back with Mrs Grant to London on the next morning.

When they had all gone Mr Trelawny, having seen the doors locked, took us into the study.

'Now,' said he when we were seated, 'I have a secret to impart; but, according to an old promise which does not leave me free, I must ask you each to give me a solemn promise not to reveal it. For three hundred years at least such a promise has been exacted from everyone to whom it was told, and more than once life and safety were secured through loyal observance of the promise. Even as it is, I am breaking the letter, if not the spirit of the tradition; for I should only tell it to the immediate members of my family.'

We all gave the promise required. Then he went on: 'There is a secret place in this house, a cave, natural originally but finished by labour, underneath this house. I will not undertake to say that it has always been used according to the law. During the Bloody Assize more than a few Cornishmen found refuge in it; and later, and earlier, it formed, I have no doubt whatever, a useful place for storing contraband goods. "Tre Pol and Pen", I suppose you know, have always been smugglers; and their relations and friends and neighbours have not held back from the enterprise. For all such reasons a safe hiding-place was always considered a valuable possession; and as the heads of our House have always insisted on preserving the secret, I am in honour bound to it. Later on, if all be well, I shall of course tell you, Margaret, and you too, Ross, under the conditions that I am bound to make.'

He rose up, and we all followed him. Leaving us in the outer hall, he went away alone for a few minutes; and returning, beckoned us to follow him.

In the inside hall we found a whole section of an outstanding angle moved away, and from the cavity saw a great hole dimly dark, and the beginning of a rough staircase cut in the rock. As it was not pitch dark there was manifestly some means of lighting it naturally, so without pause we followed our host as he descended. After some forty or fifty steps cut in a winding passage, we came to a great cave whose further end tapered away into blackness. It was a huge place, dimly lit by a few irregular long slits of eccentric shape. Manifestly these were faults in the rock which would readily allow the windows to be disguised. Close to each of them was a hanging shutter which could be easily swung across by means of a dangling rope. The sound of the ceaseless beat of the waves came up muffled from far below. Mr Trelawny at once began to speak: 'This is the spot which I have chosen, as the best I know, for the scene of our great experiment. In a hundred different ways it fulfils the conditions which I am led to believe are primary with regard to success. Here, we are, and shall be, as isolated as Queen Tera herself would have been in her rocky tomb in the Valley of the Sorcerer, and still in a rocky cavern. For good or ill we must here stand by our chances, and abide by results. If we are successful we shall be able to let in on the world of modern science such a flood of light from the old world as will change every condition of thought and experiment and practice. If we fail, then even the knowledge of our attempt will die with us. For this, and all else which may come, I believe we are prepared!' He paused. No one spoke, but we all bowed our heads gravely in acquiescence. He resumed, but with a certain hesitancy: 'It is not yet too late! If any of you have a doubt or a misgiving, for God's sake speak it now! Whoever it may be, can go hence without let or hindrance. The rest of us can go on our way alone!'

Again he paused, and looked keenly at us in turn. We looked at each other; but no one quailed. For my own part, if I had had any doubt as to going on, the look on Margaret's face would have reassured me. It was fearless; it was intense; it was full of a divine calm.

Mr Trelawny took a long breath, and in a more cheerful, as well as in a more decided tone, went on: 'As we are all of one mind, the sooner we get the necessary matters in train the better. Let me tell you that this place, like all the rest of the house, can be lit with electricity. We could not join the wires to the mains lest our secret should become known, but I have a cable here which we can attach in the hall and complete the circuit!' As he was speaking, he began to ascend the steps. From close to the entrance he took the end of a cable; this he drew forward and attached to a switch in the wall. Then, turning on a tap, he flooded the whole vault and staircase below with light. I could now see from the volume of light streaming up into the hallway that the hole beside the staircase went direct into the cave. Above it was a pulley and a mass of strong tackle with multiplying blocks of the Smeaton order. Mr Trelawny, seeing me looking at this, said, correctly interpreting my thoughts: 'Yes! it is new. I hung it myself there on purpose. I knew we should have to lower great weights; and as I did not wish to take too many into my confidence, I arranged a tackle which I could work alone if necessary.'

We set to work at once; and before nightfall had lowered, unhooked, and placed in the positions designated for each by Trelawny, all the great sarcophagi and all the curios and other matters which we had taken with us.

It was a strange and weird proceeding the placing of those wonderful monuments of a bygone age in that green cavern, which represented in its cutting and purpose and up-to-date mechanism and electric lights both the old world and the new. But as time went on I grew more and more to recognise the wisdom and correctness of Mr Trelawny's choice. I was much disturbed when Silvio, who had been brought into the cave in the arms of his mistress, and who was lying asleep on my coat which I had taken off, sprang up when the cat mummy had been unpacked, and flew at it with the same ferocity which he had previously exhibited. The incident showed Margaret in a new phase, and one which gave my heart a pang. She had been standing quite still at one side of the cave leaning on a sarcophagus, in one of those fits of abstraction which had of late come upon her; but on hearing the sound, and seeing Silvio's violent onslaught, she seemed to fall into a positive fury of passion. Her eyes blazed, and her mouth took a hard, cruel tension which was new to me. Instinctively she stepped towards Silvio as if to interfere in the attack. But I too had stepped forward; and as she caught my eye a strange spasm came upon her, and she stopped. Its intensity made me hold my breath; and I put up my hand to clear my eyes. When I had done this, she had on the instant recovered her calm, and there was a look of brief wonder on her face. With all her old grace and sweetness she swept over and lifted Silvio, just as she had done on former occasions, and held him in her arms, petting him and treating him as though he were a little child who had erred.

As I looked a strange fear came over me. The Margaret that I knew seemed to be changing; and in my inmost heart I prayed that the disturbing cause might soon come to an end. More than ever I longed at that moment that our terrible experiment should come to a prosperous termination.

When all had been arranged in the room as Mr Trelawny wished he turned to us, one after another, till he had concentrated the intelligence of us all upon him. Then he said: 'All is now ready in this place. We must only await the proper time to begin.'

We were silent for a while. Dr Winchester was the first to speak: 'What is the proper time? Have you any approximation, even if you are not satisfied as to the exact day.' He answered at once: 'After the most anxious thought I have fixed on July 31!'

'May I ask why that date?' He spoke his answer slowly: 'Queen Tera was ruled in great degree by mysticism, and there are so many evidences that she looked for resurrection that naturally she would choose a period ruled over by a god specialised to such a purpose. Now, the fourth month of the season of Inundation was ruled by Harmachis, this being the name for "Ra" the Sun-God, at his rising in the morning, and therefore typifying the awakening or arising. This arising is manifestly to physical life, since it is of the mid-world of human daily life. Now as this month begins on our 25th July, the seventh day would be July 31st, for you may be sure that the mystic queen would not have chosen any day but the seventh or some power of seven.

'I dare say that some of you have wondered why our preparations have been so deliberately undertaken. This is why! We must be ready in every possible way when the time comes; but there was no use in having to wait round for a needless number of days.'

And so we waited only for the 31st of July, the next day but one, when the great experiment would be made.

CHAPTER 17

Doubts and Fears

WE LEARN OF GREAT THINGS by little experiences. The history of ages is but an indefinite repetition of the history of hours. The record of a soul is but a multiple of the story of a moment. The recording angel writes in the great book in no rainbow tints; his pen is dipped in no colours but light and darkness. For the eye of infinite wisdom there is no need of shading. All things, all thoughts, all emotions, all experiences, all doubts and hopes and fears, all intentions, all wishes seen down to the lower strata of their concrete and multitudinous elements, are finally resolved into direct opposites.

· Did any human being wish for the epitome of a life wherein were gathered and grouped all the experiences that a child of Adam could have, the history, fully and frankly written, of my own mind during the next forty-eight hours would afford him all that could be wanted. And the recorder could have wrought as usual in sunlight and shadow, which may be taken to represent the final expressions of heaven and hell. For in the highest heaven is faith; and doubt hangs over the yawning blackness of hell.

There were of course times of sunshine in those two days; moments when, in the realisation of Margaret's sweetness and her love for me, all doubts were dissipated like morning mist before the sun. But the balance of the time – and an overwhelming balance it was – gloom hung over me like a pall. The hour, in whose coming I had acquiesced, was approaching so quickly and was already so near that the sense of finality was bearing upon me! The issue was perhaps life or death to any of us; but for this we were all prepared. Margaret and I were one as to the risk. The question of the moral aspect of the case, which involved the religious belief in which I had been reared, was not one to trouble me; for the issues, and the causes that lay behind them, were not within my power even to comprehend. The doubt of the success of the great experiment was such a doubt as exists in all enterprises which have great possibilities. To me, whose life was passed in a series of intellectual struggles, this form of doubt was a stimulus, rather than deterrent. What then was it that made for me a trouble, which became an anguish when my thoughts dwelt long on it?

I was beginning to doubt Margaret!

What it was that I doubted I knew not. It was not her love, or her honour, or her truth, or her kindness, or her zeal. What then was it? It was herself!

Margaret was changing! At times during the past few days I had hardly known her as the same girl whom I had met at the picnic, and whose vigils I had shared in the sick-room of her father. Then, even in her moments of greatest sorrow or fright or anxiety, she was all life and thought and keenness. Now she was generally *distraite*, and at times in a sort of negative condition as though her mind – her very being – was not present. At such moments she would have full possession of observation and memory. She would know and remember all that was going on, and had gone on around her; but her coming back to her old self had to me something the sensation of a new person coming into the room. Up to the time of leaving London I had been content whenever she was present. I had over me that delicious sense of security which comes with the consciousness that love is mutual. But now doubt had taken its place. I never knew whether the personality present was my Margaret – the old Margaret whom I had loved at the first glance – or the other new Margaret, whom I hardly understood, and whose intellectual aloofness made an impalpable barrier between us. Sometimes she would become, as it were, awake all at once. At such times, though she would say to me sweet and pleasant things which she had often said before, she would seem most unlike herself. It was almost as if she was speaking parrot-like or at dictation of one who could read words or acts, but not thoughts. After one or two experiences of this kind, my own doubting began to make a barrier; for I could not speak with the ease and freedom which were usual to me. And so hour by hour we drifted further apart. Were it not for the few odd moments when the old Margaret was back with me full of her charm I do not know what would have happened. As it was, each such moment gave me a fresh start and kept my love from changing.

I would have given the world for a confidant; but this was impossible. How could I speak a doubt of Margaret to anyone, even her father! How could I speak a doubt to Margaret, when Margaret herself was the theme! I could only endure – and hope. And of the two the endurance was the lesser pain.

I think that Margaret must have at times felt that there was some cloud between us, for towards the end of the first day she began to shun me a little; or perhaps it was that she had become more diffident than usual about me. Hitherto she had sought every opportunity of being with me, just as I had tried to be with her; so that now any avoidance, one of the other, made a new pain to us both.

On this day the household seemed very still. Each one of us was about his own work, or occupied with his own thoughts. We only met at meal times; and then, though we talked, all seemed more or less preoccupied. There was not in the house even the stir of the routine of service. The precaution of Mr Trelawny in having three rooms prepared for each of us had rendered servants unnecessary. The dining-room was solidly prepared with cooked provisions for several days. Towards evening I went out by myself for a stroll. I had looked for Margaret to ask her to come with me; but when I found her, she was in one of her apathetic moods, and the charm of her presence seemed lost to me. Angry with myself, but unable to quell my own spirit of discontent, I went out alone over the rocky headland.

On the cliff, with the wide expanse of wonderful sea before me, and no sound but the dash of waves below and the harsh screams of the seagulls above, my thoughts ran free. Do what I would, they returned continuously to one subject, the solving of the doubt that was upon me. Here in the solitude, amid the wide circle of nature's force and strife, my mind began to work truly. Unconsciously I found myself asking a question which I would not allow myself to answer. At last the persistence of a mind working truly prevailed; I found myself face to face with my doubt. The habit of my life began to assert itself, and I analysed the evidence before me.

It was so startling that I had to force myself into obedience to logical effort. My starting-place was this: Margaret was changed – in what way, and by what means. Was it her character, or her mind, or her nature? for her physical appearance remained the same. I began to group all that I had ever heard of her, beginning at her birth.

It was strange at the very first. She had been, according to Corbeck's statement, born of a dead mother during the time that her father and his friend were in a trance in the tomb at Aswan. That trance was presumably effected by a woman; a woman mummied, yet preserving as we had every reason to believe from after experience, an astral body subject to a free will and an active intelligence. With that astral body, space ceased to exist. The vast distance between London and Aswan became as naught; and whatever power of necromancy the Sorceress had might have been exercised over the dead mother, and possibly the dead child.

The dead child! Was it possible that the child was dead and was made alive again? Whence then came the animating spirit – the soul? Logic was pointing the way to me now with a vengeance!

If the Egyptian belief was true for Egyptians, then the 'Ka' of the dead queen and her 'Khu' could animate what she might choose. In such case Margaret would not be an individual at all, but simply a phase of Queen Tera herself; an astral body obedient to her will!

Here I revolted against logic. Every fibre of my being resented such a conclusion. How could I believe that there was no Margaret at all; but just an animated image, used by the double of a woman of forty centuries ago to its own ends . . . ! Somehow, the outlook was brighter to me now, despite the new doubts.

At least I had Margaret!

Back swung the logical pendulum again. The child then was not dead. If so, had the Sorceress had anything to do with her birth at all? It was evident – so I took it again from Corbeck – that there was a strange likeness between Margaret and the pictures of Queen Tera. How could this be? It could not be any birthmark reproducing what had been in the mother's mind; for Mrs Trelawny had never seen the pictures. Nay, even her father had not seen them till he had found his way into the tomb only a few days before her birth. This phase I could not get rid of so easily as the last; the fibres of my being remained quiet. There remained to me the horror of doubt. And even then, so strange is the mind of man, Doubt itself took a concrete image; a vast and impenetrable gloom, through which flickered irregularly and spasmodically tiny points of evanescent light, which seemed to quicken the darkness into a positive existence.

The remaining possibility of relations between Margaret and the mummied queen was, that in some occult way the Sorceress had power to change places with the other. This view of things could not be so lightly thrown aside. There were too many suspicious circumstances to warrant this, now that my attention was fixed on it and my intelligence recognised the possibility. Hereupon there began to come into my mind all the strange incomprehensible matters which had whirled through our lives in the last few days. At first they all crowded in upon me in a jumbled mass; but again the habit of mind of my working life prevailed, and they took order. I found it now easier to control myself; for there was something to grasp, some work to be done; though it was of a sorry kind, for it was or might be antagonistic to Margaret. But Margaret was herself at stake! I was thinking of her and fighting for her; and yet if I were to work in the dark, I might be even harmful to her. My first weapon in her defence was truth. I must know and understand; I might then be able to act. Certainly, I could not act beneficently without a just conception and recognition of the facts. Arranged in order these were as follows:

Firstly: the strange likeness of Queen Tera to Margaret who had been born in another country a thousand miles away, where her mother could not possibly have had even a passing knowledge of her appearance.

Secondly: the disappearance of Van Huyn's book when I had read up to the description of the Star Ruby.

Thirdly: the finding of the lamps in the boudoir. Tera with her astral body could have unlocked the door of Corbeck's room in the hotel, and have locked it again after her exit with the lamps. She could in the same way have opened the window, and put the lamps in the boudoir. It need not have been that Margaret in her own person should have had any hand in this; but – but it was at least strange.

Fourthly: here the suspicions of the detective and the doctor came back to me with renewed force, and with a larger understanding.

Fifthly: there were the occasions on which Margaret foretold with accuracy the coming occasions of quietude, as though she had some conviction or foreknowledge of the intentions of the astral-bodied queen.

Sixthly: there was her suggestion of the finding of the ruby which her father had lost. As I thought now afresh over this episode in the light of suspicion in which her own powers were involved, the only conclusion I could come to was – always supposing that the theory of the queen's astral power was correct – that Queen Tera being anxious that all should go well in the movement from London to Kyllion had in her own way taken the jewel from Mr Trelawny's pocket-book, finding it of some use in her supernatural guardianship of the journey. Then in some mysterious way she had, through Margaret, made the suggestion of its loss and finding.

Seventhly, and lastly, was the strange dual existence which Margaret seemed of late to be leading; and which in some way seemed a consequence or corollary of all that had gone before.

The dual existence! This was indeed the conclusion which over-came all difficulties and reconciled opposites. If indeed Margaret were not in all ways a free agent, but could be compelled to speak or act as she might be instructed; or if her whole being could be changed for another without the possibility of anyone noticing the doing of it, then all things were possible. All would depend on the spirit of the individuality by which she could be so compelled. If this individuality were just and kind and clean, all might be well. But if not! . . . The thought was too awful for words. I ground my teeth with futile rage, as the ideas of horrible possibilities swept through me.

Up to this morning Margaret's lapses into her new self had been few and hardly noticeable, save when once or twice her attitude towards myself had been marked by a bearing strange to me. But today the contrary was the case; and the change presaged badly. It might be that that other individuality was of the lower, not of the better sort! Now that I thought of it I had reason to fear. In the history of the mummy, from the time of Van Huyn's breaking into the tomb, the record of deaths that we knew of, presumably effected by her will and agency, was a startling one. The Arab who had stolen the hand from the mummy; and the one who had taken it from his body. The Arab chief who had tried to steal the jewel from Van Huyn, and whose throat bore the marks of seven fingers. The two men found dead on the first night of Trelawny's taking away the sarcophagus; and the three on the return to the tomb. The Arab who had opened the secret serdâb. Nine dead men, one of them slain manifestly by the queen's own hand! And beyond this again the several savage attacks on Mr Trelawny in his own room, in which, aided by her Familiar, she had tried to open the safe and to extract the Talisman Jewel. His device of fastening the key to his wrist by a steel bangle, though successful in the end, had wellnigh cost him his life.

If then the queen, intent on her resurrection under her own conditions had, so to speak, waded to it through blood, what might she not do were her purpose thwarted? What terrible step might she not take to effect her wishes? Nay, what were her wishes; what was her ultimate purpose? As yet we had had only Margaret's statement of them, given in all the glorious enthusiasm of her lofty soul. In her record there was no expression of a love to be sought or found. All we knew for certain was that she had set before her the object of resurrection, and that in it the North which she had manifestly loved was to have a special part. But that the resurrection was to be accomplished in the lonely tomb in the Valley of the Sorcerer was apparent. All preparations had been carefully made for accomplishment from within, and for her ultimate exit in her new and living form. The sarcophagus was unlidded. The oil jars, though hermetically sealed, were to be easily opened by hand; and in them provision was made for shrinkage through a vast period of time. Even flint and steel were provided for the production of flame. The mummy pit was left open in violation of usage; and beside the stone door on the cliff side was fixed an imperishable chain by which she might in safety descend to earth. But as to what her after intentions were we had no clue. If it was that she meant to begin life again as a humble individual, there was something so noble in the thought that it even warmed my heart to her and turned my wishes to her success.

The very idea seemed to endorse Margaret's magnificent tribute to her purpose, and helped to calm my troubled spirit.

Then and there, with this feeling strong upon me, I determined to warn Margaret and her father of dire possibilities; and to await, as well content as I could in my ignorance, the development of things over which I had no power.

I returned to the house in a different frame of mind to that in which I had left it; and was enchanted to find Margaret – the old Margaret – waiting me.

After dinner, when I was alone for a time with the father and daughter, I opened the subject, though with considerable hesitation: 'Would it not be well to take every possible precaution, in case the queen may not wish what we are doing, with regard to what may occur before the experiment; and at or after her waking, if it comes off?' Margaret's answer came back quickly; so quickly that I was convinced she must have had it ready for someone: 'But she does approve! Surely it cannot be otherwise. Father is doing, with all his brains and all his energy and all his great courage, just exactly what the great queen had arranged!'

'But,' I answered, 'that can hardly be. All that she arranged was in a tomb high up in a rock, in a desert solitude, shut away from the world by every conceivable means. She seems to have depended on this isolation to insure against accident. Surely, here in another country and age, with quite different conditions, she may in her anxiety make mistakes and treat any of you – of us – as she did those others in times gone past. Nine men that we know of have been slain by her own hand or by her instigation. She can be remorseless if she will.' It did not strike me till afterwards when I was thinking over this conversation, how thoroughly I had accepted the living and conscious condition of Queen Tera as a fact. Before I spoke, I had feared I might offend Mr Trelawny; but to my pleasant surprise he smiled quite genially as he answered me: 'My dear fellow, in a way you are quite right. The queen did undoubtedly intend isolation; and, all told, it would be best that her experiment should be made as she arranged it. But just think, that became impossible when once the Dutch explorer had broken into her tomb. That was not my doing. I am innocent of it, though it was the cause of my setting out to rediscover the sepulchre. Mind, I do not say for a moment that I would not have done just the same as Van Huyn. I went into the tomb from curiosity; and I took away what I did, being fired with the zeal of acquisitiveness which animates the collector. But, remember also, that at this time I did not know of the queen's intention of resurrection; I had no idea of the completeness of her preparations. All that came long afterwards. But when it did come, I have done all that I could to carry out her wishes to the full. My only fear is that I may have misinterpreted some of her cryptic instructions, or have omitted or overlooked something. But of this I am certain; I have left undone nothing that I can imagine right to be done; and I have done nothing that I know of to clash with Queen Tera's arrangement. I want her great experiment to succeed. To this end I have not spared labour or time or money – or myself. I have endured hardship, and braved danger. All my brains; all my knowledge and learning, such as they are; all my endeavours such as they can be, have been, are, and shall be devoted to this end, till we either win or lose the great stake that we play for.'

'The great stake?' I repeated; 'the resurrection of the woman, and the woman's life? The proof that resurrection can be accomplished; by magical powers; by scientific knowledge; or by use of some force which at present the world does not know?'

Then Mr Trelawny spoke out the hopes of his heart which up to now he had indicated rather than expressed. Once or twice I had heard Corbeck speak of the fiery energy of his youth; but, save for the noble words of Margaret when she had spoken of Queen Tera's hope – which coming from his daughter made possible a belief that her power was in some sense due to heredity – I had seen no marked sign of it. But now his words, sweeping before them like a torrent all antagonistic thought, gave me a new idea of the man.

' "A woman's life!" What is a woman's life in the scale with what we hope for! Why, we are risking already a woman's life; the dearest life to me in all the world, and that grows more dear with every hour that passes. We are risking as well the lives of four men; yours and my own, as well as those two others who have been won to our confidence. "The proof that resurrection can be accomplished!" That is much. A marvellous thing in this age of science, and the scepticism that knowledge makes. But life and resurrection are themselves but items in what may be won by the accomplishment of this great experiment. Imagine what it will be for the world of thought – the true world of human progress – the veritable road to the Stars, the *itur ad astra* of the Ancients – if there can come back to us out of the unknown past one who can yield to us the lore stored in the great library of Alexandria, and lost in its consuming flames. Not only history can be set right, and the teachings of science made veritable from their beginnings; but we can be placed on the road to the knowledge of lost arts, lost learning, lost sciences, so that our feet may tread on the indicated path to their ultimate and complete restoration. Why, this woman can tell us what the world was like before what is called "the Flood"; can give us the origin of that vast astounding myth; can set the mind back to the consideration of things which to us now seem primeval, but which were old stories before the days of the patriarchs. But this is not the end! No, not even the beginning! If the story of this woman be all that we think – which some of us most firmly believe; if her powers and the restoration of them prove to be what we expect, why, then we may yet achieve a knowledge beyond what our age has ever known – beyond what is believed today possible for the children of men. If indeed this resurrection can be accomplished, how can we doubt the old knowledge, the old magic, the old belief! And if this be so, we must take it that the "Ka" of this great and learned queen has won secrets of more than mortal worth from her surroundings amongst the stars. This woman in her life voluntarily went down living to the grave, and came back again, as we learn from the records in her tomb; she chose to die her mortal death whilst young, so that at her resurrection in another age, beyond a trance of countless magnitude, she might emerge from her tomb in all the fullness and splendour of her youth and power. Already we have evidence that though her body slept in patience through those many centuries, her intelligence never passed away, that her resolution never flagged, that her will remained supreme; and, most important of all, that her memory was unimpaired. Oh, what possibilities are there in the coming of such a being into our midst! One whose history began before the concrete teaching of our Bible; whose experiences were antecedent to the formulation of the gods of Greece; who can link together the old and the new, earth and heaven, and yield to the known worlds of thought and physical existence the mystery of the unknown – of the old world in its youth, and of worlds beyond our ken!'

He paused almost overcome. Margaret had taken his hand when he spoke of her being so dear to him, and held it hard. As he spoke she continued to hold it. But there came over her face that change which I had so often seen of late; that mysterious veiling of her own personality which gave me the subtle sense of separation from her. In his impassioned vehemence her father did not notice; but when he stopped she seemed all at once to be herself again. In her glorious eyes came the added brightness of unshed tears; and with a gesture of passionate love and admiration, she stooped and kissed her father's hand. Then, turning to me, she too spoke: 'Malcolm, you have spoken of the deaths that came from the poor queen; or rather that justly came from meddling with her arrangements and thwarting her purpose. Do you not think that, in putting it as you have done, you have been unjust? Who would not have done just as she did? Remember she was fighting for her life! Ay, and for more than her life! For life, and love, and all the glorious possibilities of that dim future in the unknown world of the North which had such enchanting hopes for her! Do you not think that she, with all the learning of her time, and with all the great and resistless force of her mighty nature, had hopes of spreading in a wider way the lofty aspirations of her soul! That she hoped to bring to the conquering of unknown worlds, and using to the advantage of her people, all that she had won from sleep and death and time; all of which might and could have been frustrated by the ruthless hand of an assassin or a thief. Were it you, in such case would you not struggle by all means to achieve the object of your life and hope; whose possibilities grew and grew in the passing of those endless years? Can you think that that active brain was at rest during all those weary centuries, whilst her mortal body, swathed in all the protecting environment ordained by the religion and the science of her time, waited the destined hour; whilst her free soul was flitting from world to world amongst the boundless regions of the stars? Had these stars in their myriad and varied life no lessons for her; as they have had for us since we followed the glorious path which she and her people marked for us, when they sent their winged imaginations circling amongst the lamps of the night!'

Here she paused. She too was overcome, and the welling tears ran down her cheeks. I was myself more moved than I can say. This was indeed my Margaret; and in the consciousness of her presence my heart leapt. Out of my happiness came boldness, and I dared to say now what I had feared would be impossible: something which would call the attention of Mr Trelawny to what I imagined was the dual existence of his daughter. As I took Margaret's hand in mine and kissed it, I said to her father: 'Why, sir! she couldn't speak more eloquently if the very spirit of Queen Tera was with her to animate her and suggest thoughts!'

Mr Trelawny's answer simply overwhelmed me with surprise. It manifested to me that he too had gone through just such a process of thought as my own.

'And what if it was; if it is! I know well that the spirit of her mother is within her. If in addition there be the spirit of that great and wondrous queen, then she would be no less dear to me, but doubly dear! Do not have fear for her, Malcolm Ross; at least have no more fear than you may have for the rest of us!' Margaret took up the theme, speaking so quickly that her words seemed a continuation of her father's, rather than an interruption of them.

'Have no special fear for me, Malcolm. Queen Tera knows, and will offer us no harm. I know it! I know it, as surely as I am lost in the depth of my own love for you!'

There was something in her voice so strange to me that I looked quickly into her eyes. They were bright as ever, but veiled to my seeing the inward thought behind them as are the eyes of a caged lion.

Then the two other men came in, and the subject changed.

CHAPTER 18

The Lesson of the 'Ka'

THAT NIGHT we all went to bed early. The next night would be an anxious one, and Mr Trelawny thought that we should all be fortified with what sleep we could get. The day, too, would be full of work. Everything in connection with the great experiment would have to be gone over, so that at the last we might not fail from any unthought-of flaw in our working. We made, of course, arrangements for summoning aid in case such should be needed; but I do not think that any of us had any real apprehension of danger. Certainly we had no fear of such danger from violence as we had had to guard against in London during Mr Trelawny's long trance.

For my own part I felt a strange sense of relief in the matter. I had accepted Mr Trelawny's reasoning that if the queen were indeed such as we surmised – such as indeed we now took for granted – there would not be any opposition on her part; for we were carrying out her own wishes to the very last. So far I was at ease – far more at ease than earlier in the day I should have thought possible; but there were other sources of trouble which I could not blot out from my mind. Chief amongst them was Margaret's strange condition. If it was indeed that she had in her own person a dual existence, what might happen when the two existences became one? Again, and again, and again I turned this matter over in my mind, till I could have shrieked out in nervous anxiety. It was no consolation to me to remember that Margaret was herself satisfied, and her father acquiescent. Love is, after all, a selfish thing; and it throws a black shadow on anything between which and the light it stands. I seemed to hear the hands go round the dial of the clock; I saw darkness turn to gloom, and gloom to grey, and grey to light without pause or hindrance to the succession of my miserable feelings. At last, when it was decently possible without the fear of disturbing others, I got up. I crept along the passage to find if all was well with the others; for we had arranged that the door of each of our rooms should be left slightly open so that any sound of disturbance would be easily and distinctly heard.

One and all slept; I could hear the regular breathing of each, and my heart rejoiced that this miserable night of anxiety was safely passed. As I knelt in my own room in a burst of thankful prayer, I knew in the depths of my own heart the measure of my fear. I found my way out of the house, and went down to the water by the long stairway cut in the rock. A swim in the cool bright sea braced my nerves and made me my old self again.

As I came back to the top of the steps I could see the bright sunlight, rising from behind me, turning the rocks across the bay to glittering gold. And yet I felt somehow disturbed. It was all too bright; as it sometimes is before the coming of a storm. As I paused to watch it, I felt a soft hand on my shoulder; and, turning, found Margaret close to me; Margaret as bright and radiant as the morning glory of the sun! It was my own Margaret this time! My old Margaret, without alloy of any other; and I felt that, at least, this last and fatal day was well begun.

But alas! the joy did not last. When we got back to the house from a stroll around the cliffs, the same old routine of yesterday was resumed: gloom and anxiety, hope, high spirits, deep depression, and apathetic aloofness.

But it was to be a day of work; and we all braced ourselves to it with an energy which wrought its own salvation.

After breakfast we all adjourned to the cave, where Mr Trelawny went over, point by point, the position of each item of our paraphernalia. He explained as he went on why each piece was so placed. He had with him the great rolls of paper with the measured plans and the signs and drawings which he had had made from his own and Corbeck's rough notes. As he had told us, these contained the whole of the hieroglyphics on walls and ceilings and floor of the tomb in the Valley of the Sorcerer. Even had not the measurements, made to scale, recorded the position of each piece of furniture, we could have eventually placed them by a study of the cryptic writings and symbols.

Mr Trelawny explained to us certain other things, not laid down on the chart. Such as, for instance, that the hollowed part of the table was exactly fitted to the bottom of the magic coffer, which was therefore intended to be placed on it. The respective legs of this table were indicated by differently shaped uraei outlined on the floor, the head of each being extended in the direction of the similar uraeus twined round the leg. Also that the mummy, when laid on the raised portion in the bottom of the sarcophagus, seemingly made to fit the form, would lie head to the West and feet to the East, thus receiving the natural earth currents. 'If this be intended,' he said, 'as I presume it is, I gather that the force to be used has something to do with magnetism or electricity, or both. It may be, of course, that some other force, such, for instance, as that emanating from radium, is to be employed. I have experimented with the latter, but only in such small quantity as I could obtain; but so far as I can ascertain the stone of the coffer is absolutely impervious to its influence. There must be some such unsusceptible substances in nature. Radium does not seemingly manifest itself when distributed through pitchblende; and there are doubtless other such substances in which it can be imprisoned. Possibly these may belong to that class of "inert" elements discovered or isolated by Sir William Ramsay. It is therefore possible that in this coffer, made from an aerolite and therefore perhaps containing some element unknown in our world, may be imprisoned some mighty power which is to be released on its opening.'

This appeared to be an end of this branch of the subject; but as he still kept the fixed look of one who is engaged in a theme we all waited in silence. After a pause he went on: 'There is one thing which has up to now, I confess, puzzled me. It may not be of prime importance; but in a matter like this, where all is unknown, we must take it that everything is important. I cannot think that in a matter worked out with such extraordinary scrupulosity such a thing should be overlooked. As you may see by the ground-plan of the tomb the sarcophagus stands near the north wall, with the magic coffer to the south of it. The space covered by the former is left quite bare of symbol or ornamentation of any kind. At the first glance this would seem to imply that the drawings had been made *after* the sarcophagus had been put into its place. But a more minute examination will show that the symbolisation on the floor is so arranged that a definite effect is produced. See, here the writings run in correct order as though they had jumped across the gap. It is only from certain effects that it becomes clear that there is a meaning of some kind. What that meaning may be is what we want to know. Look at the top and bottom of the vacant space, which lies West and East corresponding to the head and foot of the sarcophagus. In both are duplications of the same symbolisation, but so arranged that the parts of each one of them are integral portions of some other writing running crosswise. It is only when we get a *coup d'oeil* from either the head or the foot that you recognise that there are symbolisations. See! they are in triplicate at the corners and the centre of both top and bottom. In every case there is a sun cut in half by the line of the sarcophagus, as by the horizon. Close behind each of these and faced away from it, as though in some way dependent on it, is the vase which in hiero-glyphic writing symbolises the heart – "Ab" the Egyptians called it. Beyond each of these again is the figure of a pair of widespread arms turned upwards from the elbow; this is the determinative of the "Ka" or "Double". But its relative position is different at top and bottom. At the head of the sarcophagus the top of the "Ka" is turned towards the mouth of the vase, but at the foot the extended arms point away from it.

'The symbolisation seems to mean that during the passing of the Sun from West to East – from sunset to sunrise, or through the under world, otherwise night – the Heart, which is material even in the tomb and cannot leave it, simply revolves, so that it can always rest on "Ra" the Sun-God, the origin of all good; but that the Double, which represents the active principle, goes whither it will, the same by night as by day. If this be correct it is a warning – a caution – a reminder that the consciousness of the mummy does not rest but is to be reckoned with.

'Or it may be intended to convey that after the particular night of the resurrection, the "Ka" would leave the heart altogether, thus typifying that in her resurrection the queen would be restored to a lower and purely physical existence. In such case what would become of her memory and the experiences of her wide-wandering soul? The chiefest value of her resurrection would be lost to the world! This, however, does not alarm me. It is only guesswork after all, and is contradictory to the intellectual belief of the Egyptian theology, that the "Ka" is an essential portion of humanity.' He paused and we all waited. The silence was broken by Dr Winchester: 'But would not all this imply that the queen feared intrusion of her tomb?' Mr Trelawny smiled as he answered: 'My dear sir, she was prepared for it. The grave robber is no modern application of endeavour; he was probably known in the queen's own dynasty. Not only was she prepared for intrusion, but, as shown in several ways, she expected it. The hiding of the lamps in the serdâb, and the institution of the avenging "treasurer" shows that there was defence, positive as well as negative. Indeed, from the many indications afforded in the clues laid out with the most consummate thought, we may almost gather that she entertained it as a possibility that others – like ourselves, for instance – might in all seriousness undertake the work which she had made ready for her own hands when the time should have come. This very matter that I have been speaking of is an instance. The clue is intended for seeing eyes!'

Again we were silent. It was Margaret who spoke: 'Father, may I have that chart? I should like to study it during the day!'

'Certainly, my dear!' answered Mr Trelawny heartily, as he handed it to her. He resumed his instructions in a different tone, a more matter-of-fact one suitable to a practical theme which had no mystery about it: 'I think you had better all understand the working of the electric light in case any sudden contingency should arise. I dare say you have noticed that we have a complete supply in every part of the house, so that there need not be a dark corner anywhere. This I had specially arranged. It is worked by a set of turbines moved by the flowing and ebbing tide, after the manner of the turbines at Niagara. I hope by this means to nullify accident and to have without fail a full supply ready at any time. Come with me and I will explain the system of circuits, and point out to you the taps and the fuses.' I could not but notice, as we went with him all over the house, how absolutely complete the system was, and how he had guarded himself against any disaster that human thought could foresee.

But out of the very completeness came a fear! In such an enterprise as ours the bounds of human thought were but narrow. Beyond it lay the vast of divine wisdom, and divine power!

When we came back to the cave, Mr Trelawny took up another theme: 'We have now to settle definitely the exact hour at which the great experiment is to be made. So far as science and mechanism go, if the preparations are complete, all hours are the same. But as we have to deal with preparations made by a woman of extraordinarily subtle mind, and who had full belief in magic and had a cryptic meaning in everything, we should place ourselves in her position before deciding. It is now manifest that the sunset has an important place in the arrangements. As those suns, cut so mathematically by the edge of the sarcophagus, were arranged of full design, we must take our cue from this. Again, we find all along that the number seven has had an important bearing on every phase of the queen's thought and reasoning and action. The logical result is that the seventh hour after sunset was the time fixed on. This is borne out by the fact that on each of the occasions when action was taken in my house, this was the time chosen. As the sun sets tonight in Cornwall at eight, our hour is to be three in the morning!' He spoke in a matter-of-fact way, though with great gravity; but there was nothing of mystery in his words or manner. Still, we were all impressed to a remarkable degree. I could see this in the other men by the pallor that came or some of their faces, and by the stillness and unquestioning silence with which the decision was received. The only one who remained in any way at ease was Margaret, who had lapsed into one of her moods of abstraction, but who seemed to wake up to a note of gladness. Her father, who was watching her intently, smiled; her mood was to him a direct confirmation of his theory.

For myself I was almost overcome. The definite fixing of the hour seemed like the voice of doom. When I think of it now, I can realise how a condemned man feels at his sentence, or at the sounding of the last hour he is to hear.

There could be no going back now! We were in the hands of God! The hands of God ... ! And yet ... ! What other forces were arrayed? ... What would become of us all, poor atoms of earthly dust whirled in the wind which cometh whence and goeth whither no man may know. It was not for myself ... Margaret ... !

I was recalled by Mr Trelawny's firm voice: 'Now we shall see to the lamps and finish our preparations.' Accordingly we set to work, and under his supervision made ready the Egyptian lamps, seeing that they were well filled with the cedar oil, and that the wicks were adjusted and in good order. We lighted and tested them one by one, and left them ready so that they would light at once and evenly. When this was done we had a general look round; and fixed all in readiness for our work at night.

All this had taken time, and we were I think all surprised when as we emerged from the cave we heard the great clock in the hall chime four.

We had a late lunch, a thing possible without trouble in the present state of our commissariat arrangements. After it, by Mr Trelawny's advice, we separated; each to prepare in our own way for the strain of the coming night. Margaret looked pale and somewhat overwrought, so I advised her to lie down and try to sleep. She promised that she would. The abstraction which had been upon her fitfully all day lifted for the time; with all her old sweetness and loving delicacy she kissed me goodbye for the present! With the sense of happiness which this gave me I went out for a walk on the cliffs. I did not want to think; and I had an instinctive feeling that fresh air and God's sunlight, and the myriad beauties of the works of His hand would be the best preparation of fortitude for what was to come.

When I got back, all the party were assembling for a late tea. Coming fresh from the exhilaration of nature, it struck me as almost comic that we, who were nearing the end of so strange – almost monstrous – an undertaking, should be yet bound by the needs and habits of our lives.

All the men of the party were grave; the time of seclusion, even if it had given them rest, had also given opportunity for thought. Margaret was bright, almost buoyant; but I missed about her something of her usual spontaneity. Towards myself there was a shadowy air of reserve, which brought back something of my suspicion. When tea was over, she went out of the room; but returned in a minute with the roll of drawing which she had taken with her earlier in the day. Coming close to Mr Trelawny, she said: 'Father, I have been carefully considering what you said today about the hidden meaning of those suns and hearts and "Ka"s, and I have been examining the drawings again.'

'And with what result, my child?' asked Mr Trelawny eagerly.

'There is another reading possible!'

'And that?' His voice was now tremulous with anxiety. Margaret spoke with a strange ring in her voice; a ring that cannot be, unless there is the consciousness of truth behind it: 'It means that at the sunset the "Ka" is to enter the "Ab"; and it is only at the sunrise that it will leave it!'

'Go on!' said her father hoarsely.

'It means that for this night the queen's double, which is otherwise free, will remain in her heart, which is mortal and cannot leave its prison-place in the mummy shrouding. It means that when the sun has dropped into the sea, Queen Tera will cease to exist as a conscious power, till sunrise; unless the great experiment can recall her to waking life. It means that there will be nothing whatever for you or others to fear from her in such way as we have all cause to remember. Whatever change may come from the working of the great experiment, there can come none from the poor, helpless, dead woman who has waited all those centuries for this night; who has given up to the coming hour all the freedom of eternity, won in the old way, in hope of a new life in a new world such as she longed for . . . !' She stopped suddenly. As she had gone on speaking there had come with her words a strange pathetic, almost pleading, tone which touched me to the quick. As she stopped, I could see, before she turned away her head, that her eyes were full of tears.

For once the heart of her father did not respond to her feeling. He looked exultant, but with a grim masterfulness which reminded me of the set look of his stern face as he had lain in the trance. He did not offer any consolation to his daughter in her sympathetic pain. He only said: 'We may test the accuracy of your surmise, and of her feeling, when the time comes!' Having said so, he went up the stone stairway and into his own room. Margaret's face had a troubled look as she gazed after him.

Strangely enough her trouble did not as usual touch me to the quick.

When Mr Trelawny had gone, silence reigned. I do not think that any of us wanted to talk. Presently Margaret went to her room, and I went out on the terrace over the sea. The fresh air and the beauty of all before me helped to restore the good spirits which I had known earlier in the day. Presently I felt myself actually rejoicing in the belief that the danger which I had feared from the queen's violence on the coming night was obviated. I believed in Margaret's belief so thoroughly that it did not occur to me to dispute her reasoning. In a lofty frame of mind, and with less anxiety than I had felt for days, I went to my room and lay down on the sofa.

I was awaked by Corbeck calling to me, hurriedly

'Come down to the cave as quickly as you can. Mr Trelawny wants to see us all there at once. Hurry!'

I jumped up and ran down to the cave. All were there except Margaret, who came immediately after me carrying Silvio in her arms. When the cat saw his old enemy he struggled to get down; but Margaret held him fast and soothed him. I looked at my watch. It was close to eight.

When Margaret was with us her father said directly, with a quiet insistence which was new to me: 'You believe, Margaret, that Queen Tera has voluntarily undertaken to give up her freedom for this night? To become a mummy and nothing more, till the experiment has been completed? To be content that she shall be powerless under all and any circumstances until after all is over and the act of resurrection has been accomplished, or the effort has failed?' After a pause Margaret answered in a low voice: 'Yes!'

In the pause her whole being, appearance, expression, voice, manner had changed. Even Silvio noticed it, and with a violent effort wriggled away from her arms; she did not seem to notice the act. I expected that the cat, when he had achieved his freedom, would have attacked the mummy; but on this occasion he did not. He seemed too cowed to approach it. He shrunk away, and with a piteous 'miaou' came over and rubbed himself against my ankles. I took him up in my arms, and he nestled there content. Mr Trelawny spoke again: 'You are sure of what you say! You believe it with all your soul?' Margaret's face had lost the abstracted look; it now seemed illuminated with the devotion of one to whom is given to speak of great things. She answered in a voice which, though quiet, vibrated with conviction: 'I know it! My knowledge is beyond belief!' Mr Trelawny spoke again: 'Then you are so sure, that were you Queen Tera herself, you would be willing to prove it in any way that I might suggest?'

'Yes, any way!' the answer rang out fearlessly. He spoke again, in a voice in which was no note of doubt: 'Even in the abandonment of your Familiar to death – to annihilation.'

She paused, and I could see that she suffered – suffered horribly. There was in her eyes a hunted look, which no man can, unmoved, see in the eyes of his beloved. I was about to interrupt, when her father's eyes, glancing round with a fierce determination, met mine. I stood silent, almost spellbound; so also the other men. Something was going on before us which we did not understand!

With a few long strides Mr Trelawny went to the west side of the cave and tore back the shutter which obscured the window. The cool air blew in, and the sunlight streamed over them both, for Margaret was now by his side. He pointed to where the sun was sinking into the sea in a halo of golden fire, and his face was as set as flint. In a voice whose absolute uncompromising hardness I shall hear in my ears at times till my dying day, he said: 'Choose! Speak! When the sun has dipped below the sea, it will be too late!' The glory of the dying sun seemed to light up Margaret's face, till it shone as if lit from within by a noble light, as she answered: 'Even that!'

Then stepping over to where the mummy cat stood on the little table, she placed her hand on it. She had now left the sunlight, and the shadows looked dark and deep over her. In a clear voice she said: 'Were I Tera, I would say "Take all I have! This night is for the gods alone!" '

As she spoke the sun dipped, and the cold shadow suddenly fell on us. We all stood still for a while. Silvio jumped from my arms and ran over to his mistress, rearing himself up against her dress as if asking to be lifted. He took no notice whatever of the mummy now.

Margaret was glorious with all her wonted sweetness as she said sadly: 'The sun is down, Father! Shall any of us see it again? The night of nights is come!'

CHAPTER 19

The Great Experiment

IF ANY EVIDENCE had been wanted of how absolutely one and all of us had come to believe in the spiritual existence of the Egyptian queen, it would have been found in the change which in a few minutes had been effected in us by the statement of voluntary negation made, we all believed, through Margaret. Despite the coming of the fearful ordeal, the sense of which it was impossible to forget, we looked and acted as though a great relief had come to us. We had indeed lived in such a state of terrorism during the days when Mr Trelawny was lying in a trance that the feeling had bitten deeply into us. No one knows till he has experienced it, what it is to be in constant dread of some unknown danger which may come at any time and in any form.

The change was manifested in different ways, according to each nature. Margaret was sad. Dr Winchester was in high spirits, and keenly observant; the process of thought which had served as an antidote to fear, being now relieved from this duty, added to his intellectual enthusiasm. Mr Corbeck seemed to be in a retrospective rather than a speculative mood. I was myself rather inclined to be gay; the relief from certain anxiety regarding Margaret was sufficient for me for the time.

As to Mr Trelawny he seemed less changed than any. Perhaps this was only natural, as he had had in his mind the intention for so many years of doing that in which we were tonight engaged, that any event connected with it could only seem to him as an episode, a step to the end. His was that commanding nature which looks so to the end of an undertaking that all else is of secondary importance. Even now, though his terrible sternness relaxed under the relief from the strain, he never flagged nor faltered for a moment in his purpose. He asked us men to come with him; and going to the hall we presently managed to lower into the cave an oak table, fairly long and not too wide, which stood against the wall in the hall. This we placed under the strong cluster of electric lights in the middle of the cave. Margaret looked on for a while; then all at once her face blanched, and in an agitated voice she said: 'What are you going to do, Father?'

'To unroll the mummy of the cat! Queen Tera will not need her Familiar tonight. If she should want him, it might be dangerous to us; so we shall make him safe. You are not alarmed, dear?'

'Oh no!' she answered quickly. 'But I was thinking of my Silvio, and how I should feel if he had been the mummy that was to be unswathed!'

Mr Trelawny got knives and scissors ready, and placed the cat on the table. It was a grim beginning to our work; and it made my heart sink when I thought of what might happen in that lonely house in the mid-gloom of the night. The sense of loneliness and isolation from the world was increased by the moaning of the wind which had now risen ominously, and by the beating of waves on the rocks below. But we had too grave a task before us to be swayed by external manifestations: the unrolling of the mummy began.

There was an incredible number of bandages; and the tearing sound – they being stuck fast to each other by bitumen and gums and spices – and the little cloud of red pungent dust that arose, pressed on the senses of all of us. As the last wrappings came away, we saw the animal seated before us. He was all hunkered up; his hair and teeth and claws were complete. The eyes were closed, but the eyelids had not the fierce look which I expected. The whiskers had been pressed down on the side of the face by the bandaging; but when the pressure was taken away they stood out, just as they would have done in life. He was a magnificent creature, a tiger-cat of great size. But as we looked at him, our first glance of admiration changed to one of fear, and a shudder ran through each one of us; for here was a confirmation of the fears which we had endured.

His mouth and his claws were smeared with the dry, red stains of recent blood!

Dr Winchester was the first to recover; blood in itself had small disturbing quality for him. He had taken out his magnifying-glass and was examining the stains on the cat's mouth. Mr Trelawny breathed loudly, as though a strain had been taken from him.

'It is as I expected,' he said. 'This promises well for what is to follow.'

By this time Dr Winchester was looking at the red stained paws. 'As I expected!' he said. 'He has seven claws, too! Opening his pocket-book, he took out the piece of blotting-paper marked by Silvio's claws, on which was also marked in pencil a diagram of the cuts made on Mr Trelawny's wrist. He placed the paper under the mummy cat's paw. The marks fitted exactly.

When we had carefully examined the cat, finding, however,

nothing strange about it but its wonderful preservation, Mr Trelawny lifted it from the table. Margaret started forward, crying out: 'Take care, Father! Take care! He may injure you!'

'Not now, my dear!' he answered as he moved towards the stairway. Her face fell. 'Where are you going?' she asked in a faint voice.

'To the kitchen,' he answered. 'Fire will take away all danger for the future; even an astral body cannot materialise from ashes!' He signed to us to follow him. Margaret turned away with a sob. I went to her; but she motioned me back and whispered: 'No, no! Go with the others. Father may want you. Oh! it seems like murder! The poor queen's pet . . . !' The tears were dropping from under the fingers that covered her eyes.

In the kitchen was a fire of wood ready laid. To this Mr Trelawny applied a match; in a few seconds the kindling had caught and the flames leaped. When the fire was solidly ablaze, he threw the body of the cat into it. For a few seconds it lay a dark mass amidst the flames, and the room was rank with the smell of burning hair. Then the dry body caught fire too. The inflammable substances used in embalming became new fuel, and the flames roared. A few minutes of fierce conflagration; and then we breathed freely. Queen Tera's familiar was no more!

When we went back to the cave we found Margaret sitting in the dark. She had switched off the electric light, and only a faint glow of the evening light came through the narrow openings. Her father went quickly over to her and put his arms round her in a loving protective way. She laid her head on his shoulder for a minute, and seemed comforted. Presently she called to me: 'Malcolm, turn up the light!' I carried out her orders, and could see that, though she had been crying, her eyes were now dry. Her father saw it too and looked glad. He said to us in a grave tone: 'Now we had better prepare for our great work. It will not do to leave anything to the last!' Margaret must have had a suspicion of what was coming, for it was with a sinking voice that she asked: 'What are you going to do now?' Mr Trelawny too must have had a suspicion of her feelings, for he answered in a low tone: 'To unroll the mummy of Queen Tera!' She came close to him and said pleadingly in a whisper: 'Father, you are not going to unswathe her! All you men . . . ! And in the glare of light!'

'But why not, my dear?'

'Just think, Father, a woman! All alone! In such a way! In such a place! Oh! it's cruel, cruel!' She was manifestly much overcome. Her cheeks were flaming red, and her eyes were full of indignant tears.

Her father saw her distress; and, sympathising with it, began to comfort her. I was moving off; but he signed to me to stay. I took it that after the usual manner of men he wanted help on such an occasion, and man-like wished to throw on someone else the task of dealing with a woman in indignant distress. However, he began to appeal first to her reason: 'Not a woman, dear; a mummy! She has been dead nearly five thousand years!'

'What does that matter? Sex is not a matter of years! A woman is a woman, if she had been dead five thousand centuries! And you expect her to arise out of that long sleep! It could not be real death, if she is to rise out of it! You have led me to believe that she will come alive when the coffer is opened!'

'I did, my dear; and I believe it! But if it isn't death that has been the matter with her all these years, it is something uncommonly like it. Then again, just think; it was men who embalmed her. They didn't have women's rights or lady doctors in ancient Egypt, my dear! And besides,' he went on more freely, seeing that she was accepting his argument, if not yielding to it, 'we men are accustomed to such things. Corbeck and I have unrolled a hundred mummies; and there were as many women as men amongst them. Dr Winchester in his work has had to deal with women as well as men, till custom has made him think nothing of sex. Even Ross has in his work as a barrister . . . ' He stopped suddenly.

'You were going to help too!' she said to me, with an indignant look.

I said nothing; I thought silence was best. Mr Trelawny went on hurriedly; I could see that he was glad of interruption, for the part of his argument concerning a barrister's work was becoming decidedly weak: 'My child, you will be with us yourself. Would we do anything which would hurt or offend you? Come now! be reasonable! We are not at a pleasure party. We are all grave men, entering gravely on an experiment which may unfold the wisdom of old times, and enlarge human knowledge indefinitely; which may put the minds of men on new tracks of thought and research. An experiment,' as he went on his voice deepened, 'which may be fraught with death to anyone of us – to us all! We know from what has been, that there are, or may be, vast and unknown dangers ahead of us, of which none in the house today may ever see the end. Take it, my child, that we are not acting lightly; but with all the gravity of deeply earnest men! Besides, my dear, whatever feelings you or any of us may have on the subject, it is necessary for the success of the experiment to unswathe her. I think that under any circumstances it would be necessary to remove the wrappings before she became again a live human being instead of a spiritualised corpse with an astral body. Were her original intention carried out, and did she come to new life within her mummy wrappings, it might be to exchange a coffin for a grave! She would die the death of the buried alive! But now, when she has voluntarily abandoned for the time her astral power, there can be no doubt on the subject.'

Margaret's face cleared. 'All right, Father!' she said as she kissed him. 'But oh! it seems a horrible indignity to a queen, and a woman.'

I was moving away to the staircase when she called to me: 'Where are you going?' I came back and took her hand and stroked it as I answered: 'I shall come back when the unrolling is over!' She looked at me long, and a faint suggestion of a smile came over her face as she said: 'Perhaps you had better stay, too! It may be useful to you in your work as a barrister!' She smiled out as she met my eyes: but in an instant she changed. Her face grew grave, and deadly white. In a far away voice she said: 'Father is right! It is a terrible occasion; we need all to be serious over it. But all the same – nay, for that very reason you had better stay, Malcolm! You may be glad, later on, that you were present tonight!'

My heart sank down, down, at her words; but I thought it better to say nothing. Fear was stalking openly enough amongst us already!

By this time Mr Trelawny, assisted by Mr Corbeck and Dr Winchester, had raised the lid of the ironstone sarcophagus which contained the mummy of the queen. It was a large one; but it was none too big. The mummy was both long and broad and high; and was of such weight that it was no easy task, even for the four of us, to lift it out. Under Mr Trelawny's direction we laid it out on the table prepared for it.

Then, and then only, did the full horror of the whole thing burst upon me! There, in the full glare of the light, the whole material and sordid side of death seemed staringly real. The outer wrappings, torn and loosened by rude touch, and with the colour either darkened by dust or worn light by friction, seemed creased as by rough treatment; the jagged edges of the wrapping-cloths looked fringed; the painting was patchy, and the varnish chipped. The coverings were evidently many, for the bulk was great. But through all, showed that unhidable human figure, which seems to look more horrible when partially concealed than at any other time. What was before us was death, and nothing else. All the romance and sentiment of fancy had disappeared. The two elder men, enthusiasts who had often done such work, were not disconcerted; and Dr Winchester seemed to hold himself in a business-like attitude, as if before the operating-table. But I felt low-spirited, and miserable, and ashamed; and besides I was pained and alarmed by Margaret's ghastly pallor.

Then the work began. The unrolling of the mummy cat had prepared me somewhat for it; but this was so much larger, and so infinitely more elaborate, that it seemed a different thing. Moreover, in addition to the ever present sense of death and humanity, there was a feeling of something finer in all this. The cat had been embalmed with coarser materials; here, all, when once the outer coverings were removed, was more delicately done. It seemed as if only the finest gums and spices had been used in this embalming. But there were the same surroundings, the same attendant red dust and pungent presence of bitumen; there was the same sound of rending which marked the tearing away of the bandages. There were an enormous number of these, and their bulk when opened was great. As the men unrolled them, I grew more and more excited. I did not take a part in it myself; Margaret had looked at me gratefully as I drew back. We clasped hands, and held each other hard. As the unrolling went on, the wrappings became finer, and the smell less laden with bitumen, but more pungent. We all, I think, began to feel it as though it caught or touched us in some special way. This, however, did not interfere with the work; it went on uninterruptedly. Some of the inner wrappings bore symbols or pictures. These were done sometimes wholly in pale green colour, sometimes in many colours; but always with a prevalence of green. Now and again Mr Trelawny or Mr Corbeck would point out some special drawing before laying the bandage on the pile behind them, which kept growing to a monstrous height.

At last we knew that the wrappings were coming to an end. Already the proportions were reduced to those of a normal figure of the manifest height of the queen, who was more than average tall. And as the end drew nearer, so Margaret's pallor grew; and her heart beat more and more wildly, till her breast heaved in a way that frightened me.

Just as her father was taking away the last of the bandages, he happened to look up and caught the pained and anxious look of her pale face. He paused, and taking her concern to be as to the outrage on modesty, said in a comforting way: 'Do not be uneasy, dear! See! there is nothing to harm you. The queen has on a robe. Ay, and a royal robe, too!'

The wrapping was a wide piece the whole length of the body. It being removed, a profusely full robe of white linen had appeared, covering the body from the throat to the feet.

And such linen! We all bent over to look at it.

Margaret lost her concern, in her woman's interest in fine stuff. Then the rest of us looked with admiration; for surely such linen was never seen by the eyes of our age. It was as fine as the finest silk. But never was spun or woven silk which lay in such gracious folds, constrict though they were by the close wrappings of the mummy cloth, and fixed into hardness by the passing of thousands of years.

Round the neck it was delicately embroidered in pure gold with tiny sprays of sycamore; and round the feet, similarly worked, was an endless line of lotus plants of unequal height, and with all the graceful abandon of natural growth.

Across the body, but manifestly not surrounding it, was a girdle of jewels. A wondrous girdle, which shone and glowed with all the forms and phases and colours of the sky!

The buckle was a great yellow stone, round of outline, deep and curved, as if a yielding globe had been pressed down. It shone and glowed, as though a veritable sun lay within; the rays of its light seemed to strike out and illumine all round. Flanking it were two great moonstones of lesser size, whose glowing, beside the glory of the sun-stone, was like the silvery sheen of moonlight.

And then on either side, linked by golden clasps of exquisite shape, was a line of flaming jewels, of which the colours seemed to glow. Each of these stones seemed to hold a living star, which twinkled in every phase of changing light.

Margaret raised her hands in ecstasy. She bent over to examine more closely; but suddenly drew back and stood fully erect at her grand height. She seemed to speak with the conviction of absolute knowledge as she said: 'That is no cerement! It was not meant for the clothing of death! It is a marriage robe!'

Mr Trelawny leaned over and touched the linen robe. He lifted a fold at the neck, and I knew from the quick intake of his breath that something had surprised him. He lifted yet a little more; and then he, too, stood back and pointed, saying: 'Margaret is right! That dress is not intended to be worn by the dead! See! her figure is not robed in it. It is but laid upon her.' He lifted the zone of jewels and handed it to Margaret. Then with both hands he raised the ample robe, and laid it across the arms which she extended in a natural impulse. Things of such beauty were too precious to be handled with any but the greatest care.

We all stood awed at the beauty of the figure which, save for the face cloth, now lay completely nude before us. Mr Trelawny bent over, and with hands that trembled slightly, raised this linen cloth which was of the same fineness as the robe. As he stood back and the whole glorious beauty of the queen was revealed, I felt a rush of shame sweep over me. It was not right that we should be there, gazing with irreverent eyes on such unclad beauty: it was indecent; it was almost sacrilegious! And yet the white wonder of that beautiful form was something to dream of. It was not like death at all; it was like a statue carven in ivory by the hand of a Praxiteles. There was nothing of that horrible shrinkage which death seems to effect in a moment. There was none of the wrinkled toughness which seems to be a leading characteristic of most mummies. There was not the shrunken attenuation of a body dried in the sand, as I had seen before in museums. All the pores of the body seemed to have been preserved in some wonderful way. The flesh was full and round, as in a living person; and the skin was as smooth as satin. The colour seemed extraordinary. It was like ivory, new ivory; except where the right arm, with shattered, bloodstained wrist and missing hand had lain bare to exposure in the sarcophagus for so many tens of centuries.

With a womanly impulse; with a mouth that drooped with pity, with eyes that flashed with anger, and cheeks that flamed, Margaret threw over the body the beautiful robe which lay across her arm. Only the face was then to be seen. This was more startling even than the body, for it seemed not dead, but alive. The eyelids were closed; but the long, black, curling lashes lay over on the cheeks. The nostrils, set in grave pride, seemed to have the repose which, when it is seen in life, is greater than the repose of death. The full, red lips, though the mouth was not open, showed the tiniest white line of pearly teeth within. Her hair, glorious in quantity and glossy black as the raven's wing, was piled in great masses over the white forehead, on which a few curling tresses strayed like tendrils. I was amazed at the likeness to Margaret, though I had had my mind prepared for such by Mr Corbeck's quotation of her father's statement. This woman – I could not think of her as a mummy or a corpse – was the image of Margaret as my eyes had first lit on her. The likeness was increased by the jewelled ornament which she wore in her hair, the 'disc and plumes', such as Margaret, too, had worn. It, too, was a glorious jewel; one noble pearl of moonlight lustre, flanked by carven pieces of moonstone.

Mr Trelawny was overcome as he looked. He quite broke down; and when Margaret flew to him and held him close in her arms and comforted him, I heard him murmur brokenly: 'It looks as if you were dead, my child!'

There was a long silence. I could hear without the roar of the wind, which was now risen to a tempest, and the furious dashing of the waves far below. Mr Trelawny's voice broke the spell: 'Later on we must try and find out the process of embalming. It is not like any that I know.' There does not seem to have been any opening cut for the withdrawing of the viscera and organs, which apparently remain intact within the body. Then, again, there is no moisture in the flesh; but its place is supplied with something else, as though wax or stearine had been conveyed into the veins by some subtle process. I wonder could it be possible that at that time they could have used paraffin. It might have been, by some process that we know not, pumped into the veins, where it hardened!'

Margaret, having thrown a white sheet over the queen's body, asked us to bring it to her own room, where we laid it on her bed. Then she sent us away, saying: 'Leave her alone with me. There are still many hours to pass, and I do not like to leave her lying there, all stark in the glare of light. This may be the Bridal she prepared for – the bridal of death; and at least she shall wear her pretty robes.'

When presently she brought me back to her room, the dead queen was dressed in the robe of fine linen with the embroidery of gold; and all her beautiful jewels were in place. Candles were lit around her, and white flowers lay upon her breast.

Hand in hand we stood looking at her for a while. Then with a sigh, Margaret covered her with one of her own snowy sheets. She turned away; and after softly closing the door of the room, went back with me to the others who had now come into the dining-room. Here we all began to talk over the things that had been, and that were to be.

Now and again I could feel that one or other of us was forcing conversation, as if we were not sure of ourselves. The long wait was beginning to tell on our nerves. It was apparent to me that Mr Trelawny had suffered in that strange trance more than we suspected, or than he cared to show. True, his will and his determination were as strong as ever; but the purely physical side of him had been weakened somewhat. It was indeed only natural that it should be. No man can go through a period of four days of absolute negation of life, without being weakened by it somehow.

As the hours crept by, the time passed more and more slowly. The other men seemed to get unconsciously a little drowsy. I wondered if in the case of Mr Trelawny and Mr Corbeck, who had already been under the hypnotic influence of the queen, the same dormance was manifesting itself. Dr Winchester had periods of distraction which grew longer and more frequent as the time wore on.

As to Margaret, the suspense told on her exceedingly, as might have been expected in the case of a woman. She grew paler and paler still; till at last about midnight, I began to be seriously alarmed about her. I got her to come into the library with me, and tried to make her lie down on a sofa for a little while. As Mr Trelawny had decided that the experiment was to be made exactly at the seventh hour after sunset, it would be as nearly as possible three o'clock in the morning when the great trial should be made. Even allowing a whole hour for the final preparations, we had still two hours of waiting to go through. I promised faithfully to watch her, and to awake her at any time she might name; but she would not hear of resting. She thanked me sweetly, and smiled as she did so. But she assured me that she was not sleepy, and that she was quite able to bear up; that it was only the suspense and excitement of waiting that made her pale. I agreed perforce, but I kept her talking of many things in the library for more than an hour; so that at last, when she insisted on going back to her father, I felt that I had at least done something to help her pass the time.

We found the three men sitting patiently in the dining-room in silence. With man's fortitude they were content to be still, when they felt they had done all in their power.

And so we waited.

The striking of two o'clock seemed to freshen us all up. Whatever shadows had been settling over us during the long hours preceding seemed to lift at once, and we all went about our separate duties alert and with alacrity. We looked first to the windows to see that they were closed; for now the storm raged so fiercely that we feared it might upset our plans which, after all, were based on perfect stillness. Then we got ready our respirators to put them on when the time should be close at hand. We had from the first arranged to use them, for we did not know whether some noxious fume might not come from the magic coffer when it should be opened. Somehow it never seemed to occur to any of us that there was any doubt as to its opening.

Then, under Margaret's guidance, we carried the body of Queen Tera, still clad in her Bridal robes, from her room into the cavern.

It was a strange sight, and a strange experience. The group of grave silent men carrying away from the lighted candles and the white flowers the white still figure, which looked like an ivory statue when through our moving the robe fell back.

We laid her in the sarcophagus, and placed the severed hand in its true position on her breast. Under it was laid the Jewel of Seven Stars, which Mr Trelawny had taken from the safe. It seemed to flash and blaze as he put it in its place. The glare of the electric lights shone cold on the great sarcophagus fixed ready for the final experiment – the great experiment, consequent on the researches during a lifetime of these two travelled scholars. Again, the startling likeness between Margaret and the mummy, intensified by her own extraordinary pallor, heightened the strangeness of it all.

When all was finally fixed, three-quarters of an hour had gone; for we were deliberate in all our doings. Margaret beckoned me, and I went with her to her room. There she did a thing which moved me strangely, and brought home to me keenly the desperate nature of the enterprise on which we were embarked. One by one, she blew out the candles carefully, and placed them back in their usual places. When she had finished she said to me: 'They are done with! Whatever comes – life or death – there will be no purpose in their using now!'

We returned to the cavern with a strange thrill as of finality. There was to be no going back now!

We put on our respirators, and took our places as had been arranged. I was to stand by the taps of the electric lights, ready to turn them off or on as Mr Trelawny should direct. His last caution to me to carry out his instructions exactly was almost like a menace; for he warned me that death to any or all of us might come from any error or neglect on my part. Margaret and Dr Winchester were to stand between the sarcophagus and the wall, so that they would not be between the mummy and the magic coffer. They were to note accurately all that should happen with regard to the queen.

Mr Trelawny and Mr Corbeck were to see the lamps lighted: and then to take their places, the former at the foot, the latter at the head, of the sarcophagus.

When the hands of the clock were close to the hour, they stood ready with their lit tapers, like gunners in old days with their linstocks.

For the few minutes that followed, the passing of time was a slow horror. Mr Trelawny stood with his watch in his hand, ready to give the signal.

The time approached with inconceivable slowness; but at last came the whirring of wheels which warns that the hour is at hand. The striking of the silver bell of the clock seemed to smite on our hearts like the knell of doom. One! Two! Three!

The wicks of the lamps caught, and I turned out the electric light. In the dimness of the struggling lamps, and after the bright glow of the electric light, the room and all within it took weird shape, and everything seemed in an instant to change. We waited, with our hearts beating. I know mine did; and I fancied I could hear the pulsation of the others. Without, the storm raged; the shutters of the narrow windows shook and strained and rattled, as though something was striving for entrance.

The seconds seemed to pass with leaden wings; it was as though all the world were standing still. The figures of the others stood out dimly, Margaret's white dress alone showing clearly in the gloom. The thick respirators, which we all wore, added to the strange appearance. The thin light of the lamps, as the two men bent over the coffer, showed Mr Trelawny's square jaw and strong mouth, and the brown, wrinkled face of Mr Corbeck. Their eyes seemed to glare in the light. Across the room Dr Winchester's eyes twinkled like stars, and Margaret's blazed like black suns.

Would the lamps never burn up!

It was only a few seconds in all till they did blaze up. A slow, steady light, growing more and more bright; and changing in colour from blue to crystal white. So they stayed for a couple of minutes, without any change in the coffer being noticeable. At last there began to appear all over it a delicate glow. This grew and grew, till it became like a blazing jewel; and then like a living thing, whose essence was light. Mr Trelawny and Mr Corbeck moved silently to their places beside the sarcophagus.

We waited and waited, our hearts seeming to stand still.

All at once there was a sound like a tiny muffled explosion, and the cover of the coffer lifted right up on a level plane a few inches; there was no mistaking anything now, for the whole cavern was full of light. Then the cover, staying fast at one side, rose slowly up on the other, as though yielding to some pressure of balance. I could not see what was within, for the risen cover stood between. The coffer still continued to glow; from it began to steal a faint greenish vapour which floated in the direction of the sarcophagus as though impelled or drawn towards it. I could not smell it fully on account of the respirator; but, even through that, I was conscious of a strange, pungent odour. The vapour got somewhat denser after a few seconds, and began to pass directly into the open sarcophagus. It was evident now that the mummied body had some attraction for it; and also that it had some effect on the body, for the sarcophagus slowly became illumined as though the body had begun to glow. I could not see within from where I stood, but I gathered from the faces of all the four watchers that something strange was happening.

I longed to run over and take a look for myself; but I remembered Mr Trelawny's solemn warning, and remained at my post.

The storm still thundered round the house, and I could feel the rock on which it was built tremble under the furious onslaught of the waves. The shutters strained as though the screaming wind without would in very anger have forced an entrance. In that dread hour of expectancy, when the forces of life and death were struggling for the mastery, imagination was awake. I almost fancied that the storm was a living thing, and animated with the wrath of the quick!

All at once the eager faces round the sarcophagus were bent forward. The look of speechless wonder in the eyes, lit by that supernatural glow from within the sarcophagus, had a more than mortal brilliance.

My own eyes were nearly blinded by the awful, paralysing light, so that I could hardly trust them. I saw something white rising up from the open sarcophagus. Something which appeared to my tortured eyes to be filmy, like a white mist. In the heart of this mist, which was cloudy and opaque like an opal, was something like a hand holding a fiery jewel flaming with many lights. As the fierce glow of the coffer met this new living light, the green vapour floating between them seemed like a cascade of brilliant points – a miracle of light!

But at that very moment there came a change. The fierce storm, battling with the shutters of the narrow openings, won victory. With the sound of a pistol shot, one of the heavy shutters broke its fastening and was hurled on its hinges back against the wall. In rushed a fierce blast which blew the flames of the lamps to and fro, and drifted the green vapour from its course.

On the very instant came a change in the outcome from the coffer. There was a moment's quick flame and a muffled explosion; and black smoke began to pour out. This got thicker and thicker with frightful rapidity, in volumes of ever-increasing density; till the whole cavern began to get obscure, and its outlines were lost. The screaming wind tore in and whirled it about. At a sign from Mr Trelawny Mr Corbeck went and closed the shutter and jammed it fast with a wedge.

I should have liked to help; but I had to wait directions from Mr Trelawny, who inflexibly held his post at the head of the sarcophagus. I signed to him with my hand, but he motioned me back. Gradually the figures of all close to the sarcophagus became indistinct in the smoke which rolled round them in thick billowy clouds. Finally, I lost sight of them altogether. I had a terrible desire to rush over so as to be near Margaret; but again I restrained myself. If the Stygian gloom continued, light would be a necessity of safety; and I was the guardian of the light! My anguish of anxiety as I stood to my post was almost unendurable.

The coffer was now but a dull colour; and the lamps were growing dim, as though they were being overpowered by the thick smoke. Absolute darkness would soon be upon us.

I waited and waited, expecting every instant to hear the command to turn up the light; but none came. I waited still, and looked with harrowing intensity at the rolling billows of smoke still pouring out of the casket whose glow was fading. The lamps sank down, and went out; one by one.

Finally, there was but one lamp alight, and that was dimly blue and flickering. I kept my eyes fixed towards Margaret, in the hope that I might see her in some lifting of the gloom; it was for her now that all my anxiety was claimed. I could just see her white frock beyond the dim outline of the sarcophagus.

Deeper and deeper grew the black mist, and its pungency began to assail my nostrils as well as my eyes. Now the volume of smoke coming from the coffer seemed to lessen, and the smoke itself to be less dense. Across the room I saw a movement of something white where the sarcophagus was. There were several such movements. I could just catch the quick glint of white through the dense smoke in the fading light; for now even the last lamp began to flicker with the quick leaps before extinction.

Then the last glow disappeared. I felt that the time had come to speak; so I pulled off my respirator and called out: 'Shall I turn on the light?' There was no answer. Before the thick smoke choked me, I called again, but more loudly: 'Mr Trelawny, shall I turn on the light? Answer me! If you do not forbid me, I shall turn it on!'

As there was no reply, I turned the tap. To my horror there was no response; something had gone wrong with the electric light! I moved, intending to run up the staircase to seek the cause, but I could now see nothing, all was pitch dark.

I groped my way across the room to where I thought Margaret was. As I went I stumbled across a body. I could feel by her dress that it was a woman. My heart sank; Margaret was unconscious, or perhaps dead. I lifted the body in my arms, and went straight forward till I touched a wall. Following it round I came to the stairway, and hurried up the steps with what haste I could make, hampered as I was with my dear burden. It may have been that hope lightened my task; but as I went the weight that I bore seemed to grow less as I ascended from the cavern.

I laid the body in the hall, and groped my way to Margaret's room, where I knew there were matches, and the candles which she had placed beside the queen. I struck a match; and oh! it was good to see the light. I lit two candles, and taking one in each hand, hurried back to the hall where I had left, as I had supposed, Margaret.

Her body was not there. But on the spot where I had laid her was Queen Tera's bridal robe, and surrounding it the girdle of wondrous gems. Where the heart had been, lay the Jewel of Seven Stars.

Sick at heart, and with a terror which has no name, I went down into the cavern. My two candles were like mere points of light in the black, impenetrable smoke. I put up again to my mouth the respirator which hung round my neck, and went to look for my companions.

I found them all where they had stood. They had sunk down on the floor, and were gazing upward with fixed eyes of unspeakable terror. Margaret had put her hands before her face, but the glassy stare of her eyes through her fingers was more terrible than an open glare.

I pulled back the shutters of all the windows to let in what air I could. The storm was dying away as quickly as it had risen, and now it only came in desultory puffs. It might well be quiescent; its work was done!

I did what I could for my companions; but there was nothing that could avail. There, in that lonely house, far away from aid of man, naught could avail.

It was merciful that I was spared the pain of hoping.

Revised Ending

When *The Jewel of the Seven Stars* was republished in 1912 the book was given a new and more optimistic ending. Here is that alternative ending.

THEN THE LAST SPARK of light disappeared, and through the Egyptian darkness I could see the faint line of white around the window blinds. I felt that the time had come to speak; so I pulled off my respirator and called out: 'Shall I turn up the light?' There was no answer; so before the thick smoke choked me, I called again but more loudly: 'Mr Trelawny, shall I turn up the light?' He did not answer; but from across the room I heard Margaret's voice, sounding as sweet and clear as a bell: 'Yes, Malcolm!' I turned the tap and the lamps flashed out. But they were only dim points of light in the midst of that murky ball of smoke. In that thick atmosphere there was little possibility of illumination. I ran across to Margaret, guided by her white dress, and caught hold of her and held her hand. She recognised my anxiety and said at once: 'I am all right.'

'Thank God!' I said. 'How are the others? Quick, let us open all the windows and get rid of this smoke!' To my surprise, she answered in a sleepy way: 'They will be all right. They won't get any harm.' I did not stop to enquire how or on what ground she formed such an opinion, but threw up the lower sashes of all the windows, and pulled down the upper. Then I threw open the door.

A few seconds made a perceptible change as the thick, black smoke began to roll out of the windows. Then the lights began to grow into strength and I could see the room. All the men were overcome. Beside the couch Dr Winchester lay on his back as though he had sunk down and rolled over; and on the further side of the sarcophagus, where they had stood, lay Mr Trelawny and Mr Corbeck. It was a relief to me to see that, though they were unconscious, all three were breathing heavily as though in a stupor. Margaret still stood behind the couch. She seemed at first to be in a partially dazed condition; but every instant appeared to get more command of herself. She stepped forward and helped me to raise her father and drag him close to a window. Together we placed the others similarly, and she flew down to the dining-room and returned with a decanter of brandy. This we proceeded to administer to them all in turn. It was not many minutes after we had opened the windows when all three were struggling back to consciousness. During this time my entire thoughts and efforts had been concentrated on their restoration; but now that this strain was off, I looked round the room to see what had been the effect of the experiment. The thick smoke had nearly cleared away; but the room was still misty and was full of a strange pungent acrid odour.

The great sarcophagus was just as it had been. The coffer was open, and in it, scattered through certain divisions or partitions wrought in its own substance, was a scattering of black ashes. Over all, sarcophagus coffer and, indeed, all in the room, was a sort of black film of greasy soot. I went over to the couch. The white sheet still lay over part of it; but it had been thrown back, as might be when one is stepping out of bed.

But there was no sign of Queen Tera! I took Margaret by the hand and led her over. She reluctantly left her father to whom she was administering, but she came docilely enough. I whispered to her as I held her hand: 'What has become of the queen? Tell me! You were close at hand, and must have seen if anything happened!' She answered me very softly: 'There was nothing that I could see. Until the smoke grew too dense I kept my eyes on the couch, but there was no change. Then, when all grew so dark that I could not see, I thought I heard a movement close to me. It might have been Dr Winchester who had sunk down overcome; but I could not be sure. I thought that it might be the queen waking, so I put down poor Silvio. I did not see what became of him; but I felt as if he had deserted me when I heard him mewing over by the door. I hope he is not offended with me!' As if in answer, Silvio came running into the room and reared himself against her dress, pulling it as though clamouring to be taken up. She stooped down and took him up and began to pet and comfort him.

I went over and examined the couch and all around it most carefully. When Mr Trelawny and Mr Corbeck recovered sufficiently, which they did quickly, though Dr Winchester took longer to come round, we went over it afresh. But all we could find was a sort of ridge of impalpable dust, which gave out a strange dead odour. On the couch lay the jewel of the disc and plumes which the queen had worn in her hair, and the Star Jewel which had words to command the gods.

Other than this we never got a clue to what had happened. There was just one thing which confirmed our idea of the physical annihilation of the mummy. In the sarcophagus in the hall, where we had placed the mummy of the cat, was a small patch of similar dust.

In the autumn Margaret and I were married. On the occasion she wore the mummy robe and zone and the jewel which Queen Tera had worn in her hair. On her breast, set in a ring of gold made like a twisted lotus stalk, she wore the strange Jewel of Seven Stars which held words to command the gods of all the worlds. At the marriage the sunlight streaming through the chancel windows fell on it, and it seemed to glow like a living thing.

The graven words may have been of efficacy; for Margaret holds to them, and there is no other life in all the world so happy as my own.

We often think of the great queen, and we talk of her freely. Once, when I said with a sigh that I was sorry she could not have waked into a new life in a new world, my wife, putting both her hands in mine and looking into my eyes with that far-away eloquent dreamy look which sometimes comes into her own, said lovingly: 'Do not grieve for her! Who knows, but she may have found the joy she sought? Love and patience are all that make for happiness in this world; or in the world of the past or of the future; of the living or the dead. She dreamed her dream; and that is all that any of us can ask!'

THE MUMMY

No EVENT OF any importance occurred to our travellers in the course of their aerial voyage. They were too well provided with all kinds of necessaries to have any occasion to rest by the way, and in an incredibly short space of time they were hovering over Egypt. Different, however, how different from the Egypt of the nineteenth century, was the fertile country which now lay like a map beneath their feet! Improvement had turned her gigantic steps towards its once deserted plains; commerce had waved her magic wand; and towns and cities, manufactaries and canals, spread in all directions. No more did the Nile overflow its banks: a thousand channels were cut to receive its waters. No longer did the moving sands of the Desert rise in mighty waves, threatening to overwhelm the wayworn traveller: macadamised turnpike roads supplied their place, over which post-chaises, with anti-attritioned wheels, bowled at the rate of fifteen miles an hour. Steam boats glided down the canals, and furnaces raised their smoky heads amidst groves of palm trees; whilst iron railways intersected orange groves, and plantations of dates and pomegranates might be seen bordering excavations intended for coal pits. Colonies of English and Americans peopled the country, and produced a population that swarmed like bees over the land, and surpassed in numbers, even the wondrous throngs of the ancient Mizraim race; whilst industry and science changed desolation into plenty, and had converted barren plains into fertile kingdoms.

Amidst all these revolutions, however, the Pyramids still raised their gigantic forms, towering to the sky; unchanged, unchangeable, grand, simple, and immoveable, fit symbols of that majestic nature they were intended to represent, and seeming to look down with contempt upon the ephemeral structures with which they were surrounded; as though they would have said, had utterance been permitted to them – 'Avaunt, ye nothings of the day! Respect our dignity and sink into your original obscurity; for, know that we alone are monarchs of the plains.' Indestructible, however, as they had proved themselves, even their granite sides had not been able entirely to resist the corroding influence of the smoke with which they were now surrounded, and a slight crumbling announced the first outward symptom of decay. Still, however, though blackened and disfigured, they shone stupendous monuments of former greatness; and Edric and his tutor gazed upon them with an awe that for some moments deprived them of utterance.

The doctor, however, who was too fond of reasoning ever long to remain willingly silent, after surveying them a few minutes, broke forth as follows: 'What noble piles! What majesty and grandeur they display in their formation, and yet what dignified simplicity! Can the imagination of man conceive anything more sublime than the thought that they have stood thus, frowning in awful magnificence, perhaps since the very creation of the world, without equals, without even competitors – mocking the feeble efforts of man to divine their origin, and seeing generation after generation pass away, whilst they still remain immutable, and involved in the same deep and unfathomable mystery as at first?'

'It is very strange,' observed Edric, 'that, in this age of speculation and discovery, nothing certain should be known concerning them.'

'It is,' returned the doctor: 'but the thick mysterious veil that has rested upon them for so many ages, seems not intended to be removed by mortal hands. They remind one of the sublime inscription upon the temple of the goddess, Isis, at Sais: 'I am whatever was, whatever is, and whatever shall be; but no mortal has, as yet, presumed to raise the veil that covers me."

'Your quotation is apt, doctor,' resumed Edric, 'for both relate to nature. Indeed, nature appears to be the deity which the ancient Egyptians worshipped, under all the various forms in which she presents herself; and their strange and animal deities were but reverenced as her symbols. It was nature which they worshipped as Isis; it was nature that was typified in the Pyramids; and the good taste of the Egyptians made them prefer the simple, the majestic, and the sublime, in those works which they destined to last for ages. Formerly, from the immensity of their population, and high state of their civilisation, labour was so divided, and consequently so lightened, that multitudes were enabled to exist exempt from toil. These persons, devoting themselves to study, became *initiati*; and either enrolled themselves amongst the priesthood, or passed their lives in making themselves masters of the most abstract sciences. The consequences were natural: they followed up the ramifications of creation to their original source; they penetrated into the most profound secrets of nature, and traced all her wonders in her works: aware, however, of the taste of the vulgar for anything above their comprehension, and of the natural craving of the human mind for mystery, they wrapped the discoveries they had made in a deep impenetrable veil, and concealed awful and sublime significations under the meanest and most disgusting images.'

'You are right,' said the doctor, 'in your observations upon the religion of the ancient Egyptians; but it does not appear to me that the Pyramids were erected by them.'

'What! I suppose you draw your conclusions from the want of hieroglyphics in their principal chambers; and, from what Herodotus says of their having been erected by a shepherd, you think they were the work of the Pallic race.'

'No; though I allow much may be said in favour of that hypothesis, particularly as Herodotus says the kings under whom they were erected, ordered all the Egyptian temples to be closed, which we know the shepherd or Pallic sovereigns did; but I cannot imagine that an ignorant, Goth-like race of shepherds, men accustomed to live in tents or in the open air, and possessing no talents but for war, were capable of constructing such immense piles. No, no, the Pyramids required gigantic conceptions, highly cultivated minds, and unwearied perseverance; all qualities quite incompatible with a warlike wandering race. I do not think the Palli were capable of imagining such structures, much less of constructing them. I think they were the work of evil spirits.'

'Evil spirits!' exclaimed Edric.

'Yes,' returned the doctor. 'We are told that the evil spirits, after their expulsion from paradise, were under the command of the Sultan, or Soliman Giam ben Giam, as he is called by Arabic writers, but who is supposed to have been the same as Cheops; and I think that he employed them in this vast work.'

'I do not know by what analysis etymologists can draw the name of Cheops from that of Giam ben Giam' responded Edric, 'but supposing the fact to be correct, that they designated the same person, I think it only proves more strongly my hypothesis; for the Palli came from Mount Caucasus, where the evil spirits were said to have been enchained, and if Cheops was a Pallic king, it is possible the Egyptians might poetically call their conquerors evil spirits.'

'That is a good idea, Edric; though I do not think it by any means certain that Cheops was a Pallic king. However, we shall soon be able to see his tomb, and judge for ourselves; for we have now approached near enough to the Pyramids to descend. Foh! what a smoke and what a noise! It is enough to rouse the mummies from their slumbers before their appointed time, and without the aid of galvanism. Have you opened the valves, Edric? Oh yes! I perceive we are getting lower; we will not lose a moment before we visit the Pyramid. But what a crowd of brutes are assembled to witness our arrival! They stare as though they had never seen a balloon before. Egypt is certainly a fine country, but the inhabitants are a century behind us in civilisation.'

An immense crowd had gathered together to witness the descent of our travellers, and they did indeed stand staring, lost in stupid astonishment at the strange sight that presented itself; for though the Egyptian people had occasionally seen balloons, they had never before beheld one made of Indian rubber. The odd figure of the doctor, too, amused them exceedingly, as he sat wrapped up in the most dignified manner in an asbestos cloak, his bob-wig pushed a little on one side from the heat of the weather and the warmth of his argument; his round, red, oily face attempting to look solemn, and his little fat, punchy figure trying to assume an air of majesty. The Egyptians were amazingly struck with this apparition, and being, like most colonists, somewhat conceited and not very ceremonious in their manners, they looked at him a few minutes in silence, and then burst into immoderate fits of laughter.

The doctor was exceedingly indignant at this rude reception, and rising, shook his fist at them in anger; a manoeuvre that only redoubled the mirth of the unpolished Egyptians, whose peals of laughter now became so tremendous, that they actually shook the skies, and occasioned a most unpleasant vibration in the balloon. Edric, who was almost as much annoyed as the doctor, had yet sufficient self-command to continue calmly making preparations for his descent; and without taking the least notice of the crowd below, he screwed the top upon the propelling vapour-bottle; he let the inflammable air escape from the balloon, which rapidly collapsed as they approached the earth, and throwing out their patent spring grappling-irons, they caught one of the lower stones of the Great Pyramid, and in a few moments the car in which our travellers were sitting, was safely moored at a convenient distance from the earth for them to alight. Edric now unloosed the descending ladder, and reverentially assisted the doctor, who was encumbered with his long cloak, to reach terra firma in safety – amidst the bustle and exclamations of the crowd, who thronged round them, expressing their wonder and astonishment audibly, in broad English.

'Where the deuce did this spring from?' cried one; 'the car would load a wagon!'

'And what is gone with the balloon?' said another; 'it is clean vanished!'

'Well, I never saw such a thing in all my life before!' exclaimed a third; 'I think they must be come from the moon.'

'Hush! hush!' cried an old gentleman bustling amongst them, who seemed as one having authority. 'What's the matter? What's the matter?'

'We are strangers, Sir,' said Edric, advancing and addressing him. 'We come here to see the wonders of your country, and we wish to explore the Pyramids – but the reception we have met with – '

'Say no more – say no more!' interrupted the worthy justice, for such he was. 'Get about your business, you rapscallions, or I'll read the riot act! Here, Gregory, call out the *posse comitatus*, and set a guard of constables to keep watch over these gentlemen's balloon, whilst they go to explore the Pyramids. Eh, but where is the balloon? I don't see it. I hope neither of the gentlemen has put it in his pocket!' laughing at his own wit.

'No, Sir,' returned Edric, smiling, 'though it is a feat which might easily be accomplished, for that is our balloon,' pointing to the caoutchouc bottle, now shrunk to its original dimensions.

'Very strange, that!' said the justice; 'very curious, very curious indeed! Well, gentlemen, if you wish to proceed immediately, you'll want a guide of course. These cottages at the foot of the Pyramids are all inhabited by guides, who get their living by showing the sights. They are sad rogues, most of them, but I can recommend you to one who is a very honest man. Here, Samuel,' continued he, knocking against a small door, 'Samuel, I say!'

Samuel made his appearance, in the guise of a tall, raw-boned, stupid-looking fellow, with a pair of immensely broad stooping shoulders, which looked as though he could have relieved Atlas occasionally of his burthen, without much trouble to himself. Coming forth from his hut in an awkward shambling pace, he scratched his head, and demanded what his honour was pleased to want.

'You must show these gentlemen the Pyramids,' said the justice.

'Ay, that I will with pleasure!' returned Samuel. 'I've got my living by showing them these fifty years, man and boy; and I know every crink and cranny of them, though I'm old now and somewhat lame. So walk this way, gentlemen.'

'We are very much obliged to you, Sir,' said the doctor, bowing to the justice; who was in fact one of those good-natured, busy, bustling men, who are always better pleased to transact any other person's business than their own; and are never so happy as when a new arrival gives them an opportunity of showing off their consequence. Indeed, there is a pleasure in showing wonders to a stranger, that only those who have little else to occupy their minds can properly estimate: a man of this kind feels his self-love gratified by the superiority his local knowledge gives him over a stranger; and as it is, perhaps, the only chance he ever can have of showing superiority, they must be unreasonable who blame him for making the most of it. Justice Freemantle was accordingly exceedingly delighted with travellers who seemed disposed to submit implicitly to his dictation; and he returned a most gracious reply to the doctor's thanks.

'Don't mention it! Don't mention it, my dear Sir!' said he; 'I am never so happy as when I can make myself useful. Is there anything else I can do for you? You may command me, I assure you; and you may depend upon it, no injury shall be done to your luggage, whilst you are away.'

'What a very civil, obliging, good-natured old gentleman!' said the doctor, as they walked towards the entrance of the Pyramids; 'I declare he almost reconciles me to the country, though, I own, I thought at first the people were the greatest brutes I had ever met with.'

'Which Pyramid does your honour wish to see?' asked the guide.

'That which contains the tomb of Cheops, man!' cried the doctor solemnly; who, encumbered with his long cloak, and loaded with his walking-stick and galvanic battery, had some difficulty in getting on.

'Won't your honour let me carry that pole and that box?' said the man; 'you'd get on a surprising deal better, if you would.'

'Avaunt, wretch!' exclaimed the doctor, 'nor offer to touch with thy profane fingers the immortal instruments of science.'

The man stared, but fell back, and the whole party walked on in perfect silence.

In the mean time, Edric had advanced before his companions, completely lost in meditation. A crowd of conflicting thoughts rushed through his mind; and now, when he found himself at the very goal of his wishes, the daring nature of the purpose he had so long entertained, seemed to strike him for the first time, and he trembled at the consequences that might attend the completion of his desires. With his arms folded on his breast, he stood gazing on the Pyramids, whilst his ideas wandered uncontrolled through the boundless regions of space.

'And what am I,' thought he, 'weak, feeble worm that I am who dare seek to penetrate into the awful secrets of my Creator? Why should I wish to restore animation to a body now resting in the quiet of the tomb? What right have I to renew the struggles, the pains, the cares, and the anxieties of mortal life? How can I tell the fearful effects that may be produced by the gratification of my unearthly longing? May I not revive a creature whose wickedness may involve

mankind in misery? And what if my experiment should fail, and if the
moment when I expect my rash wishes to be accomplished, the hand
of Almighty vengeance should strike me to the earth, and heap
molten fire on my brain to punish my presumption!'

The sound of human voices, as the doctor and the guide approached, grated harshly on the nerves of Edric, already overstrained
by the awful nature of the thoughts in which he had been indulging,
and he turned away involuntarily, to escape the interruption he
dreaded, quite forgetting for the moment from whom the sounds
most probably proceeded.

'Lord have mercy on us!' said the guide; 'I declare that gentleman
looks as if he were beside himself; and see there if he hasn't walked
right by the entrance to the Pyramid without seeing it! Sir! Sir!'
halloed he.

Excessively annoyed, but recalled to his recollection by these
shouts, Edric returned.

'These Pyramids are wonderful piles,' said the doctor, as he
stumbled forward to meet him. 'I really had no adequate conception
of the enormity of their size. They did not even look half so large at
a distance as they do now.'

'Immense masses seldom do,' replied Edric, compelling himself
with difficulty to speak.

'True,' returned the doctor; 'the simplicity and uniformity of their
figures deceive the eyes, and it is only when we approach them that
we feel their stupendous magnitude and our own insignificance!'

'They give an amazing idea of the grandeur of the ancient kings of
Egypt,' said Edric, without exactly knowing what he was saying.
'Their palaces must have been superb, if they had such mausoleums.'

'How absurdly you reason, Edric!' replied the doctor peevishly; for,
being annoyed with his burthens and his cloak, he was not in a humour
to bear contradiction. 'I thought we had settled that question before.
In the first place, I think it very doubtful whether the Egyptians had
anything to do with the building of these monuments; and if they had,
I believe they were meant for temples, not mausoleums; and in the
next place, even if they were intended for tombs, their greatness
affords no argument for the splendour of the surrounding palaces; as
the Egyptians were celebrated for the superiority of their burying-
places, and for the immense sums they expended upon them. Indeed,
you know, ancient writers say they went so far as to call the houses of
the living only inns, whilst they considered tombs as everlasting
habitations – a circumstance, by the way, that strongly corroborates
my hypothesis, at least as far as their opinions go; as it seems to imply

that both soul and body were designed to remain there.'

They had now entered the Pyramid, and were proceeding with infinite difficulty along a low, dark, narrow passage.

'Observe, Edric,' said the doctor, 'how the difficulty and obscurity of these winding passages confirm my opinion: you know, the religion of the ancient Egyptians, like that of the ancient Hindus, was one of penances and personal privations; and, granting that to be the case, what can be more simple than that the passages the *initiati* had to traverse before they reached the adytum, should be painful and difficult of access. Besides this, as, you know, the bones of a bull, no doubt those of the god Apis, were found in a sarcophagus in the second Pyramid, it seems probable that it was sacred to his worship: and its vicinity to the Nile, which was indispensable to the temples of Apis, as, when it was time for him to die, he was drowned in its waters, confirms the fact. Indeed, I am only surprised that any human being, possessing a grain of common sense, can entertain a single doubt upon the subject.'

'How do you account for the tomb we are about to visit being placed in the Pyramid, if you think they were only designed for temples?' asked Edric.

'The question is futile,' said the doctor. 'A strange fancy prevailed in former times, that burying the dead in consecrated places, particularly in temples intended for divine worship, would scare away the evil spirits, and the practice actually prevailed in England even as lately as the nineteenth or twentieth century. Indeed, it was not till after the country had been almost depopulated by the dreadfully infectious disease which prevailed about two hundred years ago, that a law was passed to prevent the interment of the dead in London, and that those previously buried in and near the churches there, were exhumed and placed in cemeteries beyond the walls.'

Edric did not reply, for in fact his ideas were so absorbed by the solemn object before him, that it was painful for him to speak, and the doctor's ill-timed reasoning created such an irritation of his nerves, that he found it required the utmost exertion of his self-command to endure it patiently. The passage they were traversing, now became higher and wider, shelving off occasionally into chambers or recesses on each side, till they approached a kind of vestibule, in the centre of which yawned a deep, dark, gloomy-looking cavity, like a well.

'We must descend that shaft,' said the guide, 'and that will lead us to the tomb of King Cheops; but as the road is dark, and rather dangerous, we had better, each of us, take a torch.'

As he spoke, he drew some torches from a niche where they were deposited, and began to illuminate them from his own. The red glare of the torches flashed fearfully on the massive walls of the Pyramid, throwing part of their enormous masses into deep shadow, as they rose in solemn and sublime dignity around, and seemed frowning upon the presumptuous mortals who had dared to invade their recesses, whilst the deep pit beneath their feet seemed to yawn wide to engulf them in its abyss. Edric's heart beat thick: it throbbed till he even fancied its pulsations audible; and a strange, mysterious thrilling of anxiety, mingled with a wild, undefinable delight, ran through his frame. A few short hours, and his wishes would be gratified, or set at rest for ever. The doctor and the guide had already begun to descend, and their figures seemed changed and unearthly as the gleams of the torches fell upon them. Edric gazed for a moment, and then followed with feelings worked up almost to frenzy by the over-excitement of his nerves; whilst the hollow sounds that re-echoed from the walls, as they struck against them in their descent, thrilled through his whole frame.

No one spoke; and after proceeding for some time along the narrow path, or rather ledge, formed on the sides of the cavity, which gradually shelved downwards, the guide suddenly stopped, and touching a secret spring, a solid block of granite slowly detached itself from the wall, and, rising majestically like the portcullis of an ancient fortress, showed the entrance to a dark and dreary cave. The guide advanced, followed by our travellers, into a gloomy vaulted apartment, where longs vistas of ponderous arches stretched on every side, till their termination was lost in darkness, and gave a feeling of immensity and obscurity to the scene.

'I will wait here,' said the guide; 'and here, if you please, you had better leave your torches. That avenue will lead you to the tomb.'

The travellers obeyed; and the guide, placing himself in a recess in the wall, extinguished all the torches except one, which he shrouded so as to leave the travellers in total darkness. Nothing could be now more terrific than their situation: immured in the recesses of the tomb, involved in darkness, and their bosoms throbbing with hopes that they scarcely dared avow even to themselves; with faltering steps they proceeded slowly along the path the guide had pointed out, shuddering even at the hollow echo of their own footsteps, which alone broke the solemn silence that reigned throughout these fearful regions of terror and the tomb.

Suddenly, a vivid light flashed upon them, and, as they advanced, they found it proceeded from torches placed in the hands of two colossal figures, who, placed in a sitting posture, seemed guarding an enormous portal, surmounted by the image of a fox, the constant guardian of an Egyptian tomb. The immense dimensions and air of grandeur and repose about these colossi had something in it very imposing; and our travellers felt a sensation of awe creep over them as they gazed upon their calm unmoved features, so strikingly emblematic of that immutable nature which they were doubtless placed there to typify.

It was with feelings of indescribable solemnity, that the doctor and Edric passed through this majestic portal, and found themselves in an apartment gloomily illumined by the light shed faintly from an inner chamber, through ponderous brazen gates beautifully wrought. The light thus feebly emitted, showed that the room in which they stood was dedicated to Typhon, the evil spirit, as his fierce and savage types covered the walls; and images of his symbols, the crocodile and the dragon, placed beneath the shadow of the brazen gates, and dimly seen by the imperfect light, seemed starting into life, and grimly to forbid the farther advance of the intruders. Our travellers shuddered, and opening with trembling hand the ponderous gates, they entered the tomb of Cheops.

In the centre of the chamber, stood a superb, highly ornamented sarcophagus of alabaster, beautifully wrought: over this hung a lamp of wondrous workmanship, supplied by a potent mixture, so as to burn for ages unconsumed; thus awfully lighting up with perpetual flame the solemn mansions of the dead, and typifying life eternal even in the silent tomb. Around the room, on marble benches, were arranged mummies simply dried, apparently those of slaves; and close to the sarcophagus was placed one contained in a case, which the doctor approached to examine. This was supposed to be that of Sores, the confidant and prime-minister of Cheops. The chest that enclosed the body was splendidly ornamented with embossed gilt leather, whilst the parts not otherwise covered were stained with red and green curiously blended, and of a vivid brightness.

The mighty Phtah, the Jupiter of the Egyptians, spread its widely extended wings over the head, grasping in his monstrous claws a ring, the emblem of eternity; whilst below, the vulture-form of Rhea proclaimed the deceased a votary of that powerful deity; and on the sides were innumerable hieroglyphics. The doctor removed the lid, and shuddered as the crimson tinge of the everlasting lamp fell upon the hideous and distorted features thus suddenly exhibited to view. This sepulchral light, indeed, added unspeakable horror to the scene, and its peculiar glare threw such a wild and demoniac expression on the dark lines and ghastly lineaments of the mummies, that even the doctor felt his spirits depressed, and a supernatural dread creep over his mind as he gazed upon them.

In the mean time, Edric had stood gazing upon the sarcophagus of Cheops, the sides of which were beautifully sculptured with groups of figures, which, from the peculiar light thrown upon them, seemed to possess all the force and reality of life. On one side was represented an armed and youthful warrior bearing off in his arms a beautiful female, on whom he gazed with the most passionate fondness. He was pursued by a crowd of people and soldiers, who seemed to be rending the air with vehement exclamations against his violence, and endeavouring in vain to arrest his progress; whilst in the background appeared an old man, who was tearing his hair and wringing his hands in ineffectual rage against the ravisher.

The other side presented the same old man wrestling with the youthful warrior, who had just overpowered and stabbed him; the helpless victim raising his withered hands and failing eyes to heaven as he fell, as though to implore vengeance upon his murderer, whilst the crimson current was fast ebbing from his bosom. The dying look and agony of the old man were forcibly depicted, whilst upon the features of the youthful warrior glowed the fury of a demon.

The sarcophagus was supported by the lion, emblem of royalty, the symbol of the solar god Horus; and above it sat the majestic hawk of Osiris, gazing upwards, and unmindful of the subtle crocodile of Typhon, that, crouching under its feet, was just about to seize its breast in its enormous jaws. Neither of the travellers had as yet spoken, for it seemed like sacrilege to disturb the awful stillness that prevailed even by a whisper. Indeed, the solemn aspect of the chamber thrilled through every nerve, and they moved slowly, gliding along with noiseless steps as though they feared prematurely to break the slumbers of the mighty dead it contained. They gazed, however, with deep, but undefinable interest upon the sculptured mysteries of the tomb of Cheops, vainly endeavouring to decipher their meaning; whilst, as they found their efforts useless, a secret voice seemed to whisper in their bosoms – 'And shall finite creatures like these, who cannot even explain the signification of objects presented before their eyes, presume to dive into the mysteries of their creator's will? Learn wisdom by this omen, nor seek again to explore secrets above your comprehension! Retire, whilst it is yet time; soon it will be too late!'

Edric started at his own thoughts, as the fearful warning, 'soon it will be too late,' rang in his ears; and a fearful presentiment of evil weighed heavily upon his soul. He turned to look upon the doctor, but he had already seized the lid of the sarcophagus, and, with a daring hand, removed it from its place, displaying in the fearful light the royal form that lay beneath. For a moment, both Edric and the doctor paused, not daring to survey it; and when they did, they both uttered an involuntary cry of astonishment, as the striking features of the mummy met their eyes, for both instantly recognised the sculptured warrior in his traits. Yes, it was indeed the same, but the fierce expression of fiery and ungoverned passions depicted upon the countenance of the marble figure, had settled down to a calm, vindictive and concentrated hatred upon that of its mummy prototype in the tomb.

Awful, indeed, was the gloom that sat upon that brow, and bitter the sardonic smile that curled those haughty lips. All was perfect as though life still animated the form before them, and it had only reclined there to seek a short repose. The dark eyebrows, the thick raven hair which hung upon the forehead, and the snow-white teeth seen through the half-open lips, forbade the idea of death; whilst the fiend-like expression of the features made Edric shudder, as he recollected the purpose that brought him to the tomb, and he trembled at the thought of awakening such a fearful being from the torpor of the grave to all the renewed energies of life.

'Let us go,' whispered the doctor to his pupil, in a low, deep, and unearthly tone, fearfully different from his usually cheerful voice. Edric started at the sound, for it seemed the last sad warning of his better genius, before it abandoned him for ever. The die, however, was cast, and it was too late to recede. Edric felt worked up to frenzy by the overwrought feelings of the moment. He seized the machine, and resolutely advanced towards the sarcophagus, whilst the doctor gazed upon him with a horror that deprived him of either speech or motion.

Innumerable folds of red and white linen, disposed alternately, swathed the gigantic limbs of the royal mummy; and upon his breast lay a piece of metal, shining like silver, and stamped with the figure of a winged globe. Edric attempted to remove this, but recoiled with horror, when he found it bend beneath his fingers with an unnatural softness; whilst, as the flickering light of the lamp fell upon the face of the mummy, he fancied its stern features relaxed into a ghastly laugh of scornful mockery. Worked up to desperation, he applied the wires of the battery and put the apparatus in motion, whilst a demoniac laugh of derision appeared to ring in his ears, and the surrounding mummies seemed starting from their places and dancing in unearthly merriment. Thunder now roared in tremendous peals through the Pyramids, shaking their enormous masses to the foundation, and vivid flashes of light darted round in quick succession.

Edric stood aghast amidst this fearful convulsion of nature. A horrid creeping seemed to run through every vein, every nerve feeling as though drawn from its extremity, and wrapped in icy chillness round his heart. Still, he stood immoveable, and gazing intently on the mummy, whose eyes had opened with the shock, and were now fixed on those of Edric, shining with supernatural lustre. In vain Edric attempted to rouse himself; in vain to turn away from that withering glance. The mummy's eyes still pursued him with their ghastly brightness; they seemed to possess the fabled fascination of those of the rattlesnake, and though he shrank from their gaze, they still glared horribly upon him. Edric's senses swam, yet he could not move from the spot; he remained fixed, chained, and immoveable, his eyes still riveted upon those of the mummy, and every thought absorbed in horror.

Another fearful peal of thunder now rolled in lengthened vibrations above his head, and the mummy rose slowly, his eyes still fixed upon those of Edric, from his marble tomb. The thunder pealed louder and louder. Yells and groans seemed mingled with its roar; the sepulchral lamp, flared with redoubled fierceness, flashing its rays around in quick succession, and with vivid brightness; whilst by its horrid and uncertain glare, Edric saw the mummy stretch out its withered hand, as though to seize him. He saw it rise gradually – he heard the dry, bony fingers rattle as it drew them forth – he felt its tremendous grip – human nature could bear no more – his senses were rapidly deserting him; he felt, however, the fixed, steadfast eyes of Cheops still glowing upon his failing orbs, as the lamp gave a sudden flash, and then all was darkness! The brazen gates now shut with a fearful clang, and Edric, uttering a shriek of horror, fell senseless upon the ground, whilst his shrill cry of anguish rang wildly through the marble vaults, till its re-echoes seemed like the yell of demons joining in fearful mockery.

How long he lay in this state he knew not; but when he reopened his eyes, for the moment, he fancied all that had passed a dream. As his senses returned he recollected where he was, and shuddered to find himself yet in that place of horrors. All now was dark, except a faint gleam that shone feebly through the half-open gates; these ponderous portals slowly unclosed, and the form of a man, wrapped in a large cloak, and bearing a torch, entered, peering around as it advanced, as though half afraid to proceed. Edric's feelings were too highly wrought to bear any fresh horrors, and he shrieked in agony as the figure approached. The sound of his voice subdued the terrors of the intruder, and the doctor, for it was he, shouted with joy, as he rushed forward to embrace him.

'Edric! Edric! thank God he is alive!' exclaimed he. 'Edric! My beloved Edric! for God's sake, let us leave this den of horrors! Come, come!'

Reassured by his tutor's voice, Edric arose, and taking one hasty, shuddering glance around as the light gleamed on the sarcophagus, he hurried out of the tomb. Neither he nor the doctor spoke as they passed through the vestibule, where the colossal figures still sat in awful majesty; indeed, as their torches were extinguished, their gigantic forms looked still more terrific than before, from the wavering and indistinct light thrown upon them. Edric shuddered as he looked, and hurried on with hasty strides to the place where they had left the guide, whom they found kneeling in a corner, hiding his face in his hands, and roaring out, 'O Lord, defend us! Heaven have mercy upon us! Lord have mercy upon us! Heaven have mercy upon us!'

'He has been in that state for more than an hour,' said the doctor mournfully, 'for, after I came to myself, I tried to rouse him, but all to no purpose.'

'Then you also fainted?' said Edric, with difficulty compelling himself to speak.

'Why,' resumed the doctor with some hesitation, 'I don't know that you can exactly call it fainting; but the fact was, when I saw you touch the plate upon the mummy's breast, and start back, looking so horribly frightened, I – I thought I had better call for assistance; so as I ran for that purpose; somehow or other I fell down, and lay insensible I don't know how long. When I came to myself, I tried to rouse the guide, and when I found I could not, I came to seek you. But now that we are both recovered, I really don't know what is to become of us; for this fellow will never be able to show us the way out, and I'm sure I don't know the road.'

'Let us try to find it, at any rate,' said Edric faintly.

'Oh, for God's sake, take me too!' screamed the guide. 'If you have any mercy, don't leave me in this fearful place.'

'Take the light then, and lead the way,' said Edric. The guide obeyed, shaking in every limb, and every now and then casting a terrified look behind, whilst the quivering flame of the torch betrayed the unsteadiness of the trembling hands that bore it. In this manner they proceeded, starting at every sound, and frightened even at their own shadows, without daring to stop till they reached the plain.

'Thank God!' cried the doctor, the moment they stepped out of the Pyramid; looking round him, gasping for breath, and inhaling the fresh air with rapture.

'Thank God!' reiterated Edric and the guide, as they walked

rapidly towards the place where they had left their balloon. When arrived there, however, they looked for it in vain; and fancying themselves under the influence of a delusion, they rubbed their eyes, and again looked, but without success.

'Dear me, it is very strange!' said the doctor; 'this is certainly the place, and yet, where can it be?'

'Where, indeed!' repeated Edric, 'horrors and unaccountable incidents environ us at every step; I am not naturally timid, yet – '

'Ah!' screamed the doctor, as he tumbled over a man lying with his face upon the ground. 'Oh!' groaned he, as Edric and the guide with difficulty raised him; 'would to heaven I were safe at home again in my own comfortable little study, indulging in pleasing anticipations of that, which I find is anything in the world but pleasing in reality.'

The mummy thus strangely recalled to life, was indeed Cheops! And horrible were the sensations that throbbed through every nerve as returning consciousness brought with it all the pangs of his former existence, and renewed circulation thrilled through every vein. His first impulse was to quit the tomb in which he had been so long immured, and seek again the regions of light and day. Instinct seemed to guide him to this; for, as yet, a mist hung over his faculties, and ideas thronged in painful confusion through his mind, which he was incapable of either arranging or analysing.

When, however, he reached the plain, light and air seemed to revive him and restore his scattered senses; and, gazing wildly around, he exclaimed, 'Where am I? what place is this? Methinks all seems wondrous, new, and strange! Where is my father? And where! oh, where, is my Arsinöe? Alas, alas!' continued he wildly; 'I had forgotten – I hoped it was a dream, a fearful dream, for methinks I have been long asleep. Was it, indeed, reality? Are all, all gone? And was that hideous scene true? – Those horrors, which still haunt my memory like a ghastly vision? Speak! speak!' continued he, his voice rising in thrilling energy as he spoke, 'Speak! let me hear the sound of another's voice, before my brain is lost in madness. Have I entered Hades, or am I still on earth? – yes, yes, it is still the earth, for there the mighty Pyramid I caused to be erected towers behind me. Yet where is Memphis? Where are my forts and palaces? What a dark, smoky mass of buildings now surrounds me! Can this be the once proud queen of cities? I see no palaces, no temples – Memphis is fallen. The mighty barrier that protected her splendour from the waste of waters, must have been swept away by the encroaching inroads of the swelling Nile. But is this the Nile?' continued he, looking wildly upon the river; 'sure I must be deceived. It is the fatal river of the dead. No papyrine boats glide smoothly on its surface; but strange, infernal vessels, vomiting forth volumes of fire and smoke. Holy Osiris, defend me! Where am I? Where have I been? A misty veil seems thrown upon the face of nature. Awake, awake!' cried he, with a scream of agony; 'set me free; I did not mean to slay him!'

Then throwing himself violently upon the ground, he lay for some moments, apparently insensible. Then slowly rising, he looked at himself, and a deep, unnatural shuddering convulsed his whole frame. His sensations of identity became confused, and he recoiled with horror from himself: 'These are the trappings of a mummy!' murmured he in a hollow whisper. 'Am I then dead?' The next instant, however, he broke into a wild laugh of derision – 'Poor, feeble wretch!' cried he; 'what do I fear? – Need *I* tremble, in whose bosom dwells everlasting fire? Let me rather rejoice. I cannot be more wretched; why should I dread a change? I welcome it with transport, and dare my future fate.'

At this moment the car of the balloon caught his eye: 'Ah! what is that?' cried he; 'I am summoned! 'Tis the boat of Hecate, ready to ferry me across the Maerian Lake, to learn my final doom. I come! I come! I fear no judgment! *My hell* is here!' and, striking his bosom, he leaped into the car, and stamped violently against its sides.

At this instant Gregory awoke, and his terror was not surprising. The dried distorted features of the mummy looked yet more hideous than before, when animated by human passions, and his deep hollow voice, speaking in a language he did not understand, fell heavily upon his ear, like the groans of fiends. Gregory tried to scream, but he could not utter a sound. He attempted to fly, but his feet seemed nailed to the spot on which he stood, and he remained with his eyes fixed upon the mummy, gasping for breath, while a cold sweat distilled from every pore. In the mean time, Cheops had stumbled over the box containing the apparatus for making inflammable air, and striking it violently, had unintentionally set the machinery in motion. The pipes, tubes, and bellows, instantly began to work; and the Indian-rubber bottle became gradually inflated, till it swelled to an enormous magnitude, and fluttered in the air like an imprisoned bird, beating itself against the massive walls to which it was still attached.

'Still it goes not,' cried Cheops, again stamping impatiently. The quicksilver vapour bottle had fallen beneath his feet, and it broke as he trod upon it. The vapour burst from it with inconceivable violence, and tearing the balloon from its fastenings, sent it off through the air, like an arrow darting from a bow.

SOME WORDS WITH A MUMMY

THE SYMPOSIUM of the preceding evening had been a little too much for my nerves. I had a wretched headache, and was desperately drowsy. Instead of going out, therefore, to spend the evening, as I had proposed, it occurred to me that I could not do a wiser thing than just eat a mouthful of supper and go immediately to bed.

A *light* supper, of course. I am exceedingly fond of Welsh rabbit. More than a pound at once, however, may not at all times be advisable. Still, there can be no material objection to two. And really between two and three, there is merely a single unit of difference. I ventured, perhaps, upon four. My wife will have it five; but, clearly, she has confounded two very distinct affairs. The abstract number, five, I am willing to admit; but, concretely, it has reference to bottles of brown stout, without which, in the way of condiment, Welsh rabbit is to be eschewed.

Having thus concluded a frugal meal and donned my nightcap, with the serene hope of enjoying it till noon the next day, I placed my head upon the pillow, and through the aid of a capital conscience, fell into a profound slumber forthwith.

But when were the hopes of humanity fulfilled? I could not have completed my third snore when there came a furious ringing at the street-door bell, and then an impatient thumping at the knocker, which awakened me at once. In a minute afterward, and while I was still rubbing my eyes, my wife thrust in my face a note, from my old friend, Dr Ponnonner. It ran thus:

Come to me, by all means, my dear good friend, as soon as you receive this. Come and help us to rejoice. At last, by long persevering diplomacy, I have gained the assent of the directors of the City Museum, to my examination of the mummy – you know the one I mean. I have permission to unswathe it, and open it, if desirable. A few friends only will be present – you, of course. The mummy is now at my house, and we shall begin to unroll it at eleven tonight.

Yours ever, PONNONNER

By the time I had reached the 'Ponnonner', it struck me that I was as wide awake as a man need be. I leaped out of bed in an ecstasy, overthrowing all in my way; dressed myself with a rapidity truly marvellous; and set off, at the top of my speed, for the doctor's.

There I found a very eager company assembled. They had been awaiting me with much impatience. The mummy was extended upon the dining-table; and the moment I entered, its examination was commenced.

It was one of a pair brought, several years previously, by Captain Arthur Sabretash, a cousin of Ponnonner's, from a tomb near Eleithias, in the Lybian Mountains, a considerable distance above Thebes on the Nile. The grottoes at this point, although less magnificent than the Theban sepulchres, are of higher interest, on account of affording more numerous illustrations of the private life of the Egyptians. The chamber from which our specimen was taken, was said to be very rich in such illustrations – the walls being completely covered with fresco-paintings and bas-reliefs, while statues, vases, and mosaic work of rich patterns, indicated the vast wealth of the deceased.

The treasure had been deposited in the museum precisely in the same condition in which Captain Sabretash had found it – that is to say, the coffin had not been disturbed. For eight years it had thus stood, subject only externally to public inspection. We had now, therefore, the complete mummy at our disposal; and to those who are aware how very rarely the unransacked antique reaches our shores, it will be evident, at once, that we had great reason to congratulate ourselves upon our good fortune.

Approaching the table, I saw on it a large box, or case, nearly seven feet long, and perhaps three feet wide, by two feet and a half deep. It was oblong – not coffin-shaped. The material was at first supposed to be the wood of the sycamore (*platanus*), but upon cutting into it, we found it to be pasteboard, or, more properly, papier mâché, composed of papyrus. It was thickly ornamented with paintings, representing funeral scenes, and other mournful subjects – interspersed among which, in every variety of position, were certain series of hiero-glyphical characters, intended, no doubt, for the name of the departed. By good luck, Mr Gliddon formed one of our party; and he had no difficulty in translating the letters, which were simply phonetic, and represented the word, *Allamistakeo*.

We had some difficulty in getting this case open without injury; but, having at length accomplished the task, we came to a second, coffin-shaped, and very considerably less in size than the exterior one, but resembling it precisely in every other respect. The interval between the two was filled with resin, which had, in some degree, defaced the colours of the interior box.

Upon opening this latter (which we did quite easily) we arrived at a third case, also coffin-shaped, and varying from the second one in no particular, except in that of its material, which was cedar, and still emitted the peculiar and highly aromatic odour of that wood. Between the second and the third case there was no interval – the one fitting accurately within the other.

Removing the third case, we discovered and took out the body itself. We had expected to find it, as usual, enveloped in frequent rolls or bandages of linen; but, in place of these, we found a sort of sheath, made of papyrus, and coated with a layer of plaster, thickly gilt and painted. The paintings represented subjects connected with the various supposed duties of the soul, and its presentation to different divinities, with numerous identical human figures, intended, very probably, as portraits of the persons embalmed. Extending from head to foot, was a columnar, or perpendicular inscription, in phonetic hieroglyphics, giving again his name and titles, and the names and titles of his relations.

Around the neck thus ensheathed, was a collar of cylindrical glass beads, diverse in colour, and so arranged as to form images of deities, of the scarabaeus, etc., with the winged globe. Around the small of the waist was a similar collar or belt.

Stripping off the papyrus, we found the flesh in excellent preservation, with no perceptible odour. The colour was reddish. The skin was hard, smooth, and glossy. The teeth and hair were in good condition. The eyes (it seemed) had been removed, and glass ones substituted, which were very beautiful, and wonderfully lifelike, with the exception of somewhat too determined a stare. The fingers and the nails were brilliantly gilded.

Mr Gliddon was of opinion, from the redness of the epidermis, that the embalmment had been effected altogether by asphaltum; but, on scraping the surface with a steel instrument, and throwing into the fire some of the powder thus obtained, the flavour of camphor and other sweet-scented gums became apparent.

We searched the corpse very carefully for the usual openings through which the entrails are extracted, but, to our surprise, we could discover none. No member of the party was at that period aware that entire or unopened mummies are not infrequently met. The brain it was customary to withdraw through the nose; the intestines through an incision in the side; the body was then shaved, washed, and salted; then laid aside for several weeks, when the operation of embalming, properly so called, began.

As no trace of an opening could be found, Dr Ponnonner was preparing his instruments for dissection, when I observed that it was then past two o'clock. Hereupon it was agreed to postpone the internal examination until the next evening; and we were about to separate for the present, when someone suggested an experiment or two with the voltaic pile.

The application of electricity to a mummy three or four thousand years old at the least, was an idea, if not very sage, still sufficiently original, and we all caught it at once. About one-tenth in earnest and nine-tenths in jest, we arranged a battery in the doctor's study, and conveyed thither the Egyptian.

It was only after much trouble that we succeeded in laying bare some portions of the temporal muscle which appeared of less stony rigidity than other parts of the frame but which, as we had antici- pated, of course, gave no indication of galvanic susceptibility when brought in contact with the wire. This, the first trial, indeed, seemed decisive, and, with a hearty laugh at our own absurdity, we were bidding each other good-night, when my eyes, happening to fall upon those of the mummy, were there immediately riveted in amazement. My brief glance, in fact, had sufficed to assure me that the orbs which we had all supposed to be glass, and which were originally noticeable for a certain wild stare, were now so far covered by the lids, that only a small portion of the *tunica albuginea* remained visible.

With a shout I called attention to the fact, and it became immediately obvious to all.

I cannot say that I was *alarmed* at the phenomenon, because 'alarmed' is, in my case, not exactly the word. It is possible, however, that, but for the brown stout, I might have been a little nervous. As for the rest of the company, they really made no attempt at concealing the downright fright which possessed them. Dr Ponnonner was a man to be pitied. Mr Gliddon, by some peculiar process, rendered himself invisible. Mr Silk Buckingham, I fancy, will scarcely be so bold as to deny that he made his way, upon all fours, under the table.

After the first shock of astonishment, however, we resolved, as a matter of course, upon further experiment forthwith. Our operations were now directed against the great toe of the right foot. We made an incision over the outside of the exterior *os sesamoideum pollicis pedis*, and thus got at the root of the *abductor* muscle. Readjusting the battery, we now applied the fluid to the bisected nerves, when, with a movement of exceeding lifelikeness, the mummy first drew up its right knee so as to bring it nearly in contact with the abdomen, and then, straightening the limb with inconceivable force, bestowed a kick upon Dr Ponnonner, which had the effect of discharging that gentleman, like an arrow from a catapult, through a window into the street below.

We rushed out *en masse* to bring in the mangled remains of the victim, but had the happiness to meet him upon the staircase, coming up in an unaccountable hurry, brimful of the most ardent philosophy, and more than ever impressed with the necessity of prosecuting our experiments with vigour and with zeal.

It was by his advice, accordingly, that we made, upon the spot, a profound incision into the tip of the subject's nose, while the doctor himself, laying violent hands upon it, pulled it into vehement contact with the wire.

Morally and physically – figuratively and literally – was the effect electric. In the first place, the corpse opened its eyes, and winked very rapidly for several minutes, as does Mr Barnes in the pantomime; in the second place, it sneezed; in the third, it sat up on end; in the fourth, it shook its fist in Dr Ponnonner's face; in the fifth, turning to Messieurs Gliddon and Buckingham, it addressed them, in very capital Egyptian, thus – 'I must say, gentlemen, that I am as much surprised as I am mortified, at your behaviour. Of Dr Ponnonner nothing better was to be expected. He is a poor little fat fool who *knows* no better. I pity and forgive him. But you, Mr Gliddon – and you, Silk – who have travelled and resided in Egypt until one might imagine you to the manner born – you, I say, who have been so much among us that you speak Egyptian fully as well, I think, as you write your mother tongue – you, whom I have always been led to regard as the firm friend of the mummies – I really did anticipate more gentlemanly conduct from *you*. What am I to think of your standing quietly by and seeing me thus unhandsomely used? What am I to suppose by your permitting Tom, Dick, and Harry to strip me of my coffins, and my clothes, in this wretchedly cold climate? In what light (to come to the point) am I to regard your aiding and abetting that miserable little villain, Dr Ponnonner, in pulling me by the nose?'

It will be taken for granted, no doubt, that upon hearing this speech under the circumstances, we all either made for the door, or fell into violent hysterics, or went off in a general swoon. One of these three things, was, I say, to be expected. Indeed each and all of these lines of conduct might have been very plausibly pursued. And, upon my word, I am at a loss to know how or why it was that we pursued neither the one nor the other. But, perhaps, the true reason is to be sought in the spirit of the age, which proceeds by the rule of contraries altogether, and is now usually admitted as the solution of everything in the way of paradox and impossibility. Or perhaps, after all, it was only the mummy's exceedingly natural and matter-of-course air that divested his words of the terrible. However this may be, the facts are clear, and no member of our party betrayed any very particular trepidation, or seemed to consider that anything had gone very especially wrong.

For my part I was convinced it was all right, and merely stepped aside, out of the range of the Egyptian's fist. Dr Ponnonner thrust his hands into his breeches pockets, looked hard at the mummy, and grew excessively red in the face. Mr Gliddon stroked his whiskers and drew up the collar of his shirt. Mr Buckingham hung down his head, and put his right thumb into the left corner of his mouth.

The Egyptian regarded him with a severe countenance for some minutes, and at length, with a sneer, said – 'Why don't you speak, Mr Buckingham? Did you hear what I asked you, or not? *Do* take your thumb out of your mouth!'

Mr Buckingham, hereupon, gave a slight start, took his right thumb out of the left corner of his mouth, and, by way of indemnification, inserted his left thumb in the right corner of the aperture above mentioned.

Not being able to get an answer from Mr B., the figure turned peevishly to Mr Gliddon, and, in a peremptory tone, demanded in general terms what we all meant.

Mr Gliddon replied at great length, in phonetics; and but for the deficiency of American printing-offices in hieroglyphical type, it would afford me much pleasure to record here, in the original, the whole of his very excellent speech.

I may as well take this occasion to remark, that all the subsequent conversation in which the mummy took a part, was carried on in primitive Egyptian, through the medium (so far as concerned myself and other untravelled members of the company) – through the medium, I say, of Messieurs Gliddon and Buckingham, as interpreters. These gentlemen spoke the mother-tongue of the mummy with inimitable fluency and grace; but I could not help observing that (owing, no doubt, to the introduction of images entirely modern, and, of course, entirely novel to the stranger) the two travellers were reduced, occasionally, to the employment of sensible forms for the purpose of conveying a particular meaning. Mr Gliddon, at one period, for example, could not make the

Egyptian comprehend the term 'politics,' until he sketched upon the wall, with a bit of charcoal, a little carbuncle-nosed gentleman, out at elbows, standing upon a stump, with his left leg drawn back, his right arm thrown forward, with his fist shut, the eyes rolled up toward heaven, and the mouth open at an angle of ninety degrees. Just in the same way Mr Buckingham failed to convey the absolutely modern idea, 'Whig,' until (at Dr Ponnonner's suggestion) he grew very pale in the face, and consented to take off his own.

It will be readily understood that Mr Gliddon's discourse turned chiefly upon the vast benefits accruing to science from the unrolling and disembowelling of mummies; apologising, upon this score, for any disturbance that might have been occasioned *him*, in particular, the individual mummy called Allamistakeo; and concluding with a mere hint (for it could scarcely be considered more) that, as these little matters were now explained, it might be as well to proceed with the investigation intended. Here Dr Ponnonner made ready his instruments.

In regard to the latter suggestions of the orator, it appears that Allamistakeo had certain scruples of conscience, the nature of which I did not distinctly learn; but he expressed himself satisfied with the apologies tendered, and, getting down from the table, shook hands with the company all round.

When this ceremony was at an end, we immediately busied ourselves in repairing the damages which our subject had sustained from the scalpel. We sewed up the wound in his temple, bandaged his foot, and applied a square inch of black plaster to the tip of his nose.

It was now observed that the count (this was the title, it seems, of Allamistakeo) had a slight fit of shivering – no doubt from the cold. The doctor immediately repaired to his wardrobe, and soon returned with a black dress coat, made in Jennings' best manner, a pair of sky-blue plaid pantaloons, with straps, a pink gingham *chemise*, a flapped vest of brocade, a white sack overcoat, a walking cane with a hook, a hat with no brim, patent-leather boots, straw-coloured kid gloves, an eyeglass, a pair of whiskers, and a waterfall cravat. Owing to the disparity of size between the count and the doctor (the proportion being as two to one), there was some little difficulty in adjusting these habiliments upon the person of the Egyptian; but when all was arranged, he might have been said to be dressed. Mr Gliddon, therefore, gave him his arm, and led him to a comfortable chair by the fire, while the doctor rang the bell upon the spot and ordered a supply of cigars and wine.

The conversation soon grew animated. Much curiosity was, of

course, expressed in regard to the somewhat remarkable fact of Allamistakeo's still remaining alive.

'I should have thought,' observed Mr Buckingham, 'that it is high time you were dead.'

'Why,' replied the count, very much astonished, 'I am little more than seven hundred years old! My father lived a thousand, and was by no means in his dotage when he died.'

Here ensued a brisk series of questions and computations, by means of which it became evident that the antiquity of the mummy had been grossly misjudged. It had been five thousand and fifty years, and some months, since he had been consigned to the catacombs at Eleithias.

'But my remark,' resumed Mr Buckingham, 'had no reference to your age at the period of interment (I am willing to grant, in fact, that you are still a young man); and my allusion was to the immensity of time during which, by your own showing, you must have been done up in asphaltum.'

'In what?' said the count.

'In asphaltum,' persisted Mr B.

'Ah, yes; I have some faint notion of what you mean; it might be made to answer, no doubt – but in my time we employed scarcely anything else than the bichloride of mercury.'

'But what we are especially at a loss to understand,' said Dr Ponnonner, 'is, how it happens that, having been dead and buried in Egypt five thousand years ago, you are here today all alive, and looking so delightfully well.'

'Had I been, as you say, *dead*,' replied the count, 'it is more than probable that dead I should still be; for I perceive you are yet in the infancy of galvanism, and cannot accomplish with it what was a common thing among us in the old days. But the fact is, I fell into catalepsy, and it was considered by my best friends that I was either dead or should be; they accordingly embalmed me at once – I presume you are aware of the chief principle of the embalming process?'

'Why, not altogether.'

'Ah, I perceive – a deplorable condition of ignorance! Well, I cannot enter into details just now; but it is necessary to explain that to embalm (properly speaking) in Egypt, was to arrest indefinitely *all* the animal functions subjected to the process. I use the word "animal" in its widest sense, as including the physical not more than the moral and *vital* being. I repeat that the leading principle of embalmment consisted, with us, in the immediately arresting, and holding in perpetual abeyance, *all* the animal functions subjected to the process. To be brief, in whatever condition the individual was, at the period of embalmment, in that condition he remained. Now, as it is my good fortune to be of the blood of the Scarabaeus, I was embalmed *alive*, as you see me at present.'

'The blood of the Scarabaeus!' exclaimed Dr Ponnonner.

'Yes. The Scarabaeus was the *insignium*, or the "arms", of a very distinguished and very rare patrician family. To be "of the blood of the Scarabaeus", is merely to be one of that family of which the Scarabaeus is the *insignium*. I speak figuratively.'

'But what has this to do with your being alive?'

'Why, it is the general custom in Egypt, to deprive a corpse, before embalmment, of its bowels and brains; the race of the Scarabaei alone did not coincide with the custom. Had I not been a Scarabaeus, therefore, I should have been without bowels and brains; and without either it is inconvenient to live.'

'I perceive that,' said Mr Buckingham; 'and I presume that all the *entire* mummies that come to hand are of the race of Scarabaei.'

'Beyond doubt.'

'I thought,' said Mr Gliddon, very meekly, 'that the Scarabaeus was one of the Egyptian gods.'

'One of the Egyptian *what*?' exclaimed the mummy, starting to its feet.

'Gods!' repeated the traveller.

'Mr Gliddon, I really am astonished to hear you talk in this style,' said the count, resuming his seat. 'No nation upon the face of the earth has ever acknowledged more than *one god*. The Scarabaeus, the Ibis, etc., were with us (as similar creatures have been with others) the symbols, or *media*, through which we offered worship to the creator too august to be more directly approached.'

There was here a pause. At length the colloquy was renewed by Dr Ponnonner.

'It is not improbable, then, from what you have explained,' said he, 'that among the catacombs near the Nile, there may exist other mummies of the Scarabaeus tribe, in a condition of vitality.'

'There can be no question of it,' replied the count; 'all the Scarabaei embalmed accidentally while alive, are alive. Even some of those *purposely* so embalmed, may have been overlooked by their executors, and still remain in the tombs.'

'Will you be kind enough to explain,' I said, 'what you mean by "purposely so embalmed"?'

'With great pleasure,' answered the mummy, after surveying me leisurely through his eyeglass – for it was the first time I had ventured to address him a direct question.

'With great pleasure,' he said. 'The usual duration of man's life, in my time, was about eight hundred years. Few men died, unless by most extraordinary accident, before the age of six hundred; few lived longer than a decade of centuries; but eight were considered the natural term. After the discovery of the embalming principle, as I have already described it to you, it occurred to our philosophers that a laudable curiosity might be gratified, and, at the same time, the interests of science much advanced, by living this natural term in instalments. In the case of history, indeed, experience demonstrated that something of this kind was indispensable. An historian, for example, having attained the age of five hundred, would write a book with great labour and then get himself carefully embalmed; leaving instructions to his executors *pro tem.*, that they should cause him to be revivified after the lapse of a certain period – say five or six hundred years. Resuming existence at the expiration of this time, he would invariably find his great work converted into a species of haphazard notebook – that is to say, into a kind of literary arena for the conflicting guesses, riddles, and personal squabbles of whole herds of exasperated commentators. These guesses, etc., which passed under the name of annotations, or emendations, were found so completely to have enveloped, distorted, and overwhelmed the text, that the author had to go about with a lantern to discover his own book. When discovered, it was never worth the trouble of the search. After rewriting it throughout, it was regarded as the bounden duty of the historian to set himself to work, immediately, in correcting, from his own private knowledge and experience, the traditions of the day concerning the epoch at which he had originally lived. Now this process of rescription and personal rectification, pursued by various individual sages, from time to time, had the effect of preventing our history from degenerating into absolute fable.'

'I beg your pardon,' said Dr Ponnonner at this point, laying his hand gently upon the arm of the Egyptian – 'I beg your pardon, sir, but may I presume to interrupt you for one moment?'

'By all means, *sir*,' replied the count, drawing up.

'I merely wished to ask you a question,' said the doctor. 'You mentioned the historian's personal correction of *traditions* respecting his own epoch. Pray, sir, upon an average, what proportion of these Kabbala were usually found to be right?'

'The Kabbala, as you properly term them, sir, were generally discovered to be precisely on a par with the facts recorded in the unrewritten histories themselves; that is to say, not one individual iota of either was ever known, under any circumstances, to be not totally and radically wrong.'

'But since it is quite clear,' resumed the doctor, 'that at least five thousand years have elapsed since your entombment, I take it for granted that your histories at that period, if not your traditions, were sufficiently explicit on that one topic of universal interest, the creation, which took place, as I presume you are aware, only about ten centuries before.'

'Sir!' said the Count Allamistakeo.

The doctor repeated his remarks, but it was only after much additional explanation that the foreigner could be made to comprehend them. The latter at length said, hesitatingly – 'The ideas you have suggested are to me, I confess, utterly novel. During my time I never knew anyone to entertain so singular a fancy as that the universe (or this world, if you will have it so) ever had a beginning at all. I remember once, and once only, hearing something remotely hinted by a man of many speculations concerning the origin *of the human race*; and by this individual the very word *Adam* (or red earth), which you make use of, was employed. He employed it, however, in a generical sense, with reference to the spontaneous germination from rank soil (just as a thousand of the lower *genera* of creatures are germinated) – the spontaneous germination, I say, of five vast hordes of men, simultaneously upspringing in five distinct and nearly equal divisions of the globe.'

Here, in general, the company shrugged their shoulders, and one or two of us touched our foreheads with a very significant air. Mr Silk Buckingham, first glancing slightly at the occiput and then at the siniciput of Allamistakeo, spoke as follows – 'The long duration of human life in your time, together with the occasional practice of passing it, as you have explained, in instalments, must have had, indeed, a strong tendency to the general development and conglomeration of knowledge. I presume, therefore, that we are to attribute the marked inferiority of the old Egyptians in all particulars of science, when compared with the moderns, and more especially with the Yankees, altogether to the superior solidity of the Egyptian skull.'

'I confess again,' replied the count, with much suavity, 'that I am somewhat at a loss to comprehend you; pray, to what particulars of science do you allude?'

Here our whole party, joining voices, detailed, at great length, the assumptions of phrenology and the marvels of animal magnetism.

Having heard us to an end, the count proceeded to relate a few anecdotes, which rendered it evident that prototypes of Gall and Spurzheim had flourished and faded in Egypt so long ago as to have been nearly forgotten, and that the manoeuvres of Mesmer were really very contemptible tricks when put in collation with the positive miracles of the Theban *savans*, who created lice, and a great many other similar things.

I here asked the count if his people were able to calculate eclipses. He smiled rather contemptuously, and said they were.

This put me a little out; but I began to make other enquiries in regard to his astronomical knowledge, when a member of the company, who had never as yet opened his mouth, whispered in my ear, that for information on this head I had better consult Ptolemy (whoever Ptolemy is), as well as one Plutarch *de facic lunae*.

I then questioned the mummy about burning-glasses and lenses, and, in general, about the manufacture of glass; but I had not made an end of my queries before the silent member again touched me quietly on the elbow, and begged me, for God's sake, to take a peep at Diodorus Siculus. As for the count, he merely asked me, in the way of reply, if we moderns possessed any such microscopes as would enable us to cut cameos in the style of the Egyptians. While I was thinking how I should answer this question, little Dr Ponnonner committed himself in a very extraordinary way.

'Look at our architecture!' he exclaimed, greatly to the indignation of both the travellers, who pinched him black and blue to no purpose.

'Look!' he cried, with enthusiasm, 'at the Bowling Green Fountain in New York! or, if this be too vast a contemplation, regard for a moment the Capitol at Washington, DC!' – and the good little medical man went on to detail, very minutely, the proportions of the fabric to which he referred. He explained that the portico alone was adorned with no less than four and twenty columns, five feet in diameter, and ten feet apart.

The count said that he regretted not being able to remember, just at that moment, the precise dimensions of any one of the principal buildings of the City of Aznac, whose foundations were laid in the night of Time, but the ruins of which were still standing, at the epoch of his entombment, in a vast plain of sand to the westward of Thebes. He recollected, however (talking of porticoes), that one affixed to an inferior palace in a kind of suburb called Carnac, consisted of a hundred and forty-four columns, thirty-seven feet each in circumference, and twenty-five feet apart. The approach of this portico, from the Nile, was through an avenue two miles long, composed of sphinxes, statues, and obelisks, twenty, sixty, and a hundred feet in height. The palace itself (as well as he could remember) was, in one direction, two miles long, and might have been, altogether, about seven in circuit. Its walls were richly painted all over, within and without, with hieroglyphics. He would not pretend to *assert* that even fifty or sixty of the doctor's Capitols might have been built within these walls, but he was by no means sure that two or three hundred of them might not have been squeezed in with some trouble. That palace at Carnac was an insignificant little building after all. He (the count), however, could not conscientiously refuse to admit the ingenuity, magnificence, and superiority of the fountain at the Bowling-green, as described by the doctor. Nothing like it, he was forced to allow, had ever been seen in Egypt or elsewhere.

I here asked the count what he had to say to our railroads.

'Nothing,' he replied, 'in particular.' They were rather slight, rather ill-conceived, and clumsily put together. They could not be compared, of course, with the vast, level, direct, iron-grooved causeways, upon which the Egyptians conveyed entire temples and solid obelisks of a hundred and fifty feet in altitude.

I spoke of our gigantic mechanical forces.

He agreed that we knew something in that way, but enquired how I should have gone to work in getting up the imposts on the lintels of even the little palace at Carnac.

This question I concluded not to hear, and demanded if he had any idea of Artesian wells; but he simply raised his eyebrows; while Mr Gliddon winked at me very hard and said, in a low tone, that one had been recently discovered by the engineers employed to bore for water in the Great Oasis.

I then mentioned our steel; but the foreigner elevated his nose, and asked me if our steel could have executed the sharp carved work seen on the obelisks, and which was wrought altogether by edge-tools of copper.

This disconcerted us so greatly that we thought it advisable to vary the attack to metaphysics. We sent for a copy of a book called the *Dial*, and read out of it a chapter or two about something which is not very clear, but which the Bostonians call the Great Movement or progress.

The count merely said that Great Movements were awfully common things in his day, and as for progress, it was at one time quite a nuisance, but it never progressed.

We then spoke of the great beauty and importance of democracy, and were at much trouble in impressing the count with a due sense of the advantages we enjoyed in living where there was suffrage *ad libitum* and no king.

He listened with marked interest, and in fact seemed not a little amused. When we had done he said that, a great while ago, there had occurred something of a very similar sort. Thirteen Egyptian provinces determined all at once to be free, and so set a magnificent example to the rest of mankind. They assembled their wise men, and concocted the most ingenious constitution it is possible to conceive. For a while they managed remarkably well; only their habit of bragging was prodigious. The thing ended, however, in the consolidation of the thirteen states, with some fifteen or twenty others, in the most odious and insupportable despotism that ever was heard of upon the face of the earth.

I asked what was the name of the usurping tyrant.

As well as the count could recollect, it was *Mob*.

Not knowing what to say to this, I raised my voice, and deplored the Egyptian ignorance of steam.

The count looked at me with much astonishment, but made no answer. The silent gentleman, however, gave me a violent nudge in the ribs with his elbows – told me I had sufficiently exposed myself for once – and demanded if I was really such a fool as not to know that the modern steam-engine is derived from the invention of Hero, through Solomon de Caus.

We were now in imminent danger of being discomfited; but, as good luck would have it, Dr Ponnonner, having rallied, returned to our rescue, and enquired if the people of Egypt would seriously pretend to rival the moderns in the all-important particular of dress.

The count, at this, glanced downwards to the straps of his pantaloons, and then taking hold of the end of one of his coat-tails, held it up close to his eyes for some minutes. Letting it fall, at last, his mouth extended itself very gradually from ear to ear; but I do not remember that he said anything in the way of reply.

Hereupon we recovered our spirits, and the doctor, approaching the mummy with great dignity, desired it to say candidly, upon its honour as a gentleman, if the Egyptians had comprehended at *any* period the manufacture of either Ponnonner's lozenges, or Brandreth's pills.

We looked, with profound anxiety, for an answer – but in vain. It was not forthcoming. The Egyptian blushed and hung down his head. Never was triumph more consummate; never was defeat borne with so ill a grace. Indeed, I could not endure the spectacle of the poor mummy's mortification. I reached my hat, bowed to him stiffly, and took leave.

Upon getting home I found it past four o'clock, and went immediately to bed. It is now ten a.m. I have been up since seven, penning these memoranda for the benefit of my family and of mankind. The former I shall behold no more. My wife is a shrew. The truth is, I am heartily sick of this life, and of the nineteenth century in general. I am convinced that everything is going wrong. Besides, I am anxious to know who will be president in 2045. As soon, therefore, as I shave and swallow a cup of coffee, I shall just step over to Ponnonner's and get embalmed for a couple of hundred years.

THE RING OF THOTH

MR JOHN VANSITTART SMITH FRS of 147a Gower Street was a man whose energy of purpose and clearness of thought might have placed him in the very first rank of scientific observers. He was the victim, however, of a universal ambition which prompted him to aim at distinction in many subjects rather than pre-eminence in one. In his early days he had shown an aptitude for zoology and for botany which caused his friends to look upon him as a second Darwin, but when a professorship was almost within his reach he had suddenly discontinued his studies and turned his whole attention to chemistry. Here his researches upon the spectra of the metals had won him his fellowship in the Royal Society; but again he played the coquette with his subject, and after a year's absence from the laboratory, he joined the Oriental Society, and delivered a paper on the hieroglyphic and demotic inscriptions of El Kab, thus giving a crowning example both of the versatility and of the inconstancy of his talents.

The most fickle of wooers, however, is apt to be caught at last, and so it was with John Vansittart Smith. The more he burrowed his way into Egyptology, the more impressed he became by the vast field which it opened to the enquirer and by the extreme importance of a subject which promised to throw a light upon the first germs of human civilisation and the origin of the greater part of our arts and sciences. So struck was Mr Smith that he straightway married an Egyptological young lady who had written upon the sixth dynasty, and having thus secured a sound base of operations he set himself to collect materials for a work which should unite the research of Lepsius and the ingenuity of Champollion. The preparation of this *magnum opus* entailed many hurried visits to the magnificent Egyptian collections of the Louvre, upon the last of which, no longer ago than the middle of last October, he became involved in a most strange and noteworthy adventure.

The trains had been slow and the Channel had been rough, so that the student arrived in Paris in a somewhat befogged and feverish condition. On reaching the Hôtel de France, in the Rue Laffitte, he had thrown himself upon a sofa for a couple of hours, but finding that he was unable to sleep, he determined, in spite of his fatigue, to make his way to the Louvre, settle the point which he had come to decide, and take the evening train back to Dieppe. Having come to his conclusion, he donned his greatcoat, for it was a raw rainy day, and made his way across the Boulevard des Italiens and down the Avenue de l'Opéra. Once in the Louvre he was on familiar ground, and he speedily made his way to the collection of papyri which it was his intention to consult.

The warmest admirers of John Vansittart Smith could hardly claim for him that he was a handsome man. His high-beaked nose and prominent chin had something of the same acute and incisive character which distinguished his intellect. He held his head in a birdlike fashion, and birdlike, too, was the pecking motion with which, in conversation, he threw out his objections and retorts. As he stood, with the high collar of his greatcoat raised to his ears, he might have seen from the reflection in the glass case before him that his appearance was a singular one. Yet it came upon him as a sudden jar when an English voice behind him exclaimed in very audible tones, 'What a queer-looking mortal!'

The student had a large amount of petty vanity in his composition which manifested itself by an ostentatious and overdone disregard of all personal considerations. He straightened his lips and looked rigidly at the roll of papyrus, while his heart filled with bitterness against the whole race of travelling Britons.

'Yes,' said another voice, 'he really is an extraordinary fellow.'

'Do you know,' said the first speaker, 'one could almost believe that by the continual contemplation of mummies the chap has become half a mummy himself!'

'He has certainly an Egyptian cast of countenance,' said the other.

John Vansittart Smith spun round upon his heel with the intention of shaming his countrymen by a corrosive remark or two. To his surprise and relief, the two young fellows who had been conversing had their shoulders turned towards him and were gazing at one of the Louvre attendants who was polishing some brasswork at the other side of the room.

'Carter will be waiting for us at the Palais Royal,' said one tourist to the other, glancing at his watch, and they clattered away, leaving the student to his labours.

'I wonder what these chatterers call an Egyptian cast of countenance,' thought John Vansittart Smith, and he moved his position slightly in order to catch a glimpse of the man's face. He started as his eyes fell upon it. It was indeed the very face with which his studies had made him familiar. The regular statuesque features, broad brow, well-rounded chin and dusky complexion were the exact counterpart of the innumerable statues, mummy-cases and pictures which adorned the walls of the apartment. The thing was beyond all coincidence. The man must be an Egyptian. The national angularity of the shoulders and narrowness of the hips were alone sufficient to identify him.

John Vansittart Smith shuffled towards the attendant with some intention of addressing him. He was not light of touch in conversation, and found it difficult to strike the happy mean between the brusqueness of the superior and the geniality of the equal. As he came nearer, the man presented his side face to him, but kept his gaze still bent upon his work. Vansittart Smith, fixing his eyes upon the fellow's skin, was conscious of a sudden impression that there was something inhuman and preternatural about its appearance. Over the temple and cheek-bone it was as glazed and as shiny as varnished parchment. There was no suggestion of pores. One could not fancy a drop of moisture upon that arid surface. From brow to chin, however, it was cross-hatched by a million delicate wrinkles, which shot and interlaced as though nature in some Maori mood had tried how wild and intricate a pattern she could devise.

'Où est la collection de Memphis?' asked the student, with the awkward air of a man who is devising a question merely for the purpose of opening a conversation.

'C'est là,' replied the man brusquely, nodding his head at the other side of the room.

'Vous êtes un Egyptien, n'est-ce pas?' asked the Englishman.

The attendant looked up and turned his strange dark eyes upon his questioner. They were vitreous, with a misty dry shininess such as Vansittart Smith had never seen in a human head before. As he gazed into them he saw some strong emotion gather in their depths, which rose and deepened until it broke into a look of something akin both to horror and to hatred.

'Non, monsieur; je suis français.' The man turned abruptly and bent low over his polishing. The student gazed at him for a moment in astonishment, and then turning to a chair in a retired corner behind one of the doors he proceeded to make notes of his researches among the papyri. His thoughts, however, refused to return into their natural groove. They would run upon the enigmatical attendant with the sphinx-like face and the parchment skin.

'Where have I seen such eyes?' said Vansittart Smith to himself. 'There is something saurian about them, something reptilian.

There's the *membrana nictitans* of the snakes,' he mused, bethinking himself of his zoological studies. 'It gives a shiny effect. But there was something more here. There was a sense of power, of wisdom – so I read them – and of weariness, utter weariness, and ineffable despair. It may be all imagination, but I never had so strong an impression. By Jove, I must have another look at them!' He rose and paced round the Egyptian rooms, but the man who had excited his curiosity had disappeared.

The student sat down again in his quiet corner, and continued to work at his notes. He had gained the information which he required from the papyri, and it only remained to write it down while it was still fresh in his memory. For a time his pencil travelled rapidly over the paper, but soon the lines became less level, the words more blurred and finally the pencil tinkled down upon the floor and the head of the student dropped heavily forward upon his chest. Tired out by his journey, he slept so soundly in his lonely post behind the door that neither the clanking civil guard, nor the footsteps of sightseers, nor even the loud hoarse bell which gives the signal for closing, were sufficient to arouse him.

Twilight deepened into darkness, the bustle from the Rue de Rivoli waxed and then waned, distant Notre Dame clanged out the hour of midnight, and still the dark and lonely figure sat silently in the shadow. It was not until close upon one in the morning that, with a sudden gasp and an intaking of the breath, Vansittart Smith returned to consciousness. For a moment it flashed upon him that he had dropped asleep in his study chair at home. The moon was shining fitfully though the unshuttered window, however, and as his eye ran along the lines of mummies and the endless array of polished cases, he remembered clearly where he was and how he came there. The student was not a nervous man. He possessed that love of a novel situation which is peculiar to his race. Stretching out his cramped limbs, he looked at his watch and burst into a chuckle as he observed the hour. The episode would make an admirable anecdote to be introduced into his next paper as a relief to the graver and heavier speculations. He was a little cold, but wide awake and much refreshed. It was no wonder that the guardians had overlooked him, for the door threw its heavy black shadow right across him.

The complete silence was impressive. Neither outside nor inside was there a creak or a murmur. He was alone with the dead men of a dead civilisation. What though the outer city reeked of the garish nineteenth century! In all this chamber there was scarce an article, from the shrivelled ear of wheat to the pigment-box of the painter, which had not held its own against four thousand years. Here was the flotsam and jetsam washed up by the great ocean of time from that far-off empire. From stately Thebes, from lordly Luxor, from the great temples of Heliopolis, from a hundred rifled tombs, these relics had been brought. The student glanced round at the long-silent figures who flickered vaguely up through the gloom, at the busy toilers who were now so restful, and he fell into a reverent and thoughtful mood. An unwonted sense of his own youth and insignificance came over him. Leaning back in his chair, he gazed dreamily down the long vista of rooms, all silvery with the moonshine, which extended through the whole wing of the widespread building. His eyes fell upon the yellow glare of a distant lamp.

John Vansittart Smith sat up on his chair with his nerves all on edge. The light was advancing slowly towards him, pausing from time to time, and then coming jerkily onwards. The bearer moved noiselessly. In the utter silence there was no suspicion of the pat of a footfall. An idea of robbers entered the Englishman's head. He snuggled up farther into the corner. The light was two rooms off. Now it was in the next chamber, and still there was no sound. With something approaching to a thrill of fear, the student observed a face, floating in the air as it were, behind the flare of the lamp. The figure was wrapped in shadow, but the light fell full upon the strange, eager face. There was no mistaking the metallic, glistening eyes and the cadaverous skin. It was the attendant with whom he had conversed.

Vansittart Smith's first impulse was to come forward and address him. A few words of explanation would set the matter clear, and lead doubtless to his being conducted to some side-door from which he might make his way to his hotel. As the man entered the chamber, however, there was something so stealthy in his movements, and so furtive in his expression, that the Englishman altered his intention. This was clearly no ordinary official walking the rounds. The fellow wore felt-soled slippers, stepped with a rising chest, and glanced quickly from left to right, while his hurried, gasping breathing thrilled the flame of his lamp. Vansittart Smith crouched silently back into the corner and watched him keenly, convinced that his errand was one of secret and probably sinister import.

There was no hesitation in the other's movements. He stepped lightly and swiftly across to one of the great cases, and drawing a key from his pocket, he unlocked it. From the upper shelf he pulled down a mummy, which he bore away with him, and laid it with much care and solicitude upon the ground. By it he placed his lamp, and then squatting down beside it in Eastern fashion he began with long, quivering fingers to undo the cerecloths and bandages which girt it round As the crackling rolls of linen peeled off one after the other, a strong aromatic odour filled the chamber, and fragments of scented wood and of spices pattered down upon the marble floor.

It was clear to John Vansittart Smith that this mummy had never been unswathed before. The operation interested him keenly. He thrilled all over with curiosity, and his birdlike head protruded farther and farther from behind the door. When, however, the last roll had been removed from the four-thousand-year-old head, it was all that he could do to stifle an outcry of amazement. First, a cascade of long, black, glossy tresses poured over the workman's hands and arms. A second turn of the bandage revealed a low, white forehead, with a pair of delicately arched eyebrows. A third uncovered a pair of bright, deeply fringed eyes and a straight, well-cut nose, while a fourth and last showed a sweet, full, sensitive mouth and a beautifully curved chin. The whole face was one of extraordinary loveliness, save for the one blemish that in the centre of the forehead there was a single irregular, coffee-coloured splotch. It was a triumph of the embalmer's art. Vansittart Smith's eyes grew larger and larger as he gazed upon it, and he chirruped in his throat with satisfaction.

Its effect upon the Egyptologist was as nothing, however, compared with that which it produced upon the strange attendant. He threw his hands up into the air, burst into a harsh clatter of words, and then, hurling himself down upon the ground beside the mummy, he threw his arms round her and kissed her repeatedly upon the lips and brow. 'Ma petite!' he groaned in French. 'Ma pauvre petite!' His voice broke with emotion, and his innumerable wrinkles quivered and writhed, but the student observed in the lamplight that his shining eyes were still dry and tearless as two beads of steel. For some minutes he lay, with a twitching face, crooning and moaning over the beautiful head. Then he broke into a sudden smile, said some words in an unknown tongue, and sprang to his feet with the vigorous air of one who has braced himself for an effort.

In the centre of the room there was a large, circular case which contained, as the student had frequently remarked, a magnificent collection of early Egyptian rings and precious stones. To this the attendant strode, and unlocking it, threw it open. On the ledge at the side he placed his lamp, and beside it a small earthenware jar which he had drawn from his pocket. He then took a handful of rings from the case, and with a most serious and anxious face he proceeded to smear each in turn with some liquid substance from the earthen pot, holding them to the light as he did so. He was clearly disappointed with the first lot, for he threw them petulantly back into the case and drew out some more. One of these, a massive ring with a large crystal set in it, he seized and eagerly tested with the contents of the jar. Instantly he uttered a cry of joy, and threw out his arms in a wild gesture which upset the pot and set the liquid streaming across the floor to the very feet of the Englishman. The attendant drew a red handkerchief from his bosom, and mopping up the mess, he followed it into the corner, where in a moment he found himself face to face with his observer.

'Excuse me,' said John Vansittart Smith, with all imaginable politeness; 'I have been unfortunate enough to fall asleep behind this door.'

'And you have been watching me?' the other asked in English, with a most venomous look on his corpse-like face.

The student was a man of veracity. 'I confess,' said he, 'that I have noticed your movements, and that they have aroused my curiosity and interest in the highest degree.'

The man drew a long, flamboyantly bladed knife from his bosom. 'You have had a very narrow escape,' he said; 'had I seen you ten minutes ago, I should have driven this through your heart. As it is, if you touch me or interfere with me in any way you are a dead man.'

'I have no wish to interfere with you,' the student answered. 'My presence here is entirely accidental. All I ask is that you will have the extreme kindness to show me out through some side-door.' He spoke with great suavity, for the man was still pressing the tip of his dagger against the palm of his left hand, as though to assure himself of its sharpness, while his face preserved its malignant expression.

'If I thought – ' said he. 'But no, perhaps it is as well. What is your name?'

The Englishman gave it.

'Vansittart Smith,' the other repeated. 'Are you the same Vansittart Smith who gave a paper in London upon El Kab? I saw a report of it. Your knowledge of the subject is contemptible.'

'Sir!' cried the Egyptologist.

'Yet it is superior to that of many who make even greater pretensions. The whole keystone of our old life in Egypt was not the inscriptions or monuments of which you make so much, but was our hermetic philosophy and mystic knowledge of which you say little or nothing.'

'Our old life!' repeated the scholar, wide-eyed; and then suddenly, 'Good God, look at the mummy's face!'

The strange man turned and flashed his light upon the dead

woman, uttering a long, doleful cry as he did so. The action of the air
had already undone all the art of the embalmer. The skin had fallen
away, the eyes had sunk inwards, the discoloured lips had writhed
away from the yellow teeth, and the brown mark upon the forehead
alone showed that it was indeed the same face which had shown such
youth and beauty a few short minutes before.

The man flapped his hands together in grief and horror. Then
mastering himself by a strong effort he turned his hard eyes once
more upon the Englishman.

'It does not matter,' he said, in a shaking voice. 'It does not really
matter. I came here tonight with the fixed determination to do
something. It is now done. All else is as nothing. I have found my
quest. The old curse is broken. I can rejoin her. What matter about
her inanimate shell so long as her spirit is awaiting me at the other
side of the veil!'

'These are wild words,' said Vansittart Smith. He was becoming
more and more convinced that he had to do with a madman.

'Time presses, and I must go,' continued the other. 'The moment
is at hand for which I have waited this weary time. But I must show
you out first. Come with me.'

Taking up the lamp, he turned from the disordered chamber and
led the student swiftly through the long series of the Egyptian,
Assyrian and Persian apartments. At the end of the latter he pushed
open a small door let into the wall and descended a winding, stone
stair. The Englishman felt the cold, fresh air of the night upon his
brow. There was a door opposite him which appeared to communicate with the street. To the right of this another door stood ajar,
throwing a spurt of yellow light across the passage. 'Come in here!'
said the attendant shortly.

Vansittart Smith hesitated. He had hoped that he had come to the
end of his adventure. Yet his curiosity was strong within him. He
could not leave the matter unsolved; so he followed his strange
companion into the lighted chamber.

It was a small room, such as is devoted to a concierge. A wood fire
sparkled in the grate. At one side stood a truckle bed, and at the other
a coarse, wooden chair, with a round table in the centre, which bore
the remains of a meal. As the visitor's eye glanced round he could not
but remark with an ever-recurring thrill that all the small details of
the room were of the most quaint design and antique workmanship.
The candlesticks, the vases upon the chimneypiece, the fire-irons,
the ornaments upon the walls were all such as he had been wont to
associate with the remote past. The gnarled, heavy-eyed man sat

himself down upon the edge of the bed, and motioned his guest into the chair.

'There may be design in this,' he said, still speaking excellent English. 'It may be decreed that I should leave some account behind as a warning to all rash mortals who would set their wits up against the workings of nature. I leave it with you. Make such use as you will of it. I speak to you now with my feet upon the threshold of the other world.

'I am, as you surmised, an Egyptian – not one of the downtrodden race of slaves who now inhabit the delta of the Nile, but a survivor of that fiercer and harder people who tamed the Hebrew, drove the Ethiopian back into the southern deserts, and built those mighty works which have been the envy and the wonder of all after generations. It was in the reign of Tuthmosis, sixteen hundred years before the birth of Christ, that I first saw the light. You shrink away from me. Wait, and you will see that I am more to be pitied than to be feared.

'My name was Sosra. My father had been the chief priest of Osiris in the great temple of Abaris, which stood in those days upon the Bubastic branch of the Nile. I was brought up in the temple and was trained in all those mystic arts which are spoken of in your own Bible. I was an apt pupil. Before I was sixteen I had learned all the wisest priest could teach me. From that time on I studied nature's secrets for myself, and shared my knowledge with no man.

'Of all the questions that attracted me there were none over which I laboured so long as over those which concern themselves with the nature of life. I probed deeply into the vital principle. The aim of medicine had been to drive away disease when it appeared. It seemed to me that a method might be devised which should so fortify the body as to prevent weakness or death from ever taking hold of it. It is useless that I should recount my researches. You would scarce comprehend them if I did. They were carried out partly upon animals, partly upon slaves and partly on myself. Suffice it that their result was to furnish me with a substance which, when injected into the blood, would endow the body with strength to resist the effects of time, of violence or of disease. It would not indeed confer immortality, but its potency would endure for many thousands of years. I used it upon a cat, and afterwards drugged the creature with the most deadly poisons. That cat is alive in Lower Egypt at the present moment. There was nothing of mystery or magic in the matter. It was simply a chemical discovery, which may well be made again.

'Love of life runs high in the young. It seemed to me that I had broken away from all human care now that I had abolished pain and driven death to such a distance. With a light heart I poured the accursed stuff into my veins. Then I looked round for someone whom I could benefit. There was a young priest of Thoth, Parmes by name, who had won my goodwill by his earnest nature and his devotion to his studies. To him I whispered my secret, and at his request I injected him with my elixir. I should now, I reflected, never be without a companion of the same age as myself.

'After this grand discovery I relaxed my studies to some extent, but Parmes continued his with redoubled energy. Every day I could see him working with his flasks and his distiller in the Temple of Thoth, but he said little to me as to the result of his labours. For my own part, I used to walk through the city and look around me with exultation as I reflected that all this was destined to pass away, and that only I should remain. The people would bow to me as they passed me, for the fame of my knowledge had gone abroad.

'There was war at this time, and the great king had sent down his soldiers to the eastern boundary to drive away the Hyksos. A governor, too, was sent to Abaris, that he might hold it for the king. I had heard much of the beauty of the daughter of this governor, but one day as I walked out with Parmes we met her, borne upon the shoulders of her slaves. I was struck with love as with lightning. My heart went out from me. I could have thrown myself beneath the feet of her bearers. This was my woman. Life without her was impossible. I swore by the head of Horus that she should be mine. I swore it to the priest of Thoth. He turned away from me with a brow which was as black as midnight.

'There is no need to tell you of our wooing. She came to love me even as I loved her. I learned that Parmes had seen her before I did, and had shown her that he, too, loved her, but I could smile at his passion, for I knew that her heart was mine. The white plague had come upon the city and many were stricken, but I laid my hands upon the sick and nursed them without fear or scathe. She marvelled at my daring. Then I told her my secret, and begged her that she would let me use my art upon her.

' "Your flower shall then be unwithered, Atma," I said. "Other things may pass away, but you and I, and our great love for each other, shall outlive the tomb of King Chefru."

'But she was full of timid, maidenly objections. Was it right? she asked, was it not a thwarting of "the will of the gods"? If the great Osiris had wished that our years should be so long, would he not himself have brought it about?

'With fond and loving words I overcame her doubts, and yet she hesitated. It was a great question, she said. She would think it over for this one night. In the morning I should know of her resolution. Surely one night was not too much to ask. She wished to pray to Isis for help in her decision.

'With a sinking heart and a sad foreboding of evil I left her with her tirewomen. In the morning, when the early sacrifice was over, I hurried to her house. A frightened slave met me upon the steps. Her mistress was ill, she said, very ill. In a frenzy I broke my way through the attendants, and rushed through hall and corridor to my Atma' s chamber. She lay upon her couch, her head high upon the pillow, with a pallid face and a glazed eye. On her forehead there blazed a single angry, purple patch. I knew that hell-mark of old. It was the scar of the white plague, the sign-manual of death.

'Why should I speak of that terrible time? For months I was mad, fevered, delirious, and yet I could not die. Never did an Arab thirst after the sweet wells as I longed after death. Could poison or steel have shortened the thread of my existence, I should soon have rejoined my love in the land with the narrow portal. I tried, but it was of no avail. The accursed influence was too strong upon me. One night as I lay upon my couch, weak and weary, Parmes, the priest of Thoth, came to my chamber. He stood in the circle of the lamplight, and he looked down upon me with eyes which were bright with a mad joy.

' "Why did you let the maiden die?" he asked; "why did you not strengthen her as you strengthened me?"

' "I was too late," I answered. "But I had forgot. You also loved her. You are my fellow in misfortune. Is it not terrible to think of the centuries which must pass ere we look upon her again? Fools, fools, that we were to take death to be our enemy!"

' "You may say that," he cried with a wild laugh; "the words come well from your lips. For me they have no meaning."

' "What mean you?" I cried, raising myself upon my elbow. "Surely, friend, this grief has turned your brain." His face was aflame with joy, and he writhed and shook like one who hath a devil.

' "Do you know whither I go?" he asked.

' "Nay," I answered, "I cannot tell."

' "I go to her," said he. "She lies embalmed in the farther tomb by the double palm tree beyond the city wall."

' "Why do you go there?" I asked.

' "To die!" he shrieked, "to die! I am not bound by earthen fetters."

' "But the elixir is in your blood," I cried.

' "I can defy it," said he; "I have found a stronger principle which will destroy it. It is working in my veins at this moment, and in an hour I shall be a dead man. I shall join her, and you shall remain behind."

'As I looked upon him I could see that he spoke words of truth. The light in his eye told me that he was indeed beyond the power of the elixir.

' "You will teach me!" I cried.

' "Never!" he answered.

' "I implore you, by the wisdom of Thoth, by the majesty of Anubis!"

' "It is useless," he said coldly.

' "Then I will find it out," I cried.

' "You cannot," he answered; "it came to me by chance. There is one ingredient which you can never get. Save that which is in the ring of Thoth, none will ever more be made."

' "In the ring of Thoth!" I repeated, "where then is the ring of Thoth?"

' "That also you shall never know," he answered. "You won her love. Who has won in the end? I leave you to your sordid earth life. My chains are broken. I must go!" He turned upon his heel and fled from the chamber. In the morning came the news that the priest of Thoth was dead.

'My days after that were spent in study. I must find this subtle poison which was strong enough to undo the elixir. From early dawn to midnight I bent over the test-tube and the furnace. Above all, I collected the papyri and the chemical flasks of the priest of Thoth. Alas! they taught me little. Here and there some hint or stray expression would raise hope in my bosom, but no good ever came of it. Still, month after month, I struggled on. When my heart grew faint I would make my way to the tomb by the palm tree. There, standing by the dead casket from which the jewel had been rifled, I would feel her sweet presence, and would whisper to her that I would rejoin her if mortal wit could solve the riddle.

'Parmes had said that his discovery was connected with the ring of Thoth. I had some remembrance of the trinket. It was a large and weighty circlet, made not of gold but of a rarer and heavier metal brought from the mines of Mount Harbal. Platinum, you call it. The ring had, I remembered, a hollow crystal set in it, in which some few drops of liquid might be stored. Now, the secret of Parmes could not have to do with the metal alone, for there were many rings of that metal in the temple. Was it not more likely that he had stored his precious poison within the cavity of the crystal? I had scarce come to this conclusion before, in hunting through his papers, I came upon one which told me that it was indeed so, and that there was still some of the liquid unused.

'But how to find the ring? It was not upon him when he was stripped for the embalmer. Of that I made sure. Neither was it among his private effects. In vain I searched every room that he had entered, every box and vase and chattel that he had owned. I sifted the very sand of the desert in the places where he had been wont to walk; but, do what I would, I could come upon no traces of the ring of Thoth. Yet it may be that my labours would have overcome all obstacles had it not been for a new and unlooked-for misfortune.

'A great war had been waged against the Hyksos, and the captains of the great king had been cut off in the desert, with all their bowmen and horsemen. The shepherd tribes were upon us like the locusts in a dry year. From the wilderness of Shur to the great, bitter lake there was blood by day and fire by night. Abaris was the bulwark of Egypt, but we could not keep the savages back. The city fell. The governor and the soldiers were put to the sword, and I, with many more, was led away into captivity.

'For years and years I tended cattle in the great plains by the Euphrates. My master died, and his son grew old, but I was still as far from death as ever. At last I escaped upon a swift camel, and made my way back to Egypt. The Hyksos had settled in the land which they had conquered, and their own king ruled over the country. Abaris had been torn down, the city had been burned, and of the great temple there was nothing left save an unsightly mound. Everywhere the tombs had been rifled and the monuments destroyed. Of my Atma's grave no sign was left. It was buried in the sands of the desert, and the palm tree which marked the spot had long disappeared. The papers of Parmes and the remains of the temple of Thoth were either destroyed or scattered far and wide over the deserts of Syria. All search after them was vain.

'From that time I gave up all hope of ever finding the ring or discovering the subtle drug. I set myself to live as patiently as might be until the effect of the elixir should wear away. How can you understand how terrible a thing time is, you who have experience only of the narrow course which lies between the cradle and the grave! I know it to my cost, I who have floated down the whole stream of history. I was old when Ilium fell. I was very old when Herodotus came to Memphis. I was bowed down with years when the new gospel came upon earth. Yet you see me much as other men are, with the cursed elixir still sweetening my blood, and guarding me against that which I would court. Now, at last, at last I have come to the end of it!

'I have travelled in all lands and I have dwelt with all nations. Every tongue is the same to me. I learned them all to help pass the weary time. I need not tell you how slowly they drifted by, the long dawn of modern civilisation, the dreary middle years, the dark times of barbarism. They are all behind me now. I have never looked with the eyes of love upon another woman. Atma knows that I have been constant to her.

'It was my custom to read all that the scholars had to say upon Ancient Egypt. I have been in many positions, sometimes affluent, sometimes poor, but I have always found enough to enable me to buy the journals which deal with such matters. Some nine months ago I was in San Francisco, and there I read an account of some discoveries made in the neighbourhood of Abaris. My heart leapt into my mouth as I read it. It said that the excavator had busied himself in exploring some tombs recently unearthed. In one there had been found an unopened mummy with an inscription upon the outer case setting forth that it contained the body of the daughter of the governor of the city in the days of Tuthmosis. It added that on removing the outer case there had been exposed a large platinum ring set with a crystal, which had been laid upon the breast of the embalmed woman. This, then, was where Parmes had hid the ring of Thoth. He might well say that it was safe, for no Egyptian would ever stain his soul by moving even the outer case of a buried friend.

'That very night I set off from San Francisco, and in a few weeks I found myself once more at Abaris, if a few sand-heaps and crumbling walls may retain the name of the great city. I hurried to the Frenchmen who were digging there and asked them for the ring. They replied that both the ring and the mummy had been sent to the Boulak Museum at Cairo. To Boulak I went, but only to be told that Mariette Bey had claimed them and had shipped them to the Louvre. I followed them, and there, at last, in the Egyptian chamber, I came, after close upon four thousand years, upon the remains of my Atma, and upon the ring for which I had sought so long.

'But how was I to lay hands upon them? How was I to have them for my very own? It chanced that the office of attendant was vacant. I went to the director. I convinced him that I knew much about Egypt. In my eagerness I said too much. He remarked that a professor's chair would suit me better than a seat in the conciergerie. I knew more, he said, than he did. It was only by blundering, and letting him think that he had overestimated my knowledge, that I prevailed upon him to let me move the few effects which I have retained into this chamber. It is my first and my last night here.

'Such is my story, Mr Vansittart Smith. I need not say more to a man of your perception. By a strange chance you have this night looked upon the face of the woman whom I loved in those far-off days. There were many rings with crystals in the case, and I had to test for the platinum to be sure of the one I wanted. A glance at the crystal has shown me that the liquid is indeed within it, and that I shall at last be able to shake off that accursed health which has been worse to me than the foulest disease. I have nothing more to say to you. I have unburdened myself. You may tell my story or you may withhold it at your pleasure. The choice rests with you. I owe you some amends, for you have had a narrow escape of your life this night. I was a desperate man, and not to be baulked in my purpose. Had I seen you before the thing was done, I might have put it beyond your power to oppose me or to raise an alarm. This is the door. It leads into the Rue de Rivoli. Good-night.'

The Englishman glanced back. For a moment the lean figure of Sosra the Egyptian stood framed in the narrow doorway. The next the door had slammed, and the heavy rasping of a bolt broke on the silent night.

It was on the second day after his return to London that Mr John Vansittart Smith saw the following concise narrative in the Paris correspondence of *The Times*:

Curious Occurrence in the Louvre – Yesterday morning a strange discovery was made in the principal Eastern chamber. The *ouvriers* who are employed to clean out the rooms in the morning found one of the attendants lying dead upon the floor with his arms round one of the mummies. So close was his embrace that it was only with the utmost difficulty that they were separated. One of the cases containing valuable rings had been opened and rifled. The authorities are of the opinion that the man was bearing away the mummy with some idea of selling it to a private collector, but that he was struck down in the very act by long-standing disease of the heart. It is said that he was a man of uncertain age and eccentric habits, without any living relations to mourn over his dramatic and untimely end.

LOT NO. 249

OF THE DEALINGS of Edward Bellingham with William Monkhouse Lee and of the cause of the great terror of Abercrombie Smith it may be that no absolute and final judgement will ever be delivered. It is true that we have the full and clear narrative of Smith himself and such corroboration as he could look for from Thomas Styles the servant, from the Reverend Plumptree Peterson, Fellow of Old's, and from such other people as chanced to gain some passing glance at this or that incident in a singular chain of events. Yet in the main, the story must rest upon Smith alone, and the most will think that it is more likely that one brain, however outwardly sane, has some subtle warp in its texture, some strange flaw in its workings, than that the path of nature has been overstepped in open day in so famed a centre of learning and light as the University of Oxford. Yet when we think how narrow and how devious this path of nature is, how dimly we can trace it, for all our lamps of science, and how from the darkness which girds it round great and terrible possibilities loom ever shadowly upwards, it is a bold and confident man who will put a limit to the strange bypaths into which the human spirit may wander.

In a certain wing of what we will call Old College in Oxford there is a corner turret of an exceeding great age. The heavy arch which spans the open door has bent downwards in the centre under the weight of its years, and the grey, lichen-blotched blocks of stone are bound and knitted together with withes and strands of ivy, as though the old mother had set herself to brace them up against wind and weather. From the door a stone stair curves upward spirally, passing two landings and terminating in a third one, its steps all shapeless and hollowed by the tread of so many generations of the seekers after knowledge. Life has flowed like water down this winding stair, and, waterlike, has left these smooth-worn grooves behind it. From the long-gowned, pedantic scholars of Plantagenet days down to the young bloods of a later age, how full and strong had been that tide of young, English life. And what was left now of all those hopes, those strivings, those fiery energies, save here and there in some old-world churchyard a few scratches upon a stone, and perchance a handful of dust in a mouldering coffin? Yet here were the silent stair and the grey, old wall, with bend and saltire and many another heraldic device still to be read upon its surface, like grotesque shadows thrown back from the days that had passed.

In the month of May, in the year 1884, three young men occupied the sets of rooms which opened on to the separate landings of the old stair. Each set consisted simply of a sitting-room and of a bedroom, while the two corresponding rooms upon the ground-floor were used, the one as a coal-cellar and the other as the living-room of the servant, or scout, Thomas Styles, whose duty it was to wait upon the three men above him. To right and to left was a line of lecture-rooms and of offices, so that the dwellers in the old turret enjoyed a certain seclusion, which made the chambers popular among the more studious undergraduates. Such were the three who occupied them now – Abercrombie Smith above, Edward Bellingham beneath him and William Monkhouse Lee upon the lowest storey.

It was ten o'clock on a bright, spring night, and Abercrombie Smith lay back in his armchair, his feet upon the fender and his briar-root pipe between his lips. In a similar chair, and equally at his ease, there lounged on the other side of the fireplace his old school friend Jephro Hastie. Both men were in flannels, for they had spent their evening upon the river, but apart from their dress no one could look at their hard-cut, alert faces without seeing that they were open-air men – men whose minds and tastes turned naturally to all that was manly and robust. Hastie, indeed, was stroke of his college boat, and Smith was an even better oar, but a coming examination had already cast its shadow over him and held him to his work, save for the few hours a week which health demanded. A litter of medical books upon the table, with scattered bones, models and anatomical plates, pointed to the extent as well as the nature of his studies, while a couple of single-sticks and a set of boxing-gloves above the mantelpiece hinted at the means by which, with Hastie's help, he might take his exercise in its most compressed and least-distant form. They knew each other very well – so well that they could sit now in that soothing silence which is the very highest development of companionship.

'Have some whisky,' said Abercrombie Smith at last between two cloudbursts. 'Scotch in the jug and Irish in the bottle.'

'No, thanks. I'm in for the sculls. I don't liquor when I'm training. How about you?'

'I'm reading hard. I think it best to leave it alone.'

Hastie nodded, and they relapsed into a contented silence. 'By the

way, Smith,' asked Hastie, presently, 'have you made the acquaintance of either of the fellows on your stair yet?'

'Just a nod when we pass. Nothing more.'

'Hum! I should be inclined to let it stand at that. I know something
of them both. Not much, but as much as I want. I don't think I should
take them to my bosom if I were you. Not that there's much amiss
with Monkhouse Lee.'

'Meaning the thin one?'

'Precisely. He is a gentlemanly little fellow. I don't think there is
any vice in him. But then you can't know him without knowing
Bellingham.'

'Meaning the fat one?'

'Yes, the fat one. And he's a man whom I, for one, would rather not
know.'

Abercrombie Smith raised his eyebrows and glanced across at his
companion. 'What's up, then?' he asked. 'Drink? Cards? Cad? You
used not to be censorious.'

'Ah! you evidently don't know the man or you wouldn't ask.
There's something damnable about him – something reptilian. My
gorge always rises at him. I should put him down as a man with secret
vices – an evil liver. He's no fool, though. They say that he is one of
the best men in his line that they have ever had in the college.'

'Medicine or classics?'

'Eastern languages. He's a demon at them. Chillingworth met him
somewhere above the second cataract last long, and he told me that
he just prattled to the Arabs as if he had been born and nursed and
weaned among them. He talked Coptic to the Copts, and Hebrew to
the Jews, and Arabic to the Bedouins, and they were all ready to kiss
the hem of his frock-coat. There are some old hermit Johnnies up in
those parts who sit on rocks and scowl and spit at the casual stranger.
Well, when they saw this chap Bellingham, before he had said five
words they just lay down on their bellies and wriggled. Chillingworth
said that he never saw anything like it. Bellingham seemed to take it
as his right, too, and strutted about among them and talked down to
them like a Dutch uncle. Pretty good for an undergrad of Old's,
wasn't it?'

'Why do you say you can't know Lee without knowing
Bellingham?'

'Because Bellingham is engaged to his sister Eveline. Such a bright
little girl, Smith! I know the whole family well. It's disgusting to see
that brute with her. A toad and a dove, that's what they always remind
me of.'

Abercrombie Smith grinned and knocked his ashes out against the side of the grate.

'You show every card in your hand, old chap,' said he. 'What a prejudiced, green-eyed, evil-thinking old man it is! You have really nothing against the fellow except that.'

'Well, I've known her ever since she was as long as that cherry-wood pipe, and I don't like to see her taking risks. And it is a risk. He looks beastly. And he has a beastly temper, a venomous temper. You remember his row with Long Norton?'

'No; you always forget that I am a freshman.'

'Ah, it was last winter. Of course. Well, you know the towpath along by the river. There were several fellows going along it, Bellingham in front, when they came on an old market-woman coming the other way. It had been raining – you know what those fields are like when it has rained – and the path ran between the river and a great puddle that was nearly as broad. Well, what does this swine do but keep the path and push the old girl into the mud, where she and her marketings came to terrible grief. It was a blackguard thing to do, and Long Norton, who is as gentle a fellow as ever stepped, told him what he thought of it. One word led to another, and it ended in Norton laying his stick across the fellow's shoulders. There was the deuce of a fuss about it and it's a treat to see the way in which Bellingham looks at Norton when they meet now. By Jove, Smith, it's nearly eleven o'clock!'

'No hurry. Light your pipe again.'

'Not I. I'm supposed to be in training. Here I've been sitting gossiping when I ought to have been safely tucked up. I'll borrow your skull, if you can share it. Williams has had mine for a month. I'll take the little bones of your ear, too, if you are sure you won't need them. Thanks very much. Never mind a bag, I can carry them very well under my arm. Good-night, my son, and take my tip as to your neighbour.'

When Hastie, bearing his anatomical plunder, had clattered off down the winding stair, Abercrombie Smith hurled his pipe into the wastepaper basket, and drawing his chair nearer to the lamp, plunged into a formidable, green-covered volume, adorned with great, coloured maps of that strange, internal kingdom of which we are the hapless and helpless monarchs. Though a freshman at Oxford, the student was not so in medicine, for he had worked for four years at Glasgow and at Berlin, and this coming examination would place him finally as a member of his profession. With his firm mouth, broad forehead and clear-cut, somewhat hard-featured face, he was a man who, if he had no brilliant talent, was yet so dogged, so patient and so strong that he might in the end overtop a more showy genius. A man who can hold his own among Scotchmen and North Germans is not a man to be easily set back. Smith had left a name at Glasgow and at Berlin, and he was bent now upon doing as much at Oxford, if hard work and devotion could accomplish it.

He had sat reading for about an hour, and the hands of the noisy carriage clock upon the side-table were rapidly closing together upon the twelve, when a sudden sound fell upon the student's ear – a sharp, rather shrill sound, like the hissing intake of a man's breath who gasps under some strong emotion. Smith laid down his book and slanted his ear to listen. There was no one on either side or above him, so that the interruption came certainly from the neighbour beneath – the same neighbour of whom Hastie had given so unsavoury an account. Smith knew him only as a flabby, pale-faced man of silent and studious habits, a man whose lamp threw a golden bar from the old turret even after he had extinguished his own. This community in lateness had formed a certain silent bond between them. It was soothing to Smith when the hours stole on towards dawning to feel that there was another so close who set as small a value upon his sleep as he did. Even now, as his thoughts turned towards him, Smith's feelings were kindly. Hastie was a good fellow, but he was rough, strong-fibred, with no imagination or sympathy. He could not tolerate departures from what he looked upon as the model type of manliness. If a man could not be measured by a public-school standard, then he was beyond the pale with Hastie. Like so many who are themselves robust, he was apt to confuse the constitution with the character, to ascribe to want of principle what was really a want of circulation. Smith, with his stronger mind, knew his friend's habit, and made allowance for it now as his thoughts turned towards the man beneath him.

There was no return of the singular sound, and Smith was about to turn to his work once more, when suddenly there broke out in the silence of the night a hoarse cry, a positive scream – the call of a man who is moved and shaken beyond all control. Smith sprang out of his chair and dropped his book. He was a man of fairly firm fibre, but there was something in this sudden, uncontrollable shriek of horror which chilled his blood and prickled in his skin. Coming in such a place and at such an hour, it brought a thousand fantastic possibilities into his head. Should he rush down or was it better to wait? He had all the national hatred of making a scene, and he knew so little of his neighbour that he would not lightly intrude upon his affairs. For a moment he stood in doubt and even as he balanced the matter there was a quick rattle of footsteps upon the stairs, and young Monkhouse Lee, half-dressed and as white as ashes, burst into his room.

'Come down!' he gasped. 'Bellingham's ill.'

Abercrombie Smith followed him closely downstairs into the sitting-room which was beneath his own, and intent as he was upon the matter in hand, he could not but take an amazed glance around him as he crossed the threshold. It was such a chamber as he had never seen before – a museum rather than a study. Walls and ceiling were thickly covered with a thousand strange relics from Egypt and the East. Tall, angular figures bearing burdens or weapons stalked in an uncouth frieze round the apartments. Above were bull-headed, stork-headed, cat-headed, owl-headed statues, with viper- crowned, almond-eyed monarchs, and strange, beetle-like deities cut out of the blue Egyptian lapis lazuli. Horus and Isis and Osiris peeped down from every niche and shelf; while across the ceiling a true son of Old Nile, a great, hanging-jawed crocodile, was slung in a double noose.

In the centre of this singular chamber was a large, square table, littered with papers, bottles and the dried leaves of some graceful, palm-like plant. These varied objects had all been heaped together in order to make room for a mummy case, which had been conveyed from the wall, as was evident from the gap there, and laid across the front of the table. The mummy itself, a horrid, black, withered thing, like a charred head on a gnarled bush, was lying half out of the case, with its claw-like hand and bony forearm resting upon the table. Propped up against the sarcophagus was an old yellow scroll of papyrus and in front of it, in a wooden armchair, sat the owner of the room, his head thrown back, his widely opened eyes directed in a horrified stare to the crocodile above him and his blue, thick lips puffing loudly with every expiration.

'My God! he's dying!' cried Monkhouse Lee, distractedly.

He was a slim, handsome young fellow, olive-skinned and dark-eyed, of a Spanish rather than of an English type, with a Celtic intensity of manner which contrasted with the Saxon phlegm of Abercrombie Smith.

'Only a faint, I think,' said the medical student. 'Just give me a hand with him. You take his feet. Now on to the sofa. Can you kick all those little wooden devils off ? What a litter it is! Now he will be all right if we undo his collar and give him some water. What has he been up to at all?'

'I don't know. I heard him cry out. I ran up. I know him pretty well, you know. It is very good of you to come down.'

'His heart is going like a pair of castanets,' said Smith, laying his band on the breast of the unconscious man. 'He seems to me to be frightened all to pieces. Chuck the water over him! What a face he has got on him!'

It was indeed a strange and most repellent face, for colour and outline were equally unnatural. It was white, not with the ordinary pallor of fear, but with an absolutely bloodless white, like the under side of a sole. He was very fat, but gave the impression of having at sometime been considerably fatter, for his skin hung loosely in creases and folds, and was shot with a meshwork of wrinkles. Short, stubbly brown hair bristled up from his scalp, with a pair of thick, wrinkled ears protruding at the sides. His light-grey eyes were still open, the pupils dilated and the balls projecting in a fixed and horrid stare. It seemed to Smith as he looked down upon him that he had never seen nature's danger signals flying so plainly upon a man's countenance, and his thoughts turned more seriously to the warning which Hastie had given him an hour before.

'What the deuce can have frightened him so?' he asked.

'It's the mummy.'

'The mummy? How, then?'

'I don't know. It's beastly and morbid. I wish he would drop it. It's the second fright he has given me. It was the same last winter. I found him just like this, with that horrid thing in front of him.'

'What does he want with the mummy, then?'

'Oh, he's a crank, you know. It's his hobby. He knows more about these things than any man in England. But I wish he wouldn't! Ah, he's beginning to come to.'

A faint tinge of colour had begun to steal back into Bellingham's ghastly cheeks, and his eyelids shivered like a sail after a calm. He clasped and unclasped his hands, drew a long, thin breath between his teeth, and suddenly jerking up his head, threw a glance of recognition around him. As his eyes fell upon the mummy, he sprang off the sofa, seized the roll of papyrus, thrust it into a drawer, turned the key, and then staggered back on to the sofa.

'What's up?' he asked. 'What do you chaps want?'

'You've been shrieking out and making no end of a fuss,' said Monkhouse Lee. 'If our neighbour here from above hadn't come down, I'm sure I don't know what I should have done with you.'

'Ah, it's Abercrombie Smith,' said Bellingham, glancing up at him. 'How very good of you to come in! What a fool I am! Oh, my God, what a fool I am!'

He sank his head on to his hands, and burst into peal after peal of hysterical laughter.

'Look here! Drop it!' cried Smith, shaking him roughly by the shoulder. 'Your nerves are all in a jangle. You must drop these little midnight games with mummies or you'll be going off your chump. You're all on wires now.'

'I wonder,' said Bellingham, 'whether you would be as cool as I am if you had seen – '

'What then?'

'Oh, nothing. I meant that I wonder if you could sit up at night with a mummy without trying your nerves. I have no doubt that you are quite right. I dare say that I have been taking it out of myself too much lately. But I am all right now. Please don't go, though. Just wait for a few minutes until I am quite myself.'

'The room is very close,' remarked Lee, throwing open the window and letting in the cool night air.

'It's balsamic resin,' said Bellingham. He lifted up one of the dried palmate leaves from the table and frizzled it over the chimney of the lamp. It broke away into heavy smoke wreaths, and a pungent, biting odour filled the chamber. 'It's the sacred plant – the plant of the priests,' he remarked. 'Do you know anything of Eastern languages, Smith?'

'Nothing at all. Not a word.'

The answer seemed to lift a weight from the Egyptologist's mind.

'By the way,' he continued, 'how long was it from the time that you ran down, until I came to my senses?'

'Not long. Some four or five minutes.'

'I thought it could not be very long,' said he, drawing a long breath. 'But what a strange thing unconsciousness is! There is no measurement to it. I could not tell from my own sensations if it were seconds or weeks. Now that gentleman on the table was packed up in the days of the eleventh dynasty, some forty centuries ago, and yet if he could find his tongue, he would tell us that this lapse of time has been but a closing of the eyes and a reopening of them. He is a singularly fine mummy, Smith.'

Smith stepped over to the table and looked down with a professional eye at the black and twisted form in front of him. The features, though horribly discoloured, were perfect, and two little nut-like eyes still lurked in the depths of the black, hollow sockets. The blotched skin was drawn tightly from bone to bone, and a tangled wrap of black, coarse hair fell over the ears. Two thin teeth, like those of a rat, overlay the shrivelled lower lip. In its crouching position, with bent joints and craned head, there was a suggestion of energy about the horrid thing which made Smith's gorge rise. The gaunt ribs, with their parchment-like covering, were exposed, and the sunken, leaden-hued abdomen, with the long slit where the embalmer had left his mark; but the lower limbs were wrapped round with coarse, yellow bandages. A number of little clove-like pieces of myrrh and of cassia were sprinkled over the body and lay scattered on the inside of the case.

'I don't know his name,' said Bellingham, passing his hand over the shrivelled head. 'You see the outer sarcophagus with the inscriptions is missing. Lot 249 is all the title he has now. You see it printed on his case. That was his number in the auction at which I picked him up.'

'He has been a very pretty sort of fellow in his day,' remarked Abercrombie Smith.

'He has been a giant. His mummy is six feet seven in length, and that would be a giant over there, for they were never a very robust race. Feel these great, knotted bones, too. He would be a nasty fellow to tackle.'

'Perhaps these very hands helped to build the stones into the Pyramids,' suggested Monkhouse Lee, looking down with disgust in his eyes at the crooked, unclean talons.

'No fear. This fellow has been pickled in natron, and looked after in the most approved style. They did not serve hodsmen in that fashion. Salt or bitumen was enough for them. It has been calculated that this sort of thing cost about seven hundred and thirty pounds in our money. Our friend was a noble at the least. What do you make of that small inscription near his feet, Smith?'

'I told you that I know no Eastern tongue.'

'Ah, so you did. It is the name of the embalmer, I take it. A very conscientious worker he must have been. I wonder how many modern works will survive four thousand years?'

He kept on speaking lightly and rapidly, but it was evident to Abercrombie Smith that he was still palpitating with fear. His hands shook, his lower lip trembled and, look where he would, his eye always came sliding round to his gruesome companion. Through all his fear, however, there was a suspicion of triumph in his tone and manner. His eyes shone, and his footstep, as he paced the room, was brisk and jaunty. He gave the impression of a man who has gone through an ordeal, the marks of which he still bears upon him, but which has helped him to his end.

'You're not going yet?' he cried, as Smith rose from the sofa.

At the prospect of solitude, his fears seemed to crowd back upon him and he stretched out a hand to detain him.

'Yes, I must go. I have my work to do. You are all right now. I think that with your nervous system you should take up some less morbid study.'

'Oh, I am not nervous as a rule; and I have unwrapped mummies before.'

'You fainted last time,' observed Monkhouse Lee.

'Ah, yes, so I did. Well, I must have a nerve tonic or a course of electricity. You are not going, Lee?'

'I'll do whatever you wish, Ned.'

'Then I'll come down with you and have a shakedown on your sofa. Good-night, Smith. I am so sorry to have disturbed you with my foolishness.'

They shook hands, and as the medical student stumbled up the spiral and irregular stair he heard a key turn in a door and the steps of his two new acquaintances as they descended to the lower floor.

In this strange way began the acquaintance between Edward Bellingham and Abercrombie Smith, an acquaintance which the latter, at least, had no desire to push further. Bellingham, however, appeared to have taken a fancy to his rough-spoken neighbour, and made his advances in such a way that he could hardly be repulsed without absolute brutality. Twice he called to thank Smith for his assistance, and many times afterwards he looked in with books, papers and such other civilities as two bachelor neighbours can offer each other. He was, as Smith soon found, a man of wide reading, with catholic tastes and an extraordinary memory. His manner, too, was so pleasing and suave that one came, after a time, to overlook his repellent appearance. For a jaded and wearied man he was no unpleasant companion, and Smith found himself, after a time, looking forward to his visits, and even returning them.

Clever as he undoubtedly was, however, the medical student seemed to detect a dash of insanity in the man. He broke out at times into a high, inflated style of talk which was in contrast with the simplicity of his life.

'It is a wonderful thing,' he cried, 'to feel that one can command powers of good and of evil – a ministering angel or a demon of vengeance.' And again, of Monkhouse Lee, he said, 'Lee is a good fellow, an honest fellow, but he is without strength or ambition. He would not make a fit partner for a man with a great enterprise. He would not make a fit partner for me.'

At such hints and innuendoes stolid Smith, puffing solemnly at his pipe, would simply raise his eyebrows and shake his head, with little interjections of medical wisdom as to earlier hours and fresher air.

One habit Bellingham had developed of late which Smith knew to be a frequent herald of a weakening mind. He appeared to be forever talking to himself. At late hours of the night, when there could be no visitor with him, Smith could still hear his voice beneath him in a low, muffled monologue, sunk almost to a whisper, and yet very audible in the silence. This solitary babbling annoyed and distracted the student, so that he spoke more than once to his neighbour about it. Bellingham, however, flushed up at the charge, and denied curtly that he had uttered a sound; indeed, he showed more annoyance over the matter than the occasion seemed to demand.

Had Abercrombie Smith had any doubt as to his own ears he had not to go far to find corroboration. Tom Styles, the little wrinkled manservant who had attended to the wants of the lodgers in the turret for a longer time than any man's memory could carry him, was sorely put to it over the same matter.

'If you please, sir,' said he, as he tidied down the top chamber one morning, 'do you think Mr Bellingham is all right, sir?'

'All right, Styles?'

'Yes, sir. Right in his head, sir.'

'Why should he not be, then?'

'Well, I don't know, sir. His habits has changed of late. He's not the same man he used to be, though I make free to say that he was never quite one of my gentlemen, like Mr Hastie or yourself, sir. He's took to talkin' to himself something awful. I wonder it don't disturb you. I don't know what to make of him, sir.'

'I don't know what business it is of yours, Styles.'

'Well, I takes an interest, Mr Smith. It may be forward of me, but I can't help it. I feel sometimes as if I was mother and father to my young gentlemen. It all falls on me when things go wrong and the relations come. But Mr Bellingham, sir. I want to know what it is that walks about his room sometimes when he's out and when the door's locked on the outside.'

'Eh? you're talking nonsense, Styles.'

'Maybe so, sir; but I heard it mor'n once with my own ears.'

'Rubbish, Styles.'

'Very good, sir. You'll ring the bell if you want me.'

Abercrombie Smith gave little heed to the gossip of the old manservant, but a small incident occurred a few days later which left an unpleasant effect upon his mind, and brought the words of Styles forcibly to his memory.

Bellingham had come up to see him late one night, and was entertaining him with an interesting account of the rock tombs of

Beni Hassan in Upper Egypt, when Smith, whose hearing was remarkably acute, distinctly heard the sound of a door opening on the landing below.

'There's some fellow gone in or out of your room,' he remarked.

Bellingham sprang up and stood helpless for a moment, with the expression of a man who is half-incredulous and half-afraid.

'I surely locked it. I am almost positive that I locked it,' he stammered. 'No one could have opened it.'

'Why, I hear someone coming up the steps now,' said Smith.

Bellingham rushed out through the door, slammed it loudly behind him, and hurried down the stairs. About halfway down Smith heard him stop and thought he caught the sound of whispering. A moment later the door beneath him shut, a key creaked in a lock, and Bellingham, with beads of moisture upon his pale face, ascended the stairs once more and re-entered the room.

'It's all right,' he said, throwing himself down in a chair. 'It was that fool of a dog. He had pushed the door open. I don't know how I came to forget to lock it.'

'I didn't know you kept a dog,' said Smith, looking very thoughtfully at the disturbed face of his companion.

'Yes, I haven't had him long. I must get rid of him. He's a great nuisance.'

'He must be, if you find it so hard to shut him up. I should have thought that shutting the door would have been enough, without locking it.'

'I want to prevent old Styles from letting him out. He's of some value, you know, and it would be awkward to lose him.'

'I am a bit of a dog-fancier myself,' said Smith, still gazing hard at his companion from the corner of his eyes. 'Perhaps you'll let me have a look at it.'

'Certainly. But I am afraid it cannot be tonight; I have an appointment. Is that clock right? Then I am a quarter of an hour late already. You'll excuse me, I am sure.'

He picked up his cap and hurried from the room. In spite of his appointment, Smith heard him re-enter his own chamber and lock his door upon the inside.

This interview left a disagreeable impression upon the medical student's mind. Bellingham had lied to him, and lied so clumsily that it looked as if he had desperate reasons for concealing the truth. Smith knew that his neighbour had no dog. He knew, also, that the step which he had heard upon the stairs was not the step of an animal. But if it were not, then what could it be? There was old Styles' statement about the something which used to pace the room at times when the owner was absent. Could it be a woman? Smith rather inclined to the view. If so, it would mean disgrace and expulsion to Bellingham if it were discovered by the authorities, so that his anxiety and falsehoods might be accounted for. And yet it was inconceivable that an undergraduate could keep a woman in his rooms without being instantly detected. Be the explanation what it might, there was something ugly about it, and Smith determined, as he turned to his books, to discourage all further attempts at intimacy on the part of his soft-spoken and ill-favoured neighbour.

But his work was destined to interruption that night. He had hardly caught up the broken threads when a firm, heavy footfall came three steps at a time from below, and Hastie, in blazer and flannels, burst into the room.

'Still at it!' said he, plumping down into his wonted armchair. 'What a chap you are to stew! I believe an earthquake might come and knock Oxford into a cocked hat, and you would sit perfectly placid with your books among the ruins. However, I won't bore you long. Three whiffs of baccy, and I am off.'

'What's the news, then?' asked Smith, cramming a plug of bird's-eye into his briar with his forefinger.

'Nothing very much. Wilson made seventy for the freshmen against the eleven. They say that they will play him instead of Buddicomb, for Buddicomb is clean off colour. He used to be able to bowl a little, but it's nothing but half-volleys and long hops now.'

'Medium right,' suggested Smith, with the intense gravity which comes upon a 'varsity man when he speaks of athletics.

'Inclining to fast, with a work from leg. Comes with the arm about three inches or so. He used to be nasty on a wet wicket. Oh, by the way, have you heard about Long Norton?'

'What's that?'

'He's been attacked.'

'Attacked?'

'Yes, just as he was turning out of the High Street, and within a hundred yards of the gate of Old's.'

'But who – '

'Ah, that's the rub! If you said 'what', you would be more grammatical. Norton swears that it was not human, and, indeed, from the scratches on his throat, I should be inclined to agree with him.'

'What, then? Have we come down to spooks?' Abercrombie Smith puffed his scientific contempt.

'Well, no; I don't think that is quite the idea, either. I am inclined to think that if any showman has lost a great ape lately, and the brute is in these parts, a jury would find a true bill against it. Norton passes that way every night, you know, about the same hour. There's a tree that hangs low over the path – the big elm from Rainy's garden. Norton thinks the thing dropped on him out of the tree. Anyhow, he was nearly strangled by two arms which, he says, were as strong and as thin as steel bands. He saw nothing; only those beastly arms that tightened and tightened on him. He yelled his head nearly off, and a couple of chaps came running, and the thing went over the wall like a cat. He never got a fair sight of it the whole time. It gave Norton a shake up, I can tell you. I tell him it has been as good as a change at the seaside for him.'

'A garrotter, most likely,' said Smith.

'Very possibly. Norton says not; but we don't mind what he says. The garrotter had long nails, and was pretty smart at swinging himself over walls. By the way, your beautiful neighbour would be pleased if he heard about it. He had a grudge against Norton, and he's not a man, from what I know of him, to forget his little debts. But hallo, old chap, what have you got in your noddle?'

'Nothing,' Smith answered curtly.

He had started in his chair, and the look had flashed over his face which comes upon a man who is struck suddenly by some unpleasant idea.

'You looked as if something I had said had taken you on the raw. By the way, you have made the acquaintance of Master B since I looked in last, have you not? Young Monkhouse Lee told me something to that effect.'

'Yes; I know him slightly. He has been up here once or twice.'

'Well, you're big enough and ugly enough to take care of yourself. He's not what I should call exactly a healthy sort of Johnny, though, no doubt, he's very clever, and all that. But you'll soon find out for yourself. Lee is all right; he's a very decent little fellow. Well, so long, old chap! I row Mullins for the vice-chancellor's pot on Wednesday week, so mind you come down, in case I don't see you before.'

Bovine Smith laid down his pipe and turned stolidly to his books once more. But with all the will in the world, he found it very hard to keep his mind upon his work. It would slip away to brood upon the man beneath him, and upon the little mystery which hung round his chambers. Then his thoughts turned to this singular attack of which Hastie had spoken, and to the grudge which Bellingham was said to owe the object of it. The two ideas would persist in rising together in his mind, as though there were some close and intimate connection between them. And yet the suspicion was so dim and vague that it could not be put down in words.

'Confound the chap!' cried Smith, as he shied his book on pathology across the room. 'He has spoiled my night's reading and that's reason enough, if there were no other, why I should steer clear of him in the future.'

For ten days the medical student confined himself so closely to his studies that he neither saw nor heard anything of either of the men beneath him. At the hours when Bellingham had been accustomed to visit him, he took care to sport his oak, and though he more than once heard a knocking at his outer door, he resolutely refused to answer it. One afternoon, however, he was descending the stairs when, just as he was passing it, Bellingham's door flew open, and young Monkhouse Lee came out with his eyes sparkling and a dark flush of anger upon his olive cheeks. Close at his heels followed Bellingham, his fat, unhealthy face all quivering with malignant passion.

'You fool!' he hissed. 'You'll be sorry.'

'Very likely,' cried the other. 'Mind what I say. It's off! I won't hear of it!'

'You've promised, anyhow.'

'Oh, I'll keep that! I won't speak. But I'd rather little Eva was in her grave. Once for all, it's off. She'll do what I say. We don't want to see you again.'

So much Smith could not avoid hearing, but he hurried on, for he had no wish to be involved in their dispute. There had been a serious breach between them, that was clear enough, and Lee was going to cause the engagement with his sister to be broken off. Smith thought of Hastie's comparison of the toad and the dove, and was glad to think that the matter was at an end. Bellingham's face when he was in a passion was not pleasant to look upon. He was not a man to whom an innocent girl could be trusted for life. As he walked, Smith wondered languidly what could have caused the quarrel, and what the promise might be which Bellingham had been so anxious that Monkhouse Lee should keep.

It was the day of the sculling match between Hastie and Mullins, and a stream of men were making their way down to the banks of the Isis. A May sun was shining brightly, and the yellow path was barred with the black shadows of the tall elm-trees. On either side the grey colleges lay back from the road, the hoary old mothers of minds looking out from their high, mullioned windows at the tide of young life which swept so merrily past them. Black-clad tutors, prim officials, pale, reading men, brown-faced, straw-hatted young athletes in white sweaters or many-coloured blazers, all were hurrying towards the blue, winding river which curves through the Oxford meadows.

Abercrombie Smith, with the intuition of an old oarsman, chose his position at the point where he knew that the struggle, if there were a struggle, would come. Far off he heard the hum which announced the start, the gathering roar of the approach, the thunder of running feet and the shouts of the men in the boats beneath him. A spray of half-clad, deep-breathing runners shot past him, and craning over their shoulders, he saw Hastie pulling a steady thirty-six, while his opponent, with a jerky forty, was a good boat's length behind him. Smith gave a cheer for his friend and, pulling out his watch, was starting off again for his chambers, when he felt a touch upon his shoulder and found that young Monkhouse Lee was beside him.

'I saw you there,' he said, in a timid, deprecating way. 'I wanted to speak to you, if you could spare me a half-hour. This cottage is mine. I share it with Harrington of King's. Come in and have a cup of tea.'

'I must be back presently,' said Smith. 'I am hard on the grind at present. But I'll come in for a few minutes with pleasure. I wouldn't have come out only Hastie is a friend of mine.'

'So he is of mine. Hasn't he a beautiful style? Mullins wasn't in it. But come into the cottage. It's a little den of a place, but it is pleasant to work in during the summer months.'

It was a small, square, white building, with green doors and shutters and a rustic trellis-work porch, standing back some fifty yards from the river's bank. Inside, the main room was roughly fitted up as a study – deal table, unpainted shelves with books and a few cheap oleographs upon the wall. A kettle sang upon a spirit-stove and there were tea things upon a tray on the table.

'Try that chair and have a cigarette,' said Lee. 'Let me pour you out a cup of tea. It's so good of you to come in, for I know that your time is a good deal taken up. I wanted to say to you that, if I were you, I should change my rooms at once.'

Smith sat staring with a lighted match in one hand and his unlit cigarette in the other.

'Yes; it must seem very extraordinary, and the worst of it is that I cannot give my reasons, for I am under a solemn promise – a very solemn promise. But I may go so far as to say that I don't think Bellingham is a very safe man to live near. I intend to camp out here as much as I can for a time.'

'Not safe! What do you mean?'

'Ah, that's what I mustn't say. But do take my advice and move your rooms. We had a grand row today. You must have heard us, for you came down the stairs.'

'I saw that you had fallen out.'

'He's a horrible chap, Smith. That is the only word for him. I have had doubts about him ever since that night when he fainted – you remember, when you came down. I taxed him today and he told me things that made my hair rise, and wanted me to stand in with him. I'm not strait-laced, but I am a clergyman's son, you know, and I think there are some things which are quite beyond the pale. I only thank God that I found him out before it was too late, for he was to have married into my family.'

'This is all very fine, Lee,' said Abercrombie Smith curtly. 'But either you are saying a great deal too much or a great deal too little.'

'I give you a warning.'

'If there is real reason for warning, no promise can bind you. If I see a rascal about to blow a place up with dynamite no pledge will stand in my way of preventing him.'

'Ah, but I cannot prevent him, and I can do nothing but warn you.'

'Without saying what you warn me against.'

'Against Bellingham.'

'But that is childish. Why should I fear him, or any man?'

'I can't tell you. I can only entreat you to change your rooms. You are in danger where you are. I don't even say that Bellingham would wish to injure you. But it might happen, for he is a dangerous neighbour just now.'

'Perhaps I know more than you think,' said Smith, looking keenly at the young man's boyish, earnest face. 'Suppose I tell you that someone else shares Bellingham's rooms.'

Monkhouse Lee sprang from his chair in uncontrollable excitement.

'You know, then?' he gasped.

'A woman.'

Lee dropped back again with a groan.

'My lips are sealed,' he said. 'I must not speak.'

'Well, anyhow,' said Smith, rising, 'it is not likely that I should allow myself to be frightened out of rooms which suit me very nicely. It would be a little too feeble for me to move out all my goods and chattels because you say that Bellingham might in some unexplained way do me an injury. I think that I'll just take my chance, and stay where I am, and as I see that it's nearly five o'clock, I must ask you to excuse me.'

He bade the young student adieu in a few curt words and made his way homeward through the sweet spring evening, feeling half-ruffled, half-amused, as any other strong, unimaginative man might who has been menaced by a vague and shadowy danger.

There was one little indulgence which Abercrombie Smith always allowed himself however closely his work might press upon him. Twice a week, on the Tuesday and the Friday, it was his invariable custom to walk over to Farlingford, the residence of Dr Plumptree Peterson, situated about a mile and a half out of Oxford. Peterson had been a close friend of Smith's elder brother, Francis, and as he was a bachelor, fairly well-to-do, with a good cellar and a better library, his house was a pleasant goal for a man who was in need of a brisk walk. Twice a week, then, the medical student would swing out there along the dark country roads and spend a pleasant hour in Peterson's comfortable study, discussing, over a glass of old port, the gossip of the 'varsity or the latest developments of medicine or of surgery.

On the day which followed his interview with Monkhouse Lee, Smith shut up his books at a quarter past eight, the hour when he usually started for his friend's house. As he was leaving his room, however, his eyes chanced to fall upon one of the books which Bellingham had lent him, and his conscience pricked him for not having returned it. However repellent the man might be, he should not be treated with discourtesy. Taking the book, he walked downstairs and knocked at his neighbour's door. There was no answer; but on turning the handle he found that it was unlocked. Pleased at the thought of avoiding an interview, he stepped inside and placed the book with his card upon the table.

The lamp was turned half down, but Smith could see the details of the room plainly enough. It was all much as he had seen it before – the frieze, the animal-headed gods, the hanging crocodile and the table littered over with papers and dried leaves. The mummy case stood upright against the wall, but the mummy itself was missing. There was no sign of any second occupant of the room, and he felt as he withdrew that he had probably done Bellingham an injustice. Had he a guilty secret to preserve, he would hardly leave his door open so that all the world might enter.

The spiral stair was as black as pitch, and Smith was slowly making his way down its irregular steps, when he was suddenly conscious that something had passed him in the darkness. There was a faint sound, a whiff of air, a light brushing past his elbow, but so slight that he could scarcely be certain of it. He stopped and listened, but the wind was rustling among the ivy outside and he could hear nothing else.

'Is that you, Styles?' he shouted.

There was no answer, and all was still behind him. It must have been a sudden gust of air, for there were crannies and cracks in the old turret. And yet he could almost have sworn that he heard a footfall by his very side. He had emerged into the quadrangle, still turning the matter over in his head, when a man came running swiftly across the smooth-cropped lawn.

'Is that you, Smith?'

'Hallo, Hastie!'

'For God's sake come at once! Young Lee is drowned! Here's Harrington of King's with the news. The doctor is out. You'll do, but come along at once. There may be life in him.'

'Have you brandy?'

'No.'

'I'll bring some. There's a flask on my table.'

Smith bounded up the stairs, taking three at a time, seized the flask and was rushing down with it, when, as he passed Bellingham's room, his eyes fell upon something which left him gasping and staring upon the landing.

The door, which he had closed behind him, was now open, and right in front of him, with the lamplight shining upon it, was the mummy case. Three minutes ago it had been empty. He could swear to that. Now it framed the lank body of its horrible occupant, who stood, grim and stark, with his black, shrivelled face towards the door. The form was lifeless and inert, but it seemed to Smith as he gazed that there still lingered a lurid spark of vitality, some faint sign of consciousness in the little eyes which lurked in the depths of the hollow sockets. So astounded and shaken was he that he had forgotten his errand and was still staring at the lean, sunken figure when the voice of his friend below recalled him to himself.

'Come on, Smith!' he shouted. 'It's life and death, you know. Hurry up! Now, then,' he added, as the medical student reappeared, 'let us do a sprint. It is well under a mile, and we should do it in five minutes. A human life is better worth running for than a pot.'

Neck and neck they dashed through the darkness, and did not pull up until, panting and spent, they had reached the little cottage by the river. Young Lee, limp and dripping like a broken water-plant, was stretched upon the sofa, the green scum of the river upon his black hair and a fringe of white foam upon his leaden-hued lips. Beside him knelt his fellow-student, Harrington, endeavouring to chafe some warmth back into his rigid limbs.

'I think there's life in him,' said Smith, with his hand to the lad's side. 'Put your watch glass to his lips. Yes, there's dimming on it. You take one arm, Hastie. Now work it as I do, and we'll soon pull him round.'

For ten minutes they worked in silence, inflating and depressing the chest of the unconscious man. At the end of that time a shiver ran through his body, his lips trembled and he opened his eyes. The three students burst out into an irrepressible cheer.

'Wake up, old chap. You've frightened us quite enough.'

'Have some brandy. Take a sip from the flask.'

'He's all right now,' said his companion Harrington. 'Heavens, what a fright I got! I was reading here, and he had gone out for a stroll as far as the river, when I heard a scream and a splash. Out I ran, and by the time I could find him and fish him out, all life seemed to have gone. Then Simpson couldn't get a doctor, for he has a game-leg, and I had to run, and I don't know what I'd have done without you fellows. That's right, old chap. Sit up.'

Monkhouse Lee had raised himself on his hands, and looked wildly about him.

'What's up?' he asked. 'I've been in the water. Ah, yes; I remember.'

A look of fear came into his eyes, and he sank his face into his hands.

'How did you fall in?'

'I didn't fall in.'

'How then?'

'I was thrown in. I was standing by the bank and something from behind picked me up like a feather and hurled me in. I heard nothing and I saw nothing. But I know what it was, for all that.'

'And so do I,' whispered Smith.

Lee looked up with a quick glance of surprise.

'You've learned, then?' he said. 'You remember the advice I gave you?'

'Yes, and I begin to think that I shall take it.'

'I don't know what the deuce you fellows are talking about,' said Hastie, 'but I think, if I were you, Harrington, I should get Lee to bed at once. It will be time enough to discuss the why and the wherefore when he is a little stronger. I think, Smith, you and I can leave him alone now. I am walking back to college; if you are coming in that direction, we can have a chat.'

But it was little chat that they had upon their homeward path. Smith's mind was too full of the incidents of the evening, the absence of the mummy from his neighbour's rooms, the step that passed him on the stair, the reappearance – the extraordinary, inexplicable reappearance of the grisly thing – and then this attack upon Lee, corresponding so closely to the previous outrage upon another man against whom Bellingham bore a grudge. All this settled in his thoughts, together with the many little incidents which had previously turned him against his neighbour and the singular circumstances under which he was first called in to him. What had been a dim suspicion, a vague, fantastic conjecture, had suddenly taken form and stood out in his mind as a grim fact, a thing not to be denied. And yet, how monstrous it was! how unheard of! how entirely beyond all bounds of human experience. An impartial judge, or even the friend who walked by his side, would simply tell him that his eyes had deceived him, that the mummy had been there all the time, that young Lee had tumbled into the river as any other man tumbles into a river, and the blue pill was the best thing for a disordered liver. He felt that he would have said as much if the positions had been reversed. And yet he could swear that Bellingham was a murderer at heart and that he wielded a weapon such as no man had ever used in all the grim history of crime.

Hastie had branched off to his rooms with a few crisp and emphatic comments upon his friend's unsociability, and Abercrombie Smith crossed the quadrangle to his corner turret with a strong feeling of repulsion for his chambers and their associations. He would take Lee's advice and move his quarters as soon as possible, for how could a man study when his ear was ever straining for every murmur or footstep in the room below? He observed, as he crossed over the lawn, that the light was still shining in Bellingham's window, and as he passed up the staircase the door opened and the man himself looked out at him. With his fat, evil face he was like some bloated spider fresh from the weaving of his poisonous web.

'Good-evening,' said he. 'Won't you come in?'

'No,' cried Smith fiercely.

'No? You are as busy as ever? I wanted to ask you about Lee. I was sorry to hear that there was a rumour that something was amiss with him.' His features were grave, but there was the gleam of a hidden laugh in his eyes as he spoke. Smith saw it, and he could have knocked him down for it.

'You'll be sorrier still to hear that Monkhouse Lee is doing very well, and is out of all danger,' he answered. 'Your hellish tricks have not come off this time. Oh, you needn't try to brazen it out. I know all about it.'

Bellingham took a step back from the angry student and half-closed the door as if to protect himself.

'You are mad,' he said. 'What do you mean? Do you assert that I had anything to do with Lee's accident?'

'Yes,' thundered Smith. 'You and that bag of bones behind you; you worked it between you. I tell you what it is, Master B, they have given up burning folk like you, but we still keep a hangman, and, by George! if any man in this college meets his death while you are here, I'll have you up, and if you don't swing for it, it won't be my fault. You'll find that your filthy Egyptian tricks won't answer in England.'

'You're a raving lunatic,' said Bellingham.

'All right. You just remember what I say, for you'll find that I'll be better than my word.'

The door slammed and Smith went fuming up to his chamber, where he locked the door upon the inside and spent half the night in smoking his old briar and brooding over the strange events of the evening.

Next morning Abercrombie Smith heard nothing of his neighbour, but Harrington called upon him in the afternoon to say that Lee was almost himself again. All day Smith stuck fast to his work, but in the evening he determined to pay the visit to his friend Dr Peterson upon which he had started the night before. A good walk and a friendly chat would be welcome to his jangled nerves.

Bellingham's door was shut as he passed, but glancing back when he was some distance from the turret, he saw his neighbour's head at the window outlined against the lamplight, his face pressed apparently against the glass as he gazed out into the darkness. It was a blessing to be away from all contact with him, if but for a few hours, and Smith stepped out briskly and breathed the soft spring air into his lungs. The half-moon lay in the west between two Gothic pinnacles, and threw upon the silvered street a dark tracery from the stonework above. There was a brisk breeze and light, fleecy clouds drifted swiftly across the sky. Old's was on the very border of the town, and in five minutes Smith found himself beyond the houses and between the hedges of a May-scented, Oxfordshire lane.

It was a lonely and little-frequented road which led to his friend's house. Early as it was, Smith did not meet a single soul upon his way. He walked briskly along until he came to the avenue gate which opened into the long gravel drive leading up to Farlingford. In front of him he could see the cosy, red light of the windows glimmering through the foliage. He stood with his hand upon the iron latch of the swinging gate and he glanced back at the road along which he had come. Something was coming swiftly down it.

It moved in the shadow of the hedge, silently and furtively, a dark, crouching figure, dimly visible against the black background. Even as he gazed back at it, it had lessened its distance by twenty paces and was fast closing upon him. Out of the darkness he had a glimpse of a scraggy neck and of two eyes that will ever haunt him in his dreams. He turned and with a cry of terror he ran for his life up the avenue. There were the red lights, the signals of safety, almost within a stone's-throw of him. He was a famous runner, but never had he run as he ran that night.

The heavy gate had swung into place behind him but he heard it dash open again before his pursuer. As he rushed madly and wildly through the night, he could hear a swift, dry patter behind him, and could see, as he threw back a glance, that this horror was bounding like a tiger at his heels, with blazing eyes and one stringy arm out-thrown. Thank God, the door was ajar. He could see the thin bar of light which shot from the lamp in the hall. Nearer yet sounded the clatter from behind. He heard a hoarse gurgling at his very shoulder. With a shriek he flung himself against the door, slammed and bolted it behind him, and sank half-fainting on to the hall chair.

'My goodness, Smith, what's the matter?' asked Peterson, appearing at the door of his study.

'Give me some brandy.'

Peterson disappeared and came rushing out again with a glass and a decanter.

'You need it,' he said, as his visitor drank off what he poured out for him. 'Why, man, you are as white as a cheese.'

Smith laid down his glass, rose up, and took a deep breath. 'I am my own man again now,' said he. 'I was never so unmanned before. But, with your leave, Peterson, I will sleep here tonight, for I don't think I could face that road again except by daylight. It's weak, I know, but I can't help it.'

Peterson looked at his visitor with a very questioning eye.

'Of course you shall sleep here if you wish. I'll tell Mrs Burney to make up the spare bed. Where are you off to now?'

'Come up with me to the window that overlooks the door. I want you to see what I have seen.'

They went up to the window of the upper hall whence they could look down upon the approach to the house. The drive and the fields on either side lay quiet and still, bathed in the peaceful moonlight.

'Well, really, Smith,' remarked Peterson, 'it is well that I know you to be an abstemious man. What in the world can have frightened you?'

'I'll tell you presently. But where can it have gone? Ah, now, look, look! See the curve of the road just beyond your gate.'

'Yes, I see; you needn't pinch my arm off. I saw someone pass. I should say a man, rather thin, apparently, and tall, very tall. But what of him? And what of yourself? You are still shaking like an aspen leaf.'

'I have been within hand-grip of the devil, that's all. But come down to your study, and I shall tell you the whole story.'

He did so. Under the cheery lamplight with a glass of wine on the table beside him and the portly form and florid face of his friend in front, he narrated, in their order, all the events, great and small, which had formed so singular a chain, from the night on which he had found Bellingham fainting in front of the mummy case until this horrid experience of an hour ago.

'There now,' he said as he concluded, 'that's the whole, black business. It is monstrous and incredible, but it is true.'

Dr Plumptree Peterson sat for some time in silence with a very puzzled expression upon his face.

'I never heard of such a thing in my life, never!' he said at last. 'You have told me the facts. Now tell me your inferences.'

'You can draw your own.'

'But I should like to hear yours. You have thought over the matter, and I have not.'

'Well, it must be a little vague in detail, but the main points seem to me to be clear enough. This fellow Bellingham, in his Eastern studies, has got hold of some infernal secret by which a mummy – or possibly only this particular mummy – can be temporarily brought to life. He was trying this disgusting business on the night when he fainted. No doubt the sight of the creature moving had shaken his nerve, even though he had expected it. You remember that almost the first words he said were to call out upon himself as a fool. Well, he got more hardened afterwards, and carried the matter through without fainting. The vitality which he could put into it was evidently only a passing thing, for I have seen it continually in its case as dead as this table. He has some elaborate process, I fancy, by which he brings the thing to pass. Having done it, he naturally bethought him that he might use the creature as an agent. It has intelligence and it has strength. For some purpose he took Lee into his confidence; but Lee, like a decent Christian, would have nothing to do with such a business. Then they had a row, and Lee vowed that he would tell his sister of Bellingham's true character. Bellingham's game was to prevent him, and he nearly managed it by setting this creature of his on his track. He had already tried its powers upon another man – Norton – towards whom he had a grudge. It is the merest chance that he has not two murders upon his soul. Then, when I taxed him with the matter, he had the strongest reasons for wishing to get me out of the way before I could convey my knowledge to anyone else. He got his chance when I went out, for he knew my habits and where I was bound for. I have had a narrow shave, Peterson, and it is mere luck you didn't find me on your doorstep in the morning. I'm not a nervous man as a rule, and I never thought to have the fear of death put upon me as it was tonight.'

'My dear boy, you take the matter too seriously,' said his companion. 'Your nerves are out of order with your work, and you make too much of it. How could such a thing as this stride about the streets of Oxford, even at night, without being seen?'

'It has been seen. There is quite a scare in the town about an escaped ape, as they imagine the creature to be. It is the talk of the place.'

'Well, it's a striking chain of events. And yet, my dear fellow, you must allow that each incident in itself is capable of a more natural explanation.'

'What! even my adventure of tonight?'

'Certainly. You come out with your nerves all unstrung, and your head full of this theory of yours. Some gaunt, half-famished tramp steals after you, and seeing you run, is emboldened to pursue you. Your fears and imagination do the rest.'

'It won't do, Peterson; it won't do.'

'And again, in the instance of your finding the mummy case empty, and then a few moments later with an occupant, you know that it was lamplight, that the lamp was half turned down, and that you had no special reason to look hard at the case. It is quite possible that you may have overlooked the creature in the first instance.'

'No, no; it is out of the question.'

'And then Lee may have fallen into the river, and Norton been garrotted. It is certainly a formidable indictment that you have against Bellingham; but if you were to place it before a police magistrate, he would simply laugh in your face.'

'I know he would. That is why I mean to take the matter into my own hands.'

'Eh?'

'Yes; I feel that a public duty rests upon me, and, besides, I must do it for my own safety, unless I choose to allow myself to be hunted by this beast out of the college, and that would be a little too feeble. I have quite made up my mind what I shall do. And first of all, may I use your paper and pens for an hour?'

'Most certainly. You will find all that you want upon that side-table.'

Abercrombie Smith sat down before a sheet of foolscap, and for an hour and then for a second hour his pen travelled swiftly over it. Page after page was finished and tossed aside while his friend leaned back in his armchair, looking across at him with patient curiosity. At last, with an exclamation of satisfaction, Smith sprang to his feet, gathered his papers up into order, and laid the last one upon Peterson's desk.

'Kindly sign this as a witness,' he said.

'A witness? Of what?'

'Of my signature and of the date. The date is the most important. Why, Peterson, my life might hang upon it.'

'My dear Smith, you are talking wildly. Let me beg you to go to bed.'

'On the contrary, I never spoke so deliberately in my life. And I will promise to go to bed the moment you have signed it.'

'But what is it?'

'It is a statement of all that I have been telling you tonight. I wish you to witness it.'

'Certainly,' said Peterson, signing his name under that of his companion. 'There you are! But what is the idea?'

'You will kindly retain it, and produce it in case I am arrested.'

'Arrested? For what?'

'For murder. It is quite on the cards. I wish to be ready for every event. There is only one course open to me, and I am determined to take it.'

'For heaven's sake, don't do anything rash!'

'Believe me, it would be far more rash to adopt any other course. I hope that we won't need to bother you, but it will ease my mind to know that you have this statement of my motives. And now I am ready to take your advice and to go to roost, for I want to be at my best in the morning.'

Abercrombie Smith was not an entirely pleasant man to have as an enemy. Slow and easy-tempered, he was formidable when driven to action. He brought to every purpose in life the same deliberate resoluteness which had distinguished him as a scientific student. He had laid his studies aside for a day, but he intended that the day should not be wasted. Not a word did he say to his host as to his plans, but by nine o'clock he was well on his way to Oxford. In the High Street he stopped at Clifford's, the gun-maker's, and bought a heavy revolver with a box of central-fire cartridges. Six of them he slipped

into the chambers, and half-cocking the weapon, placed it in the
pocket of his coat. He then made his way to Hastie's rooms, where
the big oarsman was lounging over his breakfast, with the *Sporting
Times* propped up against the coffee-pot.

'Hallo! What's up?' he asked. 'Have some coffee?'

'No, thank you. I want you to come with me, Hastie, and do what
I ask you.'

'Certainly, my boy.'

'And bring a heavy stick with you.'

'Hallo!' Hastie stared. 'Here's a hunting crop that would fell
an ox.'

'One other thing. You have a box of amputating knives. Give me
the longest of them.'

'There you are. You seem to be fairly on the war trail. Anything
else?'

'No; that will do.' Smith placed the knife inside his coat, and led
the way to the quadrangle. 'We are neither of us chickens, Hastie,'
said he. 'I think I can do this job alone, but I take you as a precaution.
I am going to have a little talk with Bellingham. If I have only him to
deal with, I won't, of course, need you. If I shout, however, up you
come, and lam out with your whip as hard as you can lick. Do you
understand?'

'All right. I'll come if I hear you bellow.'

'Stay here, then. I may be a little time, but don't budge until I come
down.'

'I'm a fixture.'

Smith ascended the stairs, opened Bellingham's door and stepped
in. Bellingham was seated behind his table, writing. Beside him,
among his litter of strange possessions, towered the mummy case,
with its sale number 249 still stuck upon its front, and its hideous
occupant stiff and stark within it. Smith looked very deliberately
round him, closed the door, and then, stepping across to the
fireplace, struck a match and set the fire alight. Bellingham sat
staring, with amazement and rage upon his bloated face.

'Well, really now, you make yourself at home,' he gasped.

Smith sat himself deliberately down, placing his watch upon the
table, drew out his pistol, cocked it, and laid it in his lap. Then he
took the long amputating knife from his bosom, and threw it down in
front of Bellingham.

'Now, then,' said he, 'just get to work and cut up that mummy.'

'Oh, is that it?' said Bellingham with a sneer.

'Yes, that is it. They tell me that the law can't touch you. But I have a law that will set matters straight. If in five minutes you have not set to work, I swear by the God who made me that I will put a bullet through your brain!'

'You would murder me?'

Bellingham had half-risen, and his face was the colour of putty.

'Yes.'

'And for what?'

'To stop your mischief. One minute has gone.'

'But what have I done?'

'I know and you know.'

'This is mere bullying.'

'Two minutes are gone.'

'But you must give reasons. You are a madman – a dangerous madman. Why should I destroy my own property? It is a valuable mummy.'

'You must cut it up, and you must burn it.'

'I will do no such thing.'

'Four minutes are gone.'

Smith took up the pistol and he looked towards Bellingham with an inexorable face. As the second-hand stole round, he raised his hand and the finger twitched upon the trigger.

'There! there! I'll do it!' screamed Bellingham.

In frantic haste he caught up the knife and hacked at the figure of the mummy, ever glancing round to see the eye and the weapon of his terrible visitor bent upon him. The creature crackled and snapped under every stab of the keen blade. A thick, yellow dust rose up from it. Spices and dried essences rained down upon the floor. Suddenly, with a rending crack, its backbone snapped asunder, and it fell, a brown heap of sprawling limbs, upon the floor.

'Now into the fire!' said Smith.

The flames leaped and roared as the dried and tinder-like debris was piled upon it. The little room was like the stokehole of a steamer and the sweat ran down the faces of the two men; but still the one stooped and worked, while the other sat watching him with a set face. A thick, fat smoke oozed out from the fire, and a heavy smell of burned resin and singed hair filled the air. In a quarter of an hour a few charred and brittle sticks were all that was left of Lot No. 249.

'Perhaps that will satisfy you,' snarled Bellingham, with hate and fear in his little grey eyes as he glanced back at his tormentor.

'No; I must make a clean sweep of all your materials. We must have no more devil's tricks. In with all these leaves! They may have something to do with it.'

'And what now?' asked Bellingham, when the leaves also had been added to the blaze.

'Now the roll of papyrus which you had on the table that night. It is in that drawer, I think.'

'No, no,' shouted Bellingham. 'Don't burn that! Why, man, you don't know what you do. It is unique; it contains wisdom which is nowhere else to be found.'

'Out with it!'

'But look here, Smith, you can't really mean it. I'll share the knowledge with you. I'll teach you all that is in it. Or, stay, let me only copy it before you burn it!'

Smith stepped forward and turned the key in the drawer. Taking out the yellow, curled roll of paper, he threw it into the fire, and pressed it down with his heel. Bellingham screamed, and grabbed at it; but Smith pushed him back and stood over it until it was reduced to a formless, grey ash.

'Now, Master B,' said he, 'I think I have pretty well drawn your teeth. You'll hear from me again if you return to your old tricks. And now good-morning, for I must go back to my studies.'

And such is the narrative of Abercrombie Smith as to the singular events which occurred in Old College, Oxford, in the spring of '84. As Bellingham left the university immediately afterwards, and was last heard of in the Sudan, there is no one who can contradict his statement. But the wisdom of men is small, and the ways of nature are strange, and who shall put a bound to the dark things which may be found by those who seek for them?